Another Round

of *Presidential Spirits*

Kerry:
Thanks for all you've done for Notre Dame. And for me.
Hope you enjoy your return trip to the Saloon!
Cheers
[illegible]

Dan Coonan

Goose River Press
Waldoboro, Maine

This book is a work of fiction that depicts completely imaginary events. Certain quotes in this novel attributed to presidents or other historical or public figures may be based in whole or in part upon their actual words that appeared in speeches, letters, interviews, memoirs or other papers. In such cases, citations appear in the Sources section at the end of the book listed by chapter to enable the reader to examine the actual quote and its original context. However, all events, conversations and media reports appearing in this book are purely fictional.

Library of Congress Card Number: 2022939532
ISBN: 978-1-59713-247-3

First Printing, 2022

Cover art by Michael Hutchinson.

Published by
Goose River Press
3400 Friendship Road
Waldoboro ME 04572
e-mail: gooseriverpress@gmail.com
www.gooseriverpress.com

To Claire, Tommy & Kevin—

don't ever stop pursuing your dreams.

I mean really, who even needs Russia interfering and dividing us any longer? We seem to be doing a bang-up job of that all by ourselves. All Russia needs to do these days is act like the poets in Springsteen's epic ballad Jungleland— "just stand back and let it all be."

—Danny McFadden,
45th president of the United States

Table of Contents

Table of Contents

Table of Contents

Chapter One

Que Será, Será

January 28, 2021

Eight days after the inauguration of President Margaret Bates

Somewhere in the Solomon Islands

"Another round, Mr. President?"

"Sure, Pierre," I responded. "And don't be shy when mixing this one."

"Certainly, sir. Shall I make it a double?"

Denyse in the lounge chair next to me whirled around and shot me a bit of a look, despite being deep in conversation with Patti at the edge of the pool in front of us. It wasn't so much a look laced with attitude as it was surprise.

"Let's just call it a 'heavy pour,' Pierre," I responded, with a smile.

"Of course, sir," replied Pierre. "I'll be right back with that. And trust me, you won't be disappointed."

"He deserves every bit of that drink and more," Patti said to Denyse, but clearly intending me to hear her words over the Zac Brown playlist setting our mood. Denyse's expression quickly melted into a smile as Pierre hustled back to the bar to get me my cocktail.

Patti, now looking directly at me, added, "I'll bet it was hard to find even a moment in the past four years where you could escape and just enjoy a few drinks with friends away from it all."

"Oh, you'd be surprised," I responded with a laugh. If she only knew.

The scene in front of us took my breath away, and was almost as unlikely as anything I had experienced in the remarkable and improbable previous five years of my life. Almost.

We couldn't have been further from the Beltway—mentally or geographically. Denyse and I found ourselves sitting poolside on the deck of the *Que Será, Será*—the absurdly opulent luxury yacht owned by Silicon Valley power couple Hannah Sarner and Martin Gelpard. There was not a cloud in the sky above us, and, as if that weren't enough, the horizon on all sides of us was dotted with a spectacular collection of some the Solomon Islands' finest. If you can't relax amidst this spectacular cinematography you can't relax.

And that wasn't the half of it. Not even close. Perhaps I buried the lead here but the rest of our shipmates for this little jaunt included none other than Tom Hanks and Rita Wilson, Joe and Jennifer Montana, investment tycoon Ben Stanley and his wife Cheryl, and Bruce Springsteen and his wife—the aforementioned Patti Scialfa currently chatting up Denyse. When I bid farewell to my favorite saloon and paid my final respects just a week and a half ago, I was certain I would never again be in such distinguished company. While that may still well be true, I was beginning to think this might be a close second. And I hadn't even been out of office a month. Perhaps this post-presidency chapter of my life would be a whole lot better than I had ever imagined. It certainly seemed to be starting out on the right foot.

We hadn't been home more than a day or two in Los Gatos when I got a call from Martin and Hannah imploring us to join this illustrious group for "a little getaway." And those two are notoriously hard to turn down. They champion and fund so many urgent causes around the globe, but besides that they are just a kick to be with. I couldn't stand the thought of what we'd be missing out on if I said no, and a few of the dozen or so ideas I had for a post-presidency professional life could be aided immeasurably by the two of them.

My phone buzzed.

My first inclination was to ignore it. The phone lay upside down on the ground next to me beside a book I had brought along for the trip—Candice Millard's *The River of Doubt*, all about Teddy Roosevelt's post-presidency excursion through the Brazilian rainforest. Perhaps that selection of reading material evidenced my growing obsession with what my own post presidency would entail—as if I was actually going to read anything in the midst of this company. However, whatever my post presidency life had in store for me, I was fairly certain it wouldn't be as ambitious as TR's.

I saw that it was a text from my daughter, Kelly. I picked it up.

"*Are you guys around? I want to bring Michael home and was hoping we could spend some time with you.*"

I decided to text back. "*Mom and I are gone for a few days. How about next weekend*?"

"*No worries. Did you guys go down to Carmel or something*?"

"*No—a little further away than that.*"

"*Lake Almanor*?"

"*I'd say it's farther than that too.*"

"*Where are you? You guys just got home. What are you doing? Quit making me guess*!"

"*We may or may not be poolside sipping cocktails on the deck of a luxury yacht somewhere between Fiji and the Solomon Islands.*" That was a long sentence to type but her reaction made it well worth the effort.

"*WHAT??!! OMG. OMG. Who are you with???*"

I just laughed and allowed it to sink in further without responding.

"*Dad that is SO NOT YOU! That's crazy. Who are you with? You have to tell me more*!"

"*I won't divulge the entire guest list, but one of them might be Bruce Springsteen. I'll call later. I have to go. Love you.*"

"*What? No, wait! Whatever you do, do NOT under any circumstances tell him how many of his concerts you've been to. He'll think you're some kind of psycho stalker*!"

I laughed and flipped the phone over. She had a point.

Denyse saw me messing with the phone. "Why did you even bring that thing to the pool?"

Martin in the lounge chair to my left perked up. "Are you one who has a hard time checking out?"

Denyse chimed in before I could respond. "I'm dying to see how he answers this. Please tell us, Danny."

I took a sip of my cocktail.

"I am weaning myself off my addiction to my phones. I am proud to say I brought only my personal phone to the pool this afternoon. Now I don't expect that to impress my lovely wife here, but I consider that progress. Besides, it allowed me to answer a text I just received from our daughter."

"Kelly texted you? What did she say? Is everything alright? I didn't even tell her we were coming here."

"Oh, now that it's Kelly it sounds suddenly like it's OK for me to have my phone."

"Tell me what she said."

"Oh, just something about she and Michael getting engaged." I laughed.

"Wait," said Denyse with an unmistakable look of surprise, "she told you?"

"Hold on now," I said, now with no shortage of anger, "the two of them really are engaged and you didn't tell me? I was just kidding."

Martin yelled at Pierre. "I think we're gonna need a lot more drinks over here."

Denyse looked mortified now that she realized she had a role in spilling the beans. "Please don't blame them, honey. They're kids. They were going to tell you but with everything going on while you were president they always thought it wasn't the right time. I'm sure they were going to tell you once we got back home to Los Gatos."

"Do the boys know too?" I asked, fearful of the answer but desperately wanting to know just how offended I should be.

Denyse paused a moment while Martin, Patti and I watched her expression give it all away.

"They might."

"Might???"

"OK, but don't blame them for that either."

"Pierre, better make that a round doubles for all of us," yelled Martin.

"Or maybe just bring Danny the whole bottle," said Patti, laughing out loud.

***

The pool party broke up at about 4 and people retired to their cabins to get cleaned up for what promised to be a great evening. The positioning of the chairs around the pool had made conversation difficult, and I didn't make much of a connection with anyone aside from the initial pleasantries.

On the walk back to our suite we passed the spa, the gym, and what looked like a smoothie bar. When I saw I could get a cup of coffee there I stopped. I was going to need a little assistance recharging the battery for whatever lay ahead of us this evening. Knowing Hannah it was going to be something.

The dual marble center staircase made one hell of a statement in the front center of the boat. We enjoyed climbing the two flights up to our cabin. I'm not sure what the other guest cabins were like, but ours was pretty spectacular—much more befitting of Louis XVI and Marie Antoinette than Danny and Denyse McFadden. Our bedroom opened up to a large private balcony with 180-degree views.

Seeing it for the second time didn't diminish its grandeur. We both just shook our heads and laughed.

"I don't know what that next chapter of yours is gonna be like," said Denyse, immersing herself in that scenery, "but I'm, pretty sure it's not gonna be this."

"What? You don't think this is my style?" I answered, incapable of keeping a straight face.

"I feel guilty," she said. "I'm not sure God intended man to live quite this way."

"Well, Hannah and Martin are an absolute gift from God to the human race. If anyone is deserving of a little Heaven on Earth, I'd say it's them. Those two have made some fairly sensational contributions to the greater good of humanity. But yes, this is not us. Not even close."

***

An hour later we emerged from our suite having cleaned up and a guzzled a bit of coffee to keep us awake after the afternoon's drinks in the sun.

"We haven't discussed a gameplan or objective for tonight." I said to Denyse.

"Just have fun, Danny. You're not president anymore."

"Thanks for the reminder. I'm just better sometimes thinking a little of this through in advance."

"OK, you want my advice? Don't tell Joe Montana our collie is named after him. Don't tell Bruce Springsteen you've seen him twenty-five times."

"Actually, I'm pretty sure it's a lot more than that."

"Don't try to pretend to Hannah that you know even the first thing about her new Powershare platform. That thing is managing to actually compete with Facebook, by the way."

"Wow, for someone who professes to be my biggest supporter you really have such little faith in me. And even that might be overstating it."

"Let's just say I know you well, McFadden—the good, the bad, and everything in between. I love it all—don't get me wrong."

"Thanks for adding that last part, sweetheart."

"You can have a gameplan, babe. All I want to do is lie in the sun on that deck for the next two days. Have a massage. Maybe get a workout in. Or maybe not." She smiled and exhaled audibly.

"By the way, I think Erik and Brent are enjoying your post presidency Secret Service detail," Denyse added, motioning down to the side of the boat below our private deck where the two agents assigned to us for this trip were taking in the view while chatting with the security team for the yacht.

"Ya think?" I responded. "This has to be the worst thing possible we could have done for them. Little do they know life with the McFaddens isn't gonna be anything even remotely resembling this from here on in."

"Oh, I wouldn't be too sure about that. Maybe this is the new you. Perhaps you'll become a bit of a diva in your post presidency."

"I'll be sure to add that to my growing list of possible next chapters. That one has some real merit. Sure beats the hell out of writing my memoirs."

***

We were the last couple to arrive at the sundeck for the al fresco pre-dinner cocktail hour. In addition to the spectacular views of the islands all around us, this deck overlooked the pool and sauna below. Denyse pointed to the helicopter pad. It looked as if it had been converted to a dance floor for the evening. A grand piano sat amidst a variety of other instruments just waiting for an impeccable ensemble to show up and let them fulfill their destiny. Knowing Hannah and Martin, my guess is that just such a group was about to emerge. This promised to be an unforgettable night.

I took a moment to appreciate how much fortune continues to smile on me—even in this week when I anticipated a bit of internal depression. The view of the South Pacific and the islands surrounding us was nothing short of breathtaking. I think it is physiologically impossible to experience depression on the *Que Será, Será*. I defy anybody to prove me wrong.

As we approached the party everyone turned to look at us. They were separated into roughly three different groups, and all three appeared to be beckoning. Denyse and I split up, as we always do at these things. Her new buddy Patti was with Montana and Tom Hanks, and Denyse didn't hesitate one bit about joining them. That didn't surprise me. I've always suspected she's got a thing for quarterbacks. Didn't even matter that this one was in his mid-sixties. It's Joe Montana for god sakes. But I'm really in no position to blame her for it because truth be told I've practically got a bit of a thing for that dude too. My God—4 Super Bowls, a National Championship at ND, national spokesperson in America for the Guinness/Notre Dame campaign—how perfect is that? And then there's Jennifer. Need I go on? By the way, I wasn't a quarterback . . .

As much as I would have loved to fall in with Denyse and that group, I felt compelled to start with our hosts, even though I had already spent an hour and a half next to Martin beside the pool. Of course, I immediately heard Denyse and them laughing hysterically but I refused to second guess my choice for even a minute.

A server emerged immediately to get my order. Martin and Hannah clearly had this whole thing figured out. Even so, I opted just to start with an iced tea. I needed to pace myself.

Hannah gave me a big hug. "Let me tell you how great it is to have the McFaddens back in California!" She has a gift for making someone feel special that so many ultra-successful people seem to have. "Please put us in touch with your scheduler. Martin and I have dozens of events to add to your dance card."

"If those events are anything even remotely resembling this, Hannah, please count us in. All in."

"Oh, and I want to talk with you about your new "Alliance" political movement. I need to get involved. I've got money and I've got candidates. Please tell me you'll be leading that effort. It's just what our country needs."

"I presume I'll be involved."

"I'm gonna need a lot more than that, honey."

I laughed. "We're figuring out what that next chapter will be."

"I know you'll do the right thing, dear," she added.

At that moment Bruce Springsteen, who had been rather shielded from my view sitting on a chair at the bar talking with the bartenders, stood up and looked our way.

Hannah waved him over, then looked back at me. "Surely you've met Bruce, dear, haven't you?"

"No, I haven't actually." I responded. "But I believe I've heard of him." That line was just for my own amusement. Hannah had no idea.

"Bruce and Patti joined us last year for a week on our maiden voyage through the Greek Isles," added Hannah.

"Wow. It's hard to I imagine anything that could possibly top this trip here but I'm guessing that just might."

"Can I ask you what you really think about President Bates?" she said, looking right at me. "Or do you not want me to ask that in front of the others."

"Oh, I don't mind," I said. "I like her. She has a remarkable ability to connect with people. She has her hands full, though. Any president does these days, as I know better than anybody. But I want her to be successful—and she has a chance. I've only met her a few times. But she's incredibly sharp, and has extraordinary political skills."

"Oh good. I kind of like her too. But I don't have a good feeling about her husband," Hannah added. "And I can sense these things."

"Yes, you can, Hannah," Martin chimed in. "No doubt about that."

Then Martin, looking at the rest of us, added, "I live my life by two simple rules. Don't ever underestimate her," he pointed at Hannah and paused briefly for effect. He then stated emphatically, "and don't ever cross her."

"Don't worry—I believe you," I responded, laughing.

Hannah continued to lead the conversation—not in an overbearing way—she's just such a natural at it.

Bruce Springsteen seemed so different in this setting—away from the stage, the band and the adoring crowds. He appeared a bit meek, and almost introverted, but I can only imagine what life for this guy must be like. Eventually as our little group rearranged places a bit in conversation, I found myself standing right beside him. I took a moment to consider thoroughly the words I most wanted to say.

I turned to him. "I really admire the eulogies you gave for the bandmates you've lost—Danny and Clarence. And your tributes on the fly to people like Sinatra and Prince. As someone who is called upon to give tributes more often than I ever would have wanted, I have learned a lot from your words and your emotion in those moments. You have a gift."

He smiled back and nodded slowly without saying anything.

"Among other gifts of course," I added, perhaps awkwardly.

I felt compelled to convey one more thought. "And I think *The Rising* was the consummate artistic response to 9/11."

He nodded slowly again, his head facing down a bit but his eyes looking up to meet mine. He paused and appeared to be deep in thought. Then he opened up.

"Not too long after 9/11 I was at the beach in Asbury Park. A passenger in a car nearby recognized me, leaned out the window and yelled, 'Bruce, we need you now!' At that point we were living in a new world. What I was writing was contextualized but was what we had all experienced."

I changed the subject, as I'm certain he didn't want to talk shop. After a little bit of lighthearted small talk with the others he turned back to me.

"I respect what you are attempting to accomplish in our country—what you stand for. How you seek to make a difference."

"Thank you," I responded. "That means a great deal to me coming from you."

"I do have a question, though."

"By all means," I responded. "Fire away."

"No—this is a friendly question," he said. "I do appreciate your efforts to unify us. My question is about the symmetry you invoke in defining the problem. There may be a false moral equivalency there. Why do you view our polarization as a symmetrical problem?"

"First of all," I responded, "that's a great question. It's one I do get at times, and I'm glad you asked it."

He nodded at me with a look that seemed eager for my answer. And perhaps already a bit cynical about what he was about to hear.

"The key to achieving actual unity in the country, in my opinion, is not to attempt to assign or calculate relative blame on either side and compare fault. I'm not suggesting it's perfectly symmetrical—it may be or it may not be—to me that's actually irrelevant. The key is to get to a place where we are accepting of each other and not judging—not calling the other side socialists or deplorables, snowflakes or racists. That's not getting us anywhere. That's the first step, and maybe even the hardest step. But just getting beyond the point of disdain for one another can get us to a place where we can begin to think about true understanding of the other view, which can start to bring about healing and the possibility of unity."

Bruce seemed a bit skeptical but not dismissive. And that's all I think I could really ask for in that moment.

"I know that's hard," I added. "Some may say impossible. But I think without it, we won't ever fix this, and won't even have a prayer."

Pierre emerged with my iced tea. "On second thought, Pierre," I said with a smile. "have you got any Bourbon?" That busted both of them up pretty good. Who was I kidding?

***

After about an hour and a half of cocktailing, Martin and Hannah stepped out to the edge of the deck in front of us and called everyone's attention. The music stopped. Denyse walked over, stood next to me and held my hand as we all turned our attention toward the two of them.

Martin spoke first. "Hannah and I are thrilled that all of you could join us on this little getaway." I immediately began wondering what their big getaways must be like.

Hannah then stepped forward and spoke up. I loved watching these two Type A's collaborate cooperatively as only they can. "With Tom and Rita arriving this morning, and the McFaddens this afternoon, we are now at full strength. It warms our hearts to have all of you here with us on such short notice. We have a great evening planned ahead, and bear with us as the next few days have been kind of put together on the fly."

"Yes, Hannah," Tom Hanks chimed in, "everything here looks like it was just slapped together at the last minute." That drew a big laugh from this group, each of whom had been transported to the *Que Será, Será* from Nadi International Airport in Martin and Hannah's personal helicopter, and been pampered nonstop ever since.

"Once we realized Danny and Denyse and Tom and Rita would be with us," added Hannah. "we got a crazy idea about a little field trip we could all do tomorrow that might be of interest to some of you."

Just as I was thinking to myself that there was nothing on earth that could top this, Martin interjected. "Tomorrow we'll have two choppers arriving between 10 am and 11 to ferry anyone who cares over to Guadalcanal where three historians will be waiting there to lead us around the island on a private World War II history tour."

I laughed and looked straight at Denyse. I'm guessing that a day spent immersing herself at the site of one of World War II's bloodiest battles wasn't exactly what she had in mind when we got invited on this little junket to the South Pacific. But I was ecstatic. Wow.

I shook my head and mouthed to her, "You don't have to go."

She smiled back. "Really?"

I looked around and saw there was some excitement in the group about the excursion.

I whispered to Denyse, "Ya think after that I can get Hannah to turn this boat toward Midway or Iwo Jima?" As always I was pushing my luck. I thought it was funny, though. Sometimes that's all that matters.

Hannah and Martin split the six couples up and evenly distributed them among two tables with assigned seats in the main dining room. Of course they did. Every detail of this excursion had been carefully choreographed. They had me seated in between Tom Hanks and Cheryl Stanley—two opposite ends of the political spectrum there, I would assume.

I wasn't sure Tom would be a fan of mine given his vocal support for Hillary Clinton in '16. That provided all the more reason for me to think long and hard about what I should say to this Hollywood icon. Perhaps fortunately for me he had Hannah seated on his other side, which gave me plenty of time to consider it. She has a way of captivating one's attention that can be awful hard to turn away from. I thoroughly enjoyed my conversation with Cheryl to my left. She was so sharp, well-read and personable. I have to admit I knew so much about her husband but so little about her.

When I commented about how interesting it was to see a couple of the young servers on the yacht with very dark skin and very blonde hair, she rattled off a response that kind of blew me away.

"I'll bet those two are from right here in the Solomon Islands," she said.

"Really? What makes you say that?"

"Indigenous people from the Solomon Islands developed a gene for blonde hair centuries ago that is completely different from the Northern Europe blonde hair gene. and it runs through their population. It is actually provides a fascinating case study in genetics."

"Wow," I said. "I'm not sure whether I'm more impressed with the science of that or the fact that you know all about it."

She laughed out loud. "Don't be impressed by me. Contrary to popular belief, Ben and I really don't get out a whole lot. Consequently, I read anything and everything I can get my hands on. All subjects. All genres. Fiction and nonfiction alike. As a result, I have a lot of useless information."

"Oh, you can't convince me it's all useless, Cheryl" I added. "Try as you might, you won't be able to diminish my first impression of you!"

That's one of the reasons I love meeting people so much. If I have the time to engage with people one-on-one in a setting like this, inevitably I find I'm better off for it, and I'm guaranteed to learn something worthwhile. Or be inspired. I really liked her. I'm surprised she lived so much in her husband's shadow—but maybe that's just fine with her.

"What's next for you, Danny?" she asked. "I am fascinated to see where life takes you next."

"That is the sixty-four-thousand dollar question," I responded. "Guadalcanal tomorrow!" I said, laughing, "but I'm certain that's not what you're asking."

I looked out at the horizon. "I'm determined to find the perfect answer to that question. I am sure there are many different ideal answers. I look forward to spending time figuring that out."

Martin came over to our table to say something to Hannah, and Tom Hanks turned toward me. I wasn't exactly certain where to even begin with him, but he beat me to the punch.

"Tell me what it was like to work with John McCain?"

Wow. What a question. Completely disarmed me. That told me all I needed to know. I had a feeling I was gonna like this guy.

I started in about my dear friend and former vice president. And I ordered another cocktail.

Que será, será.

Chapter Two

A Bartender at Heart
January 28, 2021
The Saloon

The party in the Presidential Spirits Saloon was jumping. A remarkably versatile cover band was absolutely killing it on the side stage and the drinks were flowing. The saloon's elegant, majestic mahogany bar, spanning a full fifty feet end to end with a backlit backbar stocked with spirits extending all the way up to a soaring tin tile ceiling, provided such a fitting backdrop for this spectacular fete. The smoke from many active cigars blended with dimly lit gas lamps to create a mystical aura about the scene that was almost redundant, given the guest list. As impressive as this saloon clearly was, what made this centuries-old drinking establishment pop was clearly its A-list clientele—every person who had ever served as President of the United States—and no one else. All 45 former US presidents were present and accounted for, outfitted in fairly formal attire apropos of their period, with drinks to match. What a sight.

George Washington exuded an air of eighteenth century martial nobility in a coat that buttoned across the front with a long tail extending down just above his stockings to his breeches. He held court amidst a group of admirers who all drank Hot Ale Flips—a concoction served up appropriately enough, by a bartender nicknamed "Big Time," by combining molasses, egg whites, rum, and ale, finished by plunging a red hot fireplace poker directly into the mug until the drink was good and hot. That group of presidents did not appear to include any from the last 150 years, and perhaps that particular selection of drink by the Father of Our Country had something to do with that. This collection of presidents, however, appeared perfectly content to imbibe in that with him. Perhaps that explains how he convinced a ragtag assemblage of farmers, shopkeepers and settlers to take on one of the greatest military forces on earth. And win.

Some of the modern presidents had assembled in front, on the edge of the bar closest to the stage and were shouting out requests to the band between songs. Obama, George W. Bush, and Clinton appeared to be the ringleaders of that group of about a dozen.

FDR led a lively conversation of presidents seated around one of the larger oaken tables in the center of the room—a conversation enhanced no doubt by the cocktails the wait staff busily ferried over every fifteen minutes or so. Perhaps that frequency was a function more of their desire to interact with these lovely waitresses than any need for more alcohol. No, this group did not appear to be in need of any more alcohol.

Lincoln's height made him hard to miss standing near the back of the bar surrounded by Grant, John Quincy Adams, Benjamin Harrison, and a host of others from the 19th Century.

I had the sensation you get when you have just awoken in the middle of the night from a vivid dream. I attempted a quick bit of self-assessment. Things could not be so bad if I was back in this place. I had wondered for four years—obsessed, really—about whether I would be conscious of everything that happened in this saloon when I was no longer president. This scene in front of me answered that question for me rather emphatically.

This was my first night in this saloon post-presidency. I stood and marveled at the scene in front of me. It was every bit as breathtaking as it had been the night I first stumbled upon it—the night of my inauguration in 2017—four full years ago but it seemed to have gone by in an instant.

Mary Ann saw me and immediately walked over to greet me. She is always such a sweet, welcome sight.

"Danny Mac! So great to see you."

Still in a bit of a daze, I was slow to respond.

"You OK?" she asked.

"I'm sorry," I said, turning and looking right at her. "Just taking it all in."

"I know the first night in here post-presidency can be different. Scary even."

I thought about that for a second.

"Can I get you anything from the bar?" she asked.

No, I'm good right now. Maybe later."

I looked around again at the surreal scene in front of me. Then it dawned on me. I had no recollection of anything since President Bates' inaugural address. Nothing. How could that be? My brain, which had been a bit slow to process all of this, was now racing. I wondered why I was here and not back in California. We had been all set to return to Los Gatos right after the inauguration.

I spotted an empty seat at a round table of presidents nearby. I pulled the chair out, positioned it away from the table and sat down.

Yes, I had wondered so often as I came up here to this saloon during my presidency whether I would be conscious of everything happening in this place going forward—hoping so much that somehow I would. Apparently, however, it's a bit of a good news/bad news proposition. I'm thrilled that I will in fact still be able to experience all this. It is truly something to behold. But what about everything else? Denyse, the kids, Satch and all the rest? Suddenly I could feel my heartbeat.

"McFadden," a voice nearby said.

I turned and saw Martin Van Buren smiling at me. I immediately smiled back. How could I not? He had—how shall I say this—a very "unique" appearance. Bald on the top, but crazy Einstein-like unkempt hair on the sides and back, and extending down the sides of his face. I have to say though, he had a great personality that made it all work, and was one of the favorites in the saloon—particularly among the wait staff. "Old Kinderhook" is what they all call him. It was said that the women of America really loved and supported him in his time. Of course, none of them could vote. He was soundly defeated seeking re-election.

"I know what you are going through right now." he said. "Don't worry. You'll get through that phase. It will pass rather quickly, in fact."

"That's reassuring," I responded. "Might take a little longer with me, however, given my tendency toward full-tilt, bat-shit crazy at times."

He laughed. "To borrow a phrase made popular by our friend, Mr. Lincoln, 'This too shall pass.'"

I nodded in agreement, though I still wasn't entirely convinced.

He felt the need to provide me some more assurance. "The human spirit is capable of adjusting to just about anything and forging forward. I know that better than most. Keep your focus on the positive and blot out the rest. When I wrote my memoirs, I did not so much as utter a word about my presidency."

After a moment's pause, he added, "Didn't mention my wife either."

He laughed. I didn't. Wow. There's a story there. Or many. I don't think that little exchange did anything to make me feel better, but I appreciated the effort, and it was rather revealing about him.

"I've got an idea," he said, standing up and putting his hand on my shoulder. "Follow me."

We walked through the party around to the side of the massive bar, where he lifted the hinged bar flap, and we entered the bartenders' sacred workspace.

"I know you are a bit like me," he said. "A bartender at heart."

Matty, the bartender that George W. and the others call "Big Time," was back there working hard next to a new guy I had never seen before.

"Danny Mac!" Matty yelled, obviously thrilled to see me, reminding me again why I love this place.

"Big Time!" I roared right back.

"Let me introduce you to our new guy, Stephen. That's his real name, but Bush calls him Slick and most everyone else here does too. He mixes a mean drink. Damn fine martini."

"Nice to meet you, Slick." I couldn't spit that out with a straight face though. This whole place and all these nicknames really cracked me up.

"You guys look like you could use a hand," Van Buren said.

"Always a need for more bartenders, Mr. President."

Van Buren and I settled in and began pouring some ambitious cocktails. Something about that always energizes me. Each new drink comes packed with possibility. Like opening day every spring.

You really get to know someone when you work alongside them behind a bar. I like to watch how they treat people who are respectful to them and, even more telling, those who are not. I could see Van Buren's rep as a man of the people was well-earned. I loved the stories he told of growing up as the child of saloon keepers in Kinderhook, New York.

"Our tavern and inn were located along the road between New York City and Albany. I worked in the bar as a teen, and all the New York politicians would pass through. I watched each closely and learned from them all. I got to know Alexander Hamilton well. Aaron Burr too, of course. I studied each and every one of them. A splendid training ground for a life of politics."

Andrew Jackson, seeing his former vice president, Van Buren, and I behind the bar, hopped up and dashed over to join us.

"Have you room for a hard drinking Southerner back here, Matty?" asked Jackson.

"Is there any other kind?" Big Time responded. "Always room for you, Old Hickory!"

Alright. I said to myself. I might still have a long way to go yet, but I do believe it's possible I might grow to like this. I did really wonder what was up with Denyse, though. And the kids.

I put those thoughts aside for the moment, settled in and took some drink orders. Always loved tending bar, and this was the Taj Mahal of bars. For a proud bartender it had a feeling not unlike what a pitcher must feel upon first taking the mound in Yankee Stadium. The old one. We had at our disposal every liquid intoxicant ever served up in a bar in America. I loved nothing more than when someone ordered some obscure bottle from America's early days requiring me to slide one of these vintage rolling library ladders and scale it all the way to the top, if for no other reason than it gave me an opportunity to pause, twist around and catch a glimpse the magnificent canvass of American history being painted before my very eyes.

After a few moments admiring the scenery from up there, I made a mental note not to try this after a few pops—knowing full well those mental notes of mine tend not to stick very well after a few. Or at all.

Amidst all that activity, the loud and lively music, the camaraderie, and the energy clearly pulsating through the room, it's no wonder nobody noticed when the back door slowly opened—the one no one ever uses. No one, that is, except the sitting president of the United States, entering through a separate entrance that connects to the third floor of the White House . . .

Chapter Three

An Alley-oop from McFadden
Three months earlier—November 3, 2020

The election had been ground-breaking—resulting in our first female president, shattering a nearly 250-year-old glass ceiling. The Alliance political movement we had started at the end of my presidency played a small role in that. That movement, officially named the "We're Better Than This Alliance," was established in an attempt to prioritize uniting the country above all else, and draw the parties back toward the center of the political spectrum after years of becoming increasingly extreme. We chose to support a moderate Republican, Margaret Bates, in the Republican primary, and a moderate Democrat, Antonio Gutierrez, in the Democratic primary. Bates won the Republican primary, but Gutierrez was soundly defeated in the Democratic primary by the most progressive candidate, Massachusetts Senator Robert Clayton. Our movement threw our support behind Bates in the general election.

CNN Election Night Coverage
11:45 pm

ANDERSON COOPER: Welcome back to CNN's Election Night coverage. Gloria, while it's far from over, particularly with states like Pennsylvania and Michigan having so many mail-in votes yet to count, it certainly seems like Margaret Bates is now on a path to become the first woman to occupy the White House in our nation's history.

GLORIA BORGER: It certainly does, Anderson. Irrespective of your politics, Americans have to be proud tonight that the ultimate glass ceiling has been broken—shattered really—if these numbers bear out. While it's not a landslide, she looks to have won the popular vote by two and a half percentage points, and may be looking at in excess of 300 electoral college votes when all is said and done.

COOPER: Rick, it looks like it was a big night for Republicans, at least at the top of the ticket.

RICK SANTORUM: Yes, and I believe it was rejection of what many felt was a socialist agenda presented by the Democrats and Senator Clayton, the Green New Deal, Defund the Police, more taxes, more spending, bigger government.

VAN JONES: I want to urge caution here in ferreting out what this all means. While I won't deny Clayton appears headed for defeat, I'm not so sure about the House and Senate races. Democrats appear to me to be doing better in both houses than anticipated. I don't think it's fair to characterize tonight as a rejection of the progressive agenda.

DAVID AXELROD: I think Van makes a good point. Let's see how some of these House and Senate races break, but it's clear to me tonight that perhaps the Alliance political movement initiated by President McFadden on the day he announced he was not seeking re-election, had an unmistakable impact on this result. The organization that came out of that movement was able to influence the Republicans to select Bates—the most moderate of all the Republicans seeking the nomination—as opposed to the others, who were each fairly ardent conservatives, some with what I would call dangerous views.

SANTORUM: I disagree, David, I think she became the choice because she was literally the only Republican candidate in the moderate lane, and the others simply cannibalized each others' support. I'm not so sure McFadden's group had anything to do with it at all.

AXELROD: I think you are mistaken, Senator. The fact that the Alliance movement was out there and becoming a force convinced her to run in the first place, and the way that whole movement embraced her and actively worked for her, as a moderate candidate to secure the nomination, was instrumental in her emerging as the nominee.

BORGER: I believe you're right, David. Without that movement, she doesn't run, doesn't get the nomination, and we are left with a far-right candidate like Ted Cruz or Lindsey Graham facing the far left with Senator Clayton in the general election. And then of course all bets are off. The exit polls show Bates got 82% of independents tonight. That's a huge number.

AXELROD: It's worth mentioning as well, Gloria, that at least five different congressional candidates claiming to be members of the Alliance Party won races tonight as well. Five for five. I wasn't sure they were calling themselves a party but whatever they are, they now have representation in Congress and a President who certainly needs to credit their movement with some kind of an assist.

BORGER: I think it bears reminding that the Alliance movement had also simultaneously backed centrist Arizona Governor Gutierrez in the Democratic presidential primary, who, despite their assist, was unable to secure the nomination. Their entire strategy was to ensure that the parties didn't nominate from their ideological extremes. But their success with Republicans paved the way for this victory tonight.

COOPER: Let's send it back to Jake Tapper who is with Dana Bash and Abby Phillip.

JAKE TAPPER: It may have been more than a mere assist, as David Axelrod called it. I think that was a full-fledged alley-oop.

ABBY PHILLIP: I think we should be careful not to take anything away from Governor Bates, soon to be President-Elect Bates. She has shrewd political skills, and a personal charm about her that maybe we haven't seen since the way candidates like Clinton or John Kennedy were able to engage audiences and really connect at a personal level.

DANA BASH: I agree, Abby. The Alliance movement perhaps helped to begin to change the political dynamic, but Margaret Bates' victory tonight is hers. She had the vision to take advantage of that opportunity, and the political skill to make it happen. Perhaps it's better to suggest the Alliance just set a weakside pick rather than delivered an alley-oop.

TAPPER: Wow. Love the depth of the sports analogies you get on this show.

BASH: My ten-year old son is playing basketball. He went to bed long ago, but I'm sure he'd be proud of his mom for that reference.

TAPPER: Indeed, he would. Of course, Bates does have considerable skills, and she'll need all of those skills now to govern and move her agenda forward. The country might be rewarding a moderate tonight, for the second presidential election in a row now, but Congress is still deeply polarized, and weighed down heavily at the two far extremes. I think President Bates will have her hands full navigating through that. Danny McFadden could tell her all about what that's like.

Chapter Four

Peaches
Three months later—January 28, 2021
The Saloon

It opened slowly. The door that has stood there since John and Abigail Adams first moved into the Executive Mansion in 1800, even surviving the British torching the White House during the War of 1812, opened inward at a snail's pace. This door, that for 228 years had provided a private entrance into this saloon only for 45 consecutive men, was now, after all that time, opening for a woman. And no one in this room even noticed.

As it opened wider, a figure emerged, and immediately it became clear that this old boys club would never be quite the same. Standing tall, she wore an elegant yet modest, tailored navy blue St. John knit dress, knee length with three quarter sleeves and key hole neck line, slim leather belt, gold buckle, with navy blue pumps, along with her trademark pearl earrings and matching necklace. She had dark, lush, wavy brown hair that fell loosely below her shoulders. She appeared to be in her mid-forties, projecting a look that was sharp, fashionable and feminine.

She gazed upon the room with a look of disbelief and then quickly drew the door back and stood behind it, peering out with just one eye like a game of hide and seek. Who could really blame her?

Moments later she emerged again, perhaps surprisingly, and slowly this time as well. Something was obviously drawing her back in. She continued to hold the door open with one hand, looking almost like she feared that if the door closed she'd be locked inside. The light hit her now. She had sharp features, cream colored skin and very white teeth—which would certainly make her a rarity in this room. And she looked to be very fit—yet another reason she'd stand out next to many of these gentlemen. She stood there alone trying to make sense of the incredible scene before her. She glanced down at the 1792 vintage gold coin displaying the image of George Washington in her left hand.

I could see it all unfold from my place behind the bar. Mary Ann of course soon noticed her as well. She almost dropped her drink tray. She could not contain her excitement.

She let out a scream, and then yelled, "Hey Otter," looking across the saloon to George W. Bush, "it's go time!" Then Mary Ann promptly burst into tears.

It's a long story, but George W. Bush goes by the name of Otter in this saloon, after the main character in Animal House—a name given him by the other patrons here, most of whom have received one or more nicknames of their own courtesy of Otter over the years. The wait staff too. By the way, 'Mary Ann' is also a nickname. You may need a program as we go along.

Bush whirled and turned toward that door. A huge smile engulfed his face. He flashed a thumbs up sign back at Mary Ann as she scampered over toward Washington. By the way, Bush calls the Father of our Country "Big Daddy." With his personality in this place he gets away with that. Not many others even attempt that, though. Most of these guys, after all, are fairly smart.

Bush, being one of the few in this room in excellent shape—aside from the wait staff that is—hustled to the door and was at the new President's side in a flash. I wasn't far behind. Some of the others in the room noticed the commotion. Matty dropped everything he was doing from behind the bar and began to applaud.

"Gentlemen," Matty said to all those near the bar, "do you see what I see?" pointing up to the president's door.

"Oh my," uttered Van Buren.

Andrew Jackson then yelled out to the room, "Boys, looks like we've got ourselves a filly." A buzz came over the saloon.

"Welcome to the Presidential Spirits saloon, ma'am," said Bush to the astonished new patron. She couldn't seem to shake her blank expression as she continued to scan the room. When her eyes reached Lincoln nearby she fixated on him—how could you not—and began to slowly shake her head in disbelief.

"I'm George W. Bush."

"I know, we've met several times. You spoke at my nominating convention."

"This is different," Bush responded with a huge smile. "I can explain."

She turned and took a step towards the door. Bush reached out to grab her forearm but let go immediately.

"Please stay," he implored her.

George Washington began to approach. Bush waived him off.

Her jaw dropped open. "Was that . . ."

"George Washington—yes. In the flesh."

"Jiminy Christmas."

She turned again toward the door.

"Wait, please. We're here to help you," implored Bush. 'We've all been where you are."

Mary Ann, either not sensing the new president's consternation or else choosing to ignore it, wrapped her arms around her.

"Welcome!" she explained. "I'm so happy for you, and happy for us, and happy for the entire country! It's about time!"

MaryAnn's new friend remained speechless.

"I'm Mary Ann."

"I'm Margaret Bates. Pleasure to meet you. Pardon me if I'm momentarily at a bit of a loss of my manners."

By that time I was standing right behind Mary Ann. Maggie looked at me and shook her head. "Danny, I thought you and Denyse were back in California, or in Fiji with Hannah and Martin. I think I heard that."

"This is not what you think," I responded. "Please stay for a drink. And keep an open mind—pretty sure this will blow it wide open. But this little establishment will be here for you whenever you want it to be—whenever you need it—over the course of the next four years. The next eight years. It helped me immeasurably."

"What in god's name is this?" she asked, looking out at the room.

"Wait," I blurted out. "Did you say Fiji? Really?"

"Well I'll be," gasped Maggie. "Is that JFK and Franklin Roosevelt?" Her jaw fell open again.

"Have a drink, Maggie," I said again with a big smile. "I'll make it myself. What does a classy Southern belle like you enjoy at the bar?"

"I suppose a girl could have a martini," she said managing a glimmer of a smile.

"Atta girl!" I responded.

She then added, "Gin, dry, extra dirty."

I was quite pleased with that response. Otter smiled at me and winked.

"You're from Dixie?" said Bush, seemingly thrilled at this discovery. "Why I should have known, Whereabouts?"

She looked back at him with another puzzled expression. "Georgia," she said slowly, barely above a whisper, her mind racing. "Savannah. But you know that, sir."

"Oh honey," cried MaryAnn, "the presidents in this bar are not exactly the same people you have come to know on the outside. It's complicated. Really complicated. Come with me."

Mary Ann began to lead President Bates away. Then she looked back at me. "Tell Matty someone will need to cover for me for a few."

"Oh, he's got plenty of help," Bush responded. "There's no shortage of saloon expertise at his side behind the bar tonight."

"Peaches," called out George Bush. I wasn't sure who he was talking to as the two ladies had walked away and I was on my way back to the bar. I turned around.

"What are you talking about?" I asked.

"Peaches," he responded. "That's what we'll call her. Peaches."

My smile faded. "Peaches?" I said, quizzically. "You know I'm your biggest fan in here, dude, but what the hell are you talking about? Are you insane?"

"She's from Georgia. She's a peach. And boy is she a peach. That's what we'll call her."

"Love you my friend," I replied. "I really do. But are on your own on this one. I think I'll stick to Maggie. Or better yet, Mrs. President. That has a nice ring to it."

As I walked back to the bar I could still hear Bush from a distance muttering, now only to himself.

"Peaches. I like the sound of that. Peaches it will be. That settles it."

Chapter Five

A Bunch of Absolute Badasses
January 28, 2021
The Saloon

The saloon band, tipped off that President Bates hailed from Savannah, Georgia, reflexively rattled off a resounding version of "Georgia on my Mind," which they followed up with "Georgia Rain," and then finished with an absolutely heroic rendition of "Midnight Train to Georgia" that had even Jimmy Carter bobbing his head up and down and moving around like he was one of Gladys Knight's own Pips. The place was jumping, and drinks were flowing freely. In another salute to the new president, mint juleps could be seen everywhere.

President Bates emerged from her private briefing with Mary Ann, the waitress extraordinaire, and appeared now to be enjoying herself somewhat in between bewildered looks and expressions of disbelief. I would venture to say no one ever emerged from a meeting with Mary Ann without feeling at least a little bit better about themselves and the world.

Matty personally delivered another martini to our newest president as Washington motioned to Bush near the band to silence the music. Matty then let out a whistle that could probably be heard all the way to Baltimore. Washington stepped forward to address the room.

"Gentlemen," he said, "the benign Parent of the human race has been pleased to favor the American people once more. For it is through his divine blessing we welcome a new President among us—President Margaret Bates."

The group applauded. Many in the room appeared to have looks on their faces equally as dumbfounded as that of our new president. Some appeared to be agitated about her victory, but more than a few seemed delighted. Just eight years after becoming one of the first female members admitted to Augusta National Golf Club, Maggie Bates had now joined the most exclusive old boys club left in the world, leaving the glass ceiling in the room below this mystical saloon in pieces.

Washington continued. "Another peaceful transition of power—the hallmark of our republic. Let us never take that for granted."

Another round of applause.

Washington continued. "As is our tradition, I propose that we now offer thirteen toasts—one for each original state in our union—to our newest colleague. Who among us would care to offer the first?"

A few moments passed.

And then a few more.

Just as things were on the cusp of becoming awkward, President Bates herself, martini in hand, broke the silence.

"President Washington, may I offer the toast, sir?" she asked. "I appreciate the gesture, but I'd rather like to offer one of my own."

Washington, nodding his head in approval, replied "Splendid. Proceed."

"What a delightful gathering you have here," she began, flashing a bit of that trademark smile and charm, "and thank you, Matt, for the 'heavy pour'—a bartender after my own heart." The entire wait staff got a big charge out of that shout-out. Some of these guys would never give them the time of day. And I just loved her choice of words. Perhaps she and I have a lot more in common than I thought.

"I'm not quite sure what to make of all this, but I am truly mesmerized. However, as I'm the first of my gender to be invited into this exclusive club, let me acknowledge and toast a few of the great women in our history whose landmark contributions helped advance the cause of women in this country and ultimately pave the way for me to be amongst y'all here today."

Several in the room applauded amidst a chorus of "Hear, hear," although more than a few eyerolls were also seen throughout the room as well.

"So many truly devine women to choose from, of course, but perhaps the best place to start is with Susan B. Anthony, for among other things, her tireless efforts to secure for women the right to vote in the face of an onslaught of discrimination and hate. She was accosted, berated, hung in effigy and even arrested for attempting to vote in the 1872 election."

"She cast that vote for me!" yelled Grant proudly from his seat at the bar. "A fine woman indeed." The room laughed and applauded.

"She certainly was, President Grant," responded Bates. "She also attempted to right a few of America's other wrongs, including slavery and unequal pay for women, and she sought education for all."

"I hosted her at the White House on the occasion of her 80th birthday," added McKinley. "I would remind you General Grant, before you deify her, that she also fought for temperance. Which makes it rather ironic that she voted for you."

The room erupted again in laughter.

"And that we are now toasting her."

More laughter.

Priceless comments like that are what I had come to love most about this saloon.

With all eyes still on Grant, he raised his tumbler of whiskey and looked around the room. "I wholeheartedly join our newest member in toasting Susan Anthony. But here's to Margaret Bates as well. I can tell already she has the composition to handle the riff-raff in this room." More laughter.

"Thank you for that, President Grant, I think," replied Bates. "Let me add another point about Ms. Anthony. When the authorities sought to arrest her for voting, they advised her to meet them at the local police station where they would take her into custody. She refused, and instead she demanded a 'proper arrest' like they would any man, including handcuffs."

Then with an engaging smile, Bates added, "Therefore, all I ask is to be treated 'properly.' I will seek no special favor, but also no harsher treatment from the 'riff-raff' around here."

That drew a favorable response from the room, which applauded and drank, many of them aggressively, as the servers scrambled for more.

Washington, appearing very pleased at the positive turn this had taken, rose to speak again. "Thank you for that, President Bates. Let me also then seize this occasion to tender homage to a woman similarly worthy of our admiration. Our Culper Spy Ring was a sophisticated network of citizens in service of the Continental Army whose patriotism proved providential. Mrs. Anna Strong was an unlikely but indispensable component of that endeavor. She relayed messages in code by hanging laundry to dry on her clothesline in the yard of her Long Island farmstead which could be viewed by our boats in the sea. Anna was a mother whose husband was with our Continental Army, so her actions placed her at great personal risk, but she was essential to our success in our glorious victory over the British."

"Well there we have it," cried President Bates raising her martini glass, "to Anna, her clothesline, and airing of the Strong family laundry." The presidents clearly approved. The energy in the room was gathering steam. She was already winning them over.

John Quincy Adams stepped forward. "I might rightly be said to have had a blind spot when it comes to fraternizing with women," he began. "For evidence of that I would refer you to no less an authority than my wife, Louisa." That drew some laughter.

"But let me take a moment to acknowledge another trailblazing woman. When I was president, I started each day with a swim in the Potomac. Nothing better to invigorate my senses. A woman by the name of Anne Royall, the first female professional journalist in this country, doggedly sought an interview with me for many months, and I refused. One morning as I swam naked in the river she found my pile of clothes on the shore and sat on it, and would not permit me to have them back until I submitted to an interview on the spot. Needless to say, she got her interview, which I gave standing in water submerged from the waist down."

"I sincerely hope you permitted her to have a peek," yelled Cleveland, which drew many laughs.

Adams ignored him. "The woman was a force to be reckoned with. Armed with the First Amendment, her pen was as venomous as a rattlesnake's fangs. She was feared in the halls of Congress. She was decades, perhaps even a full century or more, ahead of her time."

Washington, who had walked over and was now standing alongside President Bates, raised his glass. "To Anne Royall." The room drank. President Bates seemed to be enjoying the moment immensely. I, too, was thrilled with the direction this night was now headed.

President Reagan came forward. Of course, he did. In the last four years he had rarely remained silent in moments such as this in the saloon. "Let me offer a toast to another remarkable woman who boldly blazed a trail for others to follow. Our nation had seen 101 justices appointed to the Supreme Court before my appointment of Sandra Day O'Connor. And oh what a justice she was. In her rulings she sought and found common ground, and often served as a bridge builder between the two ideological extremes. She acquitted herself so admirably, serving for twenty-five years."

Heads nodded throughout the room in approval.

Reagan continued. "May we all take a drink in honor of Justice O'Connor, and, of course, to President Bates. Maggie, may you lead this country as masterfully as another fine Maggie I knew steered hers—Maggie Thatcher." The room approved of the Gipper's words. They usually did.

Thomas Jefferson rose to speak. Though he certainly commanded the attention of the room, by reason of his legacy, his intellect, and his height, he spoke in a rather soft and high-pitched voice which always sort of startled me. "With my fellow presidents referencing these notable trailblazing women, permit me to acknowledge a woman who quite literally helped to blaze a trail—one of great consequence—Sacagawea. Our acquisition of the Louisiana Territory necessitated that we discover a passageway from the Mississippi to the Pacific. This poor Indian woman from the Shoshone tribe, just 16 years of age, made that long, dangerous and fatiguing trek with Lewis & Clark to chart a path to the Pacific and back—all the while with a newborn on her back. She provided essential navigation assistance, including the location of a gap in the Rocky Mountains, translated for them when the group encountered other Indians, and, by her mere presence in their travel party, symbolized to other tribes they encountered along the way that they came in peace. I regret to say that I do not believe she received sufficient accommodation for her efforts by me or others in that time, although I am now told her legacy is quite secure."

Most of the room raised their glass and joined in drinking to the remarkable young Native American heroine.

Before taking his seat, Jefferson added, "I must say I seem to be making a habit of confessions of regret in this saloon. I quite hope I am finished with that after this admission. Perhaps it's something about the spirits served here that elicits this sort of expressions of truth."

"Yes indeed, President Jefferson," added Nixon, "but also the fact that there are no political consequences in this saloon for speaking the truth."

That elicited a ton of laughter throughout the room.

Harry Truman stood up at his table to address the room.

"While I certainly don't make a habit of publicly fawning over another man's wife, allow me to offer a brief toast in tribute to a woman I called 'The First Lady of the World'—Eleanor Roosevelt. She was so much more than a first lady and delegate to the UN General Assembly. She was the foremost international spokesman for women. Author, columnist, lecturer, political activist, political operative, human rights advocate, civil rights advocate, presidential advisor—to name just a few of the roles she mastered. She was a tireless advocate for women, for a world without war, and for the brotherhood of man. She was a giant on the world stage, with a legacy rivaling any man in this room."

Then Truman raised his glass of bourbon, and, with a big smile, added, "To my favorite Roosevelt." That remark drew raucous laughter, including belly laughs from both Roosevelts.

"You beat me to the punch there, President Truman," John Kennedy said in his familiar Boston accent—another voice in this saloon that seemed to instantly capture the attention of the room. "I admired her so much. She served for me as our delegate to the UN and on my Committee for the Peace Corps. I asked her to negotiate with Castro for the return of our hostages following our involvement with the Bay of Pigs, and I nominated her for a Nobel Peace Prize. She was a fearless zealot for all causes she firmly believed in. And she refused to kowtow to me or any other man who stood in her way."

"I can certainly vouge for that last point, Jack," added FDR, to much laughter.

Abraham Lincoln lumbered forward slowly and cautiously to the front of the room. He wore a long dark coat with a bow tie and vest. He was so thin, making him appear even taller than six foot four. In this room full of legends, he was revered like no other, with the exception of Washington.

A hush came over the room as Lincoln addressed the crowd. "Permit me please to honor a poor uneducated slave woman who demonstrated the type of qualities you reference in the other women in receipt of our accolades tonight.

"Harriett Tubman was born into slavery in Maryland, and was severely whipped and beaten as a child, incurring injuries that included a fractured skull. At age 27 she escaped to Philadelphia. Soon thereafter she returned under cover of darkness to smuggle family members to freedom, and before long she was returning to guide dozens of others to freedom in the north as part of the 'underground railroad.' When Congress passed the Fugitive Slave Act, she simply extended her underground railroad all the way to Canada. Her crusade for freedom earned her the nickname 'Moses.'"

Lincoln, one of just a few in this saloon who chose not to drink, paused to take a sip of tea, then continued. "During the Civil War, this remarkable woman worked for the Union and even led an armed expedition of 150 black soldiers in a raid at Combahee Ferry, liberating 700 slaves. John Brown called her General Tubman.

"She was also a tireless advocate for women' rights, and worked to support the women's suffrage movement."

Lincoln raised his cup. "Let us toast, gentlemen, to the woman they called Moses, who risked her life so that others could be free." The room applauded enthusiastically.

Ulysses Grant came forward, tumbler of whiskey in his left hand.

"Thank you, President Lincoln. Let me start by saying God gave us liberty and he gave us Lincoln, and they were both worth fighting for." The room erupted again in applause.

Lincoln, smiling, approached Grant, and took his whiskey glass, held it up to his nose and took a whiff. Then Lincoln looked out at the crowd.

"Sometimes my critics and even my cabinet members would complain to me that General Grant drank too much." He then paused a second amidst some knowing chuckles. "But to that I would simply respond, 'please tell me the brand of whiskey that Grant drinks, so that I may send a barrel to each of my generals.'" That broke up the room, particularly coming from that source.

Grant waited for the room to settle down and then continued.

"Allow me to offer another toast." Grant looked over at the new president and Washington. They both nodded with approval.

"Let me tell you about a remarkable woman we called 'The Angel of the Battlefield.' We believed then, as we do now, that we had a good government and a cause worth fighting for, and, if need be, dying for. So many of our comrades paid the ultimate price to preserve our union, or incurred severe injury.

"When the war broke out this angel appeared like a gift from god to tend to the wounded and organize a large-scale medical operation. Her name was Clara Barton. She was a shy farmgirl from Massachusetts who had spent years caring for an invalid brother in her childhood after he fell from the rafters of their barn. She continued at his side long after doctors had given up. She then became a school teacher and, when she realized how few people in her community could attend school, she started a free public school.

"A Massachusetts regiment was the first to volunteer for the war, and the first to sustain casualties. Clara sprang into action to organize a relief effort, and took out advertisements in Massachusetts newspapers seeking donations to fund her operation. Soon she obtained permission to travel with the army, and before long she was a fixture at the front lines feeding and nursing the men. In the process she befriended Massachusetts Senator Henry Wilson, who would become my Vice President.

"Her raw courage was exceeded only by her compassion. At one point a bullet passed through her dress but miraculously managed to miss her. She contracted typhoid fever at the battle of Antietam. She sometimes removed bullets from soldiers using only a common pocketknife.

"She personally attended to our troops at the battles of Fairfax Station, Chantilly, Harpers Ferry, South Mountain, Antietam, Fredericksburg, Charleston, Petersburg and Cold Harbor, to name just a few. At the end of the war she organized an effort to reunite soldiers with their families and account for all the dead. She later founded the American Red Cross, and continued to work at hot spots around the world assisting victims until age 80. She finally resigned as President of the American Red Cross at age 83."

Grant lifted his glass. "To the Angel of the Battlefield, Clara Barton. Hers was truly a most consequential life of aid and service to others."

The room applauded approvingly.

Kennedy rose to speak once again. "I'd like to add another name to our illustrious list. In 1955 in Montgomery, Alabama, a seamstress by the name of Rosa Parks refused to give up her seat on a public bus to move to what was called the 'colored section,' thereby igniting a movement. She lost her job and received death threats throughout her life, but she became an international civil rights icon, and helped to bring about the end of de jure segregation. She continued to work for justice and was awarded a Presidential Medal of Freedom.

"Since nicknames appear to be a theme tonight, as they are every night in this bar courtesy of the younger Mr. Bush, let me add that Ms. Parks earned herself the moniker, 'The Mother of the Civil Rights Movement.' What a fitting testament to such an extraordinary woman."

"To the Mother of the Civil Rights Movement."

Kennedy wasn't done. He turned to the new president.

"And to President Maggie Bates. It is high time we had one from the fairer sex join this club. Your challenge will be daunting. You'll be mocked, discriminated against, pilloried and ridiculed." He paused just a second before finishing, "to say nothing of how you'll be treated outside of this saloon." The room exploded in laughter. Kennedy had a rare gift for that. He was smooth as silk.

"Welcome, dear Maggie. May you have the character of General Washington, the wisdom of Mr. Jefferson, the toughness and passion of Teddy Roosevelt, the vision of FDR, the humility, determination, and perseverance of Mr. Lincoln, and the advice, support, and encouragement of every leader in this room."

The room applauded amidst many chants of "Hear, hear."

Obama stepped forward, still chuckling at Kennedy's joke. "You would think with degrees from Columbia and Harvard I'd be smart enough not to follow President Kennedy." He smiled and looked back at JFK. These guys were good. And God I enjoyed watching this up close.

"Welcome, Maggie." Obama began. "I too am thrilled that we finally now have a woman among our ranks—even if it has to be a Republican. We wish you all the best. We are here for you."

President Bates smiled and nodded her approval.

Obama continued. "I am going to steal a page from President Truman's playbook by making a toast about another one of our colleagues' wives. I don't imagine Bill will mind."

He looked over at Bill Clinton, who smiled broadly. "Hillary Clinton surely belongs among this illustrious list of trailblazing women we have honored here tonight. A distinguished senator from New York, she served the nation so admirably in my administration as Secretary of State, and in her presidential campaigns she paved the way for Maggie and others who will follow.

"In fact, had McFadden not come along at the last minute in 2016, she certainly would have been our first female president. I cannot imagine she would have lost straight up against Donald Trump."

"That would have been something, huh Bill?" Lyndon Johnson chimed in with a grin, "Just think if you could have had her in the Saloon here right alongside you—night after night after night." Johnson was incapable of finishing that with a straight face.

Amidst much laughter, Obama, the pro that he is, moved on from that rather nasty remark immediately, sparing the room and Clinton any further awkwardness. "To a fine Madam Secretary and a distinguished Senator." The room raised their glasses in a show of respect, but a few of them were still clearly still amused at LBJ's crack.

George W. Bush, certainly a crowd favorite, addressed Washington. "May I take a turn, Big Daddy?"

The room seemed to collectively hold its breath, until Washington blurted out with a big smile, "Be my guest, Otter."

That was a bonding moment for the ages. Only in the saloon.

Bush, quite pleased with that exchange, started in. "In 2007, I had the great honor of bestowing a Presidential Medal of Freedom upon one of our true national treasures—Harper Lee. This daughter of the South wrote a novel set in the deep south just as race relations in the country were exploding in the wake of the Supreme Court case of Brown v. Board of Education. And she chose from among the most explosive subject matter imaginable—an accusation of rape by an African American man against a white woman. She was ahead of her time, and her masterpiece prodded America to catch up with her. Even six decades after its publication, her hero Atticus Finch continues to inspire every new reader. One reason *To Kill A Mockingbird* succeeded is the wise and kind heart of the author, which comes through on every page. This product of Monroeville, Alabama, had something to say about honor and tolerance and, most of all, love—and it still resonates today as much as ever."

Bush, another one of the saloon's few teetotalers, raised his glass schooner full of water. "To the Pulitzer Prize-winning Harper Lee—for her matchless contributions to humanity and to the character of our country."

Applause all around.

While I was hesitant to add my voice at first, I then asked myself what am I doing in this supernatural saloon in the first place if I can't play a key role in serving its core mission? So, with my Guinness in hand, I emerged from behind the bar and enthusiastically took a spot at the front of the room. Teddy Roosevelt, a sort of presidential BFF of mine, led a group clap as I made my way to the front.

"Welcome, Maggie," I began. "And what a perfect first night for you. I love that on your own big night you chose to honor the others whose contributions paved the way for women in this country. Speaks volumes about you. And your tendency to turn the attention away from yourself will certainly make you stand out amongst many of the others in this room." That remark drew many laughs, but notably not from every one of my colleagues.

"I consider myself somewhat well versed in our history," I added, "but I did not know the half of it about some of the backstories of these amazing women. What a bunch of absolute badasses."

That statement drew some blank stares and curious looks. Perhaps understandably.

"Rockstars," I added, which seemed to only make it worse. Sensing the translation issues with my twenty-first century vocabulary, I tried one more time. "Really, really courageous, heroic, inspirational women." That they understood. The room applauded.

"Sacagawea made that monumental exploration with a newborn on her back? At age 16? Harriet Tubman led an armed expedition of black troops in the Civil War? Clara Barton had a bullet pass through her dress and still kept returning to the front lines? Forget for a moment about all the legions of women and girls they inspired who followed them—hearing those stories inspires the hell out of me!

"I'm here to pay homage to another one of those—cut from precisely the same cloth. One we recently lost at the end of my term.

"The Babe is not the only great American treasure named Ruth. Ruth Bader Ginsberg served on the Supreme Court for nearly three decades, where she was a pioneer for gender equality. And what a force of nature she was. She stood only five feet tall, but she could do thirty pushups—even into her eighties. Nothing was capable of intimidating her. Her mind stayed sharp until the very end—at age 87. And I really love how her philosophical disagreements with Justice Scalia—her polar opposite on the bench—did not prevent them from being the best of friends—a shining example of the kind of respect and collegiality we'd hope to see in our leaders. Something that all too often seems a thing of the past.

"While the legions of us in the vast political middle in this country might not agree with every decision she crafted, perhaps that says all the more about her that someone like myself feels compelled to laud her for all she did for so many causes she championed in her remarkable career."

I raised my Guinness. "To Ruth Bader Ginsburg." Most of the room drank to that. Most.

Maggie Bates raised her hand halfway and looked to get Washington's attention. He nodded back at her.

"I love this delightful exercise, fellas. And this darling little saloon y'all have here is growing on me." She smiled broadly. "Might I add another lady to our list, President Washington?"

"By all means," Washington responded. "Splendid."

"Let me express my admiration for another hero of mine, and a political idol of sorts. Margaret Chase Smith was a Republican who served in Congress for thirty years. She was fiercely independent—a fact many in this room can attest to. She battled so many of you, Democrats and Republicans alike. And forty years before Hillary did, she was the first woman to have her name entered in nomination for president at a major party convention.

"Most notably for me, and perhaps for us at this moment in our history, she was one of the very first and loudest voices taking a stance against McCarthyism—directly calling out her fellow Republican Senator Joseph McCarthy—thereby demonstrating such fierce political courage."

Then, looking over at me, she added, "She would have been a delightful addition to your alliance, Danny. I do believe she would certainly qualify as one of those 'badasses' you refer to."

Nixon, smiling at that, responded, "I'm afraid I have a few scars left by her on my own ass that prove your point, ma'am."

"As do I," Eisenhower chimed in.

"I, too, am a member of that not-so-exclusive club as well, gentlemen," added Kennedy with a smile. "She was formidable political figure—if that is the appropriate word to use about a very fine lady."

"I reckon either term works, sir." responded Bates proudly. "Fine lady or badass indeed. They are one and the same in my book." She seemed to know just the right moments to flash that distinct accent and a touch of Southern flare.

The room paused again for a few moments. Then Teddy Roosevelt barreled forward to broad approval throughout the saloon. He may have the reputation of being the most entertaining of all the presidents to observe in action. He certainly got my vote.

"Have we thirteen yet, President Washington?" he inquired.

"Proceed," responded Washington. "No one among us is counting."

"Bring us home, Teddy!" shouted George W. Bush.

"I really have just one last point to make," he began, "but it's a salient one. What a great idea to toast the greatest and most admired women in our history." He paused briefly as the room applauded. "Thank you, President Maggie." More applause. Then he continued. "Such a pity we can't have some of these exceptional women—the greatest women in our history—in here in this fine saloon alongside us. Wouldn't that be something?"

He paused once more for effect and looked around the room. Then, now raising his voice, he barked out, "And wouldn't it be something if we could have at least a few of the greatest men too!" He burst into laughter.

That brought down the house. He always did.

Chapter Six

Do You Have any Dogs?
January 28, 2021
The Saloon

"Hey Peaches," yelled Bush as President Bates made a move toward the exit. A few of us froze, fixated on the new President's face, wondering how his chumminess would play with her. I have to say I was a bit mortified, and fearful she might take it all the wrong way.

My heart sank as she glanced over at me with a stone face. Within a few seconds, however, she broke into a smile that lit up the hazy, smoke-filled room. I exhaled. Of course. This distinguished Southern lady hadn't gotten this far without some first-rate people skills. Whether she was faking that, as women often find they have to in the workplace, or not, who knows, but that reaction spoke volumes about her.

"Yes, Mr. President," she responded, playing along.

"We'll be needing you to take a turn on vocals with the band when you return."

"Oh, am I to return to this rooster party? A lady needs a proper invitation, don't you think?"

"Now that you have graced us with your presence our group would never be the same without you."

OK, that was a great answer by Otter, I thought.

"There's only so many times we can hear Franklin Pierce's drinking songs," I added.

"We need a touch of the fairer sex in this old boys' club," added Kennedy.

"Well aren't you gentlemen precious. I suppose I might could return sometime for a hot toddy or two. Keep the light on in here for me, but don't hold your breath."

Bush, clearly pleased with himself, smiled as he returned to the party alongside Kennedy.

Seeing that we were alone, Maggie, shot me a look of astonishment and asked, "What is this, Danny? You didn't warn me about this. Goodness gracious."

"Please come back," I said. "This place can really help you. I won't pretend that any of these guys knows what it takes to be a woman in that office, but they sure as hell know what it's like to be feeling like they're under siege down there. No matter what the issue you are facing they can help."

She looked a tad skeptical but she was still listening.

"I presume it's fair to say I've got a few they haven't faced before."

"Of course," I responded, not knowing exactly what she was getting at but speculating about a myriad of possibilities.

"And your Alliance movement helped me get here—it separated me in the primaries from all the far right candidates, and helped me beat a fairly liberal Democratic ticket in the general. But there aren't many moderates left in Congress—so your group there needs to get me some help a might quickly."

"Maggie," I said slowly. "You're gonna need to get Los Gatos McFadden to help with that."

She shot me a look.

"I know, this whole thing blew my mind too."

I saw her attempting to process it all.

"Do you mean . . ." she stopped midsentence.

"Don't try to make sense of it all tonight," I cautioned.

"But come back. This place can also be an escape," I said. "This doesn't have to be just for professional development, so to speak."

At that moment Mary Ann approached us.

"You guys good, she asked?"

"Yes," Maggie responded. I nodded.

"You came here often?" Maggie asked me.

"I did," I responded. "But I didn't really drink much."

Mary Ann laughed out loud but then abruptly stopped when she saw I wasn't laughing.

"Oh, wait. You're being serious now?" She asked, trying now to contain her laughter. Unsuccessfully.

"OK, well maybe I was 'overserved' once or twice, but aside from the fun and music and wait staff and atmosphere up here you can really get a lot of emotional support and learn a lot about the issues and gain from their experience and expertise.

"Now of course it may be different for you as a woman, but the way you handled that out there tonight I think you'll have these guys eating out of your hand. I can't imagine much of anything intimidates you. This might not be your cup of tea, but come for the wait staff if you don't love these old guys. They are a kick. And I'm guessing a University of Georgia sorority girl like you is right at home at a party. And I hear such good things about Savannah."

"You have to come for St. Patrick's Day, Danny. Savannah has the finest St. Patrick's Day celebration in all the land. Someone like you would love it. I know your type. I know it all too well, I'm afraid." She smiled. I decided to take that as a complement no matter how it was intended.

"The point is we have been given a great gift in this place. On all my worst days in that office, like after the violence in Raleigh, or the mass shooting in Mayton, or when gridlock and polarization was at its worst, this place was such a welcome escape. There's a camaraderie here, and they all want you to be successful—and this country."

"That's nice to hear. By the way, do y'all have a pool table in this bar?"

"No," I answered Not yet at least. But just say the word and I'm sure one can be arranged."

"OK, Danny. You have me convinced. I'll come back. At least once." She flashed me that smile that America fell in love with. Or at least 52.7% of America.

"One more thing," I asked. "Do you have any dogs?"

"We certainly do. Two—one's a Georgia bulldog and the other's a mix."

Mary Ann shrieked with delight.

"Why would you ask? You are the fourth person in here tonight to ask me that question."

"You'll find out," I said. "Just keep that Washington coin handy at all times and come back to see us."

Chapter Seven

An Utter Abdication of Leadership
February 4, 2021

Call me "old school," but I had planned to more or less stick to the "Presidents' Creed," which is to refrain from critiquing the current president, except in extraordinary circumstances. Having sat in that Oval Office and agonized over decisions, I had great sympathy for anyone who found themselves in that role, and didn't want to contribute to their woes. By the same token, while I anticipated taking on some incoming fire from the new administration as they set a new course, I more or less expected such criticism to be respectful and somewhat low key.

In light of that, I was taken aback, to say the least, to see this headline in the Washington Post only a week after I had left the White House. So much for the presidents' creed.

WASHINGTON POST

VICE PRESIDENT MARGEL DENOUNCES MCFADDEN ADMINISTRATION'S NORTH KOREA POLICY AS "FECKLESS"

(February 4, 2021, Washington DC) By Javier Martinez
In a speech in front of a gathering of US veterans today in Washington, Vice President Charles Margel openly criticized the McFadden administration's North Korea policy over the past four years as "feckless," chastising President McFadden for adopting a policy toward North Korea that neither prevented North Korea from further progress toward producing deliverable nuclear weapons capable of reaching the United States, nor achieving any sort of

diplomatic solution of any kind.

In his first address as Vice President, the former Ohio Senator did not mince words, stating as follows: "The North Korean people have endured no shortage of humanitarian hardship at the hands of its leader Kim Jong-un, as the United States sat idly by. The previous administration failed both with respect to our moral compass as well as our strategic interests. What resulted was four years of further progress toward North Kora becoming a nuclear power coupled with for years of continuing crimes against humanity."

The Vice President chided McFadden for both refusing to meet with the North Korean leader and ruling out a military strike to disable the hermit kingdom's missile installations and nuclear facilities. "I might understand choosing one path over the other," stated the Vice President, "but to pursue neither of the two strategies strikes me as an utter abdication of leadership."

Vice President Margel's remarks caused quite a bit of rumbling on Capitol Hill. Later in the day he appeared with Laura Ingram on *The Ingram Angle* on the Fox News Channel, at which time some expected that perhaps he may soften his criticism. Instead, he doubled down.

"After four years of the utter absence of a coherent foreign policy," Mr. Margel concluded, "North Korea remains a humanitarian nightmare, and is apparently now on the verge of becoming the next nation to possess intercontinental ballistic missiles. Do not expect the same from the Bates-Margel administration. "

The Vice President, whose political brand has always been to speak his mind, served for years on the Senate Foreign

Relations Committee, and believes this is one of his areas of expertise. Reporters sought a reaction from President Bates on her vice president's comments but as of now there has been no response.

Chapter Eight

Fortini Loop
February 4, 2021

Dripping wet and peddling feverishly on my Rockhopper mountain bike that I dusted off after four years of neglect, I looked back but saw no sign of Erik. I don't believe he expected me to linger for him. Closing in on the summit at the Fortini Loop of the Santa Theresa trail south of San Jose, I wasn't about to slow down now and sacrifice my momentum. Besides, there wasn't another soul in sight—not a human at least. Just me and the elements. The closer I got to the top, the more spectacular the view of the Valley. The rolling hills all around were green today as they typically are in February after the rains. Most of the year they appear brown with yellow vegetation. Occasional oak trees dot the hills these switchback trails meander through. And plenty of sagebrush. I saw a few owls, some deer and a couple coyotes, but far and away the highlight was the bald eagle soaring high above me, as if to welcome me back home to California. I appreciated that hospitality. How delightfully thoughtful.

Was it possible that I had forgotten how much I missed this trail, this bike, this view and this feeling? And how those elements all seem to combine to feed my spirit and fuel my imagination. This setting sits just a few miles from trendy, techy Silicon Valley, but up here that seems a state or two away. Whatever my next chapter, I had to make this a part of my routine—I hope Erik is down with that. He's gonna have to be. He's gotta be in much better shape than me, but he's never been a biker. It dawned on me that this beautiful, mind-clearing, everythings-gonna-be-OK mountain hideaway of mine might just play a role in the process of ferreting out exactly what that next chapter for me will entail. So many possibilities await anxiously. And this little recurring bit of exercise and spiritual awakening might even make it worthwhile to take my sweet time with those decisions.

I stopped at the top, took my helmet off, wiped the sweat from my face and forehead with my shirt, and allowed the scenery and wildlife to sweep me away and permit my thoughts to carry me wherever they cared to take us. It was good to be home.

***

Following my ride, I grabbed an extra-large organic juice at Nine Lives Juicery, one of my favorite spots on Santa Cruz Avenue—the main drag in downtown Los Gatos. Los Gatos is a tony little enclave tucked into the eastern base of the Santa Cruz Mountains about fifty miles south of San Francisco. A creek winds through the town, which is loaded with cute little shops, restaurants and parks, and is a perfect spot just to walk around and explore on a Saturday night.

I hadn't been to Nine Lives in five years, but at one point it was my post-workout go-to spot—back when workouts used to be a thing in my life. They forgot my usual order but who could really blame them. I posed for a photo with the two young baristas—Kaitlyn and Martina. The girls asked me about my son Brett. I got a kick out of that. I told them I'd send him in one day, even though he'd never in a million years order one of these concoctions. It was the first time I had entered any place of business since I'd been home. It felt good, even as Erik and Brent lingered outside. I meant to treat each of those guys to my standard order—coconut milk base, blueberries, pineapple, bananas, oranges, strawberries, spinach and carrots. It was the first thing they made for me fifteen years ago when Denyse and I strolled in after I joined her down the block for yoga and I've never waivered from it since. That tells you a lot about me, actually. Now that I think of it, I should have asked Matty or Ginger to whip one of these up in the Saloon. That would have blown their minds. I'm surprised that never occurred to me. I'm certain they could have pulled it off. I miss that place. Nothing like it. Maybe I'll get back someday. Highly unlikely though.

I sat down for a moment and checked my phone for messages. There were many, as there always are, but one kind of jumped out and demanded my attention. It was from unnamed number I didn't recognize.

"*Pardon my French, Danny Mac, but what the fuck?? Did you seriously intend to spring Thomas Jefferson out onto the world two centuries after his death? Are you kidding me? It took all I had to clean up after that little mess.*

If I didn't love and respect you so much I swear I'd hate you for that."

I took a deep breath. That was Tina, the Mensa-caliber waitress from the Presidential Spirits Saloon while I was President who seemed to be, along with Chief White House Usher Satch Davis, somehow the keepers of everything necessary to make that secret mystical establishment going. I had availed myself of that wonderful nightly party fairly often during our years in the White House. I'm sure more than most. Tina had somehow broken the seal of that place and now had a role on the White House staff. I still don't understand it all but I stopped wasting time wondering a few years ago. In that sense I think Albert Camus would be quite proud of my approach to those profound mysteries.

A follow-up text came immediately after the first one.

"*I got your number from Satch. This is my cell. Please call me, Mr. President. Heard you and Denyse were in Fiji or something yachting with a bunch of one-percenters. Really? Have you changed already? :) Miss you. Cheers.*"

Hearing from Tina got me thinking about the Saloon again, wondering what was happening up there, who was busting whose chops. God I missed that place. I wondered if Maggie had made it up there yet, what her reception would be like in there—particularly without Tina holding all those guys accountable. And if there was a version of me in there. How could there be? I had to stop thinking about it all before the whole thing blew my mind. I tried to make a mental note to get back to her, although that mental notebook of mine seems all too often these days to be attached to a shredder.

When I got back to the house I saw Denyse out on the back deck with a cup of coffee and her laptop scrolling through the news of the day. She motioned for me to join her. It looked like something was up. I put my shower on hold and pulled up one of the high deck chairs next to hers. Viewing the peaceful Los Gatos neighborhood morning before us felt as if I was reacquainting myself with an old friend. Our yard didn't offer a view of the whole valley but we had an elevated view of much of our gorgeous tree-lined neighborhood. Another serene California setting I had sorely missed.

Denise looked up from her laptop. "Nice to be back on your morning ride?"

"So nice. Unbelievably nice."

"Did our new friends tag along for the ride?"

"Erik followed me on a bike. Aaron stayed at the trail entrance. Brent circled the park in a separate vehicle."

"Did Erik put you to shame?"

"Wow. Nothing like the unwavering support of my biggest fan. Who needs Twitter bashing me up and down when I can just have you?"

"C'mon now. You know I love you, but that guy's twenty years younger than you and looks like he spends all his waking hours working out."

"I'll have you know I beat him to the summit. Beat him pretty good actually."

"Did I mention he's not stupid either?" she responded, laughing. "I think that's worth remembering right about now before you entertain visions of taking on Lance Armstrong."

Suddenly I was a whole lot less impressed with myself.

She had a look on her face suggesting she had something to tell me.

"Have you seen the latest?"

My heart kind of instinctively jumped at that. With this world these days absolutely nothing will ever surprise me about anything or anybody.

"What," I asked, "is my buddy Margel ripping me openly again? That guy won't stop crushing me in the press until I'm in the grave—and I'm not sure that would put an end to it either."

"Oh no. This isn't about him. But you are right. I'm sure he just wants to feed some red meat to that far right base of his to keep his own ambitions alive. I can't believe she selected him as running mate."

"I don't blame her. She needed that wing of the party to come out for her on election day. She had to. Unfortunately that's kind of how it works."

"Seems like Maggie's husband has a bit of a mess on his hands."

"Our 'First Dude'? Literally nothing would surprise me about that guy."

"I'd have left you years ago if you did one tenth of what he gets away with."

"What has he done now?"

"Looks like he missed a few hush payments to a coworker he had an affair with and she has now gone public with it. Suing him and his company for sexual harassment. Pretty ugly story."

"Wow. Dammit. I hardly know her but, man I feel for Maggie. I never trusted that dude. Something about him."

We both paused in thought.

"My heart breaks for her," I said, "going through all this right out of the gate. All the world watching."

"Should you call her, Danny?

"I don't know if she wants to hear from me. We're not exactly BFFs. And her VP continues to take an occasional shot at me. If it were a mess more related to the job like the Middle East or North Korea maybe I'd lob her a call of support, but I'm not sure when it comes to her marriage."

"Maybe a note of support or encouragement."

"Sure. Of course. That's probably about right."

"Why would somebody cheat on her?" Dense wondered out loud. "I mean, my gosh, she's smart, charming, beautiful . . ."

"Really?" I responded. It was more of a statement than a question. "Are you not paying any attention to the world in front of you? Haven't you noticed that so many women who have so much going for them end up falling for the wrong guys?" I responded. "Well . . . like you, for example."

"Did I actually ever *fall for you*? I kind of think you just sort of took me off the dating market and then proceeded to just wear me down over time. After all that I basically had no other options. And I wasn't really in the mood to reenter the dating world."

"That's not exactly how I intend to the tell the tale of our storybook romance to my biographers. We may know the truth, but posterity will think it was really quite idyllic. A fairy tale."

"I'm OK with that. As long as I can approve of all the photos."

I went in to take a shower. But I couldn't stop thinking about Maggie Bates. What a way to start.

WASHINGTON POST

CO-WORKER CLAIMS PRESIDENT'S HUSBAND SEXUALLY HARASSED HER, PAID HER OFF

(February 4, 2021, New Orleans) By Kristen Leigh
Vanity Fair Magazine is reporting that First Gentleman Dwight Bates engaged in an affair and subsequently sexually harassed a young female coworker between June of 2018 and January of 2020, and paid her off privately via

negotiated settlement. Sherise Dunphy, a 28-year old analyst in Bates' New Orleans-based international trade corporation, Bates International, alleges that Dwight Bates initiated a relationship with her, promoted her twice, and then froze her out of any meaningful role in the company when she started dating another man. She maintains that a private settlement was reached with Dwight Bates personally to silence her, without the knowledge or participation by Bates International. A spokesperson for the company denied that any improper relationship or harassment occurred and described Ms. Dunphy as a disgruntled former employee hoping to exploit Dwight Bates' new status as the husband of the President of the United States. The company asserts that she never complained or filed any grievances while employed with the company, and that these allegations are merely an attempt to tarnish the Bates family politically. The company refused to comment further. Ms. Dunphy left the company in March of last year.

Lawyers for Ms. Dunphy assert that they intend to file an action against Bates International for sexual harassment and wrongful termination.

The White House has thus far declined to comment on this story.

I couldn't stop thinking about the implications of this story for Maggie and the country. And I couldn't come up with a meaningful precedent in American history to compare it to. Unfortunately, I didn't think Maggie would be able to get much help in the way of advice from my friends in the saloon on this one. And I was afraid there might just be quite a few of those such issues lying ahead of her.

Chapter Nine

There's Nothing More Pathetic in Life Than an Ex-president
February 12, 2021

My phone buzzed. I looked down and saw it was my favorite historian.

"Professor Harris," I answered, "thanks so much for calling me back so quickly."

"I'm sorry I couldn't respond earlier. We were at a birthday party for my granddaughter."

"Not a problem, professor. I'm quickly getting used to people not taking my calls any longer. And I can't conceive of a finer excuse than that. I have been meaning to reach out to you ever since the Inauguration Day."

In a monumental lapse of memory, I had left the professor alone with Thomas Jefferson in the Blue Room of the White House on the morning of President Bates' inauguration, and never returned. It caused a bit of a brouhaha that ultimately Tina had to step in and fix. That's a long story too . . .

"Yes. Let's talk about that next time we get together. I might one day forgive you for that—if I manage to live another ten years. But I have so many questions."

"And I don't blame you. I have to make it up to you somehow."

"That's not really necessary. But an explanation would be appreciated."

"Come on out sometime and bring Carol. Denyse and I would love to spend a couple of days in Napa with you two. I would think that would begin to pay you back for the spot I put you in."

"That sounds tempting," he replied, "but you must have so other many better, more productive ways to spend your time."

"Well, funny you should say that. We are not really sure what that next phase of life will entail. We have so many compelling possibilities."

"I can imagine, sir."

"Tell me, Professor, what are some of the more memorable and impactful roles presidents have found for themselves post-presidency."

"My goodness," he responded. "What a question. It's hard to know even where to begin. So many spend time trying to find ways to influence history's view of their presidency and legacy—writing memoirs, building their libraries."

"Start with the best and most admirable," I asked.

"There's a great humility about some of them that made for some of the more admirable post-presidencies. Let me begin with John Quincy Adams—perhaps my favorite post-presidency president, to coin a new term. Quincy Adams is the one, of course, credited with saying 'There is nothing more pathetic in life than a former president.' Ironic that he should have said that, as his post-presidency was anything but pathetic. He served ten years representing Massachusetts in the House of Representatives, and became the most prominent anti-slavery voice in the nation. He also represented the Africans from the slave ship Amistad in that famous case before the Supreme Court and won their freedom back."

"It is remarkable that all that happened after he had been president."

"Yes, and he had left the office rather bitter, as his father had. The two Adamses both refused to attend their successors' inauguration. Hard to imagine that happening today."

"Carter has done so much for the world in his post-presidency—and for his legacy in the process. He has embraced humanitarian causes, founding The Carter Center. He's been called upon to engage in international diplomacy, for which he was awarded a Nobel Peace Prize. At age 92 he was still building homes for the needy in Mexico as part of the Habitat for Humanity. It's fair to say he has completely remade his reputation and standing after leaving office."

"Yes—he is certainly an inspiration to us all—not just to presidents."

"Teddy Roosevelt traveled the world, and took an expedition with his son Kermit to navigate their way through the River of Doubt in Brazil—the tributary of the Amazon which now bears his name. It nearly killed him."

"Wow—perhaps it was worth it though. He has both a river with his name on it and a portion of a mountain in South Dakota with his face on it."

"Yes. If it wasn't so dangerous he wouldn't have wanted to attempt it in the first place."

"That's my boy there."

"We are going to have to have that long conversation about all that."

"We'll do that when you come to Napa."

"Alright. Maybe we'll have to come soon. I really need to know what that is all about."

"Who and what else is noteworthy?"

"Taft served as Chief Justice of the Supreme Court for ten years after his presidency, which is remarkable to think about. And Thomas Jefferson founded the University of Virginia. Both of them clearly figured out significant ways of making valuable contributions.

"Many of course were not so noteworthy. As you know, eight presidents died in office. And not all those who survived to a post presidency enhanced their reputations. Van Buren ran for president and lost three times. Buchanan kept trying in vain to defend his presidency and his troubled legacy. Nixon did a series of famous paid interviews to restore his reputation, but in doing so uttered the unfortunate statement, 'When the president does it, that means that it is not illegal.' After the interviews, nearly 70% of the public felt he was still trying to cover up for his actions.

"And Carter and Clinton both tried their hand at fiction in retirement, releasing novels that both pretty much got panned by the critics."

"Ha! I don't imagine I'll be attempting to write the great American novel. But this has been very helpful. Fascinating stuff. It does give me something to think about. I have no idea what's next but it's great to hear what some of the others have done, for better and for worse."

"I am happy to oblige, sir."

"You have given me some ideas and, more importantly, a little inspiration. I always come away from our conversations feeling a whole lot better informed and a little smarter."

I really did. This guy was a great blessing in my life as a student at ND so many years ago, but had arguably served an even greater role informing so many of my decisions as president with the history behind some of this stuff. And he had been an invaluable source of information regarding the history behind many of my new drinking buddies in the saloon.

"Let's make sure we plan that Napa trip soon, professor."

"I will discuss it with Carol right away."

"Please do."

As I prepared to hit the red dot on my cell phone to hang up, he spoke up again.

"There's one more that might be particularly noteworthy to you, sir," he said.

"Oh yeah? Who is that?' I responded.

"Grover Cleveland."

"What did he do in his post-presidency?"

"He moved to New York, practiced a little law, and pursued his main passion quite a bit—fishing."

"And how is that instructive to me?"

"Well, it's not that part. It's what he did four years later."

I had a feeling I knew where this was going, but I asked just the same to play along.

"What did he do?"

"He became president again."

Chapter Ten

Testing a Lot More Than Their Missile Systems
February 15, 2021

North Korea wasted no time in testing the first female president in American history.

ASSOCIATED PRESS
NORTH KOREA CONDUCTS A BATTERY OF MISSILE TESTS, INCLUDING ICBM LANDING JUST 85 MILES OFF GUAM

(February 15, 2020, AP) By Ray Newell
North Korea launched four missiles on Saturday in its latest attempt to further test its nuclear missile capabilities, including a long range ICBM that fell into the Pacific Ocean roughly 85 miles off the island of Guam, an American territory in the Western Pacific Ocean. The aggressive actions are thought to be an attempt to test United States President Margaret Bates, who has not yet even completed her first month in office. Additionally, North Korea launched three short range missiles, one from Sinori in the North Province and two from Sondok in South Hamgyong Province. All three short range missiles fell in the Sea of Japan. The missile originating from Sinori may have been a Russian Iskander, which is a missile capable of making course corrections midfight. The other two short range missiles appear to be a new design. The missile launches prompted the Japanese government to alert its citizens via cell phone messages.

The United States condemned the ballistic missile test, citing relevant UN Security Council resolutions in a statement issued by Vice Chairman of the Joint Chiefs of Staff, General John Hyten. President Bates has yet to issue a statement.

THIS WEEK WITH GEORGE STEPHANOPOULOS

ABC Sunday February 15, 2020

ANNOUNCER: *From ABC News in Washington, it's This Week with George Stephanopoulos. Here now is George Stephanopoulos.*

GEORGE STEPHANOPOULOS: *Good morning and welcome to This Week.*

We begin this week with North Korea, which over the weekend conducted multiple missile tests by launching both a long range ICBM that landed close to the American territory of Guam in the Pacific, and three short range missiles into the Sea of Japan— all in clear contravention of UN Security Council Resolutions.

One can't help but wonder whether Kim Jong-un's regime was sending a message directly to the White House. They may have been testing a lot more than their missile system this weekend. The whole world awaits President Bates' response.

We are joined now by the President's newly approved Secretary of Defense Stanley Reming.

Mr. Secretary, thank you so much for joining us this morning. You have barely moved into your new office, sir, and here you are dealing with a potential international inci-

dent initiated by North Korea. Welcome to Washington.

SECRETARY STANLEY REMING: *This is what we are here for, George. This is what we are hired for. The United States military is prepared to deal with precisely this sort of provocation by this brutal dictator. It is nothing we didn't expect from this despot.*

STEPHANOPOULOS: *Are you suggesting a military response is appropriate?*

REMING: *It is fair to say anything and everything is on the table. We believe they are gearing up for another nuclear test as well. They have to be stopped. No one desires a world where this madman has nuclear weapons at his fingertips.*

STEPHANOPOULOS: *Did all the tough talk by the new administration, particularly your own words and those of Vice President Margel lead to this? Or is this an attempt to test the new President, our first female Commander in Chief.*

REMING: *I don't know if it's because she's a woman, although anything is possible with Kim, but more likely it is because she is a new president, and having been a governor, they may mistakenly perceive this administration as lacking foreign policy resolve. Let me tell you, they do so at their own peril.*

No, our words did not lead to this. The failed policies of the past two decades—Bush, Obama and McFadden—led to a situation where North Korea felt emboldened to do this. And they now have the capabilities. They are charging full speed ahead with their nuclear program, their biological weapons and their cyber warfare capabilities. We will put a stop to all of that. The US policy of appeasement toward the Korean Peninsula ends with this administration.

STEPHANOPOULOS: *But we didn't see a whole lot of this sort of thing from Kim Jong-un during the last administration.*

REMING: *That's the point George. Kim Jong-un had four years of clear sailing to quietly advance his nuclear capabilities. These latest tests, at least on initial analysis, seem to suggest they have significantly upped their game during those years, and might be getting ready to take their seat at the table of countries with nuclear capabilities. The prudent assumption for us to make is that the North Koreans now possess all the components and expertise to miniaturize a nuclear weapon and place it on an ICBM. We simply cannot afford to let another four years go by without reversing that and eliminating that threat. Thankfully you'll see a different policy from this administration.*

STEPHANOPOULOS: *The world awaits your response, Mr. Secretary. Thanks for joining us.*

REMING: *My pleasure, George.*

STEPHANOPOULOS: *Tough talk here this morning from the new Defense Chief. It remains to be seen if a new approach can make a meaningful difference, but it appears as if we may find out soon. Stay tuned.*

Chapter Eleven

Hannegan's
March 15, 2021

I heard my phone ringing as I exhaled, trying with everything I could possibly muster to get that last rep up on the weight bench in our multipurpose room that I had kind of taken over for a gym. The phone distracted me a tad—just enough to put me in jeopardy of not being able to push the bar up. More than a few times in my life I've gotten stuck without a spotter on the bench with the bar on my chest. I'm always able to roll it off my body the long way—down over my midsection and below—but it's kind of a brutal process and not something I want to have to do again. We're done having kids and all, but there are still two real good reasons I try as hard as I can to avoid that predicament. I wasn't about to ask Denyse to spot me—she does enough heavy lifting for me in every other phase of my life.

I managed, just barely, to get the bar up and secure, and looked at my phone. It was Kelly. I answered it before it went to voicemail. The music was kind of loud on both her end and mine, and we struggled a bit to hear each other.

"Dad what are you doing?" she blurted out, fast enough that it sounded all like all one word.

"I'm getting better. In our new gym. You've gotta come check it out. It's gonna allow me to make this body a finely tuned machine once again. At least that's the plan."

"Come meet us! I'm with all the girls at Hannegan's and they want you to come out."

Hannegan's is a classic old Los Gatos Irish pub that doubles as a sports bar as well and kind of transforms at the end of each day into a night spot for the younger generation—and somehow manages to pull all of that off without sacrificing any authenticity.

"I love that place," I responded. "Haven't been there in five years. But come on, Kelly, I can't just waltz into Hannegan's these days with no advance notice or detail of any kind."

"Why not? What good was it to be president and go through all that stress if it's just gonna prevent you from being the real you the rest of your life?"

"You think the real me is hanging out in bars with kids 25 years younger than me?"

"Do you want me to answer that? Are you kidding me right now? I know you want to come be with us. C'mon Dad. Your better than this!" She cracked herself up pretty good with that line.

"That's just not fair, Kelly!" I laughed. "I was just gonna watch college hoops with Mom. Do they have the games on there?"

"Yes! Every tv is going."

"Alright. Do me a favor. Is Gil there? Is he still working there?" Gil was the long-time bartender who might just be the most popular guy in all of Los Gatos but is just so unassuming and humble you could never tell. I hadn't seen him since the thirty seconds I spent with him when he came to the California Ball following my inauguration four years ago.

"Yes—he's here. We all love Gil."

"Everybody does. Please give him a heads up. They don't need to do anything for us. Tell them we don't want anything special. But give them fair warning that I'll be coming and accompanied by some security."

I wondered for just a fraction of a second if I was doing the wrong thing, but how could I have really said no to Kelly? I have a feeling she knew that. That's my girl. Within twenty minutes I was showered, dressed and on my way to my second favorite saloon.

It was a nice night in the Bay Area. I could have walked, but Brent and Erik scrambled to accompany me and insisted on making the three-minute drive down to Santa Cruz Avenue. As much as I thought it was overkill, I stayed with Brent in the car while Erik went inside just to get a sense of the place.

"I'm so sorry I dragged you guys out tonight." I said to Brent.

"Are you kidding? This is what we're here for. Looks like a place we would love. We might be coming back without you sometime soon."

"Don't you guys dare come without me!" I'm not sure if they knew about my major league FOMO.

We walked through the front door with the classic Hannegan's logo etched in glass, proceeded through the dining area and up the stairs to the perennial party that surrounded the beautiful mahogany bar. I could see Kelly and her girlfriends amidst a crowd of twenty-somethings. A gentleman met us as we were ascending the stairs and ushered us into a private room off the bar where two servers awaited.

Moments later Kelly and a sea of young adults came streaming into the room, followed by no shortage of trailers. Kelly ran over to me and gave me a big hug, then immediately turned to her friends. "Dad, this is Juliane, Shelby, Emma, Keeley, Kristen, Vanessa . . ." She seemed to go on and on. She is in her last year nearby at Santa Clara, and must have invited the whole sorority. That really shouldn't surprise me. Out of the corner of my eye I could tell Brent and Erik were enjoying the scene.

I motioned to the server, who darted over immediately.

"I'll take care of anything in this room tonight," I said. I think I still knew how to pick up a tab. It had been a while.

"Oh no, Mr. President. Mr. Hannegan is on his way here, and he'll have none of that. This one is on the house."

"I hope he knows what he's getting into. You don't want to underestimate the potential of these Santa Clara coeds." I laughed as many more filed in, followed by two more servers.

Kelly had just recently turned 21, and while I had seen her drink at the lake each summer with the entire McFadden extended family, I really hadn't been with her in a setting like this before. She seemed oddly right at home with it all. Clearly in her element. That was telling.

All Kelly's pals ordered cocktails. Before returning to the bar the server looked at me.

"What can I get for you, Mr. President?"

"Well, I would have just had a draft beer but I guess if all these lovely ladies are drinking cocktails . . ." I thought for a second. "You know I just got back from the South Pacific and I had a few really good mai tais. Do you have a good dark rum—maybe some Meyers, a little Malibu, pineapple and orange. And just a cap full of Grenadine."

"Dad," Kelly blurted out, "Pretty sure they know how to make a mai tai here. That's not exactly something that can't be served in any bar in America."

"Wow," I said, looking at our server, who was trying in vain to hold back a smile. "Nothing like the undying love and respect of a daughter."

"We'll make it precisely as you ask, Mr. President."

I turned to Kelly and her friends. "So ladies," I said, "tell me about Kelly's friend Michael. They all turned their heads in perfect unison and looked at Kelly. I tried to read their faces but they all immediately burst into smiles. All, that is, with the exception of Kelly, who was somewhat mortified. I convinced myself she deserved it because of her snarkiness about my drink order.

"You would love him," said Juliane.

"He came to our Super Bowl party," added Emma.

"Did you have to explain the rules to him?" I asked, laughing.

Kelly's friends laughed.

Kelly smiled too, but added, "That's not funny, Dad."

"I wasn't trying to be funny. I'm perfectly ok with him not being a sports fan."

"You are not and neither are the boys. He's learning though. I'm teaching him. That tells you something about him, right?"

"Yes. All we care about is that he makes you happy. I just wish he wouldn't keep avoiding me."

Our server returned with our drinks. I took a sip of my mai tai.

"This is perfect," I said to him. "Great job. Well done."

"Dad," Kelly said. "Do you know how rude it is to compliment someone for making such a great drink after you directed them specifically how to make it?"

Kelly's friends howled. I think they got such a kick out of seeing her have no compunction about laying into me.

I looked up at the at the televisions suspended from the ceiling in front of us.

"Oh my god," I exclaimed.

"What's wrong, Dad?" Kelly asked. Everyone turned to the look at the television. The scroll at the bottom of the CBS screen showing the basketball game was flashing an 'Urgent News Alert,' and proceeded to describe a missile attack being carried out by the U.S. against North Korean nuclear systems all across that country.

I pulled out my cell phone. Twitter was lighting up.

Kelly looked over at me and saw the look on my face.

"What's going on, Dad?"

"It looks like we've acted preemptively to destroy the North Koreans' nuclear missile capabilities."

Now Kelly's friends, sensing something was up, gathered close to hear our conversation.

"What does it mean?" Kelly asked.

"I'm not saying it wasn't justified—that's the last country we want to have nuclear weapons capability. And they've been all but daring us to do this with their recent testing. But I fear for what may happen now. It quite literally could trigger a nuclear war."

One of the servers noticed what we were focusing on. He approached the television just as CBS News broke into the game. He turned down the music and turned up the volume on the television.

We could hear Nora O'Donnell beginning her report.

> *This aggressive action by the Bates administration is in direct response to the missile tests over the course of the past weekend in violation of UN Resolutions. The intent is to accomplish by surgical strike what previous administrations have been unable to accomplish with sanctions and diplomacy—curtailing North Korea's nuclear capabilities.*
>
> *The United States executed the attack using aircraft, including both bombers and stealth aircraft, and sea launched missiles. B-1 bombers carried bunker-buster bombs to take out underground facilities. Stealth aircraft like the B-2 and F-22 are thought to have been used as well. The attack was supported by three US aircraft carriers in the Western Pacific, the USS Nimitz, The USS Ronald Reagan, and the USS Theodore Roosevelt, and various accompanying warships in the region.*
>
> *CBS News received an embargoed report providing much of the detail we are giving you now just ninety minutes ago*

> *and we were instructed to hold it. CBS and other news outlets honored that request.*
>
> *The attack is already being condemned by the Chinese. China is North Korea's biggest trading partner.*
> *This is not the first US administration to contemplate such an attack. However, each previous administration to consider this type of action ultimately determined that the risks, including instability within the region and beyond, and the virtual certainty of retaliation against South Korea and US installations in the region, far outweighed the benefits.*
>
> *These next 48 hours will be crucial as the world braces for what could be a massive military response from North Korea.*

I motioned to Erik and Brent. I could see a look of disappointment engulf Kelly's face. This wonderful little bonding moment was about to come to an end.

"I'm so sorry, sweetheart. I'll make it up to you. I've got too many emotions kicking in to be any fun to you and your friends. I'm gonna go home, say a few prayers and watch this thing unfold. I hope cooler heads prevail, but I fear it may be a bit too late for that."

Chapter Twelve

An Eye for an Eye
March 16, 2021

I had a brutal night, running through all the doomsday scenarios, worried sick for Maggie, wondering if somehow I could have contributed in some way to avoiding this predicament. My morning ride was just what I needed. There's something about the night and the darkness that tends to amplify problems, which can make life difficult for all those humans who don't ever sleep very well—like me for example. But there is also something about a morning workout that tends to operate as an antidote to that nighttime effect, dispelling those demons, calming the nerves and soothing the soul.

Denyse had been asleep when I left. Upon my return home I walked through the house and saw the three tvs were all on, each tuned to a different news channel. That's my girl—seeking out a diversity of news sources. Now if we could just get the rest of the 300 million other US citizens to do the same.

I saw Denyse and her best friend Wendy out on the back deck enjoying another pleasant Los Gatos morning. Wendy saw me coming and got up to give me a big hug and a kiss.

"It is so great to have the McFaddens back in town! We missed you so much!"

"It's been way too long," I responded. "You look identical. I'm afraid I can't exactly say the same."

"You look a little more experienced," she smiled. "But now with the weight of the world off your shoulders you'll get younger again."

"I don't think the weight of the world ever leaves his shoulders." Denyse added. Scary how well she knows me.

"Any good news?" I asked. "I'm afraid to even bring it up. It was so nice to take that ride this morning. Just what the doctor ordered."

“They’re saying we didn’t get all their missile sites,” Denyse responded. She wasn’t a newsaholic when we met and first started dating, but she sure as heck is now.

“We got a lot though, and hit the nuclear sites we knew of, including the underground ones. They’ve been retaliating with all that’s left. Sounds like our Patriot missiles have intercepted a lot of their attempts to hit Seoul, but even so they are estimating there may be several thousand dead in South Korea from what made it through. There’s wall to wall coverage of it on every station.”

My heart sank, though none of it surprised me.

“We’re hitting them again to take out anything that is still working for them. And if I’m reading between the lines well enough I’d say it’s possible we may have hit Kim.”

I was devastated by it all. Not because I felt it was wholly unjustified. No, this was one of five well-thought out and detailed options that had been laid out to me in my first year for dealing with the nuclear threat of North Korea. All were flawed. This one had the highest chance of successfully bringing their nuclear program to a halt, but it also was the riskiest option on the table. It could lead to world war, including nuclear war, and could turn much of the world against us—even our allies.

“Are we getting crushed in the world press?” I asked.

“I think everyone’s just asking why at this point. Why this. Why now. But yes, they anticipate we’re about to get crushed in world opinion.”

All that jumpstarted my emotions again. I was devastated. For me, for the country, for the world, and for Maggie.

Chapter Thirteen

Call Me Jack
March 20, 2021
The Saloon

Maggie returned to the Saloon much sooner that anybody expected. Perhaps we hadn't scared her off. Shocker.

It was Country Music Night, and a cover band that appeared to be plucked right out of Nashville's Wild Horse Saloon was killin' it on the side stage, to the delight of most of the room. I don't go incredibly deep on country, but deep enough to love everything I heard. An angel of a lead vocalist with a voice like Linda Ronstadt was singing her way straight into our hearts. A lot of Kenny Chesney stuff. Loretta Lynn. Willie Nelson. Faith Hill. Patsy Cline. Dolly. Zac Brown. Shania Twain. Maybe I go deeper than I thought. A lot of songs about broken hearts, first romances, blue jeans, pickup trucks—and revenge. Beer and whiskey everywhere too. Not the ideal soundtrack to pair with the conversation that was to follow. Or, on second thought, perhaps the perfect pairing.

Maggie marched straight in this time. Amidst this collection of patrons she stood out like the Milky Way on a moonless desert night. Such a pleasant site against a backdrop of aging, weathered males. On closer look, however, she looked a little different this time. Could this job already be getting to her?

Matty called out to her as she approached the bar.

"What can I get for a sweet Southern Belle on a night like this?"

She brightened up. "Well, a little Gentleman Jack would do just fine, kind sir."

Haskell, the young bartender next to Matty, greeted her. "So, Madam President, you were the first female governor of Georgia, one of the first women admitted as a member at Augusta, the first woman president—does it ever get tiring breaking down all of society's gender barriers?"

She turned around to see if anyone else had heard that. Garfield was the nearest president sitting at the bar nearby. "Is this guy for real?" she asked, fully aware that Haskell could hear her every word in front of her.

"He's the reason I sit right here on this barstool every night," Garfield replied.

Then, looking back at Haskell, Garfield said, "Can I get another beer here, young man."

"Anything for the Union hero at the battle of Middle Creek, General," shot back Haskell. "Such a brilliant victory against almost insurmountable odds. People still can't believe how you managed to pull that off."

The general smiled broadly and looked over at the new president. "I should think you'll come to like young Haskell, my dear Maggie."

Otter approached in his usual host-with-the-most role. Maggie whispered something to him and they walked over together to a small table in the corner to talk. Ginger tried to interrupt to take their drink order but Bush waived her off. I could tell something was up.

After about five minutes of what appeared to be a very serious conversation they came back to the center of the saloon. Bush sat her down at the big front table and started hand-selecting presidents to sit around her. I loved watching him operate. Our frat president at work.

I studied the group he was assembling. Washington, Kennedy, FDR, Reagan, Obama.

He didn't appear to be looking my way, and it's not my style to elbow my way into a gathering like that without an invitation, so I proceeded to the bar and took a seat within earshot. I had no idea what was up, but I had a feeling it might be compelling. And there's always something alluring to me about sitting at a bar anyway, particularly this one.

Before their conversation commenced, President Bates excused herself and walked over to me at the bar.

"Tell me again, Danny, does anyone in here know anything about what's is going on in the world out there?"

"Only what you inform us of."

"Of course. And I know the answer to this next question, but I have to ask anyway. Nothing I say inside this saloon can ever be known outside this room?"

"Not unless you yourself divulge it. You know how you always think your senior staff meetings will be air tight until you read about them in the New York Times the next day? Well that could never happen here—and you'll find the advice you'll get will be the unfettered truth—devoid of any personal agenda. Treat this like the greatest senior staff meeting you could ever have. Go ahead—bare your soul if you care to. I did. Many times. And it felt good."

Maggie took it all in. I'm not sure I convinced her, but I don't blame her a bit for her skepticism. I can't say I ever really figured this place out even after four years of regular visits. I was pleased she trusted me enough to ask.

She returned to the table. I could tell instantly Otter had teed them all up. I wasn't sure about what, but I was dying to know.

Mary Ann behind bar saw me sitting down and came over to say hello. I love that about her, but I wanted to hear every word of this.

"Let me begin, President Bates," said Washington. The whole room seemed to always look to him first in here on nearly every issue. Except maybe those hot ale flips. His voice didn't necessarily command respect, but the aura around him demanded it.

"Moments of self-doubt were plentiful in my years leading the Continental Army and as President. To this day and with the utmost sincerity I do not think myself equal to the command I was honored with. Do not despair. Rely upon the goodness of the cause, and the aid of the supreme being, in whose hands victory rests."

"Oh my," she replied. "Your faith is refreshing. I sincerely hope the Good Lord smiles upon me like you. Perhaps you could put in a good word for me." She smiled, but it was clear she was masking an awful lot.

"I fear I put my trust in some folks I might regret."

Washington appeared to be quite taken with her, and clearly wanted to help.

"I believe my own experience might be instructive here, President Bates," JFK stated. "In the first days of my administration I made the decision to back military action involving 1500 Cuban exiles trained and supported by our forces. I had what must have been fifty of the smartest and most experienced people planning the operation. But five minutes after it started we all looked at each other and asked 'How could we have been so stupid?' I guess you get walled off from reality when you want something to succeed too much."

I saw Maggie slowly nodding her head. She seemed pleased to hear what JFK had to say.

He continued. "I learned many valuable lessons from our failure with that Bay of Pigs invasion, when so many of those 1500 were killed or captured. Challenge the advice you get. Assume at least the potential for the worst. Create an environment where advisors are unafraid to offer you the truth, even if they know it's not what you want to hear. Especially then. Make certain several options are presented to choose from. And finally, if, despite it all, failure comes, step up and publicly assume full responsibility. Success has a thousand fathers, but failure is an orphan. Own it and move on."

I was transfixed by all of it, and could see that Maggie was too. Such great lessons in leadership. With all the attention the Cuban Missile Crisis seems to get, and deservedly so, you forget about the Bay of Pigs and what a terrible setback that was for Kennedy right out of the gate. But what a moment. There is nothing quite like hearing about it directly from him.

"Move on you did, President Kennedy," added Obama. "Quite capably."

"Those early lessons served me well," Kennedy responded. "It gave me the confidence to reject the advice of the military brass during the Cuban Missile Crisis to simply wipe out the Soviet missiles in Cuba with a military strike."

I was thrilled that Maggie was seeing here tonight the very best benefits of this place. I wasn't sure what she was going through or contemplating, but this had to be comforting as well as educational.

"I'm afraid I'm learning some early lessons of my own. Remarkably similar to yours, Mr. President," said Maggie, looking directly at JFK.

"Call me Jack, please, Madam President."

Her stern face burst into a smile.

"Alright then, Jack. I will do that." she responded. Kennedy smiled back at her. Then she added, "And you be a dear and call me Maggie."

"Well then that settles it." Kennedy responded.

That exchange alone was worth the price of admission.

"Take advantage of the fellows in this room, Maggie," said FDR. "There is a whole lot of wisdom in this saloon. Everyone here has made mistakes you can learn from. The men here will give you the unvarnished truth, and deliver it straight from the shoulder."

"I appreciate that, sir. Although I may have some unique challenges those in this room didn't have."

"So did I, Maggie." Obama added. "And you are correct, they can't help you with that. But you seem to have navigated that one fairly well to this point. It's worth hearing what this group can offer you as advice for all the rest."

Maggie seemed appreciative of that. She sat there taking it all in. I could see the wheels spinning inside her mind. And all the while she kept occasionally glancing back at JFK. They seem to have made a connection.

Mary Ann came over, turned a bar stool around to face the main table like mine and sat down next to me. Many of the other presidents were now gathering around that table as well.

"It appears as if she's getting the advice and support she was seeking tonight," I said.

"Yes it does," Mary Ann replied. "And I have to say—God it's great to have a woman as a member of this club, don't you think," she whispered to me.

"You don't have to convince me of that," I responded.

"Oh I know that. You're one of the good ones. *You get it.*"

"I think Kennedy is as pleased about it as you," I said. "Looks like he's kind of turned on the charm up to eleven, as they say. It appears to be working, too."

"Oh, is that what you see?" she smirked. "I see just the opposite. I think she'll have him and the whole lot of you eating out of her the palm of her hand in no time."

I laughed. Of course. That's why I love this place. For all the allure a room full of presidents holds, I always tended to find I learned as much from the wait staff as I did from all my predecessors. Or more. What a valuable lesson.

Chapter Fourteen

Lori Summer's Kid
March 23, 2021

With the international news consuming me, I needed to tend to my own mental health. The fact that this international mess was not on my watch was of little consolation. I was invested in this country as never before—perhaps, in a weird way, even more so now that I was no longer the occupant of the Oval Office. I turned immediately to my *go to* sources of hope and life affirmation—my kids. And baseball.

I watched the last part of Brett's practice from beyond the left field fence adjacent to the track on the Jesuit College Prep campus in San Jose. I didn't want to be a distraction, and tried to remain as inconspicuous as an ex-president could possibly be. But I could tell Brent, Erik and I had clearly been noticed. Even though it was just a practice the stands were full of parents, members of the freshman and jv teams, and a few girls in softball and track and field practice garb. I hadn't seen any of my kids at a practice in the past four years, and I was surprised at all the spectators—particularly the parents. But that's youth baseball these days. All of youth sports, really. I guess I can't be too critical because here I was right alongside all of them watching a practice. I couldn't keep myself away. But I felt so guilty about moving this kid 3000 miles away from all his friends right smack in the middle of his high school years. I desperately needed some evidence that he was acclimating to ease my conscience. And of course it wouldn't hurt if I could also catch him hitting a double off the wall while I was here.

I watched alone from out past the outfield fence and remained there after practice broke up perusing The Drudge Report on my phone for the latest news on Korea and everything else. I texted Brett to meet me out there when he was ready to leave.

A little while later Brett and a teammate appeared, followed by a stream of others.

"What's up gentlemen?" I said. "Good practice?"

"It was OK," said Brett. "Hey Dad, this is my friend Sean. He says you know his mom."

"Oh really."

"Yeah. My mom went to school with you at Notre Dame."

"Wow. That was a long time ago."

"Every time she sees you on the tv she says things like "if you only knew what I knew" and "wait until my book comes out."

I laughed out loud. "I'm sure she's just kidding."

"She said you once pulled her and her friend out a of a moving cab to get them to come back to a party."

Brett, who had started talking nearby with another kid whirled around at that.

"Wait a second. What was that?"

I ignored him.

"Dad…Dad…"

"Now that just doesn't sound like me at all," I said, trying my damnedest to keep a straight face. "I'm certain she has me mixed up with someone else."

"Sean, what was that?" asked Brett.

"Who is your mom?" I asked quickly, hoping he wouldn't repeat that scurrilous allegation.

"Lauren Steele."

"Lauren Steele. No. I do not recall her. Is that her maiden name?"

"No."

"What was her maiden name?"

"Summer."

"Oh my God. You're Lori Summer's kid?"

I did a bit of a double take as my mind raced back in time twenty-five years.

"We all loved her. She was a kick. How could she not be with a name like that? I don't know how much she loved us but she and her friends kept coming back to our parties. She had a lot of friends. And we had good parties."

Throughout the duration of this little exchange Brett couldn't keep his eyes off me—trying to ascertain if I was telling the truth or not.

"What is Lori doing these days?" I asked—a desperate attempt to shift the focus of this particular exchange to the present day.

"She runs a nonprofit in Palo Alto. It works with local companies to find employment for people in homeless shelters."

"Wow. Good for her. Doesn't surprise me a bit."

"Please tell her I said hello. No wait. On second thought tell her I said she is a bold-faced liar and I have absolutely no idea who she is."

He smiled. "I think I'll do that. I can't wait to say that actually. She mentions it so much we're all kind of tired of hearing about it—especially my dad."

Two of the coaches approached. Brett looked a little frustrated—I think he wanted more information—but he nonetheless did the right thing and moved on.

"Dad, this is Coach Tyler and Coach Murtaugh."

"Thanks for having Brett in the program," I said, shaking their hands, "I know he missed all of fall ball so I appreciate you letting him try out late."

"It's a pleasure having him with us," said Coach Murtaugh. "And we're honored to have you out here as well."

"Brett tells me you served in Afghanistan," I said.

"And Iraq," he responded. "Two tours of duty in each actually."

"Wow. How admirable. Thank you so much for your service. With that background I'm guessing you can handle any issues these boys might present."

"Oh, they don't give me any trouble. As long as they all stand for the anthem. We had a little issue with that last year."

"Oh did you now?" I said. I had thought I was off duty but I guess there's really no such thing.

"I assume that won't be a problem with Brett," he said. It was clearly a statement rather than a question.

"To be honest I have no idea," I responded. "I really admire his outlook on the world—and it's uniquely his, not mine. I think he respects the hell out of our military and all that people like you have done throughout our history to preserve our way of life. There's deep appreciation there. I think he fully understands why many would view anything other than reverence for the flag and anthem a slap in the face of everyone who ever served our country or died defending it.

"And I think at the very same time he's very sympathetic to the plight of African Americans and others who confront hardships and challenges due to their race. And I think he fully understands why many people whose ancestors were forced into slavery in this country, and who may still have to face various forms of racism and discrimination even today, might not share in that same reverence in light of that, and might opt for a peaceful form of protest—exercising a right all our military veterans fought hard to protect.

"But I'm sure at a place like this you engage them in a dialogue about these issues and handle it in the most thoughtful, sensitive manner possible."

That was a mouthful, but the best I could do on the fly. He seemed annoyed by that answer, though. I tried to remember whether Brett's high school team back in DC even played the National Anthem before each game. I felt a bit like I was back in the White House Press Room. As luck would have it, before the coach could respond two more people came upon us.

"Good afternoon, Mr. President, my name is Joyce McClendon and this is Principal Alberts."

I shook their hands, but could tell the coach felt my answer left him hanging a bit. In that way he was certainly in good company—Jake Tapper and John Roberts may have felt less than satisfied at times with my answers as well. I was all too happy not to complete that conversation—with the coach who determined my kid's playing time. There's a lot to be said for getting the last word in and moving on without taking any more questions.

I turned to address the two school administrators. "What is your connection to the school, Joyce," I asked.

"Director of Development," she responded.

I turned back to finish my conversation with Coach Murtaugh.

Chapter Fifteen

Let Me Say What Everyone Else Is Afraid to
March 24, 2021

While President Bates' decision to take out North Korea's nuclear capacity was fairly universally criticized in the national press, particularly in light of their response and the resultant loss of life in South Korea, one commentator felt compelled to link his criticism to her gender, causing others to pile on as well.

The Lance Crenshaw Show

(Nationally-syndicated Political Talk Radio Host)

Lance Crenshaw: I am going to get right to the point today. The national media will be reluctant to say this, ladies and gentlemen, and you won't hear this anywhere else. Let me say what everyone else is afraid to. I believe President Bates took that preemptive strike against North Korea because she is a woman. She felt she needed to prove her chops to the world—that she deserves the respect of the world leaders who are naturally questioning her bonafides. Her only executive experience is as Governor of Georgia. And let's face it, Georgia will never be invaded by Florida, or any other state. She is out of her league, and wanted desperately to demonstrate that she belongs at the table with the other world leaders. What she has is the equivalent of little man syndrome.

Unfortunately, she is learning on the job on our watch and at our expense. I am afraid that the Republicans' attempt to nominate a moderate rather than a true conservative forced this upon us, and look where it has gotten us. She'll no doubt need the help of a lot of people to extricate us from this mess. And that could be literally decades in the making.

Now I can already see the hue and cry from the Twitter mob that I am a misogynist, a bigot, a male chauvinist. What I am, ladies and gentlemen, is a truth teller, and a patriot. And that is why we have the national following that we do. I trust that by speaking out in this manner, I give political cover to others who were reluctant to call this what it is, a desperate attempt to earn some degree of instant international credibility and gravitas.

I will continue to deliver to you the truth every morning for three hours, you can count on that.

Chapter Sixteen

The First Arrows Are Coming from Inside the Reservation
March 25, 2021

The more I paid attention to the news and read between the lines of some of the coverage of our new Vice President, the more my suspicions of him seemed to be confirmed. To put it lightly, I was not a fan.

WASHINGTON POST

SOURCES SAY VICE PRESIDENT HAD URGED BATES NOT TO STRIKE NORTH KOREA

(Washington DC, March 25, 2021) By Javier Martinez
Sources in the Bates administration, speaking to the Washington Post on the condition of anonymity, have indicated that Vice President Margel was the lone dissenting voice in the Situation Room urging caution rather than aggression the night President Bates made the final decision to order preemptive strikes to take out North Korea's nuclear capabilities. That unilateral action by the US has met with international disdain and caused instability throughout the world.

Margel, who has been openly critical of the Obama and McFadden years of employing a policy of strategic patience, often suggested on the campaign trail that further US inaction will only lead to a world where North Korea possesses nuclear weapons, which he has described as "unthinkable." This long-time public stance of Mr. Margel towards North Korea caused immediate speculation that he was a leading behind-the-scenes advocate of the preemptive strike executed by the US last week that seems to have thrown the world dangerously close to world war, and caused virtually all major global stock markets to plummet. The situation has placed the new administration into immediate crisis mode. Our sources indicate he was not advocating for the preemptive strike.

***.

CNN'S NEWDAY
(Cable News morning show)

March 26, 2021

ALISYN CAMERATA: Welcome back to New Day. Alyson Camerata here with John Berman. We welcome back our friend Rachel Hale from the New York Times who has done some interesting behind the scenes sleuthing relating to the recent reports in the Washington Post suggesting that Vice President Margel was privately arguing against the recent US preemptive attack against North Korea that has triggered such brutal retaliation by North Korea against both South Korea and now Japan, and has caused instability across the globe.

Good morning, Rachel.

RACHEL HALE: Great to be with you, Alisyn.

CAMERATA: Tell us what you have learned.

HALE: We all thought it odd that a report so favorable to the vice president would leak so quickly after the events. And with something like this there's really typically a few reasons this might leak. It may be someone leaking in order to undermine the president, someone leaking who is philosophically opposed to the action, or perhaps someone intending to make the vice president look good, or maybe a combination of those. I can't divulge our sources of course, but we have reliable sources that trace the leak directly back to the vice president himself through his Press Secretary, Stanley Kirwan. But what's even more amazing, Alisyn, is that we have several credible sources that dispute the veracity of the underlying story itself. What we are learning is that there were no dissenters in the room with the president—the joint chiefs, the National Security Adviser, the Defense Secretary, the Chief of Staff and the Vice President—when the options were presented to the President and the decision was made, which raises serious questions about the motivation of the leaker.

CAMERATA: Let's be clear about what we are talking about here. These are anonymous sources outing other anonymous sources.

HALE: Yes, that's precisely what this is.

CAMERATA: If what you and your colleagues are reporting is true, Rachel, then that means Vice President Margel is intentionally undermining his boss, seeking to distance himself from this decision, and perhaps worst of all, being deceitful about the underlying content of the leak. You are reporting that he did not in fact argue against the military action.

HALE: You are correct, Alisyn. I'm trying hard to recall a Vice President who has engaged in this sort of action to undermine a president and I'm coming up short. Maybe you can get John Avlon to look into that. Certainly states have had Lieutenant Governors do this from time to time, but those are typically split party arrangements, not two from the same party who run together on the same ticket.

CAMERATA: Yes—it makes you wonder if they were ever on the same page even in the beginning.

HALE: Well, it's worth remembering that the choice by candidate Bates to make Senator Margel her running mate was largely bowing to pressure from the far right to balance the ticket, with a secondary motivation of helping her win Ohio. She already had the support of McFadden's independent minded Alliance movement—who preferred her to the very liberal Democrat nominee—Massachusetts Senator Robert Clayton. Voters on the far right certainly preferred her to Clayton, whom they refer to as a socialist, even though many consider her what they call a RHINO—Republican in name only. But to motivate them to actually come out on election day, she ran with Margel. While I don't know that anyone expected Margel to play the role of the dutiful vice president—wholly supportive of his boss and her agenda—it's safe to say that few expected this sort of thing from him, particularly this soon after the election.

CAMERATA: I'll just throw something out here that maybe some others are thinking this morning too. Do you think we'd be hearing this story if the president he was serving was a man? Would he be that quick to undermine a male president with a leak like this?

HALE: I think that's a fair question, Alisyn. Are you asking with respect to Margel in particular or society in general?

CAMERATA: Either, really. How about both.

HALE: Well of course it's impossible to tell for sure.

Margel is his own man, and one might wonder whether he could fall in line with anyone as president. But we've had other strong personalities through the years as vice president—guys like Lyndon Johnson for example—who have fallen in line, and perhaps even reshaped their own views to those of the president. Maybe Dick Cheney comes to mind, but he did all his pushing behind the scenes to get George W. Bush to do what he wanted, rather than privately undermine him in the press, and when they disagreed he kept it quiet. I think your question is worth considering. It will certainly be something worth keeping an eye on as we go forward here.

CAMERATA: Yes, indeed. We all knew it might be challenging for the first woman to ascend to the presidency. I just don't think anyone contemplated that the first arrows would be coming at her from inside the reservation.

AP
VICE PRESIDENT DISMISSES LEAK ALLEGATIONS AS "FAKE NEWS'

(Washington DC, March 27, 2021) By Amy Selcin
Following an appearance and speech at the National Press Club this afternoon, Vice President Margel paused just long enough to answer a reporter's question shouted at him, asking for a comment about a New York Times report that his office had leaked details of a private meeting with the President during which the decision to take preemptive action against North Korea was given the go ahead. Vice President Margel emphatically denied all aspects of the report, dismissing it as "fake news."

The White House has thus far declined to comment on the story.

Chapter Seventeen

When Can You Start?
March 28, 2021

I had a good long workout in our makeshift gym at the house—such a luxury of being kind of retired—but so necessary to my sanity and general happiness. Having more time on my hands tends to provide my mind more time to go searching for new reasons to be stressed. I'm gonna fix that soon when I figure out my next chapter in life.

Denyse and Montana were relaxing on the deck. I mixed myself a post-workout smoothie—not the quite the quality of a Kaitlyn and Martina special but pretty good nonetheless—and joined them.

Denyse turned and shot me a look that screamed both amusement and bewilderment.

"Am I imagining it, or were you just working out to the soundtrack from Hamilton?"

I laughed. "I've got about a dozen playlists, and just felt like something completely different."

"Broadway, really? If I tweeted out that you work out to show tunes perhaps you'd get a higher percentage of the gay vote if you ever run again." She amused herself with that comment.

"I think you'd need to get a twitter account first. I don't see that happening anytime soon."

"You get inspiration from show tunes written about your drinking buddies?"

"Well Hamilton wasn't in the saloon of course, so I never got to know him. Although he would have been a great addition. Burr kind of took him out of the running. And effectively took himself out of the running with the same shot."

"Hamilton really couldn't have been president anyway, right? Born in Haiti?"

"Actually I think it was somewhere in the West Indies. But how did you know that?"

"Hey I was paying attention during that Broadway show—'immigrants, we get the job done.'"

"Yes! He and Lafayette. Lafayette's name came up a lot in the Saloon. Washington loved him. And Washington's dogs were mixed with Lafayette's French stag hounds."

"Alright, that's enough saloon talk now. You're scaring me."

"You're the one who brought it up, sweetheart. I know how much you hate that subject."

"I don't hate it. I've just come to accept it. I don't like to think that the man I love and respect has this side of him, but I made my peace with it long ago. I tend to allow myself to forget about it, and actually kind of prefer it that way."

"Speaking of which, have you got anything going tomorrow? I've got to meet a woman who worked on the White House staff and I may just do it here to make it easier on everyone."

"Sure, just do it here. What did you mean, speaking of which? You were talking about the saloon, right?"

"No, um . . . I just mean we were talking about the White House and it reminded me I've got to figure out a way to meet her tomorrow."

"No problem. I'll be gone most of the day volunteering at Jesuit. More auction stuff. They've got quite a sophisticated operation. Do I know the staff member?"

"I don't believe so. I don't think you'd remember her."

"What's the meeting about."

"I'm not sure actually. She works for President Bates now back there. But I'm happy to help people who worked for me in any way I can."

"Well if she works for Maggie now be careful. That could be politically dangerous."

"To be honest I'm not certain Maggie even knows who she is. But she really should. She's really sharp. I'm looking forward to seeing her."

***

I was reading the *Wall Street Journal* in the living room the next afternoon when Aaron knocked on the open door.

"Sir, your guest, Tina, is here to see you."

Tina is a complicated one to explain. She was a waitress extraordinaire in the saloon during my presidency. It's rather impossible for me to imagine the saloon without her, actually. Not only is she brilliant, but she had provided a refreshingly strong female voice that was otherwise lacking in that exclusive club of men.

It had only been two months but I was so excited to see her—partly because I had kind of thought I was saying goodbye to her for good when we bid each other farewell my last night with all the presidents, only to learn the next day that she had successfully left the saloon. That's a long story too—one I'm not entirely sure I myself understand.

"Well, what have we got here?" I said with a big smile as she gave me a hug.

She was out of her waitress duds, in jeans, a turtleneck and boots with her hair down. Rather startling after four years of seeing her hair up in that familiar black, pencil skirt and white knit, scoop neck shirt.

She looked above the fireplace and saw our huge print of Emanuel Leutze's epic painting of Washington crossing the Delaware. She couldn't help but laugh.

"You guys all respected him so."

"Monroe's in that too—the guy holding the flag."

She looked closer. "You're right. There he is. I liked him too. He was nicer than a lot of those guys."

"We took a very memorable trip to New York when the kids were young and we just loved seeing this painting when we visited the Met," I said.

"Oh, so that's why you've got that up," she responded. I could see her mind working, appearing as if she wanted to say something but holding back. Moments later she couldn't help herself.

"Does Denyse know about the saloon?" She paused briefly. "And more importantly, the clientele that frequent that place?"

"Well, yes—sort of. We kind of have an understanding," I responded. "I think she's happier just pretending it doesn't exist, and that it's not a big part of my life." I smiled. "So we don't really talk about it."

"But it sounds like she does know something about it."

"Enough to know she doesn't want to know anymore." I laughed. "And sometimes she'll refer to the past presidents as my 'imaginary friends.'"

She laughed good and hard. "God I adore your wife. And I don't even really know her. That's priceless though. I love how your marriage has just figured out a way to handle something enormous like that. Quite admirable, really. Although it sounds a bit like "don't ask don't tell, don't you think?"

Now I was the one laughing hard.

"Right?" she added, quite pleased with herself. "How the hell did that ever fly by the way? What kind of genius does it take to come up with that?"

OK, that was a little unsettling that Tina boiled my entire marriage coping and sustainability mechanism down to the Clinton-Gore gays-in-the-military policy. I felt I was skating dangerously close to violating some aspect of my vows by divulging all this and figured I'd better move the conversation along. Quickly.

"Can I fix you a drink?" I asked. "In fact, I'd love to make you a drink for a change—after all you did for me in the last four years."

"Sure. But you know that's not the first time, right?"

"What?"

"Don't tell me you don't remember."

"You're messing with me right now, I know it."

"Ha!" She screamed. "Of course you don't remember. It was that night you and your buddy Teddy and Grant were rolling pretty good, and Cleveland maybe, and you guys took over the bar and the staff all sat at the front table with FDR, Lyndon Johnson, Clinton and Kennedy. It was pretty memorable for us. Can't believe you don't remember it."

"I had quite a lot on my plate, as I recall."

"Well that night you had quite a lot in your schooner too, and in your wine glass, and in your tumbler."

"I blame Grant. You have to admit that didn't happen often."

"Yes, I'll grant you that. Not with you."

Moments later I brought her a lemon drop martini.

"See, I knew you remembered." She smiled proudly.

It felt good to serve someone else for a change. I got myself a Corona. Still wondering exactly what was up with her, I decided to get to the point.

"What brings you here, Tina? Someone as sharp as you always has a plan."

"I had a plan, but I'm questioning it a little."

She looked serious. That really peaked my interest.

"I think it was the right thing to do to leave the Saloon. It was time. But I'm not sure working with this administration is the best role for me."

"You should be a presidential scholar, Tina. Who one earth could possibly know them all any better than you?"

"I know what they drink!" She laughed. "I don't want to study history. I want to be history. And besides, I'm not exactly an expert on their record in office."

"Who did you like?" I asked.

"I liked the good ones, the decent guys, not the smarmy or creepy ones."

I laughed. "So who does that leave?"

Guys like Gerald Ford. Monroe, Carter. Otter was fun and I actually like that he didn't drink. Van Buren was fun. Kennedy had all that charm. Obama was a good guy. Those were probably my favorites."

"How about Lincoln?"

"He was hard to get to know. More serious too—or melancholy even. Of course all you guys revered him so much too for all he did. Most of what I know about them is what they are in that saloon."

"How about Washington?" I asked.

"Yeah—but it's kind of a cliché to say you like him, right?"

"What do you think of Maggie?"

"I like her personally, but my goodness she's got some problem people around her, beginning with her husband. Then add her Vice President. Not a fan. And her Chief of Staff, too."

I decided it was better to just listen without adding to the conversation. This certainly wasn't surprising.

"Here's what I'm getting at," she said. "I respect you, what you stand for, what you were trying to do, and the kickstart you gave that effort nationally. I thought Maggie was going to be part of that. I think she wants to, but she's being pulled in different directions. Pulled hard."

"I would not underestimate her," I said. "She is sharp, determined, persuasive. You could try to effect some change in her—like you changed me in my four years."

"I'm nobody there. And I won't be able to break through to her."

Again, I just looked at her without saying a word.

"Here's what I'm getting at. I want to work for you, Danny. I don't know what you have planned, but I'd love to be part of it. I believe in that cause, and it's the reason I left the saloon. The chance to be a part of real change in the country. And there are thousands of others just like me."

"Wow. I'm flattered. I am a little surprised. I don't think it's too far-fetched to say we aren't perfectly aligned politically."

"That's where you are wrong. I respect your integrity, your civility your decency, your desire to speak the truth, to do what you think is right, what's in the best interests of the country regardless of party. That's the crucial part. It's so lacking in our politics. And in that manner in a way you transcend any political branding. I know progressives and conservatives alike that respect you. That's why your approval ratings always hovered around 60%, even though you wouldn't be either party's top choice."

I thought for a second. "I'm not sure I know what I'll be doing, how active I'll be politically or with the Alliance. That grass roots effort we started is growing all its own."

"That's perfectly fine with me—for now. I want you to consider me on your office staff. But in time I know you'll get back involved. That cause and this country is too important. Particularly at this moment."

"You think so, do you?"

"I know so," she replied. "And you do too. In the end you'll do the right thing."

I laughed. She had some undeniable skills of persuasion.

"Maybe I know you better than you know yourself," she added.

"Now you are starting to talk like Denyse."

"What a nice complement."

I love that I've managed to surround myself with smart women who tend to think more of me than I think of myself. Surely that's because they tend to focus on the very best version of me, and block out the rest. That's much more like "see no evil, hear no evil" than it is like "don't ask don't tell."

"Please promise me you'll consider me when building your staff for whatever your post presidency entails."

"Okay. Done. I considered it."

"And?"

"When can you start?"

Chapter Eighteen

Sand Hill Road
March 30, 2021

Aaron, Brent and I made the short drive in two vehicles from Los Gatos up the western edge of Silicon Valley on 280 to Sand Hill Road—a street and location practically in the shadow of Stanford and its Hoover Tower. Unusual that the ultraconservative Hoover Institute resides here, amidst a bastion of progressives and what many might refer to as "coastal elites." And of course, Sand Hill Road has taken on almost mythical significance as the venture capital and private equity center of the United States, or, in their minds here, the universe.

The building that was our destination certainly looked the part. Aaron and I entered the large spacious lobby of this gorgeous six-story, largely glass office building sitting atop an incline packed with oyster cream marble. Objects of modern art dotted both the exterior and interior—none of which really did it for me. In the center we found an elegant circular staircase next to a beautiful glass elevator that scaled the building's west side, displaying the Santa Cruz Mountains in all their glory. The place appeared empty, in the way all these buildings seemed to every time over the years I found myself here. Very few people coming to pay house calls. But the few that do I'm certain pack a mighty punch, and that makes all the difference.

I motioned to Aaron that I wanted to take the stairs. I never seem to be sure if I'll have time for a workout on any given day. But my post presidency track record in that area so far was fairly impressive.

We entered a suite on the fifth floor. Brent had beaten us there, but I immediately saw another familiar face—my Executive Assistant Cathy. Cathy had been there through it all—my early days at the tech firm, my start-up, my brief stint in the Senate, and had come with me to DC to work along-side me at the White House, before moving back to nearby Almaden in January.

"Welcome!" Her greeting reassured me that I hadn't said goodbye to all the parts of the past four years I had loved.

"Come on in." she said, looking at Aaron. "It's such a beautiful space. And get a load of that view."

"I love this side of the peninsula," I responded. "Such spectacular scenery. I can do without some of that debris though cluttering up the lobby and outer ground."

She shrieked with what I believe was laughter. "Are you referring to the priceless objects of modern art, Mr. President?" She never called me that, by the way, except those times when she's being really sarcastic. Which I guess is kind of a lot, now that I think about it.

"Just give me those iconic photos of Jackie stealing home and our G.I.s storming Normandy beach on their way to saving the world. It'd be even more meaningful and would have saved them a ton of dough. Perhaps throw in that print of Washington crossing the Delaware for good measure. But I will grant you I have fairly simple tastes."

"Oh, I wouldn't say that," she responded before adding, "necessarily."

"Some of these folks around here may have slightly more, shall we say, *sophisticated* taste in art, perhaps."

She was talking to me of course as if I was eight. I began to wonder why exactly it was that she had been with me all these years.

This certainly wasn't a hill I wanted to die on, as I often say, but I needed to press just a bit more to make my point. It didn't hurt that Brent was listening nearby and a vet of Afghanistan.

"I'm serious, Cathy," I said, though I was smiling now at the absurdity of it all. "This isn't like our conversation about wine, where I say I have no desire to be that guy that needs a $200 bottle of wine to be happy. In this case I really do believe the images I described contain more beauty and pack a far more powerful message than those pieces—which might be the best term for them—downstairs. And do so without a hint of pretentiousness."

Cathy looked at Brent and Aaron, who remained poker faced through it all. "I don't know why I bother to even argue with him sometimes. It always seems to end like this."

The suite was broken up into four offices and a conference room, all separated by glass that extended floor to ceiling. I could see Tina in the conference room talking with three young adults.

She saw me and jumped up immediately to come out to greet me.

"Ok, Boss," she said with a smile. She had called me by a few different names, as that's just what happens in the Saloon, but never 'Boss'. I think we both got a kick out of it. When she was serving up drinks to us up there I never could have imagined this scene in front of me now. But if there's one thing that Saloon taught me it's that anything is possible. Absolutely anything.

"I've assembled for you in just one short week three young, certifiable superstars—each of whom would die to have the chance to work with us. I believe the proper term for them, if I was paying attention to you in the Saloon properly, which I was, is *badasses*. That's not language I learned listening to your buddy Thomas Jefferson."

Then she added, "And I do think I used it properly in a sentence."

I laughed. "I'll be the judge of that."

"And I want to reiterate that I did just as you asked—they come from a variety of places along the political spectrum, or rainbow as I like to call it."

"Alright," I said. "Let me meet these three rockstars."

I walked right past her and I heard her quietly say to herself, "Rockstars," with a bit of a pensive look. "Now that's a new one."

***

I walked in and sat across from them. There is something about meeting with young adults—kids college age or right out of college. So much promise, idealism, innocence. Like opening day. They haven't been beaten down by life. Yet.

I dove right in.

"How can we move past our polarization?"

They looked at each other and smiled.

"What?" I asked.

"You're not even going to ask our names?"

I smiled back. "Let me see how you answer this and then I'll get a sense of whether I want to know your names."

They laughed. That was the correct response. I liked them already.

"How did we get to this place? And I want to know what you think yourself—not what you think I want to hear or what you may have heard others say." I saw the lights going on in their heads.

"How *the hell* did we get here?" I asked again.

"I think it's the internet, And the media," said the young beach blonde gentleman seated on the right.

"Actually," I interrupted, "Before you get rolling, I really do want to know your name and where you are from. I was kidding earlier."

"I'm Noah. I graduated last May from Stanford. I grew up in Newport."

"Newport Beach?"

"Yes."

"What have you been doing since graduation?"

"I've been doing some research for the Hoover Institute. I'm also involved with a startup along with a couple of Stanford friends that combines artificial intelligence with database management. And I created a nonprofit that serves disadvantaged youth in East Palo Alto."

"Wow. Incredible. Good for you. OK—the media. You were saying—"

"Well, yes. I believe it's the natural result of media conglomerates and Big Tech seeking big profits. There's no profit in playing it straight. Everyone, kids included, are seeking their own platform—whether it's viewers, clicks, subscribers, or likes. Everyone needs an angle to separate themselves. Everyone wants to make a splash. They need to survive in the marketplace. You make a lot of noise or you die.

"And like any good story they all need a villain. Liberal media wants you to believe all Republicans are racists. Conservative media wants you to think liberals are all communists. And each side views anyone in the middle as either irrelevant or a part of that enemy.

"On top of all this people now go years without hearing a news broadcast that may challenge their views or help expand their worldview."

What a great response.

"Thank you for that," I replied. "That is an excellent start. I think you are spot on."

I looked at the others. "What do you two make of that?"

"I won't say I disagree with it," said the young African-American man seated on the left. "But I think it's missing a big piece of this."

"Let's hear it, I said. But tell me who you are first.

"My name is Deion. I just graduated from San Jose State after the fall semester."

"Great to meet you, Deion. Where are you from?"

"I grew up in Hercules."

"That's East Bay? Right?"

"Kind of. Ten miles north of Berkeley."

"I was raised by my mom and my sister. My dad was murdered when I was two years old."

"I am so, so sorry to hear that."

"Thank you. I've had one job or another since I was thirteen to help the family out. I'm determined bring about a better life for all of us."

"From the little I know about you I'd say you are well on your way."

"I appreciate this opportunity, sir."

"I'm honored to have you here. Give me your thoughts on our polarization."

"I understand that there is genuine disdain on each side for the other that has created a really nasty political and cultural divide, but I really think there's more to it than that. On the left the fears and some of the hatred results perhaps, at least for many minorities, from a brutal history in this country of a few hundred years of the most despicable mistreatment imaginable. Mistreatment which persists today in so many ways, including the form of police brutality, workplace discrimination, income inequality, inequities in housing, education and health care. All that is tangible and real, with indisputable facts and supporting evidence.

"On the other side I would argue it's fear as well, but not fear based on a demonstrated track record over two centuries. I really believe it's a fear of the unknown. We have segregation in this country—racial and cultural segregation. Red states and blue states. Urban life versus rural life. Consequently, many conservative white people might not ever interact with other groups. If you don't know any gay people, or have any African Americans in your social circle, you may be uncomfortable with talk of things like diversity as a value in and of itself, and gay marriage. And you may really resent it when people call you a bigot and make it clear they believe they are superior to you because you don't embrace such concepts."

Deion paused.

"Well stated," I answered. "And I like how you attempt to understand why those who might see things differently than you do so. I think that is exceedingly fair-minded. We need a lot more of that today."

Now all of us turned toward the tall woman in between them.

"Hello, gentlemen" she smiled broadly. "I'm Sarah. I'm from Manhattan Beach. I graduated from UCLA in 2018."

"What have you been doing since then?" I asked.

"I was studying in England."

"Whereabouts?"

"The University of Oxford."

"I've heard of it."

They laughed.

Then, more seriously, "Holy cow. Were you Rhodes Scholar?"

"Yes, I was," smiling again.

These three superstars Tina delivered were unbelievable.

"What did you study?"

"I got a Masters in Philosophy on Global Governance and Diplomacy."

"Good for you. But even more so, good for the world."

"Did you play a sport in college like most Rhodes Scholars?"

"Volleyball."

"I could have guessed that. Manhattan Beach. Of course. What's your take on how we got here?"

"I'm not sure if this is a cause or a symptom of polarization, probably both, but my first thought is just about the wildly different realities in which people exist today. There is no longer a shared baseline, a basic agreement on *objective facts*. We've seen this time and time again on so many issues. It's become so easy for these parallel universes to spring up because people can now choose where to receive their information, and millions source their 'news' exclusively from an inherently biased source, either Fox News and the *Wall Street Journal* or MSNBC and The *New York Times*. Or worse yet—from Facebook, where their clicking patterns ensure that the algorithms produce for them only news that feeds their biases. And in many cases, particularly with social media, it's purely false information. Conspiracy theories have crept into the nightly broadcasts and regular media diets of millions of Americans. And the more nasty and outrageous the opinions expressed, the more attention the voice seems to attract, and also the more advertising dollar."

She continued. "I don't think it helps that the two major parties seem to be getting more and more extreme, and there is no party really in the middle—or at least there never had been really until recently with you—seeking to promote a more balanced political agenda."

"Nicely done. All three of you. Very concise statement of our predicament. I think you each make a solid case as to how we got here. What can we do about it?"

"Part of the reason I'm here today is that I think you are one who is doing something about it," said Noah. "But the deck is stacked against us. Red states are getting more red and blue states more blue. I think this movement you have started, which rejects the temptation to demonize either side, has a chance to be a bridgebuilder, and serve as an alternative path for millions of people seeking a better way."

"I agree," said Sarah. "When I see how much media figures and politicians can influence the minds and views of millions of people, I think if we just had more inspirational voices like yours out front showing people that alternative path, inevitably that message would resonate and pick up steam.

"I also agree with Deion that somehow we have to get people to understand those who hold vastly different views, and what it is about their lives and experience that informs those views. That's only the first step, but it's a critical one. I wish I knew how to do that. But I am here today because I think the momentum you have started around this has a genuine chance of making a difference."

Deion jumped in again. "I really think the one thing that can genuinely make a difference is a charismatic leader who embodies all these values—integrity, respect, decency, country over party. And if I may be so bold, sir—I think you offer us all of that and more. It's not just the Alliance and the grass roots organization, it's you out front. You are popular with both sides and you somehow artfully manage to transcend the parties. You are not viewed as hostile to either side, and that puts you in a unique position to unify us."

Through the windows I saw Cathy approaching the conference room. She opened the door halfway and knocked. We all looked over.

"I think there's a call you might want to take."

I stood up reluctantly. "Excuse me for a minute if you don't mind. I love hearing your take on these issues and I'm impressed with your thoughtful analysis of how we got here. I'm not sure what's up but I'll do my best to be quick."

As I got up I looked at Tina. She was smiling ear to ear. "Not bad, huh?"

she whispered.

"You weren't kidding," I responded.

As I got to the door, Cathy whispered in my ear "It's President Macron."

"I'm sure there's no secure lines here," I replied.

"They know that. They said he simply wants to say hello and wish you well."

Tina took over the meeting as I took the call in an empty office.

We spoke for no more than ten minutes, but I appreciated the gesture and the personal touch very much. He had been my favorite leader to hang with at the G8, and Denyse and I both got a kick out of Brigitte. I think Denyse just loves the thought of a powerful man linked with an older woman, as opposed to one decades younger. I think Macron saw a bit of a kindred spirit of sorts in me politically, as he had come from the left but tacked a bit to the right landing or attempting to land at least firmly in the center.

He asked me if what he heard about us being on a yacht with Bruce Springsteen in the Solomon Islands was true. I was all too happy to confirm that for him. Turns out he's a huge fan. New Jersey of course couldn't possibly be more different than France, but I got a kick out of hearing that. The conversation was mainly breezy and light, but that made the question he slipped in at the end all the more surprising.

"How active do you plan to be with your new Alliance?"

The kind of took me aback. My immediate response was just to laugh.

Moments later I mustered a response. "Oh, I don't know. It's possible I may be content now to leave some of the politics to the others. I might remain connected, but perhaps as more of a figurehead."

"I would encourage you to be more than that, Danny. The world is watching your democracy. You made some progress. Demons may be lurking below in your country that could soon surface. Natonalistic demons. History sometimes threatens to take its sinister course again. I implore you not to abandon what you have started."

I couldn't get my mind off of that exchange as I hung up the phone. Tina saw that I was done with the call and popped into the office. My head was still spinning a bit from his parting words.

"What did you think of the 3 amigos?" she asked.

"You mean that Dream Team you assembled? My god, what's not to love?"

"And did you notice what they all have in common?"

"What's that?"

"A firm belief that you, sir, are on to something. They want to be a part of that solution to this problem plaguing our country."

"You are making it harder and harder for me to dial it all back."

"What would your pal Teddy say? I may be mistaken, but I don't recall 'dial it back' being one of his signature phrases."

I laughed out loud. "Wow. You sure know which buttons to push. That's scary. Hard to say no to that."

"Can I hire them?"

"Yes. Can any of them write?"

"You better believe it."

"Great. They can help with political essays, Op eds, speeches, releases, letter writing, any behind the scenes lobbying we'll do, social media—especially that."

Cathy joined us in the office.

"How'd that go?" she asked.

"The call with Macron? It went well. He wants me to stay active with the Alliance. And by that I mean he wants me to be leading the charge."

I thought for a second. "Wait," I said, looking at Tina. "Were you somehow behind that call?"

She howled. "I love that you think that. I'm good, Boss, but not that good."

I wasn't convinced. She is formidable.

"Whatdja think of the kids?" asked Cathy.

"Loved 'em. Three homeruns. I'm not so sure about these digs, though."

"Murph predicted you would say that," Cathy responded.

"Let's finish talking about these three first," said Tina. "Do you want me to bring them on?"

"Yes. I think they'll be great. Nicely done."

"I think they are the cream of the crop," Tina declared. "Politically, the three of them might not be precisely where you are on the political spectrum—"

"Actually I kind of prefer it that way."

"—but they all believe in your cause, as you call it. And, while we're on the subject, I'm not really sure I'm where you are on the political spectrum either, and I'm here and all in. I'm a tad left of you."

"A tad?"

"Here's the thing, Boss—I've been thinking about this a lot, and reading a lot about people's perceptions of you. There are people on both ends of the spectrum who identify with you and swear by you, even though they won't see eye to eye with you on every issue—including some issues that might mean a lot to them. And I think it's because there's a purity about your motive—the good of the country—and an absence of an agenda. That resonates with people. It really does. And you know who it doesn't resonate with? Those that have an agenda. The two parties. Which is why you're here and not in the White House. But you have tapped into something real, and people really believe in you. Even those with diametrically opposing views."

"I like her, Danny," Cathy said, looking at Tina. "Great hire."

"So do I," I said. "But I kind of fear her too." They both laughed.

"So did I just hear you say you don't like this suite?" asked Cathy.

"There's a tight window of time on this space, Boss," said Tina. "If we want it we can have it, but we need to notify them right away. This little loaner arrangement is very temporary."

"Are there any other possibilities you're looking at?"

"Well as you know, not every building has the potential to be secured properly, so it's challenging. This place is really perfect. I think the political people love this spot. All the venture capital people are in this neighborhood, of course. And your old tech firm, Aengus, is less than two miles from here. But yes, we've got one we are looking at in downtown San Jose a few doors down from the Fairmont. There's another on The Alameda near Santa Clara University that's promising, and a third near the corner of Bachman and Santa Cruz."

"Santa Cruz Avenue?"

"Yes."

"In Los Gatos?"

"Yes."

I thought for a second. "Wait—isn't that right around the corner from Hannegan's?"

"What's Hannegan's?"

Chapter Nineteen

My New Offices on Santa Cruz Avenue
April 4, 2021

My first official meeting in our brand new offices on Santa Cruz Avenue was with freshman Congressman David Gonzales. Cathy brought him in.

"Congressman Gonzales, congratulations on your victory in November. Nicely done."

"It is an honor to meet you, Mr. President. Thank you so much for agreeing to meet with me."

"Anytime at all. You went to Cal, is that right?

"Yes I did."

"I have a niece there right now. Go Bears!"

"Yes! Roll on you Bears!"

"The birthplace of the free speech movement."

"Yes indeed, sir. I had some professors there who swear that Berkeley is the center of the universe."

"Well, for a year or two in the mid-sixties I'm not sure they were wrong. I can only imagine what that must have been like."

"Yes, Mr. President. You can still sense the presence and impact of the sixties when you walk around Berkeley."

"And you are an Afghanistan vet? Do I have that right?"

"Yes, I am sir. I volunteered after 9/11."

"Wow. Thank you for your service and your deep love of this country. I am happy to help you in any way I possibly can."

"Thank you so much, Mr. President. That means a great deal to me. I came here to see if I could get your thoughts and maybe some advice on a few things I'm kicking around."

"Sure. What's on your mind?"

"Let me begin my saying that you have been an inspiration and a hero to me. Your involvement in politics motivated me to run for Congress. And

I know I'm not the only one who feels that way."

"That's great to hear. But please don't blame me if you soon find yourself bitter and beaten down."

He laughed. "I have my eyes wide open. But it's funny you should say that. I'm already being squeezed by the House Democratic leadership in several ways."

"How so?"

"I've been befriending several other new members, including the five Alliance representatives who are getting so much attention, and they've invited me to attend their Alliance caucus meetings. I think you know they've managed to get about two dozen additional House members attending those —the five Alliance reps but also many Democrats and Republicans as well—all of whom are taking considerable heat from their party."

"That doesn't surprise me. Both parties are notoriously proficient at getting every last one of their ducklings to fall in line. Or sheep might be a better metaphor."

"I'm already catching flack from the Speaker's staff about it, to put it mildly."

"Of course. As presently constructed, the parties are not really built for bipartisanship. Those in the extremes tend to fear it."

The new congressman arose and paced a bit, then gazed outside for a moment. I could see his mind was racing. He looked back at me.

"I think I'm ready to formally, publicly change my party affiliation to the Alliance."

Wow. I looked right at him and chose not to respond just yet.

"To be honest," he continued, "I've studied the speech you gave on the Senate floor on St. Patrick's Day, and that speech you gave at Mount Vernon when you announced you would not be running again, and your farewell address. I can recite them in my sleep. They inspired me to run for office and serve this country. I think you convinced an enormous amount of people that we are better than this."

I smiled. "I'm flattered. I love your passion."

I thought for a second. "I have a several thoughts. First, you have to know what will be coming your way—a whole lot of venom. Party money and organization helped get you elected, and many will likely want to inflict some damage on you for that reason."

"My first loyalty, as you often put it, is to the country and the people who elected me and everyone else in my district."

"Well of course you know I love hearing that. But as I've told many others like you, it was easier for me to take that principled stand because we had a pretty nice fallback position. We will never want for money or a job. The risk of course is that they vote you out in two years."

"I know that well. I like my chances though. Running as an incumbent will be far easier than challenging a sitting Democrat or Republican. But in the end this is not a political calculation on my part. It's just pure and simply the right thing to do. When I was waking up every day in Afghanistan in life or death situations and promising myself that if I returned I'd live fully and do things like run for Congress, I never envisioned that I'd immediately be bowing to pressure to curtail my attempts to create more unity and national consensus in this country."

My face brightened. "Wow, I could not have put it better myself. What a great message. You might just be my new favorite congressman."

He seemed thrilled with that response.

"My final caution for you," I said, "would be pertaining to expectations. Any single congressman has such limited power and authority. I know some may feel that ultimately they'll get more done and have greater influence working within the party organization, even it entails a tremendous amount of compromising to the will of the party over time."

"Of course. I realize I'm only one of 435, so I don't have an inflated sense of my own importance. Or my influence for that matter. However, that doesn't mean I won't try. The Alliance members are already getting a ton of attention. They get interviews. And they're doing some fairly creative things on social media. And that caucus is going to generate a lot of media attention."

"I like a lot of what they are doing."

"People are starting to call it the McFadden caucus. You know that, right?"

"Ha! I'm not sure I like that. I have to think they can come up with better branding."

He ignored my attempts to laugh that off.

"I predict more Alliance candidates will run, and more sitting congressmen and women from both parties will switch parties and join your cause.

I'm looking to make an announcement fairly soon. What advice do you have for me?"

"Don't do what I did on the Senate floor. I kind of bashed the whole system. I would advise you to make it completely positive. You're not running from something, you are running to something. Take no shots at the two parties, but lay out exactly what appeals to you about this move. The numbers speak for themselves—there are more voters who now affiliate with neither of the major parties than there are in either party. That's significant. Many will still hit you, and hit you hard, but I suggest you stay positive."

"Great. That is so helpful."

"And if I can help you further in any other way please let me know."

His expression changed but he didn't say anything.

"What?" I asked. "Is there something else?"

"Well, yes."

"What is it?"

"Would you be willing to campaign for me?"

"Yes, of course!" I said. "Anything for the cause! You just let me know when the time comes. Denyse would love a trip to Napa."

"Napa's not in the district, but it's close."

"Really? What's your district? North of San Francisco, right?"

"Yes, but all along the coast. It extends from the Golden Gate Bridge all the way to the Oregon border."

"Wow—that is quite a district. Good for you. Let us know about anything you might be doing in Sausalito or Tiburon and Denyse and I will be there. Or maybe you'd just want Denyse—she's probably more popular than me anyway."

I walked him out to the lobby of our suite to say goodbye.

Cathy saw us coming and arose to meet us. "Can I get you a cup of coffee for the road, Congressman?"

"Oh, no thank you. I'm not going back up there today. I have a fundraiser in San Jose tonight."

"What are you doing between now and then?" I asked.

"I'll probably just find a spot to get a bite to eat and answer some calls and emails," he replied. "Anything nearby you'd recommend?"

"A coffee shop?" Cathy asked?

"I was thinking more of a beer and a sandwich."

Cathy looked right at me and saw my big smile.

"Gee I don't know," I said, through my grin. "If only there were a place like that around here. An Irish pub, perhaps."

Cathy stared back at me with a bit of an annoyed look. I couldn't believe she wasn't playing along, and it showed on my face.

"Oh, I'm sorry do you want me to participate in your little charade?" She glanced at the congressman and then back at me.

"Oh Mr. President," she said, "I think there's a wonderful Irish pub right around the corner. The one your car is usually parked in front of. You might just want to walk him over there to make sure he doesn't get lost along the way."

"You know," I responded, "now that you mention that I think I remember hearing good things about that place. And yes, maybe I'll walk you over there myself."

She then turned to David. "It was a pleasure meeting you, Congressman Gonzales. I hope we see you again."

We walked out of the suite, preceded by Aaron and Brent. I looked back at Cathy.

In the loudest whisper I've ever heard, she asked, "Was that more like what you had in mind, Mr. President?"

"Perfection," I responded. I did get a kick of her.

***

On the short walk to Hannegan's he told me more about the fundraiser.

"Who are you meeting with?" I asked.

"Oh, just handful of Silicon Valley's A-listers. Some of the world's richest and most powerful people."

"Another piece of advice, then," I responded. "You may want to give them a bit of a heads up on the plan you told me about."

"Oh I have sir."

"And?"

"It's the reason they are holding the fundraiser. They are so fired up."

A rush of adrenaline came over me. I thought to myself, maybe we've created a monster. A really, really, good kind of monster.

Without fully thinking about it, almost involuntarily, I blurted out, "Let me know if you'd like me to swing by."

He did a bit of a double take, and then shot back, "Yes. Absolutely, unequivocally, yes."

Just like they had in all the most meaningful moments of my life, my emotions were clearly manning the controls rendering futile all considered thought or reason. If I had thought it through I may have reconsidered making such an appearance at this time. But the thought of this type of event happening rather organically in the name of the Alliance energized me. I couldn't help but think this might just be the beginning of something big. . .

Chapter Twenty

Hannah Calling
April 5, 2021

My cell phone rang. I was a little busy. I had brisket going in my brand new smoker and some Jackson Browne rolling on the deck speakers as I squeezed some limes for a few scratch margaritas for me, Denyse, Wendy and her husband Mark. But not many people had my new cell phone number. One thing I missed the most during our White House years was exactly what I was doing in this moment. I decided to take a quick glance and see who it was anyway, knowing there was no way on earth I was going to answer it now.

I saw that it was Hannah.

"Hannah how are you?"

"Is this a bad time?"

"For you, Hannah, I've got all the time in the world."

"If I had known you were doing fund-raisers I would have been right there at your side last night."

I froze for a second. Word travels lightning fast. Of course it does. Who am I kidding? Nonetheless I felt a little bit outed.

She didn't wait for my response. "That wasn't much of a retirement. I'm thrilled you're back in the game. I just heard an audio of your speech last night. Perfection. And how devine to have elected officials abandoning the two parties and joining your cause. How can I get involved?"

At this point my three dinner and drink partners on the deck stared at me, no doubt curious about the startled look on my face. I walked down the deck steps into the backyard quickly to get out of earshot of them. I don't think Denyse knew I attended that fundraiser. Actually, I know she didn't because I didn't tell her.

"How did you hear about it?"

"It's all over the internet, honey. I saw it first on Drudge. Don't tell me you meant it to be below the radar."

"It was a small group. I don't think I felt it would go viral or anything, but of course I knew it might leak. Maybe not so quickly. I have to say I was a bit overcome by the crowd's enthusiasm for the concept. Some of these people run companies that have the power to shape public opinion."

"I think you have a lot of people excited about this, Danny. Martin and I are donating to Gonzales today. I think this is just what the country needs. And I think Gonzalez and the others in the center, to the extent they want to use us, can wield an inordinate amount of power, force the two extremes to come closer to the middle and prevent some of the wild left-right swings we seem to experience after each election. I applaud you. You are a genius."

I laughed. "I have nothing to do with this," I protested. "I'm on the sidelines now."

"What you did last night does not smack of someone being on the sidelines, my friend. What are our next steps? I know you have to have thought this all out. I need to know how you want me to plug in to this effort. I'm ready to play a major role."

I laughed again. Hannah is absolutely unbelievable. Type A squared. At least that. More energy— and competence—than anyone I know. So glad she was on my side.

I wasn't about to dampen her enthusiasm.

"I would love to meet about it, Hannah. We are just now in the process of figuring all that out. Let's get together to discuss it in further detail." I was just spitballing here.

"Perfect," she replied. "I'll have my assistant contact your office tomorrow. By the way, did you move into that delightful spot on Sand Hill Road?"

"No," I said. "We passed on that one."

"That's a shame. That would have been ideal if for no other reason than all that big money nearby."

"You are right, of course," I replied. "But I'd say the place we ended up with has perhaps even more advantages nearby."

Chapter Twenty-One

A Chasm Between the President and Vice President
May 12, 2021

WASHINGTON POST
VICE PRESIDENT MARGEL NOW THE SUBJECT OF MULTIPLE HOUSE INQUIRIES

(Washington DC, May 12, 2021) By Javier Martinez
The number of Congressional investigations into Vice President Margel for any one of a variety of reasons has swollen to five recently—remarkable given the new administration is still in its first year. Investigations are being conducted by the House Oversight and Reform Committee, House Ways and Means Committee, House Intelligence Committee, House Judiciary Committee, and House Financial Services Committee. Margel has steadfastly refused to cooperate with any of the inquiries, ignoring subpoenas for documents and instructing staff members not to comply with subpoenas to appear before the committees in person. His posture toward the inquiries was apparently unimpacted by President's Bates publicly urging him to cooperate. She has long claimed that her administration will be the most transparent in history. Mr. Margel's defiance of the subpoenas certainly belies that claim.

The White House, on the other hand, is fully cooperating with all Congressional Committee inquiries into the Vice President, at times following negotiations pertaining to scope and relevance. The result is a chasm between the

President and Vice President the likes of which Washington has not seen in decades. The running feud, once carefully hidden from public view, has now spilled out into the open, with aides in both offices no longer going to great lengths to conceal their disdain for one another. This new dynamic threatens to consume Washington, at a time when the Bates Administration is already reeling from its missteps in North Korea that has destabilized much of the globe.

Chapter Twenty-Two

The Proper Care and Feeding of a Vice President
May 13, 2021
The Saloon

I decided it was high time I order a hot ale flip. Why not? At this point, what exactly did I have to lose? I had somehow managed to avoid it for four years. I had a few other things going in my life. To tell you the truth, now that I find myself rather permanently on this side of this mystical drinking establishment, I was kind of looking forward to it.

I got Otter's attention from a distance and sauntered up to the bar, although he had no idea what I was up to. Ginger happily greeted me.

"What do you need, Danny Mac? They all seem to be drinking mead in here tonight."

"Not tonight, Ginger. I've decided the time has come for me to order a hot ale flip."

She shrieked with delight, then turned and yelled down to the other end of the bar.

"Hey Big Time, we need one hot ale flip over here."

"Alright!" he shouted back with a big smile. He looked at Slick bartending next to him.

"You're gonna need to get a dozen or so hot ale flips ready."

"Didn't she just ask for one?" he responded.

Matty shot him a look. "You don't think I know these guys? A twenty-first century guy has never ordered one of these before. Trust me, this night may have just taken a turn."

A group of presidents started approaching the bar, as a palpable burst of energy seemed to pulsate throughout the room.

Slick lined up a dozen large mugs on the bar, while Matty hustled over to the fireplace and stuck several fire pokers directly into the roaring fire. I wasn't certain I wanted to observe this process closely. I couldn't be sure, but I imagined it must be something akin to sausage being produced. Or legislation.

Slick then assembled what looked to be molasses, raw egg whites, rum and ale, and at that point I figured it'd be better to just look away.

Madison, Jefferson, Adams, and Van Buren gathered behind me approvingly. Otter approached with a huge smile.

"Hey Big Time," he yelled, "make sure you mix up one of those for me."

That itself caused more buzz throughout the room.

I looked back at him. "Dude, you haven't drunk in decades."

He laughed and shook his head. "Don't worry, Rook. I'm only gonna have a few sips. But this is for the boys. For the country. United we stand."

I laughed. Now Ginger was lining up at least another dozen giant mugs. Matty put more pokers into the fire.

When all the mugs were full the wait staff brought them in trays over to the fireplace. The music stopped and the entire bar followed behind them. Matty gleefully pulled the redhot iron pokers out of the fire and plunged them one at a time directly into the into the mugs until the each concoction was piping hot. Our early presidents cheered.

I thought to myself, I saw a lot of crazy stuff in college—hell, I did a lot of crazy stuff in college. But I have to say this is about as batshit crazy as anything I've ever seen. And somehow it was a badge of honor in this ultimate men's club.

Matty handed the first finished drink to Washington himself, who waited until all the other mugs had takers, and then raised his to the crowd.

"Gentlemen, let us thank Matt and the staff, for these libations from days of yore. I daresay my friend Samuel Fraunces, whose tavern on Pearl Street in New York so frequently and capably hosted my officers, could not have produced a finer looking hot ale flip himself."

Obama walked over. He did not have one of these drinks in his hand, and seemed proud of that fact. He then leaned in and said to me in a soft voice only Otter and I could hear, "You are a world class suck up!"

I laughed hard and so did he.

Then Bush added, "Yes, he does have some political skills, doesn't he?"

By the way, I fought mine down—it was rancid—but I never saw Bush take so much as one sip.

***

The party had decidedly less energy and many had already left an hour later when the door from the White House third floor flung open. Maggie entered and walked directly to the big oaken table in the center of the room where FDR sat in a wheelchair, his trademark long cigarette holder in his left hand. A hot ale flip mug sat unattended to in front of him. All his attention was on the Bermuda rum swizzle next to it, and the collection of admirers around the table.

Maggie confidently approached the four-term president as he was regaling the table with stories of Winston Churchill. He happily paused as President Bates appeared beside him.

"How can I help you, my dear?"

"I think you might be the one in here I am most in need of advice from. I'm fit to be tied."

"Of course. Do we need privacy?"

"No sir. Maybe some of these other gentlemen can help too."

"Certainly, Madam President. What is the general nature of your troubles?"

"My vice president."

FDR smiled. "Ah, you have chosen the right counsel indeed. Have a seat, my dear. I could have penned a treatise on the topic."

"Oh, I don't need all that sir. I just need your advice. Or a gun."

"I can happily provide both."

FDR looked back at the table. "Gentlemen, as much as I'd care to continue on and on about Sir Winston," he broke into a smile at the mere mention of the name of his fellow "Big Three" Allied leader, "my duty to our beloved country calls." He clearly relished his role in this tavern and basked in the glow of the admiration of his fellow presidents.

Meanwhile, I enjoyed observing the goings on behind the bar. Matty handed one of the large hot ale flip mugs to Slick.

"I need you to take this up to the fireplace and finish it by plunging one of the hot pokers deep into the mug and keeping it there until the drink is plenty hot. Then take it over and serve it to President Bates over there at the center table."

"Did she order one?"

Haskell couldn't contain his laughter any longer and immediately turned and walked away.

Mary Ann, sensing this may have been some mild form of hazing tried to interject.

Matty quickly added, "Yes. Everyone here is having them tonight. It's a bit of a tribute to Washington, I believe."

Slick did as he was told. As he left to carry out his orders Mary Ann slugged Matt in the shoulder.

"Hey!" he yelled. Sure, Matty was ripped, but Mary Ann was masking a bit of might herself in those well-toned arms of hers.

Taft, Arthur and Cleveland sitting at the bar had a front row seat to this priceless moment and could not contain their laughter. Not that they tried too hard. They then turned around to focus their attention on the delivery of this creation.

While that drama had been playing out, FDR motioned to Otter who had been hovering a bit awaiting just such a moment.

"Please summon if you would Mr. Jefferson, Mr. Adams, Mr. Lincoln, Mr. Johnson—Lyndon, and Mr. Nixon. Bush happily complied, and within minutes these presidents all joined FDR and President Bates at the big center table.

"Colleagues," FDR began, "Madam President is seeking counsel on the proper care and feeding of a vice president." He roared with laughter.

I bellied up to the bar and took the nearest stool within earshot of the center table. JFK and Clinton soon joined me. Most of the rest of the room came over and surrounded the main table.

Maggie managed a smile in response to FDR's opening but I'm not sure she really felt it was funny.

"Let me paint a bit of a picture for y'all," President Bates began. Before she could complete the thought, Slick appeared over her shoulder with a hot ale flip. When she didn't flinch, he slowly lowered the now piping hot mug and placed it right in front of her. It reeked of molasses, which I could smell from several feet away at the bar.

"Here you are, Mrs. President."

All eyes in the saloon now fixated on our newest colleague. The room hung on her response.

Without skipping a beat or even turning her head, she struck a slight smile, shook her head just a tad, and then simply proceeded, completely ghosting the new server and that ludicrous libation in front of her. I thought, all things considered, it was pretty savvy in-the-moment response by her. The worst thing she could have done was get upset. But that bit of a smile she flashed ever so quickly as she ignored him spoke volumes to us all. It took Slick several seconds to conclude he had been played by Matty.

She continued. "I relied too heavily on all the so-called experts in choosing a vice president. I ended up with a gentleman who, while he 'balanced the ticket' and helped us win Ohio, does not really share my vision, my political ideology or my desire to reach across the aisle. Perhaps worse, he is apparently undermining me in the press, sometimes surreptitiously, sometimes overtly. He's certainly become a bit too big for his britches. They tell me the way our Constitution is written I can't fire him."

She looked around the room. "Where's our Mr. Madison?"

That question triggered a round of hearty laughter that started slowly and then grew louder and longer.

Jefferson, clearly enjoying the moment more than most, pointed out his buddy Madison in the back of the room.

"Stand up, Madison," Andrew Jackson yelled, to more laughter. The diminutive Madison was already standing. More laughter.

Madison, backed into a corner here, fought back. "Contrary to popular opinion, our Constitution, which I might add, has stood the test of nearly 250 years now, was not unilaterally penned by my hand. I don't seem to recall the delegates to our Constitutional Convention ceding me the sole authority to establish that seminal document. Are your memories failing you, Mr. Jefferson, Mr, Adams, Mr. Monroe and General Washington?"

Jefferson shot right back, "You are the one lacking in memory, James, for you will certainly recall that I was in Paris for the duration of the Convention."

Clinton leaned over and whispered to Kennedy and me, "If he is in need of an alibi for that, I believe Maria Causeway might do the trick."

To me, the fact that Clinton uttered that line was as hilarious as the comment itself.

"Don't look at me," John Adams added. "I was in England serving as Ambassador to Great Britain."

Otter chimed in. "My goodness, Peaches. If we just had a Constitutional scholar in the house." He then turned and looked directly at Obama. "If we only had someone who taught Constitutional Law amongst us . . . maybe a Harvard-educated Constitutional lawyer who might have taught that, say, at the University of Chicago, perhaps?"

Obama smiled broadly. "Ha, ha! OK, I'll take the bait. I believe a few of our brilliant colleagues here are minimizing their roles."

He continued. "As I have always understood it, President Bates, the Vice President, like the president, is removed only by impeachment in the House and conviction in the Senate. Vice Presidents of course are elected by the people, just like presidents. In fact, the Electoral College has a separate ballot for the vice president. Thus, there exists a much higher standard for removal."

"Alright then. Short of impeachment, what would you gentlemen suggest?"

"Perhaps no one in this room can sympathize with you more than yours truly, Madam President," replied FDR. "My Vice President, John Nance Garner, was also selected for political purposes. In our second term, while he was still my vice president, mind you, he publicly opposed some of my most critical initiatives, and called me 'the most destructive man in all American history."

That broke up the room like nothing else could. I had never heard that, but how utterly hilarious to think of a sitting VP saying that of his president. I couldn't really sympathize, having had two of the very best possible vice presidents in John McCain and then Leon Panetta. But that clearly struck a chord with so many in the room. I looked around and virtually everyone here was beside themselves. I tend to pay attention to history's account of some of these guys now, and most historians rank FDR in their top five. So to have anyone say that about Roosevelt is pretty funny. But his own Vice President? That's priceless.

"And I don't think he was too enamored of the office itself," added FDR. "He called it as worthless as a warm bucket of spit." More laughter.

"I apologize for correcting you, Franklin, added LBJ, "but I believe the word he used was piss."

"I know that, Lydon. I was cleaning it up a bit in front of our fine southern lady guest here."

"Oh, thank you, Mr. President, but for heaven's sake I've heard worse."

She smiled. “Hell, I’ve often said much worse.” FDR returned her smile and nodded.

“What could you do about it?” she asked.

“He became my former Vice President. I dropped him from the ticket when I ran for re-election in ’40. I did it again when I ran in ’44. I dropped Henry Wallace for Mr. Truman here.”

“What if I can’t wait until I run for re-election?”

“Let’s see if some of the fellows here can advise you about that.”

There was a brief pause as many in the room looked around to see who would respond.

Richard Nixon seemed happy to break the silence. “You could have him indicted.”

That brought about much laughter.

“I had tried to replace Vice President Agnew on the ticket with Treasury Secretary John Connally. Connally declined and I decided to run again with Agnew. He then resigned following a felony tax fraud investigation.”

“You may have something there, Mr. President. My guy likely has many skeletons in that closet of his that could merit indictment, bless his heart.”

“You could just freeze him out, ma’am,” added Lydon Johnson. “I don’t believe I’d be telling tales out of school to say that Jack here and his little brother more or less did that to me. Made me feel like a goddamn raven hovering over their shoulders every time I was near, which wasn’t much after he discontinued our weekly meeting.”

Kennedy took that slight quite in stride. “As you know, we needed you working the halls of Congress, Lyndon. You were far too valuable to us on Capitol Hill to tie you up with the endless meetings and bureaucracy of the White House.”

That response to Johnson’s obvious dig impressed me. I guess I’ve become jaded watching what Washington has morphed into with the nonstop verbal warfare these days. I could learn a lot watching Kennedy at work.

Jefferson weighed in—another voice like JFK’s in this Saloon people were always eager to hear. Or maybe that was just me. “I must admit to perhaps a singular expertise on this subject, as I had plenty of experience at both being frozen and then perpetrating the freezing.” I don’t think he was trying to be funny but that elicited some laughter.

No laughter was heard from John Adams—the president for whom he served as vice president— who was quick to respond. "I will avow, my dear friend Mr. Jefferson, that I then believed, and now believe, that your actions, which caused considerable anxiety, brought about your own frost. So to that look for no other causes."

"I should think the election of 1800 quite settled the matter, Mr. Adams," responded Jefferson. "The people spoke. There can be no higher authority than the electorate itself."

The room buzzed following that painful dig.

Again, maybe it's just me, but this was really entertaining stuff. What I loved most about the saloon. Particularly these two. A complicated love/hate relationship involving a couple of giants of American History.

Even so, our Ms. Bates seemed a bit aghast at that exchange. Eisenhower, noticing her expression, added, "I think you'll find the saloon to be just like love and war, Madam President. All is fair."

The group applauded that sentiment.

Otter, our frat president and the one most proud of the dynamic in this place, looked quite pleased with himself.

I fought down another swig of my hot ale flip. God it was nasty.

Another classic night in the saloon.

Chapter Twenty-Three

It's Never Too Late to Become Who You Might Have Been
May 15, 2021

The Berkeley sun was unseasonably hot for mid-May as I approached the center of the stage erected on the field in Cal's Memorial Stadium. Luckily I had spent much of the long graduation ceremony in the airconditioned press box, basking in its breathtaking views of the San Francisco Bay, Coit Tower, Alcatraz, Sausalito, and the Golden Gate all in full bloom on this crystal-clear spring day. My phone started blowing up just moments before I had risen to speak, and it continued to vibrate now as I geared up mentally to address this crowd of nearly 30,000.

Vibrations continued throughout the speech. I should have turned it off. I have to say it did distract me ever so slightly as I wondered if something was happening with the North Korea situation or the Middle East perhaps.

In light of the extreme heat I kept it under ten minutes, but I really enjoyed addressing these kids. What I love most is that so many of them have no idea how bright their future is. I don't know for sure, but I'm guessing most of these commencement addresses are fairly similar. But in my mind that doesn't make them any less meaningful. I love all those messages. And everyone needs to hear them—not just on graduation day but every couple years or so for the rest of their lives. Life has a way of sucking some of the inspiration out of us at times, and then next thing you know a decade has gone by.

My favorite quote—British author George Eliot's "It's never too late to become who you might have been," works even better perhaps for someone my age than it does for these graduates. Actually, if I'm not mistaken I think "George" was really a "Mary Ann." How perfect is that, by the way. But either way, he or she absolutely nailed it. And in that sense, today I could have just as well have been delivering that whole address right into a mirror.

I also hit on many of my other themes. Of course, I covered our political and cultural division. I implored them to seek out the unvarnished truth from a wide variety of daily sources in getting their news and filter out all the blowhards bloviating opinions masked as news. And of course I told them we are indeed better than this—so much better.

And I asked them to take a few moments every now and then to record in a journal or diary their thoughts about themselves, their family, country, the world, and the human condition—beginning today if they haven't already started one. They'll never regret that as they grow older and reflect back upon this day.

I think my message was well received. I settled back into my seat after my talk but my phone continued its intermittent buzzing. However, the last thing on earth I was going to do was pull that thing out on this stage just to satisfy my curiosity. I gazed up at the bluff above the stadium they call Tightwad Hill, where those too cheap to spend money on a ticket take in football games every fall. It appeared to be standing room only up there today too, no doubt spillover family members. The view I had looking east from the Stadium—of the Berkeley Hills dotted with Eucalyptus trees and Monterey Pines—was fairly magnificent as well. This spectacular setting provided a backdrop befitting those lofty academic accolades that had just been earned.

After a brief post-graduation ceremony at the Chancellor's house on campus, I finally settled in to the back of the town car for the ride back to Los Gatos.

The phone rang right as I was about to check my texts. It was Brett.

"Dad, did you get any of the texts?"

"No," I replied. "I've been tied up for three hours. What's up?"

"I hit a walk-off three-run homer in the tenth to beat Serra."

Wow. I was overcome with a rush of emotions. I was thrilled for him. Oh my God I was thrilled. But at the same time my heart sank. I can't believe I wasn't there for that. How could I possibly let that happen? I felt I had failed him as a father. And failed myself to boot.

I did my very best to carry on the conversation but there was a part of me that just wanted to cry.

"Good for you. That is so awesome."

"You know that's where Tom Brady and Barry Bonds went to high school, right?"

"Yes, I know."

"When we played them at their pace earlier this year we saw all the plaques they've got up for those guys. A ton of other MLB guys went there too."

I continued on of course, compartmentalizing the disappointment—a trait I've become all too good at, but I was crushed.

"You're showing them what you can you do, Brett. Proving you belong. All your hard work is paying off. I am so happy for you. So proud of you. Tell me about it."

"We tied it up in the bottom of the seventh on a double by Preston. It remained 6-6 until the top of the 10th when they got one. I came up in the bottom of the tenth with runners at first and third and one out."

"Take me through the at bat."

"I was just looking for something to drive, Dad. I wanted so badly to win this thing for us 'cause their bench was riding me about you all day. He started me with a sinker in the dirt and then a slider outside. With that count I figured I could afford to guess fastball. I got one middle of the plate a little bit up and I barreled it. It cleared the center field fence and disappeared into that big tree out there. As you would say, Dad, it was 'properly struck.' "

I was so fired up for him but so devastatingly disappointed in myself. Here I had missed one of the most memorable moments of his life. I wasn't gonna let myself off the hook for this. Not anytime soon at least.

"Make sure you text Satch," I said. "I'm sure he'd love to hear about this."

"He called me right after the game. Mom and I talked to him for twenty minutes. He and Christy were watching the live stream on the internet. He thinks I should be batting higher than seventh in the order. I'm just happy I'm in the lineup."

"Pretty sure you've secured your spot, dude."

I hung up as thrilled for him as I was devastated I missed it. And of course Satch was watching—still showing me the way even from afar. I vowed then and there to be present for him while I still had time. The last four years had caused me to be absent for a lot of the kids' high school moments. I still had a chance to be there for what was left. I owed that to them. And to me.

***

"Are you alright over there?" Denyse asked. It was 3:14 a.m., and I had been tossing and turning for a good couple of hours.

"I'm just a little out of sorts," I responded.

"Is this still about missing the game today?"

The way she asked that made it all the more clear how ludicrous it was that I was so distraught. But even that realization didn't make it any better.

"It is. And I know. I'm not proud of how I feel."

She sat up. "Alright, let's talk this through. I'm certain if we analyze it we can get you to a better place."

"Thank you. I appreciate that." I really did.

"Let's approach this logically."

"I'm game for that."

"I may have to ask you some tough questions."

"Fire away. I'm used to tough questions."

"Alright. I know a little something about baseball and the McFaddens, but I don't pretend to know the half of it."

"In fairness to my family, and to baseball for that matter, let's not pretend it's just us. Go watch Field of Dreams and then tell me it's just a McFadden family thing."

"OK. I'll grant you that. Not that it's something rational but that it affects more than just your family."

"Thank you. I think. And I feel I need to add it's your family too."

"Yes, it is. I married into this. When you said you are not proud of how you feel, what is it you're not proud of? Are you afraid you are living vicariously through Brett?"

"Wow. No. I hate that you might think that but it's really not it."

"Do you feel unappreciated by him?"

"No, that's not it at all."

"I'm struggling to get to the root of where you believe you failed here."

"I do get such personal satisfaction in seeing the kids succeed at things they are most passionate about, and when I think about it, their greatest moments are really my greatest moments. That was how my mom was. And that's not living vicariously through them, it's wanting to see them find joy in life and achieve their dreams.

"And I'm just sitting here thinking about how my dad was at every one of my games growing up. Even when I had a JV baseball game an hour and a half away that started at 3:15 on a Thursday afternoon, our bus would pull up at the field and there would be my dad already there sitting in the stands with his fold up bleacher chair and ND cap reading a book—most likely something about American military history.

"And you know what else?" I said. "Satch was watching today. Of course he was. He gets it. You'd think after spending four years alongside him at the White House I would have learned a little something. Brett will remember this day all his life. And I wasn't with him. And it wasn't because I was off trying to broker peace in the Middle East or anything."

"OK, well I'm glad you said that," she responded, "I have two responses to that. First of all, don't you think it's even more important to be there the game after he gets the walk off homerun? The one when he goes 0 for 5 and grounds into a double play with the bases loaded to end the game?"

"Wow. Looks like you've got about as much faith in him as you do in me."

"No, I'm serious now. They don't need their parents when they're on top of the world. They need us when the world is beating them down, as it does so often. Particularly for teenagers. And particularly for teenagers who are the son of a president and are saddled with all those expectations.

"And secondly, look what you did today. Now I have no idea what you said to those thousands of graduates, but knowing you, it was inspirational and life affirming and hopeful. I am guessing you touched hundreds of them today if not more, and made a difference that matters. But even if it were only one of them, wouldn't that alone have been worth it?"

I thought for a second. "OK. I can accept that. I'm not done mourning though, but that helps. You know I wound easily. But I recover quickly."

"Great. There's no reason to beat yourself up. Really there isn't. Now get some sleep."

With that she rolled over. Away from me.

"There were a couple brutal questions in there, by the way." I had to add that. It was true.

"Oh c'mon. No more brutal than you would have gotten from the White House press corps. I'm no John Roberts or Kaitlyn Collins. You're used to that. What's the difference?"

"What's the difference? There's a huge difference! I'm not sleeping with the White House press corps."

Moments later I added, "Or should I say attempting to sleep with."

I don't think she heard that last part. She was sound asleep.

Chapter Twenty-Four

El Tarasco
July 11, 2021

I walked into El Tarasco on Main Street in El Segundo—a little beach town just south of Los Angeles, and saw that Hannah hadn't arrived yet. Brent positioned himself outside in the front and Aaron grabbed a table near the back door. I walked in and took an empty table in the front corner. It was midafternoon, and the tiny place was virtually empty. None of the patrons or staff seemed to recognize me, and I was just fine with that.

For a few months Hannah had been trying hard to book something with me. She and Martin invited us to join them on another trip, but Denyse and I didn't want to go away for any extended period of time with Brett and Jack still being at home. Hannah had long offered to take me to any restaurant in the world. All I had to do was pick the time and place. After much thought I chose a time we would both be in LA. She was building a bit of a media conglomerate and was spending a good deal of time down here, and I was meeting with Mayor Garcetti and some of the Los Angeles City Council members to talk about the homeless crisis throughout California. We compared calendars and landed on today.

I had eaten here may times over the course of my life and career. Authentic Mexican in every respect. It was established in the sixties by Mexican immigrants Moises and Celia Palomo. A classic "dive" of course, but it had achieved legendary status through the years. Back in the day you may get your food served on plates inscribed "International House of Pancakes." Huge burritos are the specialty, but all the other entrees are noteworthy. In addition to being tremendous, the food is also as cheap as you can get in LA, and they hand you enough chips and salsa to last a couple weeks.

I was well into those chips, salsa and guac when Hannah came rolling in fifteen minutes late. I smiled and studied her face, uncertain of how she was going to react to my choice of venue.

"OK, I do love it," she admitted, sitting down across from me after taking it all in. We could hear one of the cooks in the kitchen singing along to the Spanish music coming from an old transistor radio by the cash register. The walls were peppered with random old photos and posters with no apparent common style or theme, but it all worked.

"I'm glad you like it—but just wait until you get your food. You can't beat this spot for bona fide Mexican food."

"I'm so glad to learn of it. Martin and I just bought a little place not too far from here."

"Really? You bought a place near here?"

"Yes—Manhattan Beach. We figured since we're going to be spending a lot more time down here we may as well have a home base."

"Wow. What street? We have a lot of friends who live there."

"The Strand."

"What? You bought a *little place* on the Strand?"

I just smiled and shook my head. Only Hannah could have put it exactly like that. There are no "little places" on The Strand in Manhattan Beach, by the way. And no places of any kind that run you anything less than about $15 million.

"Let us know if you ever want to use it."

I wasted no time answering that. "The answer to that is yes, Hannah. Unequivocally yes. You can count on that."

"Great. It has several master suites so even if we are there you and Denyse are always welcome."

She was priceless. As much as I was dying to find out what "several master suites" means for a "little place on the strand," I didn't want to appear too star struck so I moved along and suggested we proceed to the menu. But yes, we are coming back.

I ordered a Super Deluxe Burrito—the house specialty—as big as a junior high football—and ordered a Junior Super Deluxe for Hannah. We also ordered a ton of sides, knowing there was no possible way we'd finish. I ordered a full spread for Aaron and Brent as well. Hannah looked a little intimidated when all the food showed up. It's fair to say I had never before seen that look on her face. But the food more than lived up to the billing.

"So tell me," I asked, "how is your media empire shaping up?"

"I don't think I've ever been so excited about a project in all my life.

We have about a dozen movies in production or in the pipeline and a handful of original series. You would love so much of it. Our cable and streaming channels launch October 1. That's actually one of the things I wanted to talk to you about."

"Really? I never thought of myself as much of a leading man, but perhaps with the help of a really spectacular hair and makeup person . . ."

She didn't bother to laugh. She was all business.

"No, I need your advice and direction. We are planning some nightly world and political news and opinion programming to compete with the likes of MSNBC, CNN, and Fox News."

"Terrific. We need that. The media, I believe, is a big part of the problem of the division in this country, and can and should be a big part of the solution."

"I want something with a little less judgement and a lot less hate—something that doesn't just see all these issues as binary but acknowledges there is a vast middle ground that is too often lost."

"Good for you," I said. "I can't believe where we are as a country. I mean really, who even needs Russia interfering and dividing us any longer. We seem to be doing a bang-up job of that all by ourselves. But turning that around will be a tall order."

"I'm well aware of that. But Martin and I are going to throw some money at it, and a great deal of our energies. This is going to be successful."

"I have no doubt about that, Hannah. I would not bet against you. How can I help the cause?"

"Well, you've done a lot already. You ignited this fire. We won't be running politics and news 'round the clock like the others. But we'll devote some prime time to it. This whole channel will be right up your alley, Danny. There is a nuance and a middle ground that is being completely ignored. The world is just not just black or white. You have tapped into something that could actually change the toxic political dynamic in this country."

"Thank you," I responded. "I agree that we now have a window of opportunity here. The Alliance candidates having so much success last election confirms that. And being in the middle as they are, they are wielding some power and making a difference in Washington. And I still think that's just the tip of the iceberg."

"Would you be interested in hosting something?"

I laughed, but then I looked and saw she was serious. "I'm flattered you think I could pull that off."

"Of course you could. You could use it as a platform for your movement. You can conduct interviews, deliver your opinion, and shine a light on all those who are making a difference."

"I appreciate that very much, but I hardly think I'm the best one to do this. I love the concept though. And I think it's a piece of this puzzle. A vital piece."

"My vision—pulling a page right from your opus, Danny, is for a network that is relentlessly focused on the best of us, and all that has made this country special through the years and can do so again to get us to a better place. I want both the creative content we'll produce as well as the nightly broadcasts to be absent the hate you see and the disdain by both sides for the other, but seeking not only common ground when it's achievable but, perhaps as importantly, a genuine understanding of the other side."

"That is such an admirable vision, to be sure. Easier said than done, however. But what a service it could provide. People need hope. And people need to see and understand that it's not all right versus left—there's so much more than just the two extremes—that 42% of their fellow citizens fall in the middle, and an even larger group just wants their politicians to do what's best for the country regardless of party. But to do this effectively above all it needs to be authentic—always—to make it credible. It can't be in any way syrupy like some past attempts to do this. But what a boon for all of us if you can pull it off."

"Watch me."

"Oh I will! I can't wait to. And I'm guessing people of all stripes will as well. If we could just get people to seek more balance in their news sources every day this country wouldn't be at the mercy of these corporations and talking heads that get filthy rich off of dividing us. Go make some people rich by bringing us together, Hannah. What a legacy that would be."

"Are you saying you don't want to be directly involved?"

"I will happily help you get guests, provide advice, and serve as a guest commentator if you like from time to time, but I don't think I can be more front and center on it than that at this particular point. Denyse and I are focusing a lot on family right now, as we wind down the last few years of the kids being at home. Besides, I think it's important for people to hear powerful voices that aren't mine delivering this more unifying message."

"I'll take that as a 'no' for now. A temporary no. We'll reconvene on this when the boys leave for college."

I laughed. She is not an easy person say no to.

"I love the concept, Hannah. It is a big piece of the solution here. And you are the best possible person to be taking this on."

"Thank you. I'm not saying it won't be a challenge, but it's one I will relish every single day."

"If anyone has a chance to pull it off, Hannah, it's you."

We did our best with the food in front of us but didn't really come close to polishing it all off. She looked around the room.

"Great choice of restaurant, Danny," she exclaimed as we rose to leave. Just then I saw her limo pull up in the street in front of the restaurant. Like magic.

She paused on our way out to look at an old vintage poster hanging partly askance on the wall. It advertised a bullfight in Tijuana, displaying a massive bull emerging from under a red cape extended by a colorfully-dressed matador.

"I'm not much a fan of this," she said.

"Always makes me think of Hemingway," I responded.

"Maybe there was romance about it in his day, but are they still doing these?" she asked. "Must we really glorify something where the only possible outcomes are the maiming of a human being or the death of a bull?"

"Maybe you can fix that too, Hannah," I said. "Can't we all just get along?"

She laughed.

"But do me a favor," I added, "promise me you'll wait until you've managed to help me solve our own inane national death match first."

"Deal."

I swear, if anyone could do it she could.

Chapter Twenty-Five

The Hostess City of the South
August 15, 2021
The Saloon

I was late to the party—something I always deeply regret. But the mood in the saloon seemed dramatically different tonight. The dimly lit gas lamps provided the only source of light. The jukebox was playing but barely audible. I think it was a Roy Orbison playlist. Kind of fit the scene in front of me. Not many people here. Perhaps that's why I wasn't drawn to it. I came around the bar and saw Maggie and a few of the presidents on barstools engaged in what appeared to be a fairly serious conversation.

I approached Slick and Mary Ann at the end of the bar.

Mary Ann brightened up when she saw me. "Danny Mac! Great to see you tonight."

"What's up here, M.A.?" I asked.

"Some heavy stuff it appears. I'm not trying to eavesdrop, though. Why don't you join them? You might be just what they need. Looks like they could use a little infusion of your joie de vivre. So to speak." Mary Ann always made me feel like a million bucks.

"I think that's a lot more your role in life than mine," I responded, "but you know I'm always up for a challenge."

I made the long walk to the other end of the bar and hopped on an open barstool. Now that I was near them all I could see it was Maggie, Truman, JFK, John Quincy Adams, Carter and Obama. Their barstools faced away from the bar toward a table where FDR sat in a wheelchair next to Washington, Teddy Roosevelt, Eisenhower, Harding and Reagan.

"Good to see you, Danny," Maggie said. "We are talking a little bit about where and how a president can possibly get away from it all. I'm not ashamed to tell y'all that at times I'm really struggling. And I mean mentally—emotionally. I'm certain many of you can sympathize. It's not the just the job. I have a few things in my personal life I'm working through as well, and while I may be no mental health expert, I'm just not sure the White House fish bowl is the best place to get my head right when I'm running all over hell's half acre trying to run this country."

She smiled. "My mom used that expression all the time. Maybe it's a southern thing. I think I repeat expressions like that from time to time just to keep her memory close to me."

A brief bit of silence followed as we all took a moment to appreciate what we were seeing, and respect the fact that this charming, accomplished woman who had ascended to the highest office in the land was laying it all out to bare in front of these gentlemen with no compunction about displaying her vulnerability. And oh my god that accent—I could listen to that all day—not to mention those endearing expressions.

John Quincy Adams broke the pause. "I found that a swim in the Potomac first thing each morning invigorated me and cleared my head."

"I agree with that," added Truman. "I began each day with a shot of Bourbon followed by a brisk walk around Washington or just the White House compound to reset my mind each day."

"I get that, fellas. I'm not really talking about that—although I kind of like the Bourbon idea." The group smiled and laughed. I could tell she already had us all pulling for her.

"But I have my Peloton for that daily exercise," she added. "and that helps. However, the kind of help I am talking about is much bigger than that."

"Churchill and I spoke of this," said Eisenhower, "and he warned me that I had to find some mechanism to escape mentally. Like him, I found that in painting. I was a deliberate dauber. My works of art were woefully bad, but it gave me an excuse to be completely alone, and interfered not at all with my contemplative powers."

"Thank you, President Eisenhower," replied Maggie. "But while I am a woman of many talents," she paused and looked around, eliciting precisely the response from these old guys she was aiming for, "painting certainly is not among them."

"I took to boxing," declared Teddy. "What a glorious sport. Just you and your opponent. Nowhere to hide. The ultimate test of skill, strategy, stamina and mental toughness."

"Hold on there, Teddy,' replied Harding. "Didn't you literally lose an eye boxing in the White House?"

"Indeed I did, sir. I didn't say there aren't risks, but the sport's rewards are truly exhilarating."

"Surely you aren't suggesting I take up boxing?" asked President Bates.

"Perhaps not. Although I think it would provide the release which you seek, and I suspect you'd be quite a formidable opponent."

Maggie beamed. She had many of the most challenging characters in this Saloon eating out of the palm of her hand.

"Rather, I would suggest in your case that you take time to explore nature, my dear," he added. "There is a delight in the hardy life of the open. There are no words that can tell the hidden spirit of the wilderness that can reveal its mystery, its melancholy and its charm. I took a glorious couple of weeks on horseback through Yellowstone, a park which had a rejuvenating effect on me. I excluded all press and everyone else, including the Secret Service. At times I was alone with just the great outdoors and my own thoughts. Splendid time indeed. And we traveled there and back by rail on the Roosevelt Special—the rolling White House. I wholeheartedly recommend it for you, Maggie."

"Oh how I would delight in ditching the press corps for two weeks," replied Maggie.

Kennedy laughed. He seemed to get as much of a kick out of Teddy as I did. "Maggie," he said, "We had at our doorstep in Hyannis the New England equivalent of Yellowstone—the sea. I would always go there to be revived, to know again the power of the ocean and the master who rules over it and all of us. Sailing, whether alone or with mates, I found to be a singular source of inspiration."

FDR applauded. "Yes, indeed, Jack, my boy. I too fancied myself a bit of an ancient mariner. Of course, I relished spending time away from Washington at Warm Springs down in your neck of the woods, Maggie. But I also loved to sail along Jack's New England coast to our summer retreat on Campobello Island in New Brunswick. Sailing is always so good for the soul. And I found sailing to be quite like politics—the fun of the sport was that if you're headed for somewhere and the wind changes, you just change your mind and go somewhere else."

That drew great laughter among the group.

Maggie's solemn expression brightened. "Yes," she declared emphatically. She looked over at FDR and then back at Kennedy next to her. "That might just do the trick." Then, eyeing the rest of us, "I spent so much of my youth sailing all around Savannah. What a devine way to spend a day. We'd sail to the Isle of Hope. Why you haven't lived until you've seen the azaleas in full bloom in the spring from the water, gloriously ornamenting the breathtaking mansions along the high bluffs."

Kennedy and FDR both beamed at the revelation that we had another sailor in the room. Not to mention one that seemed capable of matching their charm. These two first ballot Hall of Fame Democrats were clearly thrilled to have stumbled upon some common ground with this new Republican president.

Maggie then looked over at Teddy. "I can't think of a better place to enjoy one of your beloved mint juleps than on a spectacular veranda atop a hill on the Isle of Hope at a proper Southern cocktail party."

Teddy smiled. "Why I don't doubt that for a second my dear."

"There's a reason they call Savannah the Hostess City of the South."

I cast a quick glance in the direction of our resident Georgian, Jimmy Carter. He flashed me a quick thumbs up accompanied by a big smile.

Kennedy jumped into the conversation again. I think he was quite taken with our new president. "I spent many a winter day in Palm Beach."

"Oh bless your heart. But Honey, that's not the South."

JFK smiled amidst the laughter in the rest of the room. Nice to see he could take that in stride.

The room fell to a hush as Washington rose to address the group. Sometimes there was a noble formality about him that I really enjoyed watching.

"I traveled by carriage throughout the South in 1791," he began. I saw that even the wait staff around us had stopped in their tracks with their ears peeled to listen to what the Father of Our Country had to say.

"We traversed 1,900 miles over three and a half months. The road conditions were quite difficult and crossing the waterways was treacherous at times. But what a journey. I relished the time with the countrymen we encountered. I found very pleasing the manners of the people.

"We enjoyed a very memorable week in Charleston full of balls, teas, attending church services and other gatherings. A group of the most respectable southern ladies requested a proper visit. That was the first honor of its kind I had ever experienced and it was as flattering as it was singular. I must say, I should think that particular gathering would be quite pleased with our new president here."

All eyes turned to Maggie, who brought both hands up to cover her mouth. She was speechless. I had some experience being on the receiving end of a compliment from President Washington—or Big Daddy, as Otter and Matty call him. There is really nothing quite like it. I can vividly recount word for word every conversation I ever had with him in the saloon, and the night he took my side in an open debate among the presidents. I don't believe I ever felt more worthy of being an American than in that moment.

This was a whole new vantage point for me on the value of this saloon. Maggie and the presidents carried on for another hour of storytelling and reminiscing about sailing and everything else that was joyful about their lives. I had wondered if this saloon and these good old boys were capable of having the same impact on a woman that they clearly had on me in my presidency. To my great surprise and to their great credit, Maggie seemed to be finding some of that which she desperately needed from this place, just as I had. Of course, her approach to them had everything to do with it. But I was thrilled. For her, for the country, and for me.

Chapter Twenty-Six

ESPN College Gameday
October 23, 2021

From the campus of The University of Notre Dame, in front of the Hesburgh Library in advance of the USC v. Notre Dame football game.

ESPN COLLEGE GAMEDAY
ESPN Saturday October 23, 2021

RECE DAVIS: Welcome back to ESPN's College Gameday. We are broadcasting live outside of iconic Notre Dame Stadium— "The House that Rockne Built." This site is to college football fans what The Sistine Chapel is to Catholics.

LEE CORSO: Not so fast. This place might just be even more hallowed, Rece.

DAVIS: It certainly is to the legion of Irish faithful behind us.

(*camera pans the huge crowd forming a sea of green behind the stage going crazy*)

DAVIS: It's time for us to bring in this week's Celebrity Guest Picker. We've got someone who needs no introduction certainly to this partisan crowd here, or anyone else for that matter. College Gameday proudly welcomes former president Danny McFadden. One of Notre Dame's own.

(Applause as the camera pans the crowd of roughly 5,000 students and fans gathered behind the stage. The camera zooms in on a student wearing a Notre Dame jersey with "McFadden" on the back displaying the numbers: 45 and 47.)

DAVIS: That reaction has to make you feel pretty good, Mr. President.

DANNY MCFADDEN: No question about that Rece. And it's fair to say I might not get quite that reception in a lot of other parts of the country.

KIRK HERBSTREIT: This is your base, right here.

MCFADDEN: Ha! Yes indeed. I had a feeling it would be a sympathetic crowd. Thanks so much for allowing me the privilege of being with you. I love what you guys do, and the enthusiasm you bring to it all.

DAVIS: Before we get to today's picks, I think Bear has a trivia question designed specifically with you in mind. We waited until you arrived to roll it out.

CHRIS "BEAR" FALLICA: I think many of us know that a handful of US presidents played college varsity or jv football, or at least were members of the squad even if they never saw the field. What two US presidents coached college football?

HERBSTREIT: Oh, Bear, you're killing me.

DESMOND HOWARD: Well, wait a second. It might not be that hard. I'm gonna jump in right away and say my fellow Wolverine, Gerald Ford. I know he was a baller for Michigan back in the day. Maybe he coached too.

BEAR: You are correct, sir.

MCFADDEN: I did not know that.

DAVIS: Did he coach at Michigan?

BEAR: No. He coached at Yale. After graduating from Michigan he turned down offers to play professionally and instead enrolled at Yale Law School where also served as an assistant coach for the football team while he studied law.

HERBSTREIT: Now that's a full plate. Yale Law School and assistant football coach. I wonder what he did in his spare time?

MCFADDEN: I'm pretty sure I know who the other is.

CORSO: How about the Gipper?

HERBSTREIT: That's a great answer. Was it Reagan?

BEAR: A good guess. He was one of several who played college football. He played offensive line at Eureka College. But no, he did not coach.

MCFADDEN: I think it was Ike at Army.

BEAR: Yes—Eisenhower. His injuries kept him from being a football star at Army, but he played until his career was cut short. He coached some at Army and later became Head Coach at St. Louis College in San Antonio, which is now St. Mary's College. By all accounts he was viewed as a very successful coach.

MCFADDEN: He was obviously an inordinately distinguished leader of men.

CORSO: Ya think?

***

(Later in the show, and following a commercial break)

DAVIS: Welcome back. Now it's time to pick this marquee game here today.

(Crowd going crazy behind the stage)

DAVIS: As the great Keith Jackson used to say, "nothin' gets the blood a boilin' like the Irish and the Trojans."

HERBSTREIT: Get a load of some of these signs.

(*Camera pans the crowd signs, showing one that reads "McFadden/Corso 2024"*)

MCFADDEN: We might actually fare better with Lee at the top of the ticket.

(*Camera finds a "Corso/McFadden" 2024 sign, Desmond Howard bursts into laughter*)

CORSO: That's more like it, sweetheart!

(*Crowd starts chanting "four more years"*)

HERBSTREIT: Now there's an idea, Mr. President. Sounds like your approval ratings are as high as ever. And I know you've got some eligibility left. You got another run in you?

MCFADDEN: (*Laughing*) That's very flattering. Although this crowd is not exactly a scientific sample. It's nice to be away from the constant day to day fight, living in that fishbowl, and all the scrutiny that comes with it.

DAVIS: We had Head Coach Brian Kelly on here with us an hour ago. I think he's living the life you are describing.

(*Desmond Howard laughing out loud again.*)

MCFADDEN: Yes, he certainly knows a little something about living that life. In fact, he may have it even worse. I'm just fine in my new role as ex-President, thank you. I've got my sons here for this game and a ton of other family. And we're all going to the Bears/Packers game tomorrow night at Lambeau Field as well.

CORSO: What a weekend!

MCFADDEN: You're telling me! The best. This is the kind of stuff it was really hard to do in my prior role. I'm savoring every moment of it. Wouldn't trade it for the world.

***

The more words like that kept coming out of my mouth, the more I started to really believe them...

Chapter Twenty-Seven

This Is Gonna Blow Your Mind
November 10, 2021

I blew into the office at about 10:15. I saw the bank of televisions which were tuned to news channels across the political spectrum. That was symbolic more than anything—we weren't going to be sitting here each day watching cable news. But it made the right statement about getting news from a diversity of sources.

Tina saw me and belted out a huge, welcoming "Danny Mac!" that would have made Matty and Mary Ann proud. I flashed back immediately to the saloon. God I missed that place. I allowed myself a moment of sadness for the memory of that spectacular establishment and all its patrons. And the staff. Especially the staff.

I stuck my head in her office and glanced around at the barren office walls. "I admire what you've done with the place."

She laughed.

"Do you have any diplomas you can put up in here, Tina?" I asked. "By the way, just when did you graduate, anyway? Someday, somebody's gonna ask those questions. And where exactly did you graduate from?"

"One of the very best schools, of course."

"Oh I'm certain it was. But which one would that be? An Ivy League school? Patriot League? Big Ten?"

"One of the finest. Everybody says so."

"Oh I have no doubt about that. You might have to work on that backstory of yours."

"Speaking of great schools, Boss, how did it go at Berkeley?"

"Oh, well . . ." I hesitated for a second. "It went great."

"What happened?"

"Nothing. It went well. It was great. I was flattered to be asked and enjoyed having the chance to address them."

"Something went wrong. I can tell."

"Nope. I was happy with it, and flattered to be asked to do it. It was great."

"I'll find out."

I turned to walk out of her office.

"You can't snow me, Danny Mac. You didn't hire me just to punch a clock. I can't have your back if you're not letting me all the way in."

***

An hour later I heard her screaming for me. She was in the front lobby looking up at the bank of televisions.

I came running out from my office. Our Next Gen Dream Team kids were alongside her. I heard some howling.

As I settled in alongside them, Tina said, "This is gonna blow your mind."

Each camera showed a version of the same shot. Four sitting congressmen were conducting a joint press conference. The chyron at the bottom of the screen said "Four House Members Announce Joint Decision to Join Alliance Party."

"Take a bow, Mr. President," Tina shouted, as she high fived each of the our Next Gen Wonder Kids.

The other six House members who were already registered in what they are calling the Alliance Party were also present for the press conference. Together they now numbered 10.

My phone started blowing up.

Representative Tessa Fisher of Connecticut was speaking on behalf of the others. "We'll be caucusing together as a group now, and we encourage any Democrats or Republicans interested in pursuing bipartisan solutions and putting country over party to join us, whether or not they formally shed their party affiliation. We'll take all comers. We'll answer not to any party leaders but to the American people, with particular attention to the 42% of Americans that do not identify themselves as either Republican of Democrat, and heretofore have had no representation in this body. Those days are over. Democrats, with just 31% of the country, and Republicans, with just 27%, should not and cannot maintain their stranglehold on the levers of power in our democracy. That dynamic is one of several factors contributing to our debilitating political divide in this country."

The group stood there for 45 minutes taking questions. It was exhilarating to watch. Had we created a monster? I certainly hope so.

Tina beside me was already working the phone.

Fox News' Mike Emanuel asked the Congressmen what I thought to be the most obvious and pertinent question.

"What are your next steps?"

"This has all been so fast-moving," responded Walker Guthrie, the freshman Congressman from Highland Park, Colorado, "but it looks like this weekend we'll get together for a bit of a retreat with a whiteboard or two and map this out. It's fair to say the sky's the limit. And I do want to add, without mentioning any names, that others in both the House and Senate are contemplating joining our cause."

CNN's Sunlen Serfaty posed the next question. "Where will you be conducting your retreat, and will the press be invited to any portion of it?"

"Thank you for asking that, Sunlen. I should have mentioned the venue—we won't be doing this in Palm Beach or Half Moon Bay. For this important gathering, we felt it was most appropriate to go right to where it all started—Independence Hall."

"Oh my," I yelled at the televisions. "I love this so much!"

I could see the Dream Team got a charge out of seeing Tina and I so fired up about something like this.

Tina yelled over at me. "Hey Boss, I've got Murph on the phone." Christina Murphy had been my Chief Congressional Liaison during my administration. "This group has been working with her a bit on this. She's begging you to come to Philly this weekend. They didn't want to approach you until all of them were on board and this was a done deal."

I smiled but didn't say anything. I had glanced at my phone a few minutes earlier and quickly saw there was a text from Kelly, in addition to many from Murph. I breezed over Murph's and opened Kelly's.

"*Dad, can Michael and I meet you and Mom for dinner Sat night? Mom said it's fine but asked me to check with you. I thought maybe we could go to Shadowbrook in Capitola maybe. I know you love that place. LMK.*"

Tina was on to me. She walked over so she and I could talk out of earshot of the others.

"I really think this could be huge for your cause, Boss. These are more than little sparks, this has the makings of a full-on bonfire."

"It does," I responded. "I agree. I just don't know about me joining them. At least not yet."

"Don't fail us now, Danny Mac. This could be something big. Really big. I don't have to tell you how the abysmal state of our politics and public discourse is crushing this country. You set in motion a solution. This cause is rolling because of you. And you remain their hero."

"Why don't you and Murph go?" I said. "And maybe take one of the Wonderkids here. I might be taking a step back a bit. I had my time. But my office can still be all in. I know that's not the answer you want to hear but it's the best I can do."

"Alright," she said. "I'm not going to hide my disappointment but of course I will go. But I want you to know Danny Mac. . ."

I was looking at my phone.

"Look at me, Danny," she said. "I want you to know that as far as the state of things in this country goes, there are not many paths out of this abyss. But one of those—maybe the only one—is controlled by you and you alone. You got on a pretty high horse about all this stuff over the last four years, so don't tell me this cause doesn't mean the same to you now that it did then. I don't accept that. Not for one minute. And I'm not asking for me, I'm asking for this country. For the left, the right and the middle."

"It's great to have you working with me, Tina," I responded. I meant that. Oh, how I meant that. "Having you on my team is everything I thought it would be. Don't ever change."

I could sense her bitter disappointment. It's as if she couldn't even hear the compliment in that sentence.

"You guys go," I said. "Take the staff. Take all three of the Dream Team. Call me as often as you want. I am supportive. Just do me a favor and don't make promises about my own involvement."

I walked back to my office and texted Kelly.

We'd love to meet you guys for dinner Saturday night. I can't wait to meet Michael.

Chapter Twenty-Eight

An Intervention. At Hannegan's
November 21, 2021

I walked into Hannegan's right at 3:00 just as Tina had asked me to. For some reason she wanted to meet with me there—a request I was all too happy to comply with. She and the entire staff were excited because they had all been so well received at the Alliance summit in Philadelphia last weekend, and they were quite energized by that. As disappointed as they all were that I didn't accompany them, their meetings went well and the cause appears to be gaining some serious momentum nationally.

I had no regrets about missing the summit. As much as I believed in the cause, I was slowly coming to the conclusion I should be focusing more on family than anything more formal with that movement, believing I could still be a factor from a distance without being quite so hands on. I don't think it hurts to have a new generation of leadership assume the mantle of that cause. The other reason I had passed, of course, was to finally meet this Michael character, but that had fallen through when they canceled at the last moment. They offered an excuse, but once I had heard they were canceling I'm not sure I really focused much beyond that. In fact I know I didn't. Pretty sure he'll have to go through me eventually if he wants to continue on with Kelly. Maybe not. What do I know?

My bartender buddy, Gil, approached me when he saw me enter the bar.

"Good afternoon, Danny. They're all in the Presidential Room waiting for you." He was pointing to the side room they had put me in when I was here with Kelly and her Santa Clara friends.

"Who's they?" I asked. "I'm just meeting Tina, right?" I suddenly got a little nervous.

"Tina is in there, sir."

I swung around the dining room corner to enter the "The Presidential Room." It was packed. The first person I recognized was Representative

David Gonzales. Then I saw the Congressmen and women from the press conference last week—the ones who had re-registered their party affiliation to name the Alliance. Then I noticed Hannah. And Martin.

Tina approached me with two Irish Bucks in her hands— one for me and one for her. Just like old times.

The room was all abuzz. It didn't take a genius to figure out what this was all about. It wasn't my birthday. This had everything to do with the Alliance.

"This is unbelievable, Tina," I said softly as I scanned the room. Everywhere I looked there were political people who had embraced the Alliance along the way.

Tina's smile was every bit as big as the ones that must have been on the faces Crazy Horse and Sitting Bull as Custer's 7th Cavalry rode into the Little Big Horn Valley one sunny afternoon in June, 1876. She had me surrounded.

I leaned over and whispered in her ear, "You bitch." She laughed out loud. I couldn't say it without smiling myself, since I knew full well if I tried to resist this crowd I'd meet a fate that equaled Custer's that day.

"Just think of this as an intervention," she said. It was so clear she was quite proud of herself. I was toast.

"An intervention?" I responded. "In a bar." I paused to let that sink in. "At Hannegan's of all places. You don't think that's even mildly ironic?"

"I have to play the hand you dealt me," she replied. "And this is just the best way I knew of to play my hand."

"I think you just played a royal flush."

"I don't know what that is, but it sounds pretty good so I'll take it."

***

An hour later we were right smack in the middle of a blue-sky brainstorming session—fueled by a few cocktails and a whole lot of passion. They were looking for me to go all in and devote genuine time and attention to the new cause. I couldn't very well say no—not in this crowd, and besides, I didn't want to say no. I was fired up to see all this energy and progress. But I didn't exactly express a firm commitment either.

Tina approached me. "Danny Mac," she said softly so no one else could hear, "you know they need to hear directly from you. They are eager to follow your lead here. Don't fail me now, Boss."

"I got you, Tina," I responded. "I'm fired up about this turnout. I obviously didn't prepare anything, but I could give this talk in my sleep."

I downed the last portion of my Irish Buck— not my first of the afternoon—and turned to the room. "Thank you for coming. I am so touched, and excited for where this is going. I love the progress you have made. It's really remarkable and rather unprecedented in modern American political history. We have a core set of common values and principles that guide us, an identifiable brand—one that polls exceedingly well, and we have a viable caucus in the House which can now boast ten Alliance representatives and two dozen more that caucus with us.

"I think for the upcoming midterms, we need to do both of the following: identify candidates that embody our values to run in the coming elections in independent leaning districts for the House formally as Alliance party members; and support moderate Democrats and moderate Republicans in all the many districts where an Alliance candidate would not have any chance of victory.

"But an even bigger goal, and one more important to our ongoing viability, is to run and win a few Senate races. Easier said than done of course, but that is the holy grail. We need to establish a beachhead right in the center of the Senate. What power and influence they would yield—particularly if we can get enough seats to prevent either side from having a majority. Heck, in that case we may even end up with a majority leader."

We spent the rest of the afternoon brainstorming, trading ideas and mapping strategy. The whole experience was exhilarating for everyone involved. The excitement in the room was far more intoxicating than anything Gil and his staff were putting in our drinks. This was the center of the political universe as far as we were concerned. And God it seemed like we were on to something.

Eventually we arrived at an appropriate stopping point. Tina approached me. "Why don't you wrap this up with some eloquent words and then commit to leading them all to the Promised Land."

I laughed. "Tina, I didn't hire you so you could use that brilliant mind of yours to cajole me into doing things I'd rather not do."

"Do not for even a second pretend that you are not as excited as everyone else in this room."

"You're right," I responded. "This is really something special."

"Where is the Dream Team?" I asked.

She laughed. "OK, you're gonna love this.

"What is it?"

"They were worried about how you would react to all of this. Don't get me wrong—they helped plan and coordinate it, and even picked people up at the airport this morning. But they weren't sure how you'd react to it all so they didn't want to be visible for this part."

"God love those three!" I responded. "That makes my day."

"I'm glad for their sakes you're happy, because I was inclined to fire them all over it."

"No, don't you see what great political instincts they demonstrated. They let you take all the risk and meanwhile they maintain the appearance of loyalty to me. They each have such bright futures in politics. They'll go far."

"OK, but isn't that the polar opposite of the political courage we are celebrating here with this? Are you saying loyalty to you should be placed before political courage and doing what they think is right?"

She had a point. She always does.

We were interrupted by the sound of a spoon tapping against a glass. We looked up to see Hannah had taken center stage and was about to address the group. Of course she was.

"To all our elected officials who made the trip here for this, thank you for your courage. Political bravery is the scarcest of all commodities these days—an old-fashioned notion really. In rare instances political bravery begets social transformation. We are on the cusp of just such a phenomenon. We are all foot soldiers in this great crusade, albeit in the case of Martin and me, foot soldiers who just so happen to possess a king's ransom with which to bankroll this whole effort. Please use us to fund whatever it is you may need. And, best of all, it's clear to me we now have our champion to head up our cause."

With that her eyes and all the other pairs in the room turned to me.

I wasn't exactly sure what they felt I was committing to, but I didn't want to rain on their parade. And I was so moved by all of this.

The room was now packed, as almost everyone from the bar and restaurant had filed in as well.

I just started talking— not really sure what I was going to say. That's usually not a good thing.

"The most important thing to remember in all this is that the goal is a great country rather than a great party." They applauded for that.

"I think that's crucial, and perhaps antithetical to what parties have come to be all about. We won't judge ourselves by how many seats we hold but by how much we can move the dial in uniting the country and countering the partisan divide." More applause.

"And please, keep in mind what we agreed upon this afternoon—if we find that congressional districts and states already have great, fair-minded Republican or Democrat incumbents who embody our principles and values and want to reach across the aisle at times, we won't oppose them with an Alliance candidate."

They seemed to be applauding at everything I said now. Maybe I finally located my true political base—the happy hour patrons at Hannegan's.

I thanked them profusely for embracing this cause, told them I would gladly help lead the effort, and parked myself at the door so I could say a proper goodbye to everyone on their way out. Cathy was the first to engage with me. She had a rather quizzical look on her face.

"Please don't take offense by this, Danny, but are you really all in on this? I know you pretty well, and I sort of saw you pulling back a bit on this to let others take the lead. Or did I get that wrong?"

Just then Congresswoman Tessa Fisher appeared in front of us.

"Thank you so much for coming, Congresswoman," I said. "Your involvement means so much to this cause. Please let me know if I can ever help you."

"Oh my gosh, yes, Mr. President. I would welcome your help." Congressmen Guthrie, Parks and Gonzalez joined us.

"Would you be willing to come to my district to campaign for me?" Congressman Fisher asked.

"Of course I would," I said. "Whereabouts in Connecticut are you?"

"Danbury. Maybe come once in August and again in October right before the election. The leaves will be breathtaking. Nothing like you've ever seen out here."

"Of course I'll come. You can count on me." I looked over at Cathy as the words came out of my mouth. She was laughing and shaking her head.

Congressman Parks perked up. 'Would you come to Minnesota, sir? It would make a world of difference."

"Of course," I responded. I turned my back to Cathy. I didn't want to see the look. To be honest, I really didn't need to see it in order to know it was there.

Out of the corner of my eye I caught a glimpse of Tina and Hannah, looking remarkably like Frank and Jessie James dividing up the loot following a well-planned and executed bank heist.

Kelly and her Santa Clara girlfriends emerged from the crowd to say hello. I hadn't even seen them there in the back.

"Thank you so very much for coming, guys," I gushed. "I'm so glad young people are getting behind this cause. How did you guys learn about this gathering?" I didn't think Tina knew them or would have had their contact information. And I'm pretty sure if she had gone through Denyse to contact them Denyse would have certainly told me.

They all burst into smiles and looked at each other but said nothing. After a few seconds, as the silence began to morph into awkwardness, I had a sense perhaps there was a joke here and it may have been on me.

"What's up?" I asked, scanning the group. Kelly wasn't saying a word and looked away to hide her big smile.

I looked at her buddy Juliane. She couldn't ghost me like Kelly had. And she couldn't lie either.

"Well, Mr. McFadden, we . . ." she paused, not knowing how to finish the thought, searching for precisely the right words.

"Ok," she continued, "I'll just tell you the truth. We had no idea this was happening here today."

She kind of squinted as she looked up at me, braced for some reaction she thought that might trigger in me.

I thought for a second and then busted out a big smile all of my own.

"That is priceless!" I said, laughing out loud. "Of course—it's 4:30 on a weekday afternoon. Why wouldn't you all be at Hannegan's anyway?"

Kelly turned back around to look at me as her friends howled with laughter.

"But don't get us wrong," added Shelby. We totally believe in your cause."

"Ha! Which cause what that be? The struggling brewers of America?"

I looked at Kelly.

"Dad, promise me you won't tell Mom."

"Don't worry. I won't tell her, sweetie," I responded. "But I can't promise she won't read about it on the internet."

Kelly gave me a big hug. "Great seeing you, Dad," They all added their goodbyes.

"I certainly hope you guys can survive this semester. I'm just worried sick about your grueling academic workload. you know. I don't know how you all manage." I was trying to maintain a straight face. "Please do me a favor and make sure you take a little time out for yourselves."

"Thanks so much for your concern, Mr McFadden," responded Emma. "But I think we'll be OK." It's possible she thought I was serious.

I continued to watch them as they walked away. The front door and exit to the street was to the left from the room we were in. The short flight of stairs to the bar was to the right. As they left the room they all turned right.

I could only laugh. I don't think that group ever has to buy a drink in here. And that has nothing to do with me, by the way.

I saw Cathy standing nearby, taking all of this in.

"I think the party is just getting started for them," I said.

"No question about that," she responded.

"To be young again . . ."

"Who do you think you are kidding, Danny?" Cathy actually looked mildly annoyed at me. "We both know you're gonna wait until you've said goodbye to every last person in this room and then hightail it up there to join them."

"Holy Cow," I responded. "You've got me there. Busted." This was perhaps one of those moments where I didn't appreciate that my assistant knew me so well. Would it have killed her not to say anything?

"Well you know, Mr. President," she added, "you really have been meaning to spend more time with the family lately. This would seem a wonderful opportunity to spend a little time with Kelly. You really are such a wonderful father."

OK—that was a heck of a recovery by her. And a nice touch, even adding a "Mr. President" for good measure. That's the genius of Cathy. She delivers her zinger with a marksman's precision but in the next breath softens the blow with a blatant appeal to my ego—as feigned as it was appreciated. Nicely played.

I said my goodbyes and did my best to convey to each and every last guest my appreciation for their involvement and attendance.

And then, of course, I exited the room to the right to join Kelly and her friends at the bar . . .

Chapter Twenty-Nine

The Miller's Tale
November 23, 2021
The Saloon

Maggie walked into the saloon just in time to save me from any further embarrassment. Thomas Jefferson had engaged us all in a bit of what he referred to as a "Monticello parlor game" he had created, and many in the room were quite engrossed in it. Me, not so much.

He had divided us all into roughly 15 teams of three, all seated at different tables. It looked like almost all of the presidents and some of the wait staff were participating. The object was for each team to come up with a question, any question, about science, history, music, art, literature, mythology . . . you name it, that half the groups would get right and half would get wrong. His theory was that it's easy to come up with a question no one would get right, and easy to craft one everyone would get right. The real skill, he explained, and the beauty of the game, is in evaluating each of the other teams, analyzing their strengths and weaknesses, and then crafting the perfect question to split the room precisely in half—with seven teams answering correctly and seven incorrectly. The closer you get to splitting the room, the more points you earn. Your team also earns points for each correctly answered question. Leave it to Thomas Jefferson . . .

Oh sure, I would have enjoyed it a lot more if I had done better at it. I didn't contribute much to the cause. I was paired with James Polk and Warren Harding. I'll just say we didn't end up on the podium and leave it at that.

I think I only contributed a couple correct answers the entire afternoon—I knew that Ganymede was Jupiter's largest moon and that Pheidippides was the name of the courier who ran from Marathon to Athens to deliver the news of the victory over the Persians in what is considered the first marathon. But my proudest moment was clearly when I knew that the story from Chaucer's Canterbury Tales that featured ass-kissing and farting prominently was The Miller's Tale. My high school British Lit teacher, Mr. Baldetti, would be so pleased. He loved that tale in particular. That question happened to come from John Quincy Adams's group, and since he and I had discussed Chaucer before I think he had factored in that our group would get that right. Some of these guys really know how to play this game.

It made my day, however, when Mary Ann proudly answered a question about what American author achieved fame writing novels about collies. She proudly answered "Albert Terhune" on behalf of her team. It made her day too.

Some of the top players were Jefferson himself of course, JFK, and Clinton—the former Rhodes Scholar. But the guy who really stole the show was Haskell, our bartender extraordinaire. My god, he crushed it. He was paired with Nixon and Lincoln and they ran away with it. I want to bring that guy into the real world and put him on Jeopardy. He'd instantly become the Jeopardy GOAT.

In fact, Haskell, in his own indomitable and endearing way, took it too far. Just one example of that is when he correctly answered that the famous ship captained by Vicente Yáñez Pinzón was the Nina. Anyone else would have been thrilled just to come up with that. But then he just couldn't help himself— doing what he does best.

"His brother captained the Pinta. The original name for the Nina was The Santa Clara, because, well, as I'm sure you know, all Spanish ships were named for saints. She was also Columbus's personal favorite ship . . ."

The room ultimately just moved on as Haskell kept right on talking.

The question my group asked which came the closest to splitting the room was who is the only US president to have served as Speaker of the House. The answer was sitting at my table—Polk. We figured correctly that a few of those not hailing from his era nonetheless might guess him. Eight of the fourteen got it right. Our other questions were either answered by far too many or too few.

The game broke up when Maggie arrived. This time she looked a bit better, and instantly began working the room with all the skill of a bride at her wedding reception. She had a way of connecting in a very direct way with all of these folks, and it showed. And the greetings she received upon entering the saloon were becoming increasingly rapturous.

When she came upon our table she burst into a smile as she caught sight of me.

"How did y'all do in the parlor game?" The tone of her voice could easily have been interpreted as mocking our little afternoon activity.

"We're so sorry you missed it, ma'am," replied Polk.

"Oh I'll just have to make certain I'll be here for it next time. How could I miss out on this?" Again, her delivery was susceptible to multiple interpretations, but then she shot me a knowing look that gave it all away.

Harding stood up and placed his hand on her shoulder. "It's great to have a Republican in the White House, Madam President."

He looked away moments later and Maggie quickly caught my attention and mouthed to me, "Who was that?"

He looked back right away before I could respond.

"President Harding carried our table today, Mrs. President." I said.

"If that's true, McFadden, then I certainly didn't carry it too far. I would say it was a dismal effort indeed by the three of us."

Minutes later, as it appeared Maggie was about to proceed to the next table, I couldn't help but ask another question.

"Have you heard anything from California lately?"

She seemed puzzled for just a brief second but then responded, "Oh, from Danny and Denyse? No, I'm afraid I haven't. I wouldn't blame him, however. A few in my administration have not been kind to you, or I guess I mean him . . . or perhaps the two of you, in the press. I can't say I'm proud of that. I want to tell you that much. I don't control them all, you know—Mr. Margel in particular. I didn't know what I was being talked into when I asked him to join the ticket."

I believed her sincerity. She looked directly into my eyes and I think she sensed my despair. She struck me as quite sharp, and perceptive that way.

"Would you like me to reach out to them, Danny?"

"No, no, no. Stop. You have enough on your mind. This is not about me. Don't worry about me."

She nodded. "But just say the word and I'll try to reach out to him."

"No need to do that," I responded. "But if you find anything out about how he's doing . . . how Denyse and the kids are doing, don't be shy about passing that along to me."

"Oh, I'd be happy to do that for you. I'll try to plan on making contact with him."

"If you happen to ever need some advice, I would think he'd be willing to help. At least I would hope so, if you sought him out."

"You mean advice different from the advice you'd give me?"

I think she had me there. That was a very good question. And again, I couldn't immediately tell if she was mocking me a little or playing it straight up. I just smiled and laughed.

"Who knows," I added. "Maybe it would be different. If he's trapsing around the South Pacific with Hannah and Martin and the rest of the one per-centers, maybe you're better off not interacting with him at all."

She smiled. "Tell you what, I'll give him a call. I can make up a reason. Besides, I think one of the White House staff just went to work for him."

"Really? Who was that?"

"Oh I can't remember her name. She was helping to run the White House staff office. Brunette. Smart and pretty . . ."

"Tina?"

"Yeah—that's her name I believe."

"Tina's working for McFadden?"

"Yes."

Oh my God.

Chapter Thirty

Jefferson and Madison's 'Literary Cargo'
November 23, 2021
The Saloon

My head was still spinning with the thought of Tina moving to California for a spot in the McFadden post-presidency office. If I haven't mentioned this before, I'm one of those guys with major league FOMO. And it didn't necessarily have anything specifically to do with her—it was just the whole thing—missing all of the goings on out there. Not that I didn't love this—all the perks of the saloon without the headaches of the presidency. But I wasn't any closer to mentally adjusting to it all. At least not yet.

One thing I had learned about my new life in this saloon was that in those moments when I felt a little down, it was always best to just bounce up and engage with one or more of these folks around me—the presidents or the staff. With all the classic characters in this place, typically all the distraction I ever needed was only a barstool away.

In this instance it was a table away. I traded my teammates Polk and Harding in for Madison and Jefferson, who were seated alone now at the table to our right. I pulled up a chair.

"That's quite a parlor game you concocted there, Mr. Jefferson," I said.

"Did you fancy that, McFadden?"

"Oh, absolutely." I may have been fibbing a little. Or a lot.

"You guys split the room well." I added, perhaps pandering just a tad. Why not, it was Thomas frickin Jefferson for God's sake. His response was professorial.

"John Adams' question about the Nina was superbly constructed. Binary questions, 'yes or no' and true or false' are not permitted you know, because they are too easy to divide the room. So a question like his, about a ship captain with a Spanish name who had a brother with a similar name, and both captained boats in the same fleet with similar sounding names, is simply ingenious. Half the room guessed Nina and the other half guessed

Pinta—splitting the room. Brilliant."

"I'm not sure our team could muster up either of those two answers."

He laughed out loud.

"Tell me something," I asked. "I've been meaning to ask this of both of you. I'm having a little trouble adjusting mentally to our predicament here. As much as I do love this remarkable place and the camaraderie."

I paused for a second to let that sink in. They were now listening intently.

"I figured I'd raise this with you two. You guys are clearly the two smartest in this room."

"Perhaps, now that Tina is no longer here." responded Jefferson. It didn't appear that he was kidding.

"How have you adjusted mentally to the finality of this?" I asked. "Particularly you two, of all people in here. Each of you in your lifetimes had such a profound influence on the creation of this country and thereby managed to have an enormous impact on human history as well. How do you go from all of that to this? From charting a new course for self-government, freedom and democracy in the world, to playing the "split the room game"—and then try to even begin to come to terms with that?"

They smiled. "Our adjustment was long, long ago," responded Madison.

"First of all," Jefferson added, "this is all still so very new to you. It will take time to completely come to terms with it. More importantly, you are missing your family and your life outside the saloon while all of that is still in full swing. That is no longer the case for us. We had our day, and it was sensational. We were each blessed in ways very few men have ever been fortunate to know. We drank from the cup of life. We have deep appreciation for that. Indeed the world owes us nothing.

"That profound realization, coupled with the passage of time, provides us a perspective and appreciation for this that will be yours too in time."

"And, perhaps most importantly, we relish the new opportunity—this 'predicament,' as you call it— provides us, for through our interaction with each new president we do continue to be afforded momentous impact on the country we love and indeed upon the world itself. And thanks to a truly benevolent arrangement of things, we do all that from our barstools in this grand saloon.

“When one contemplates all that, it is quite easy in the end to, how did you phrase it—‘mentally come to grips with it.’”

Madison jumped in. “We see this not as a loss to be mourned, McFadden, but as a great and glorious gift.”

I knew I had picked the right people for this discussion. These two philosophers could be great wingmen for me in this place—to go along with Otter and Teddy of course. No one’s taking their places. Not any time soon at least.

Mary Ann appeared out of nowhere, like an angel from above, to take our drink order.

“Thanks for including me in your wonderful game, Mr. Jefferson,” she said.

“It was our sublime delight, madam.” She always burst into a smile when Jefferson called her madam. Although many things that come her way over the course of a day produce that same engaging smile.

“I can just close my eyes and picture the scene at Monticello in the afternoon with you entertaining important people from all over the world playing that game.”

“You would have been a welcome addition to any of those gatherings, Mary Ann.”

“You are too kind, sir,” she responded. “Can I assume the Virginia delegation here would like more wine?”

“Impeccable instincts, my dear,” responded Madison.

“What’s your preference?”

“Would you happen to have the white Hermitage of M. Jourdan of Tains?” inquired Jefferson.

“Fellas, we’ve got everything.”

“Two please,” responded Jefferson. “And McFadden?”

“That’s not Andrew Jackson’s Hermitage?” I asked.

“No, no.” responded Jefferson. “Hermitage in Marseille.”

I wasn’t about to take even one sip of any wine made by Andrew Jackson. Fine wine wasn’t really his personal ‘brand. Now if it were whiskey, on the other hand . . .

“Great,” I responded. “That’s more like it—for wine at least. French wine, of course.” As much as I wanted to order a California Cabernet just to make a statement to these two I went along. That’s the diplomat in me.

"Make it three."

"It is the finest wine in the world without a single exception," declared the Author of the Declaration of Independence. Who was I to argue? Although I'm certain this wine would be wasted on me.

"Was she right about you playing that game at Monticello?" I asked Jefferson.

"Indeed. We enjoyed it quite often at Monticello. Each man playing by himself rather than in teams. Ben Franklin was the best I've ever seen play it."

"I'm sure he was a kick to be around."

Just the thought of Franklin brought a smile to his face. "He was my beloved and memorable friend. He worked closely with me as I drafted the Declaration of Independence. And I followed him as our Minister to France. He had made quite an impression on the French. And yes—it was altogether pleasing to be in his presence. The men loved him almost as much as the ladies did. And he made one and all laugh. I was honored to give a eulogy for him."

"A brilliant fellow," added Madison. "Every conversation with him was like a brilliant feast to me. I never passed half an hour in his company without hearing some observation or anecdote worth remembering."

Then, Jefferson added, "Upon arriving in Paris, a Frenchman said to me, 'So it is you, sir, who is here to replace Dr. Franklin.' To which I responded, 'No one can replace him, sir; I am only his successor."

Madison shook his head. "Yes, but Mr. Jefferson neglects to add that he made quite an impression of his own in Paris."

"I should say so," I added. "They erected a statue of you there."

"In Paris?" asked Jefferson.

"Yes."

"Splendid. Where did they place it? In the Tuileries Gardens?"

"No. Nearby though. Over on the river bank on the other side of the Seine. It depicts you looking towards the Hotel de Salm."

Jefferson was speechless. A smile grew across his face as he imagined it.

"How marvelous. I walked on that route every day as I consumed that glorious city. A walk about Paris will provide lessons in history, beauty and in the point of life. Man has not yet created a work of art or a piece of music that can match a magnificent city like Paris."

"I feel that way about great saloons," I responded. They both laughed out loud.

"Do you know Paris well, McFadden?" Jefferson asked.

"Yes, thanks to my wife, Denyse. She feels about it the same way you do. Each new generation of Americans still fall in love with the romance of it all. Maybe you and your buddy Franklin have something to do with that. I suspect that's at least partially true."

"The dome I had erected at Monticello is a replica of the one at the Hotel de Salm," added Jefferson.

"Pretty sure your Paris sculptor knew that," I responded. "The statue of you is not only looking at the hotel, you're holding a quill in one hand and a sketch of Monticello in the other."

He smiled. "It is a charming thing indeed."

"What else did you bring with you back from France." I asked.

"What didn't he bring back?" responded Madison. "Mr. Jefferson sent me books and treatises— numbering more than 200 in all—on the ancient and modern federal republics, on the law of Nations, and the history both natural and political of the New World. Written by great philosophers and thinkers and by consequential Greek and Roman authors, all of which we fondly called our 'literary cargo'."

"Yes, I sent him all such papers I had the favor of securing," added Jefferson. "However, my role was easy. Mr. Madison studied and mastered them all, and then authored his own paper, 'Notes on Ancient and Modern Confederacies.' His studies led him to produce the Virginia Plan for the Constitutional Convention, where he assumed his seat in the front and center of the room, as the foremost authority on all such matters. And his Virginia Plan, I'm proud to declare, formed the basis for the new Constitution. He also authored many of what we now call the Federalist Papers to secure its passage."

"Wow," I responded. "I think I knew a lot of that but it's fairly awe-inspiring when you put it all together end to end like that."

"When weighing the relative contributions of the men in this room toward the success of this grand experiment in self-government, McFadden," added Jefferson, "do not underestimate the contributions of this gentleman next you, for his diminutive stature certainly belies his mammoth legacy."

Madison looked at me and smiled but shook his head. "When evaluating the merits of those assertions, kindly bear in mind that Mr. Jefferson is my fondest acquaintance, and that he has a tendency toward embellishment after a few glasses of the grape. In truth, to me he was always the professor and I his student."

"He is correct on only one account," responded Jefferson. "Our enduring friendship. When I became president I asked James to be my Secretary of State. The Madisons came to Washington and promptly moved right in to the Executive Mansion with me. It was only a few weeks later when Dolley gave James an ultimatum that he began to seek another lodging arrangement nearby."

They both roared with laughter. So did I.

I was mesmerized. I'm like this, but I found this conversation so enthralling that for a brief period I had completely forgotten the sinking feeling I had earlier. And that is precisely what I was looking for in seeking out these two legends of American history in the first place.

I'd say my "mental adjustment" was well underway.

Chapter Thirty-One

A Coral Island of Bipartisanship Emerging Amidst a Sea of Polarization
February 12, 2022

Permitting my staff to attend the Alliance summit in Philadelphia, and then allowing Hannah to meet Tina, had combined to create a force of nature that simply was not about to be denied. The de facto national headquarters for the Alliance was now a suite of offices around the corner from Hannegan's—my offices, that is.

Our workplace had come to resemble a national campaign war room. In addition to the televisions that didn't seem to have any off button, the walls were decorated with congressional maps in every district where an Alliance candidate was in play in the midterms, together with candidate posters, polling data, and event calendars. On days I would come in to the office I was just as likely to be greeted by one of Hannah's staffers as my own. It had absolutely taken on a life of its own.

I would have attempted to slow it all down if I wasn't so inspired by it. And there's no conceivable way I really could have brought a halt to it even if I had wanted to. But it seemed to be ever so slowly making a difference. Some days not so slowly.

NEW YORK TIMES

SIGNS OF AN INDEPENDENCE AND BIPARTISANSHIP EMERGING IN THE HOUSE

(Washington DC, February 12, 2022) By Cedric Urias
Signs of independence and bipartisanship appear to be emerging in Congress like a coral island amidst a sea of polarization. The ten members of the House of Representatives who now formally claim to be members

of the Alliance party, together with the Alliance Caucus, are emerging as power players, whose votes are often necessary for either Republicans or Democrats to get a bill passed in the House. Additionally, as we've seen recently, bills proposed by Alliance members can often draw support from both sides in sufficient numbers to pass. An example of this is the recent federal minimum wage bill. When the Democrats' bill to increase the minimum wage by more than double, from $7.25 to $15, failed, several Alliance members proposed a hike to $11, which passed with enough support from both Republicans Democrats, even though a large number of more conservative Republicans voted against it, as did many progressive Democrats who felt it wasn't high enough.

Sources within the Bates administration have stated that the White House is divided over whether to embrace the Alliance as a political strategy to promote a portion of their agenda, particularly in cases where bills otherwise would be dead on arrival, or to declare war on the Alliance. Those sources indicate that the main proponent of the latter view is Vice President Margel, who has hardly hidden his disdain for former President Danny McFadden and the Alliance movement which grew out of the last year of his presidency.

To be sure, the House of Representatives remains tremendously divided, but this independent caucus has some power and is unafraid of wielding it, and that is a new and different political development worth watching in the coming months and years.

***

Articles like this one added some legitimate credibility to the Alliance effort. It was now being seen not only as real but as a force to be reckoned with. Now if we could just achieve in the Senate what we had started to establish in the House ...

Chapter Thirty-Two

General Lee, We Are All Americans
April 8, 2022
The Saloon

I took my Virginia colleagues' advice to heart. Missing my family terribly, I decided to geek out on the saloon. Each night presented a brand new opportunity to explore a different facet of American history, and do so in a way Ron Chernow, Ken Burns and Doris Kearns-Goodwin would die for—with first-hand accounts from direct sources.

This new endeavor of mine was aided by the fact that I was no longer the bride at this nightly party. We had a new bride, and she was ravishing—and nicely took the focus away from me as I scoured the room seeking a new chance to revisit an epic chapter in American lore.

Tonight I spotted just such a promising chance and decided to seize the moment. With a versatile cover band taking us through the history of Motown, I noticed Grant and some of the other presidents who had been generals sitting off by themselves at the table in the far corner. I made my way over to them.

Ike saw me coming and motioned for me to join them.

"Can a civilian join this illustrious group?" I asked.

"Pull up a chair, McFadden," Eisenhower replied, "and learn a little something about how these gentlemen preserved our republic through the years."

"And expanded it," added Jackson, to some laughter.

Speaking of expansion, the group was discussing the Mexican American War, with Zachary Taylor doing most of the talking.

Ulysses Grant chimed in, "I was bitterly opposed to the occupation of Texas, and to this day regard the war which resulted, as one of the most unjust ever waged by a stronger against a weaker nation."

Taylor nodded, in seeming agreement. He was one of the smallest men in the room—though not nearly as tiny as Madison. However, he spoke in a manner that commanded attention.

"President Polk had directed us to occupy territory in Texas specifically in order to provoke a fight. That we did. I took our 'Army of Occupation' right to Corpus Christi. Mexico did indeed fire first of course, and war naturally ensued. We won decisive victories at Monterey and Buena Vista."

President Taylor paused and looked around the room. He then whispered to Grant next to him, "where is President Polk?"

"I don't see him in the room," responded Grant.

Taylor proceeded. "I then became ensnared in a political tussle, and found myself relieved of my command over the war. General Winfield Scott was placed in charge."

President Taylor looked over at me. "Politically I was much like you, McFadden. I shunned the deal making and promises of most of the political people, and openly declared I would not be the mere president of a party, but would act independent of party denomination, and would administer the government untrammeled by party schemes."

"You're speaking my language, General," I happily replied.

"You know how much I admired you, General Taylor," said Grant. "I learned a great deal from both you and General Scott. The difference being I thoroughly enjoyed serving alongside you." Grant's words drew a bit of a delayed laugh from the others as they processed precisely what he was saying.

President Hayes laughed hardest. "So, I take it by that you preferred the company of "Old Rough and Ready" to that of "Old Fuss and Feathers."

"Your words, General Hayes, not mine," replied Grant, but with a smile.

Then Grant, placing his hand on the shoulder of Taylor, his former commanding officer, continued. "Let me add clarity to this lest there be any mistaking it. The general here was known to every last soldier in his army, and was respected by all. He possessed an air of humility that belied his station and accomplishments. There was no man living whom I admired and respected more highly than Zachary Taylor."

"Would it be fair to say that Robert E. Lee more closely identified with Winfield Scott, and you with General Taylor?" Eisenhower asked.

"I suppose so. Yes," replied Grant. "Lee was very formal in both his manner and attire, like Scott. General Taylor was not," Grant added, laughing, "and I was not. It was said we dressed more like farmers than generals."

The generals around the table got a kick out of that.

"General Scott had offered Lee the command of the Union army, even though Lee at the time was merely a colonel. Scott considered Lee to be the finest soldier in the entire U.S. Army. As Lee's mentor, he was devastated when Lee resigned his post to assume command of the Army of Northern Virginia."

Then General Washington, who had been quietly taking it all in, broke his silence. "I'm afraid many of my fellow Virginians through the years have tended to place the Commonwealth above the country."

The others at the table appeared to be enjoying this discussion as much as I was.

"What did you think of Lee?" I asked Grant. Why not, I figured. That question was borne of my new resolve to take full advantage of every night in this establishment.

Grant thought for a second. I looked around the table and all eyes fixated on him in breathless anticipation of his response.

"To be honest, I could never see in his achievements what justifies his reputation."

Wow, I thought to myself. That was a heck of a way to begin his summation of his arch rival, who I know is still revered as a general in so many circles. I looked over at Ike, who had kept a photo of Lee up in the Oval Office while president, alongside a portrait of Washington and a bust of Lincoln. Eisenhower seemed captivated now watching Grant talk of Lee.

Grant continued. "To be honest, I never ranked Lee as highly as some others of the army—that is to say, I never had as much anxiety when he was in front as when Joe Johnston was in my front. Lee was a good man, who had everything in his favor. He was a man who needed sunshine. He was supported by the unanimous voice of the South. He was also supported by a large voice in the North. He had the support and sympathy of the outside world. All this of immense advantage to a general. Lee had this in a remarkable degree. Everything he did was right. Our generals had a hostile press, lukewarm friends, and a public opinion outside. The cry was in the air that the North only won by brute force, that the generalship and valor were in the South. This has gone into history with so many illusions that are historical. Lee was of a slow, conservative, cautious nature, without imagination or humor, always the same, with grave dignity. But the illusion that nothing but heavy odds beat him will not stand the ultimate light of history. I know it is not true."

How telling. If I had thought about it, perhaps it's not so surprising that Grant would utter these words about Lee. I'm sure he grew tired of the mythology surrounding Lee, and the narrative that the South was a decided underdog fighting insurmountable odds.

Grant wasn't finished. Hardly. "The southern generals were seen as models of chivalry and valor— our generals were venal, incompetent, coarse. Everything our opponents did was perfect. Lee was a demigod. Jackson was a demigod, while our generals were brutal butchers."

Andrew Jackson left the table for the bar. But others in the room began to join us and listen in.

"Contrary to the popular belief, the South had the position of advantage," added Grant. "The South was unified from the outset. In the North we had cracks, divisions—enemies in our midst. We had to send troops to suppress riots in New York. In every Northern State there was a strong party against the war, always rejoicing over disaster, always voting to paralyze our forces, ready for any concession or surrender. The South often fought on its own familiar soil, and it's white population could leave the farms to be tended to by their slaves to maintain the economy while they fought in the war."

I was riveted. I didn't want to say a word and interrupt his roll. Most of the other presidents were now surrounding our table. The staff too.

I saw Maggie had joined some of the others standing behind my chair. Almost instinctively I hopped up and motioned for her to take my seat. I was gambling that she isn't the type to view it as a slight when a man makes such an offer.

Flashing that smile that won over the country she responded, "Well how about this! Wherever have you been all my life, Danny?"

Jackpot. Occasionally following my gut pays off. Sometimes I'm just better when I don't take the time to think.

"Attaboy, Rook!" pronounced Otter from the back of the pack. "Nicely played."

"I see what you're trying to do here to the rest of us, McFadden." barked LBJ.

"I daresay we could all take a lesson from McFadden," added JFK.

Unfortunately, the whole exchange with Maggie had prematurely stopped Gant in his tracks. He sat back, took a generous sip from his whiskey tumbler and a long draw from his cigar. Was he finished? I hoped not.

Eisenhower came to our rescue with another great question. "Tell me about Appomattox."

Wow. Perfect follow-up question.

Grant took another sip and flashed just a hint of a smile.

"I assumed Lee's offer to meet about terms of surrender was genuine," he continued. "When I informed General Sheridan, he immediately responded, 'Damn them. I wish they would have held out an hour longer and I would have whipped the hell out of them.' Sheridan had left Lee no other option. He felt, however, that Lee's overture was a ruse. I believed otherwise.

"I arrived at the Courthouse on the back of my favorite horse, Cincinnati, dismounted, and noticed Lee's horse, Traveller and another in the front yard. Lee and his staff awaited us inside. Far from my headquarters, I could not dress for the occasion. I had an old suit on and dirty boots, without my sword, and without any distinguishing mark of rank, except the shoulder straps of Lieutenant General on my woolen shirt. I was afraid Lee might think I meant to show him studied discourtesy by so coming—at least I thought so. General Lee, by contrast, was magnificently dressed. A gray suit that appeared brand new buttoned to the top. A dress sword at his side with gilded hilt, embroidered buckskin gauntlet, silk sash, and high boots ornamented with red silk and spurs.

"Seeing how he was dressed, I apologized for my appearance. I began by recalling that we had met once before, while we were serving in Mexico, and that he had made an impression on me I would not forget. He acknowledged that he knew we had met, but admitted he could not remember anything about the meeting.

"He was outwardly cordial, but what his true feelings were I do not know. As he was a man of great dignity, with a face difficult to read, it was impossible to say whether he felt inwardly glad that the end had finally come, or felt sad over the result, and was too manly to show it. Whatever his feelings, they were entirely concealed from my observations. But my own feelings, which had been quite jubilant on the receipt of his letter, were sad and depressed. I felt like anything rather than rejoicing at the downfall of a foe who had fought so long and valiantly, and who had suffered so much for a cause, though that cause was, I believe, one of the worst for which people ever fought, and one for which there was the least excuse.

"Lee inquired about the terms I would accept for his surrender. We agreed to the terms, and he asked that I write them out, which I did right there. I did not ask for his sword. I did not utter the words 'unconditional surrender.' His officers and men were to be paroled, and permitted to return to their homes not be disturbed by the United States authority. Arms, ammunition and supplies were to be delivered up as captured property. Officers were permitted to retain sidearms. Rebel soldiers who owned their horses or mules could retain them. The general was relieved to learn that, and told me that was 'more than he expected.'"

Grant paused and looked around, seeing now that the entire saloon had gathered around the table with rapt attention. What a moment. He took another sip from his tumbler.

Obama spoke up. "General Grant, is the story that's told of the Senecan gentleman on your staff accurate, and can you fill us in on that?"

Grant nodded. "It is indeed. I had asked my aid, Ely Parker, to write out the terms of surrender in ink. He was indeed a Senecan Indian, with dark skin, and could have been mistaken for mulatto. Lee's reaction to meeting him made some of my staff believe he at first felt he was a negro. Upon learning he was a member of the Senecan tribe, Lee seemed relieved, and told him he was glad to see there was one 'real American' there. To that, Ely replied, "General Lee, we are all Americans."

"Good for Ely!" shouted Maggie. The room applauded.

Eisenhower then asked, "Did you not also agree to feed his army as well?"

Grant again nodded. "Yes. He requested 25,000 rations and we fully accommodated them."

To that Ike responded, "Rarely, if ever, in human history has a conqueror extended such compassion to a defeated foe."

"Much is made of the human toll of the war," continued Grant. "I should mention that all three groomsmen who stood alongside me as I married my sweet Julia served in the Rebel Army, including my best man, my dear friend General Longstreet, as well as General Cadmus Wilcox."

That floored me. Grant and Longstreet were "dear friends?" Wow. How did I not know that? There was a collective audible gasp in the room, followed by silence for several moments, No one wanted to destroy the moment.

"One last remembrance about that day," added Grant, who though he appreciated the interest and support, may have been uneasy with all the attention. "As he made his exit, Lee seemed almost in a trance in front of the courthouse waiting for Traveller to be bridled, appearing not to even notice the Union soldiers around him. As he rode away slowly to return to his army, I watched from the steps and lifted my hat to him, and others did as well. Lee responded by tipping his own hat in return. The Pennsylvania regimental band was playing Auld Lang Syne as he rode away. That image will stick with me for all eternity."

"As it will us now, too, General Grant," added Ronald Reagan. "Thank you so much for sharing those priceless memories."

After a few moments, the presidents resumed small chatter amongst themselves and the band picked up again. The band that had absolutely crushed their Motown setlist earlier in the evening now segued into *Travelin' Soldier*, and the female lead singer's heart-wrenching vocals sucked me right in—particularly after that discussion. She had me practically on the verge of tears when I saw Maggie arise.

"Another fascinating evening, fellas," she exclaimed. "Thanks for all your hospitality. At many different stages of life I'd be poised to go all night with y'all, but not at this particular one."

She smiled. I don't think any of us doubted her. I looked around. The room seemed to buzz now every time she spoke, as some of these normally sullen faces beamed. Many of them implored her to stay—Cleveland, Harding, and Pierce among them. I didn't have the heart to tell them they didn't stand a chance. Perhaps a trio like Jefferson, Kennedy and FDR would have had more success.

Then she added, "A lady needs her beauty sleep."

She caught my eye briefly as she excused herself, and motioned for me to follow.

As we neared her exit she grinned a bit. "I'm very fond of your bar here, Danny."

"Oh, it's my bar?" I laughed. "Looks to me like you own this place as much as anybody."

"I'm beginning to really enjoy myself here." She looked at the small table with two chairs near her exit. “Hey, do you have a second. Let’s sit down for a minute.”

We both took a seat.

“That was fascinating to hear what Grant had to say there,” she said.

“I think there are some real lessons there for us, and for the country,” I responded.

“I couldn’t agree more.”

Just then Mary Ann appeared.

“You guys good?”

“Oh honey, I’m just about to turn in, but thank you,” said Maggie.

“One of these nights I want to see that party girl version of you that you were referencing back there,” I said.

She laughed. “That Maggie would love it here! We’ll have to make that happen one night. Let’s plan on it.”

“I’d be careful going toe to toe with some of these guys if you are going deep into the night,” I cautioned.

She very slowly turned her head my way with a look of disdain. Then smiled and looked at Mary Ann. “Bless his little heart. This sorority girl from deep in the heart of the SEC will do just fine up against whatever these Yankee boys have to offer.”

I regretted immediately my doubting her. “I’ll make certain I’m here for that,” I responded, with a new found respect for this formidable lady.

Mary Ann was gleeful with that exchange.

“And anything for you, Danny Mac?”

“Sure—how about a whiskey sour?” She gave me a bit of a double take. “It was my mom’s favorite drink,” I added.

“Perfect. What was her name?”

“Kay.”

“OK then, One Kay McFadden special coming up.”

We both then watched Mary Ann scurry back to the bar.

“I think I love her even more than I love this bar,” I gushed.

“The girl certainly has a gift,” Maggie replied.

Her expression turned serious again. “Tell me more about what you are gleaning from Grant’s words tonight.”

“Well,” I said, “you heard what he said about how he felt about the cause the South was fighting for —I think he called it one of the worst for which people have ever fought. However, even considering that, and how brutal that war was, he still was inclined to show compassion in the end, and respect. He did nothing to exact revenge or even express judgement or attitude of any kind. His immediate instincts were to begin to heal the country. I think there are lessons that apply to our political divide today."

"I like how you are approaching this, Danny. That's intriguing. But people today are not inclined to feel any sort of empathy or compassion for the other side. Demonizing their political opponents is much more their stock in trade."

"That's my point. Somehow we've gotta get past that."

"Good luck."

"I know. But I think there's something to it. When I gave my stump speech about partisanship, oftentimes people would say they agree, but that their side is honorable and the other side is despicable—either ignorant socialists or deplorable racists."

"In Grant's case, he clearly knew many of his enemy well," Maggie responded. "He said each of his groomsmen fought for the South."

"Yes—and two were distinguished southern generals. I never knew he and Longstreet were so close. That might have a lot to do with that compassion he demonstrated."

"People today inevitably know and love others on the opposing side too, but that doesn't seem to reduce the venom."

"Well, there's a whole media enterprise on both sides getting rich off of feeding that divide, which makes it all the harder."

"I'm not disagreeing, Danny. I just don't know how we can get people on either side to feel compassion or understanding for those that they have genuine contempt for. They'll resist that."

"And by the way," she added, "I'm no historian, but I don't believe his goal of unity and healing worked out so well in the end after Appomattox."

"Well," I said, "Booth had something to do with that, and a lot of others too, as America failed to fully heal, unite and embrace civil and voting rights for the freed slaves."

"My only point," I added, "is that I think Grant was on to something in his approach."

"OK, Mr. Political Genius. You may well be right about all that, but how would we even begin coerce or incentivize people on both sides to adopt

Grant's approach?"

"Ha," I laughed. "I'm not saying I have all the answers. Or even that I have any answers, but I think I may be asking the right questions."

After a few seconds of thought, I added, "Go ask our friend in Los Gatos." Then, laughing, "Let's put this to that political genius."

That cracked her up. "If he'd even take my call. Not sure he's a fan of mine."

"Really, Maggie, how could he possibly not be?"

***

After Maggie left I returned to the table of generals just in time to catch Ike regaling the group, including Grant and Lincoln, with stories about Gettysburg, where he and Mamie bought a farm and retired after he served his two terms. He talked about walking the battlefield with world leaders, including French Prime Minister Charles de Gaulle and British Field Marshall Bernard "Monty" Montgomery. But the highlight by far was his detailed account of a very memorable tour of the battlefield he hosted from above by helicopter for Winston Churchill, concluding with the stretch Pickett's Division took from the Spangler farm to the location of the Union line on Cemetery Ridge. What an image to conjure up—those two iconic world leaders at that venerable spot. Wow.

I settled in for what I knew would be a long, entertaining night. I wished so much that all of America could have witnessed this priceless evening right alongside me.

I took a sip of my Kay McFadden special. Just another night in my favorite saloon.

Chapter Thirty-Three

Of Mice and Men
July 6, 2022

If I mentioned earlier that I was planning on pulling back a bit from the Alliance effort and focusing a bit more on the family, file that under the best laid plans "of mice and men." Mice and men don't stand a chance when up against forces like Hannah, Tina and Murph.

THE MICHAEL SMERCONISH PROGRAM

Interview Between Former President Danny McFadden and Talk Show Host Michael Smerconish of Sirius XM Radio's POTUS Channel, July 6, 2022

Michael Smerconish: Ladies and Gentlemen, we are privileged today to welcome back to the program President Danny McFadden. Listeners may recall he was a guest of ours back in 2016 as a new California Senator. An awful lot has transpired between then and now—more for him than us of course. Thank you so much Mr. President for making time for us.

President McFadden: It's my pleasure, Michael. Thank you for having me. I have so much admiration for the unique niche your program has carved out within the political media landscape. I love what you stand for. I only wish there were more like you.

Smerconish: Thank you for the kind words, but nobody other than me wants to hear that.

We'll get to the media landscape a little later. But first let me ask you this: we had you as a guest six years ago shortly after your now-famous St. Patrick's Day speech on the Senate floor, where you railed against the present state of the two parties and our polarization. If I'm not mistaken our interview was the first one you did following that speech—and it took place just as people were first beginning to mention that you might be an independent alternative to Hillary Clinton and Donald Trump. I don't want to sound like a blowhard, but is it fair to say our interview may have helped jump start the national movement to get you on the ballots in all fifty states?

McFadden: Ha! I do think that is fair to say. That whole period of my life was rather surreal. But I do believe that speech of course, and all the media attention it generated, beginning with our interview, set in motion this whole unlikely chain of events.

Smerconish: So much about your path to the presidency and your presidency itself have really broken the mold, so no one should be surprised that you are doing so in your post-presidency as well.

McFadden: Yes, well, it's not really how I planned it, to be honest. I think Denyse and I pictured a more leisurely couple of years in California before I dove back into anything in particular.

Smerconish: In the past five weeks by our count you've campaigned alongside at least fifteen different candidates. I wouldn't call that leisurely.

McFadden: Well, again, that's not how we drew it up. But in the end I couldn't bring myself to sit these midterms out. I have a real soft spot for candidates determined to genuinely get us beyond our great political divide. But we had not planned on that much campaigning.

Smerconish: Did you feel an obligation to the Alliance movement you started?

McFadden: Yes—to the Alliance but even more so to the country. Anyone paying attention lately can see little rays of hope amidst all our polarization and dysfunction. I think we have a window of opportunity now to capitalize on that and make further inroads. I felt if I didn't act now we may miss out on our only chance. I can be all in for five weeks and then go back home and relax on the back deck of our place in Los Gatos.

Smerconish: Another way you are breaking the mold is by campaigning for others outside your Alliance party. I think I know why but I'd love to hear you enunciate your thinking to our audience.

McFadden: Our whole purpose in putting together our movement was simply to lessen our polarization and bring our politics in from the extremes. How we go about achieving that may differ by state and by district. In some cases running a centrist candidate from the Alliance may not have a realistic chance of success and may in fact increase the chance that a candidate from one of the two parties with extreme views will be elected. For that reason I'll happily step in and get involved in races where we are not running candidates to support people from either of the two parties who embody our principles of civility, bipartisanship and country-over-party, particularly when they are up against a candidate who is part of the problem and only seeks to divide us. Consequently, in some races we encourage an Alliance candidate to run and in others we'll support the one that best aligns with our philosophy.

Smerconish: Again, I understand that well but it is still remarkable to see it. I don't recall anything quite like it in my thirty-plus years of following this closely.

McFadden: Well I think this batshit-crazy political dysfunction we're living in screams out for solutions that perhaps no one has ever tried before. Because what we've been trying sure as heck isn't working.

I hope I don't get you in trouble for my use of colorful language there.

Smerconish: Ha! It's satellite radio. You may speak freely. We actually encourage it.

So am I to understand that when the midterms are over you don't plan on being active further with the movement you started?

McFadden: Correct—for the most part. I may always keep a bit of a hand in it, but I think the movement has organization now and momentum and will not only survive but in fact thrive with someone else leading the charge and bringing new and fresh ideas.

Smerconish: With or without you at the helm, where do you think this Alliance movement is headed in the next five to ten years? Do you actually envision a workable three-party system in this country?

McFadden: We are taking this one election at a time, and seeing where that leads us. Our goal isn't necessarily to control Congress and statehouses, but to influence those that are in power and get us back to an atmosphere of mutual respect, civility and working together in this country, including crossing the aisle to achieve reasonable compromises on key issues that move the country forward. If we elect a lot of Alliance candidates in the process, that's great. But the overriding goal will always be to bridge our cultural and political divide, make government work again, make it less confrontational, and restore some of the public confidence in Washington. And in democracy.

Smerconish: Gee, is that all? (Laughing) Nothing like shooting for the stars.

McFadden: Yes, it's kind of the definition of a big hairy audacious goal.

Smerconish: It is an intriguing concept, and a very creative approach. You've had a great deal of success galvanizing support, which only seems to be growing as frustration with our present dynamic continues to simmer. You certainly have a lot of support from my listeners, most of whom are untethered to either of the political extremes.

McFadden: Yes, we have some real momentum. But as you well know these things can be fleeting. It's critical to take advantage of it now before the political winds shift.

Smerconish: Will you be devoting time to the construction of a McFadden Library?

McFadden: (Laughing out loud) No! I don't suspect you'll see me spending my time and energy soliciting donations to erect a multi-million dollar monument dedicated to the glorification of me.

Smerconish: How refreshing. How about your memoirs?

McFadden: Same answer. I may decide to write a book

someday. Maybe a new iteration of JFK's Profiles in Courage. While our polarization has created so many new opportunities for elected officials to demonstrate courage, all too few have chosen to avail themselves of such chances.

Smerconish: Sounds like a great topic for a new book.

McFadden: Yes. And maybe I'll write something else relating to our history.

Smerconish: Perhaps a book on the presidents?

McFadden: Yes! I'd love to do that.

Smerconish: I would imagine after your four years in office you'd be uniquely qualified to profile the presidents.

McFadden: Yes. You have no idea . . .

Smerconish: Promise me you'll come back as part of your book tour. I have a book club podcast now.

McFadden: It's a deal.

Smerconish: I wish you all good things.

Chapter Thirty-Four

My Dear Winston
July 28, 2022
The Saloon

Maggie turned to me among the crowd of presidents gathered around her, as she often does. "Just like you, Danny, I'm not sure my route to re-election runs through either of the parties. So many moderate Republicans have fled the party to become independents. My efforts to seek bipartisan solutions have hurt me with the far right wing of my party. I'm quite convinced Margel will run against me and be the choice of those remaining, which now amount to only 24% of the overall electorate."

"Establish your own party and run. I did." Said Teddy Roosevelt. "Or run with McFadden's new party."

"I'm a Republican. Always have been. I think it would be political suicide to switch."

"It might possibly be political suicide not to switch," I added.

"I began as a member of the Whig Party," said Lincoln. I was an old line Whig, and disciple of Henry Clay, and served in the House as a Whig. Only later did I became a Republican. Then in 1864 we created a party we labeled the National Union Party when I ran with Johnson to be re-elected that year," said Lincoln. "I was a Republican and he a Democrat."

"I was a Federalist like my father when I served as a Senator from Massachusetts," said John Quincy Adams. "Then I was a Democratic Republican as President, and a Whig for the last four years of my career in the House of Representatives. I believe I managed to disappoint each of them. Quite purposefully, of course."

"I started out as a Democrat, believe it or not," said Ronald Reagan. "I like to say I didn't leave the Democratic Party, it left me."

"Winston Churchill switched parties." Said FDR. "Twice as a matter of fact. He left the Tories—the Conservative party—to join the liberals, and twenty years later rejoined the Conservatives. I wouldn't recommend it, but it worked for my dear Winston."

"Were you in fact friends, Mr. President?" asked Obama. "Or was it more something borne out of necessity?"

Obama spoke loudly, as he was standing behind the seated presidents at the other end of the table opposite FDR. Most of the room heard the question, and it seemed to silence them all as they anticipated his answer.

FDR smiled, enjoying the moment. He motioned to Mary Ann, "My dear, I will require another little sippy," pointing at his martini.

"I first met him in 1918 in London at a dinner for the War Cabinet. I was Assistant Secretary of the Navy, and Winston was in the War Office as Secretary of State for both War and Air. When I mentioned it to him decades later he had no recollection of it. Of course I had great fun reminding him of that and brought it up constantly.

"Yes, we were good friends. We had to be, for the sake of our nations and for the world, but ours was a genuine friendship. We spent 113 days together during the war. We exchanged over 2000 letters. We had a great working relationship, and plotted war strategy and post-war strategy. But we spent time on so many other pursuits. We went hunting and fishing. We drank and we smoked. We frequently went to church with each other—we both enjoyed the hymns immensely."

Clinton joined the conversation. "There exists today a mythology about Churchill that pervades popular culture as a bit of a drunk, albeit a smart, witty and eloquent drunk, and a fierce and stubborn and obstinate leader. Did you find that to be true?"

"Ha," FDR laughed. "I certainly did. All of it. When we received the telegram in the Cabinet Room notifying me of his selection as Prime Minister, I remarked to the others that I suppose Churchill is the best man England has—even if he is drunk half the time."

That broke up the room, much to FDR's delight.

"When he took over in 1940, Churchill and Britain were the very last hope for Europe and indeed the world. And I suspect any Prime Minister other than Churchill would have acceded to Hitler's wishes. Winston is indeed a heroic figure, and yes, he rather matches the mythology that you say is attached to him, President Clinton. However, he was wrong about a lot of things—terribly wrong. India for example. Of course, Gallipoli. Tragic. And he initially favored an invasion in central Europe up through the

Mediterranean rather than our Normandy Invasion. But he got on board in the end.

"In fact, he wanted to accompany the boys on the raid on D-Day and watch the landings in person. Who could tell him no?" FDR laughed out loud.

"Eventually King George declared that if Churchill was going, then damn it he was going too."

"Sounds like my kind of fella," declared Teddy Roosevelt.

"You have got to be kidding," remarked Clinton.

"No, sir. Churchill only backed down as a means of preventing the King himself from going as well."

"Churchill felt the same about you," added Truman. "He said you, Franklin, were the greatest American friend Britain has ever had."

FDR smiled again. "I'm not sure that's a long list." He and many others laughed at that, Washington included..

"But it was great fun to be in the same decade with him."

I found it fascinating to hear FDR's thoughts about Winston Churchill. This was the Presidential Spirits Saloon at its very best. A moment like that really has no equal anywhere in the universe.

I vividly recalled a night in the saloon from my first year in office back in 2017 when the Founders were confronted with some challenging questions about race and slavery, during which Thomas Jefferson had even admitted the truth of the rumors that had persisted for two centuries about he and a young slave his daughter's age, Sally Hemmings. Back then those issues kind of just came up in conversation, without me being so bold as to ask them directly—much as I would have liked to. Although I might have been steering the conversation that way. Four years later I now had a much better relationship with these gentlemen, and really no longer had anything to lose. I decided to raise what I thought perhaps was another one of those taboo topics.

"President Roosevelt," I began, "if I'm overstepping my bounds here, please tell me, but your ascent to the governor's mansion, then to the presidency, and then on to become the most powerful leader in the world, leading us out of a terrible depression, and then confronting and defeating Hitler and Japan is, to me, made all the more astounding by your disability. Can I ask you how you managed to overcome that challenge in your life, and how it impacted your political ascent and the position you came to occupy on the world stage?"

Just as Obama's question about Churchill had instantly brought the entire room to a halt, so too did this. However, a good part of that this time may have been sheer astonishment that someone would "go there" with him. It may have been to my advantage that he'd had a few "sippys," as he calls them. He may not have drank quite like his buddy Winston, but he clearly enjoyed having a few.

He paused for a second in thought. It seemed more like a minute as the room hung in the balance. I looked at Otter and he flashed me a look that screamed, "How could you, McFadden?"

"I was stricken with it at age 39, while we were at our summer home on Campobello Island. At the time I was still strong, athletic and vigorous. I had five children, and had just run for Vice President on the Democratic ticket with Cox. It was devastating."

He was looking right at me with those brilliant blue eyes. I didn't dare look away but with my peripheral vision I could tell the other presidents were absolutely transfixed.

"At first they thought it was just a cold or a muscular condition, but pretty soon they surmised it was much more than that. They diagnosed it as infantile paralysis and told me I would not walk again. I must say I never accepted that. I simply refused to believe it. I never stopped striving to conquer it, and in spite of the crippling nature of my affliction, never let it defeat me."

I had a thousand questions but I didn't dare utter a word for fear it would somehow make him stop talking. He seemed to be on a roll, and I wanted to hear everything he had to say.

"I tried everything I could—electric belts, healing lights, massages, muscle packs. physical therapy. When I heard about the healing powers of the mineral-rich waters in Warm Springs, Georgia, I had to give it a try. The water temperature is 88 degrees year-round. In just three weeks spent there staying nearby at an old broken down Victorian inn I made more progress than I had in the previous three years. So I bought the place." He laughed, and looked around the room as everyone else did as well.

"We transformed it into a facility equipped to provide care and support for others with this ailment. I established the Georgia Warm Springs

Foundation to generate awareness and seek a cure. That led the National Foundation for Infantile Paralysis to coordinate all aspects of the fight against the illness. And of course the March of Dimes grew out of that, bringing over two and a half million dimes to the White House."

"All those efforts, Mr. President," added Eisenhower. "led to Jonas Salk's vaccine, announced while I was President."

"I recall the boys had quite a celebration in the saloon the night we heard that news," responded FDR. "Particularly some of the more bibulous amongst us, of which I proudly include myself."

That drew more laughter.

"It has to be said here, Mr. President," said Obama, "that your accomplishments would have been unparalleled in human history even if you had no disability. How could you possibly muster the physical and mental strength not only to carry on after that diagnosis but to lead us out of depression and then proceed to save the world?"

"I remained optimistic. I never let it be seen that this affliction hampered me in any way. I had great assistance. With my crutches or with my braces and the assistance of one of my sons I could walk across a stage to a podium and stand holding on with both arms to deliver a fiery speech. Whether I was nominating Al Smith at the conventions of '24 and '28 or giving an inaugural address, or anything in between, I met the occasion physically."

He thought for a second. "I suppose the mental hurdles were every bit as challenging as the physical. It changed me—in some ways for the better. Eleanor often said it made me a stronger and more courageous person. Perhaps we all need to be tested in order to increase our strength.

"She also felt it made me more empathic. That is undoubtedly true. I mingled often with the other poor victims and their families at Warm Springs. My first real exposure to rural poverty. And so many of them crippled with this condition. That can't help but make a man more empathetic. And compassion for people certainly drove our policies. In that sense my affliction did impact my presidency.

"And I suppose it enabled ordinary Americans to relate to me better—particularly the forgotten man. This upper class socialite with Harvard and Columbia Law School credentials suddenly became a whole lot more like them in their daily struggles."

"To what extent did they know about your condition?" asked Maggie. "Wasn't that a sort of state secret, shielded from the public?"

"We minimized it. We did not shield it. We tried not to permit photographs of me in a wheelchair, but some were taken. Time, Life and the New Yorker all ran features on me which mentioned my paralysis and the wheelchair. I even gave a speech in Rochester where I acknowledged my condition and held myself out as an example of what people with disabilities can accomplish when properly supported.

"And I told you about my Foundation, which certainly was very public. I raised a million dollars for the Foundation with annual balls on my birthday around the country, and spoke openly of it in my radio address. That might not be a lot by the standards of the new boys in the room and you, my dear Maggie, but in my day that was king's ransom.

"And my opponents used it against me of course. Evidently politics is a lot like love and war. All is fair. They raised it when I ran for governor. And in my first race for president Liberty Magazine ran a piece that asked whether a crippled man can possibly be fit for that office. Some spread rumors that the cause of my illness was syphilis."

"How about world leaders? What impact did it have?"

"Well, Mussolini of course famously declared that never in the course of human history has a nation been led by a paralytic. But it was not the issue one might think. Oh, of course the German press hit it hard, but for the most part leaders respected the United States, our military might and our boys, and that made it irrelevant what they felt about me."

"You are demonstrating an inordinate amount of humility, Mr. President," said Kennedy.

"Well then how utterly uncharacteristic of me!" Roosevelt laughed hard, and so did the room. "Don't get used to it, boys!"

I found myself under his spell. Yes, he enjoyed hearing himself talk, but so did all of us. And what a compelling narrative he had.

"Certainly an occasional cameraman would have snapped a photo of you in a wheelchair, would they not?" asked Clinton.

"That's what the secret service was there for," FDR responded.

"To make sure no one was in position to take such a photo?"

"No, to confiscate the camera and destroy the film after it was taken." He laughed, along with many others. Not all of us.

"A perfectly appropriate use of the executive power," added Nixon. Perhaps kidding. Perhaps not.

"Most of the boys in the press had enough good sense and regard for the country not to focus on such impertinent items." FDR added.

"That wouldn't fly today," I responded.

"It flew in Mr. Adams' day," responded Jefferson. "As a matter of record he routinely threw newspaper publishers in jail for criticizing his administration."

"He even threw a Congressman in jail for criticizing him— Matthew Lyon," said Madison, quick to come to the support of his Virginia mentor.

Adams rose in his defense. "They were punished, and rightfully so, for uttering falsehoods, and seditious statements. Not for criticism of me."

Jefferson had the last word on the matter, "My dear Mr. Adams, I do believe that your Alien and Sediton Acts may explain why you were our first and last Federalist president. For that, the Democratic Republicans amongst us, who occupied the presidency for 24 consecutive years following you, owe you an enormous debt of gratitude." He glanced at Madison and then over at Monroe, who did not attempt to shield their delight.

OK, that was mean, but funny. But also fair, in my mind. We tend to think that the founders were all in on freedom of the press, free speech, and all our other critical freedoms in the Bill of Rights, but that wasn't always the case. Adams, Wilson and even Lincoln had their moments that would make us cringe today.

Adams chose not to respond to his friend and rival's zinger. Perhaps wisely.

Kennedy, looking now directly at Jefferson and Madison, chimed in. "I think it's worth noting here as a postscript that Mr. Lyon, who was born in Ireland, and was a great Revolutionary War hero, won re-election from inside that very jail cell—demonstrating, of course, that it's the voters who wield the ultimate power in this democracy you gentlemen created."

I love that Kennedy knew that story of Matthew Lyon, and was proud of it.

Maggie was looking a little antsy. "Do you need to get back, Maggie?" I asked. If so, I certainly knew how she felt.

"Well, this place is unbelievable, but I should be heading back. Walk me out, Danny, if you would be so kind."

We got up to leave.

George H. W. Bush, I think sensing the moment would be lost, spoke up.

“I proudly signed the Americans With Disabilities Act in 1990, the world's first comprehensive declaration of equality for people with disabilities.

“It was powerful in its simplicity, and ensured that every man, woman, and child with a disability can now pass through once-closed doors into a bright new era of equality, independence, and freedom.”

FDR looked skeptical. “Are you saying, gentlemen, that someone with disabilities today would not face discrimination in the workplace or in politics.”

Obama jumped back in. “The Act is making a difference, but just as the Civil Rights Act didn’t put an end to all racism, a level of discrimination against those with disabilities persists, but the world they live in is much more friendly and accommodating than in your time or any time before.”

Maggie worked the room masterfully on her way out. She high fived Otter and Clinton and fist-bumped Obama. She layed it on thick with some of them. Andrew Jackson beamed as she told him she wanted to come back to have some of his Tennessee whiskey. As she circled the table behind Jefferson, she said, “I want to play your Split the Room Game sometime soon.” And the smiles she and Kennedy flashed at one another emitted more than a few sparks that illuminated this dimly lit saloon.

Her last goodbye was to FDR. “Well, my weren’t you the belle of the ball tonight, sir.”

FDR beamed.

She continued. “Thank you for your candor and for opening your heart. I’m so pleased you could find your own little version of paradise in my beloved Georgia.”

Then, shooting a glance at Carter, she added, “We think it’s pretty special, don’t we Jimmy?”

Carter laughed. “We certainly do, ma’am.” He appeared to be blushing.

I accompanied Maggie as she walked out.

“That was nothing short of a clinic there, Maggie,” I said. “Wow.”

“Oh, please, Danny. They all love you more than they’ll ever love me.”

“That’s a lie.” I responded. It was easy to see how she had so rapidly ascended to the summit of American politics.

"OK, Danny, I just love President Roosevelt. Don't you?"

"Yes—both Roosevelts. But I've spent more time with Franklin lately than I ever did while I was president."

We looked back and saw that he was still holding court. The soft light amidst the hanging smoke cloud made the surreal scene all the more dramatic.

"My goodness," she said, "if he's not the embodiment of the American spirit, battling back from his paralysis to save the free world, I'm not sure what is. How extraordinary that he managed to remain cheerful and optimistic. Such a pity he couldn't bring himself to be more up front about it at the time."

"Oh my god, yes. I have newfound respect for him too after hearing that. By any measure his is one of the most consequential American lives ever lived."

Maggie let her guard down just a little with me as we neared her exit. She looked back at the saloon.

"I do love this place," she said. "Maybe not as much as you, but this is special. But I'm struggling, Danny. The job, some personal issues, you name it. I've had a bit of a bad spell here lately."

That floored me. How could she put on that charm offensive I just witnessed with anything internally ailing her?

"Is there anyone you can confide in at the White House who can help you calmly assess things?" I asked.

"I'm having a hard time trusting anyone. The staff is leaking. I'm convinced all of DC has their own personal agenda that takes priority over all else. I'm being undermined by my Vice President. No, there's really no place to turn. I guess except here . . . and you and a few of your buddies out there."

I thought for a second.

"I've got an idea," I said.

"Great. I knew you would. I'm pretty much ready to try anything."

"Ask one of your staffers to locate a guy by the name of Eugene Davis. Most people call him Satch. He's an ex-Marine, and a Medal of Honor recipient. Prince of a dude. He's a National frickin Treasure. He served for three decades as Chief White House Usher. But he was so much more than that for all the presidents he served. He was my rock during my time here—he and

Denyse. I am so lucky I had both of them at my side. He retired as I left. You should be able to find him not too far away in Virginia.

"And for that matter, while you're at it, how about reaching out to your friend in Los Gatos?"

"I'm not sure he views me as a friend. And I'm not certain those overtures would be so welcome. Some of my staff and supporters see him as a threat and have been hitting him hard at times."

I didn't respond, but that crushed me. God that sucks. Life is much easier in this saloon, that's for sure.

"Contact Satch," I said. "Tell him I said hi."

Then, as she opened the door to leave, I added, "by the way, I'm pretty sure he knows everything about this place too, but whatever you do, do not tell him I told you that."

Chapter Thirty-Five

The Midterms: A Big Step Forward for the Alliance
November 5, 2022

Then came the midterms, which offered an ever-so-slight glimmer of hope for the Alliance—and the country.

WASHINGTON POST

DEMS TAKE HOUSE, SENATE STAYS GOP, ALLIANCE GAINS GROUND

(Washington DC, November 5, 2022) By Celest Markid
America rendered a split decision yesterday with divergent outcomes in the House and Senate—a Democratic takeover in the former chamber, Republicans holding the latter. But the big story might just be the gains made by the new Alliance party. What began as an idea tossed out by President McFadden in a speech at Mt. Vernon during which he announced his decision not to seek election, has taken hold and can now boast not only 22 members of the House of Representatives, but two new members of the United States Senate.

The different outcomes in the House and Senate exposed the ever-widening gap that now exists between America's cities and its suburbs.

The gains made by Democrats in the House came largely in densely populated, educated and diverse communities, particularly those in and around traditional Democratic strongholds like Philadelphia and New York. But gains were also made in some traditionally conservative large cities among college educated whites voting with minorities. Republicans made gains among whites in more rural areas among voters without college degrees that previously had leaned Democratic.

Perhaps the biggest news of the night was the Alliance party landing Senate seats in Alaska and Maine—two states which have instituted "ranked choice voting"—voting systems designed to be more amenable to third party candidates by enabling voters to rank their top choices in order of preference.

In Alaska's new single open all-comers primary, the top four finishers regardless of party advance to a rank-choice general election, all but eliminating the chance to be "primaried" within a party. Alliance candidate Betsy Carig won yesterday in convincing fashion. Maine also utilizes a rank-choice voting system, which worked to the benefit of first-time candidate Nelson Carmichael, who bested the field to become the state's junior senator.

The House now stands at 211 Democrats, 202 Republicans and 22 from the new Alliance party. This new dynamic for the House means no party will have an absolute majority, elevating the profile and power of the new Alliance members. Democrats will be unable to elect a new Speaker of the House without at least seven Alliance party representatives voting with them. Alternatively, the Alliance could broker a deal with Republican House members to combine to reach the 218 votes necessary to elect a Speaker, and could possibly do so with an Alliance member taking the gavel. The mere threat of that possibility of a deal with Republicans of course, would provide the leverage for a similar arrangement for an Alliance Speaker of the House in a deal with Democrats. Less likely but still possible is a deal with enough House Democrats and Republicans to produce an Alliance Speaker of the House with a bipartisan vote—or tripartisan, to coin new phrase in our national political lexicon.

Yesterday's vote was hailed by some voices who have been decrying the state of our political divide. However, it remains to be seen whether this will signal any new movement in the direction of national political unity. Either way, former President Danny McFadden's Alliance undeniably took a big step forward yesterday. Pundits disagree tonight as to whether this is evidence of a new trend or just a blip. However, these results do signal a new political dynamic in Washington.

Chapter Thirty-Six

Now This Little Cause Is Getting Somewhere
December 24, 2022

"This is big, Boss," said Tina as I walked through the front door of our office suite.

"I assume it is," I responded, "and really it better be, to be summoned here on Christmas Eve."

"You won't be disappointed."

"OK," I responded. "I'm prepared to have my socks knocked off."

Tina had called me last night telling me I needed to come in to the office today for a videoconference with Murph, who had been working it day in and day out for us and for the Alliance on Capitol Hill.

Moments later Murph appeared on the big screen, with a big smile on her face.

"Hey Tina," she said, "thanks for putting this together on short notice. Great to see you, Mr. President."

"How are all my friends in Congress?" I said, before adding moments later, "That's a joke."

"Well, as you're about to find out, I'm not sure how much of a joke it is."

I looked at Tina, who was smiling ear to ear.

"OK, you've got my attention. What's up?"

"I've been working closely with our nearly two dozen Alliance representatives in the House in behind-the-scenes negotiations over the next Speaker vote. There's been some pretty fascinating developments."

Tina beside me could hardly contain herself.

"Would you like to tell him, Tina?"

"No, no, no—you've done all the work on this. You do it."

"Both of the two parties appear deathly afraid that we'll work a deal with the other party to make one of them Speaker."

"Of course," I replied.

"Well, since neither party has a majority in the House, the Republicans came to us offering for their entire membership to vote for an Alliance representative for Speaker. They see it as a way to avoid a Democrat Speaker. With their 202 votes and our 22 that would give us the Speakership."

"I love it."

"It gets better. The Democrats got wind of that and then offered to do the very same, even proposing they'll work with us in naming the Alliance representative we want as Speaker. They want to avoid the fallout from having Republicans being seen as the one working the deal with us."

"Wow—either way we get the Speakership. That's huge. Exactly what I was hoping for. You are the very best at what you do, Murph."

"It gets better still. Did you know there is no requirement that the Speaker be a current member of the House of Representatives?"

"No. And I'm not sure I even believe that."

"It's not in the Constitution and the idea has been floated many times before."

"OK. So what are you getting at?"

"One scenario that is a possibility is for them to vote you in as Speaker. And with our present bargaining power we could make that happen. Several of the Alliance representatives met with me yesterday to propose the idea, and I figured I'd get with you about it immediately. I think we could make that happen."

"Wow. That's surprising. I know many of those Congressmen in the two parties aren't big fans of mine."

"Well, while that may be the case they still like you 1000 times more than they like every member of the opposing party. While they know you won't promote the hardcore aspects of their agenda they do in fact respect you and some even admire you as one putting the best interests of the country first."

"Wow. How telling is that?"

"Think about it, Boss," added Tina.

"I'm flattered. And gosh, thanks for all your work, Murph. But I think it's huge that we'll have an Alliance Speaker regardless of who it is. I say you push Congressman Crawford forward if he is up for it. He'd be great. It's crucial that whoever we choose be someone with the charisma and political skills to pull it off. That job will be a monumental challenge—but what a moment for our cause. As for me, not only is it not where I want to be right now personally, but I think if I took it that might be so unusual and out of the ordinary that it could end up hurting the cause. Just because something like this is possible doesn't mean it's the right thing to do. I think people would consider it an overreach to put me in there and it would backfire on us. Let's keep making solid, incremental progress. The tortoise rather than the hare. Besides, I'd like to see some new faces emerge in our leadership to really carry our torch forward as I gradually step aside. But regardless, what a phenomenal day this is for us."

"And for the country," added Tina.

"Was that sufficiently flabbergasting?" asked Murph.

"Without a doubt," I responded, "and well worth the trip in here. Can't think of a finer Christmas gift. Now this little cause of ours is getting somewhere."

Chapter Thirty-Seven

Landing Denyse Struckmeyer
December 29, 2022

Denyse shrieked as she watched the car pull up to the small gate the Secret Service had erected beyond our driveway. The City of Los Gatos had redone the section of Bungalow Drive that wrapped in front of our home, and added the gate and tiny guard house.

"Danny, come quick. You *have* to see this!"

I hustled in to the front room and looked out our Bay window. Our dear friends Satch and his wife Christy were pulling up in a red convertible. Satch laid on the horn as Denyse threw open the front door and she and Montana both dashed across the lawn to meet them. Satch stopped the car abruptly to avoid hitting Montana, who then lept into the vehicle. He can recognize a couple of dog people when he sees them, and I think he remembered Satch from the White House.

I called the boys to come out and grab their bags and we met them as they parked at the top of the driveway. They were both beaming.

"Sick ride," said Brett. He reached out to shake hands but instead the tall and lanky Satch engulfed him in a big broad bear hug while Christy and Denyse embraced nearby. Somehow in just four short years Satch had effortlessly carved out a prime place within each of our hearts, and Christy was well on her way to joining him there.

I would have greeted Christy first, but it didn't appear that she and Denyse would be concluding any time soon. Satch smiled broadly as we embraced.

"You and your girl are traveling in style," I said. "You are all class, my friend."

"Well sir, I figured since I finally found someone worth celebrating life with, by golly I'm gonna celebrate life with her. Besides, it's our first time in California. Had a feeling a convertible might just be the right call."

As I walked over to greet Christy I heard Satch get right to the heart of it with Brett. "Tell me how you're hittin 'em, son."

"Screaming line drives to all fields, sir." That put a big smile to my face.

The whole scene in front of me brought a rush of pure joy. Life had not been easy for Christy Manzanetti. She had been the wife of Satch's best Viet Nam buddy—the one who had saved his life, but ultimately didn't make it home. Her only son passed away a few years ago of respiratory failure brought about by opioid addiction. After a rough period of grief she assumed responsibility for raising her grandson, Dom. My boys had gotten to know Dom when Satch had stepped in to take care of him after his father's death. Satch had been alone for a decade since the death of his wife. The two of them coming together this late in life had rather instantly turned their sometimes-tragic lives into the stuff of fairy tales. And after the two of them, no one was happier about it than Denyse and me—in that order.

Before we entered the house, Aaron, Ricky and Erik all emerged to pay homage to Satch, like Catholic pilgrims greeting the Pope.

Now I had thought I had a great repartee with these dudes, but Satch of course put me to shame. I wasn't jealous in the least, mind you. I admired that about the man and relished the opportunity to observe it first-hand all over again. It was a thing of beauty, and something to aspire to. God it was good to see him again.

Denyse and I pulled out all the stops for dinner out back on the deck. I had ribs going in the smoker and salmon on the barbecue, and but we started with some brown sugar bacon wrapped scallops.

As we sat down to eat Satch eyed the spread.

"You two have really gone above and beyond."

That of course fueled Denyse's "go-to" criticism of me. "Danny tends to always take things a step too far."

"Well it's a good thing for you I do," I responded. "If I weren't programed like that I may never have attempted to land the likes of you. Denyse Struckmeyers don't exactly come around every day in a man's life."

"Oh, is that what you did to me? Land me? My what a hopeless romantic you are."

Christy appeared to be slightly mortified until she saw Satch roaring with laughter.

"Whatever he did, Denyse, to win your hand," said Satch. "it was surely his finest hour."

"Thank you Satch," responded Denyse, staring right at me. "I much prefer the way you put it."

Interesting to see how Satch was still schooling me even two years away from the White House. Evidently I hadn't yet mastered all the wisdom he had attempted to impart to me in the course of my term.

We sat on the deck for hours on a flawless Northern California evening. We turned our patio heaters on but I'm not sure we even needed to. And that ambitious meal turned out. But the real star of the night wasn't the food but the company. Nothing nourishes the soul quite like a lazy, lingering evening with great friends.

It was getting close to 11, and the ladies were still hanging in there with us. God love 'em. I figured the least I could do was to give them a cue to let them know I wouldn't be offended if they turned in. But everyone seems to somehow know that when around me, if they don't eventually decide on their own to call it quits the party may well never come to an end.

"Don't feel like you need to stay on this deck all night."

"And you realize he will be out here all night if one of you accompanies him," Denyse added.

"Yes— we should be getting to bed," said Satch. "Heck, it's 2:00 am our time."

I looked at Christy and she had a look on her face that seemed to scream "*Hello*!" But I love that she wasn't about to be the one to put an end to the night.

"One more thing before we head in, sir." Satch added.

"Sure, what is it?"

"I was invited to meet the President last week. You know they had the G-7 meetings at Hilton Head. I had coffee with her right after the meetings concluded. We met in a private room at her hotel."

Believe it or not, we had gone the whole night without really mentioning a word about her, national politics or the country really. It was kind of refreshing.

"That's great. Good for her. What a great call on her part to connect with you."

"Here, let me get Christy settled in the guest room," interrupted Denyse, "and you two can carry on as long as you like."

Christy flashed a smile that evidenced I'm sure a feeling of sheer relief, and the two ladies excused themselves.

"Tell me about your meeting," I asked. "Do you like her?"

"Yes. I do. Like you, she sought my advice. That's always a humbling feeling, and didn't happen a whole lot in my years in the White House."

"Good for her. That speaks volumes about her. Someone must have been giving her some first-rate advice."

"Someone indeed," responded Satch, looking straight into my eyes.

It was an awkward moment. I thought for a second.

"It wasn't me," I responded.

"That may depend, sir, on how broadly you are defining the word 'me.'"

He kept staring at me, as if he was saying something without saying something. Either way, I wasn't picking up on what he was attempting to convey.

Then I kind of did a double take. I hadn't had a lot to drink, but I had certainly had a little—several glasses of wine over the course of several hours. So maybe I wasn't thinking as quickly as usual, which, but the way, isn't all that quick to begin with.

Then it hit me like a fast ball to the middle of my chest—if Margaret Bates has stumbled upon the Saloon, and if there is a version of me there, perhaps that presidential spirit has advised her to go meet with Satch.

I stood up and just started walking. I tend to do that when I'm a bit freaked out. Like now. I walked into the backyard. I looked up at the full moon and I swear instead of the "Man in the Moon," I distinctly saw an image of George Washington in there. Being away from the Saloon these past couple of years it had become so easy to just kind of put it out of my mind. Almost as if it never happened. Had it really happened? Of course it did. Tina is evidence of that. But I'm better not dwelling on such mysteries. Not unlike life itself.

I don't think Satch quite knew how to react to my response. From the yard I saw him slowly get up, clear a bunch of plates from the table, and head back into the house.

I soaked up the California night air and thought hard about what I just heard. As president I had often wondered what my post presidency spirit would be like. Would I be conscious of it? Obviously not—I had that answer. What would that spirit be like and stand for? Tina and I both had openly wondered about that, and even discussed it. And perhaps most importantly, would I be proud of him?

I paced around the back yard a bit more and Montana pranced along behind me as collies tend to do. Looking now at the rear view of my house I could see Denyse through the windows to our bedroom upstairs to the right, and the lights on in the spare bedroom on the far left. I felt strangely at peace. The more I thought about it, the more at ease I became with the whole notion of Bates in that saloon. If the Danny Mac of the Saloon was taking the time to befriend President Bates, and if on top of that he was encouraging her for whatever reason to reach out to Satch, I guess I can only be proud of the role he is assuming in there. How interesting now to catch even this ever-so-brief glimpse of what might be going on in that Saloon. I wondered if it was possible that Bates was becoming even nearly as besotted with that place as I immediately had been.

Focusing on it now for a few minutes made me realize that God I missed that Saloon. But how reassuring to hear, even cryptically, about that mystical place again. While I'm no fan of the Bates administration, it's encouraging to know she is availing herself of at least some of what that magical saloon has to offer. Good for her. And good for the country.

Chapter Thirty-Eight

Fight On!
December 30, 2022

The next day Satch and I arose early and made the short drive to Quicksilver Park, accessible from a beautiful residential neighborhood in nearby Almaden Valley. We hiked a challenging five mile winding trail through the hills and beneath the immense Live Oaks with views of San Jose and the Guadalupe Reservoir. I worried whether Satch would be up to it physically but he definitely was. We didn't exactly set the course record, but it was a great hike.

Brent, Erik and Aaron all accompanied us. I think they are a bit enamored of Satch. In fact, I know they are. Brent was several yards ahead of us and Aaron behind, with Erik positioned at the entrance to the trail off of Whispering Pines Drive. It was great to have a solid block of time alone with this gentleman I had come to love and admire so much.

"How is Christy doing?" I asked. I knew she had really gone through some depression following the death of her son.

"She's fantastic. Oh, she misses Dom terribly with him being off at college, but I believe she feels that she has been able to fill that void in his life following his dad's death. He's very happy, and that gives her tremendous satisfaction. And she and I are thrilled to have each other. I don't believe either of us ever dreamed we'd find this type of relationship again so late in life."

"I am so happy for you, my friend. They say good things happen to good people. I don't know if I always believe that but it couldn't be more true in your case."

We paused for a water break as we came to a shaded area where the trees on either side of the trail formed a natural canopy against the steep hill we were scaling.

Satch guzzled a good portion of his water bottle and looked over at me.

"I don't believe I've ever seen you this relaxed, sir."

I laughed. "Those four years we were together were the exception for me in my life, not the rule. I used to be a fairly chill guy before DC." I smiled. "The Beltway has a way of chewing you up and spitting you out."

"What's next for you? Will you be plugging back in to Silicon Valley?"

"I don't know. Maybe not. I'm enjoying a variety of things at the moment. Taking it slow. Focusing a bit more on parenting."

"You'll never regret that."

"No question about that."

We started walking again.

"Do you have a bucket list?" he asked.

"Not so much of a bucket list, but two life goals stand out amongst all others."

"What's that?"

"One is to see Normandy."

"You've never been there? I don't believe that."

"Don't you remember? We were in France preparing to do a big event on the beaches at Normandy and then go to Ireland when the school shooting in Mayton Florida happened. We came right home."

"Well that one should be easy enough for you to pull off. What's the other?"

"To stay healthy long enough to be able to walk Kelly down the aisle."

"I want to be there for that, too. I'll be cheering both of you on."

"That would be special."

We walked in silence following that exchange for the next few minutes.

"I see you've been involved in your political cause too, and doing a good bit of campaigning."

"Yes—I got pulled in. A little bit reluctantly, I should say. But not exactly kicking and screaming. I just want to do all I can to get that fire burning and see where it can go eventually without my direct involvement."

"Good luck with that, sir." He smiled, and I slowed down.

"What are you getting at?" I asked. "Good luck getting the fire burning or good luck pulling back?"

"Both. I'm no expert, but I've observed these things for a few decades now. I just don't know if this fire is ready and capable of burning without your involvement."

We rounded a bend on the trail only to see an even stiffer incline awaited us as the morning sun seemed to instantly begin to burn a few degrees warmer.

"I love that it has picked up some steam. My goodness, we now have representatives in Congress, for God sakes. And we're about to have the Speaker of the frickin House. But these forces behind our polarization are fierce and entrenched. I think it's a tall order with or without my involvement."

Satch looked over and smiled and didn't say a word.

"And I'm enjoying a little time for the kids and Denyse."

He looked over again and smiled again.

"What?" I asked.

"I'm not saying anything," he responded.

"The hell you aren't."

He burst out laughing.

"I've been a little overcome lately with guilt about the kids," I said. "I worry that I haven't been there as much as I should have been for them."

"That's just because they're leaving the nest, right?"

"No—I really wish I could have been alongside them more as they went through a lot of their stuff —especially the stuff brought about by my high profile."

"You're kidding me right now, right?"

"No. I'm totally serious. I really struggle with that."

Moments later a fit young couple coming the other direction approached us at an impressive clip.

"Mr. McFadden, I mean . . . President McFadden," the young woman said as they got close. Brent and Aaron appeared in a flash. I had my ND hat pulled down and sunglasses on but there's only so much you can do.

"It's Alexa—Lexi Aiken. I went to school with Kelly. You coached our 5th grade volleyball team."

I signaled to Brent and Aaron all was good. "Lexi! Wow, great to see you. That was a pretty good team as I recall."

"Thanks to Kelly. We got most of our points off of her serve."

"There was a lot of talent on that team the way I remember it. You had a nice little developing jump serve yourself for a fifth grader."

"This is Bobby. We both just graduated from USC. Fight On!"

"I think I've heard of it." I laughed. So did they. "Congratulations. Good for you guys. And I promise I won't hold that against either of you."

"How's Brett?" she asked. "He was in my brother David's class. I think you coached their Little League team one year too."

"Absolutely. I remember David as well. Brett is good. He'll be off to college next year. Jack will be the only one left at home. None of us are happy about that. Least of all, Jack."

"I follow all your kids on Instagram. They all seem great."

"How are your folks, Lexi?"

"They split a few years ago but we're alright. I think David took it harder than me. But it's all good."

"Look, I don't want to hold you up," she added. "Promise me you'll say hi to Kelly for me. I'd love to connect with her."

"I will do that. Good luck to you, Lexi. And you, too, Bobby. Congratulations. Go Irish!" They laughed.

A few moments later, Satch, turned and said, "You understand what just happened there, don't you?'

"What?"

"That was very telling sir. And impeccable timing."

"What?" I asked again. "Not sure I follow."

"Sometimes the good Lord sends us brilliant, glowing neon signs and all we want to do is shield our eyes and look the other way."

I shot him a puzzled look.

"I know you're smarter than this, my friend. You were president of this country."

More silence.

"Here's what I saw," he continued. "In the middle of you moaning about some cockamamie notion that you were an absent father, that young woman just exposed that for the lie it is. That was Jesus himself, who just appeared to you in the form of Lexi and Bobby to set you straight."

I slowed my pace to a crawl.

"Or are you going to try to tell me you managed to neglect your kids while you were busy coaching their teams? I don't think so. Doesn't sound like any absent father I know."

I didn't respond. And he wasn't finished.

"Yes sir. That was Jesus himself right there. You can choose to ignore me all you wish, but you best not ignore Jesus as well. Do that, my friend, at your own peril."

With that, he picked up his pace and walked ahead of me.

He's very good. Boy, is he very good.

A little further on, as the trail began to descend a bit, Satch picked back up where we had left off the previous night.

"President Bates specifically asked me if I would reach out to you for her."

He saw the look of surprise that engulfed my face.

"She said she needs to appeal directly to your Alliance. Particularly with all the inroads you're making."

Oh does she really?" I said. "We would welcome that. We are a big tent—at least we'd certainly like to be."

"But that's not the only reason she came to see me," added Satch. "She had heard I was a good sounding board and calming influence for a sitting president. Someone evidently told her that."

He looked over at me and smiled.

"You do make one hell of a president whisperer," I responded. "Although I don't know how I feel about that secret getting out. But I definitely know how I feel about the bastard who spilled the beans."

"I'll have you know I have tremendous respect for that particular bastard, Mr. President." He couldn't contain his laughter.

"Then that makes one of us."

That kind of teed up a pregnant pause of sorts. I waited to see if he would volunteer anything without me asking a question. I should have known better. I decided then that I was gonna be the one to take to take the plunge.

"So about that saloon . . ."

He was walking on the outside of the trail, and he turned away from me and looked at the view of San Jose below.

"If I'm not mistaken," he said, "that's San Francisco way off in the distance there, is that not?"

I just shook my head. "Now wait just a second. What is the deal with that? We both know exactly what I'm getting at, yet we can't openly acknowledge it? Tina can talk to me about it. Why can't you?"

"How is Tina?" he asked.

"See right there—how would you even know who Tina is if it weren't for the Saloon?"

He didn't respond.

"See—I got you there with that one."

No response.

"You're not even going to respond? The old man with all the wisdom is suddenly without words?" I smiled as I said it. I didn't have the heart to pressure this wonderful gentleman any further though.

Finally he looked over at me and flashed a big smile. "Plausible deniability."

I laughed out loud.

"That's all you got? Really? That's the best you can do?"

"Presidents aren't the only ones who get to use that term very strategically."

With that we kept walking. I respected the man way too much to make him uncomfortable even in the least. My desire to know more—which was overwhelming at times—took a back seat to my affection for him. No regrets.

Chapter Thirty-Nine

The Collective Works of John Locke
February 22, 2023
The Saloon

Maggie walked into the Saloon and did a major double take. The room was lit up well beyond what the dim gas lamps typically emit. We could have been performing surgery. And there was no music, which was highly irregular and a little suspicious.

All the presidents were dispersed throughout the room, about five to a table. John Tyler stood alone in front addressing the group.

Maggie saw me and I motioned for her to come sit near me. She stopped at the bar to get her martini first. God love her.

As she as sat down at my table she whispered to me. "What the hell is going on?"

I leaned over to answer, but I didn't think I needed to keep my voice to a whisper. Many at the other tables were talking amongst themselves.

"It's book club night," I answered. I couldn't say it with a straight face. I showed her the cover of the book we all had in front us. It was Adam Smith's *Wealth of Nations*.

She flashed me the most priceless "what the actual fuck?" look I think I've ever seen.

"You have got to be kidding," she responded. Slowly. Incredulously.

"What?" I said, smiling, "it's not like all we do is just drink every night in here."

Our table mates couldn't help but follow this exchange and thought it was hysterical.

"Adam Smith," she said, nodding her head and pursing her lips. "Okay."

I couldn't help but laugh.

"It's not always this dry," I said.

"You're right," added Clinton. "Sometimes it's worse."

"That's true," I said. "Madison had us reading *The Collective Works of*

John Locke.

Clinton may have been joining us in mocking it a bit but I think deep down he enjoyed all this stuff—even the Greek and Roman philosopher/thinkers some of these guys select.

"Coolidge had us reading Cicero last week," I said.

"Danny you've gotta warn me about when these nights happen so I don't bother coming up here. I'll just have a few glasses of wine and be in bed by 9:30."

"Do all these guys read this stuff?" she asked.

"I'm not entirely sure Jackson or Taylor do," I responded.

Obama heard our little exchange and had to chime in. "Pretty sure the next book those boys read will be their first."

She looked at him and laughed.

"Then there's a guy like Jefferson," Obama added. "He had the biggest private collection of books in the country. When the British burned the Library of Congress in 1812 the library replaced their stock by buying a good portion of his collection."

"We have had some books I think you would love, Maggie," Clinton added. Those two often bonded over novels they were reading. "Hoover brought *David Copperfield*. Ike brought Mark Twain's *A Connecticut Yankee in King Arthur's Court*. Lincoln always selects something from Shakespeare. Reagan had us read *The Hunt for Red October*. Kennedy brought Ian Fleming's *From Russia With Love*."

"That sounds about right for JFK," Maggie added. "I imagine he and James Bond have quite a bit in common." I thought that was pretty funny. And spot on.

"Don't get me wrong," she added. "I'm all in on the novels. I go pretty deep there. John Locke I'm not so sure though."

"What book would you select, Maggie?" asked Clinton.

"Great question." She paused in thought. "Oh, I suppose something from Flannery O'Connor." She seemed quite happy to have been asked.

"A fine Georgia girl," Clinton added.

"Savannah," she declared proudly.

"Of course," responded Clinton. He and Obama go a heck of a lot deeper with these novelists than I do. Most people go a heck of a lot deeper than I do.

"What was your opinion of *Midnight in the Garden of Good and Evil?*" asked Clinton.

"I didn't care much for the portrait it painted of our town, but it kind of put us on the map at the same time in the eyes of the world. It added to the aura and mystery of Savannah, and that's not a bad thing."

We were all just speaking out loud now. Tyler had kind of lost control of the room, and each table seemed to have lively conversations going—and I'm not sure how many of them were about Adam Smith.

"Why is it that so many of our great American novelists hail from the South?" I asked. I kind of intended it to be rhetorical but you can't utter that in front of a couple of proud Southerners and not expect an answer.

Clinton seemed just about to offer up an answer when Maggie beat him to the punch. "For so many of us through the years," she said, "to grow up in the American South is to have been born right smack in the middle of an epic American novel. Every direction you look you see humanity in its most raw form—and all of man's most gripping themes—family, love, triumph, tragedy, pride, regret, shame, betrayal, perseverance, vindication, to list just a few."

What an answer. Holy cow.

I looked at Clinton. "Did you want to add something?" I asked.

"Are you kidding? I'm smarter than that, don't you think? I won't even begin to try to add one bit to that." That drew some laughter.

"And we're all such story tellers by nature in the South," Maggie added, seemingly oblivious to the awestruck response at the table to her synopsis. I tried to recall a time where I had received such impeccable response to any question I had ever asked of anyone my whole life.

We sat through another ten or fifteen minutes of discussion in the room about classical economics and the Industrial Revolution.

Maggie looked at me and Clinton. "Hey, I actually had a few points I wouldn't mind getting some advice from the group on. Would that be awkward?"

"Not at all," responded Clinton. "That's what we're here for."

"Let me get Otter over here," I said. "You can tell him and he'll mention it to Washington."

I got George W. Bush's attention and he instantly jumped up and he sprang into action. Within five minutes our bookclub had adjourned until next time.

Otter then spoke to Washington and returned to our table.

"Big Daddy will get the attention of the group here in a just a second."

She gave him a puzzled look.

"George Washington. That Big Daddy." He smiled and winked.

"Oh, thank you so much. You're a sweetheart."

"Anything for you, Peaches," he responded. Clinton practically busted a gut at that. I tried hard not to laugh, but once her smile emerged I couldn't help myself.

As Bush walked away, I had to ask her about him.

"Does it bother you when he calls you that?"

"Maybe at first," she responded, "but then I thought about it. He gives everyone else a nickname. If he treats me differently than the others then some will likely call him sexist. On the other hand, given where we are with men and women these days, if he gives me a nickname he could be accused of being disrespectful or perhaps even mysoginistic. So he really can't win, can he?"

I nodded.

"To me, it's all about the spirit in which he says it," she added. "I've seen all the very worst of men in my career. He's not ogling me or undressing me with his eyes, as so many men would do— especially those who have tasted a little success in life. In his case, his intentions are pure as the magnolias that line the Savannah River in late spring." She smiled at the thought of that. "I'm good with it. And even mildly amused by it."

"I understand all that," I responded, "but I just can't bring myself to go along with it. If he had named Chester Arthur Peaches, for example, of course I'd be calling him that." I laughed for a second at the sheer absurdity of that. "But for some reason I can't do that in your case."

She thought for a second. "Well, what I didn't say is that I'm fine with gentlemen choosing specific instances to treat a woman differently than they would a man. We shouldn't be fighting courtesy, chivalry and good manners. Those differences help make the world go round."

At that moment Washington stood to address the group. These were always some of my favorite moments in the Saloon. I relished observing the universal respect and admiration he elicited in this group—from all political stripes. He commanded the undivided attention of the room, including the servers, without so much as uttering a single word.

"Gentlemen," he said, "We have been summoned to provide advice and counsel to President Bates as she considers executive actions and policy.

"I am informed that the magnitude and difficulty of her task is formidable, with factions lining up in opposition. Please permit her to consult this assembly, and recommend to her such measures as you may deem necessary or expedient, for this is our seminal mission and purpose."

He then turned to Maggie, who was now standing at his side.

"President Bates, you have our collective attention."

Maggie appeared quite moved to have received that preamble from the Father of our Country. I have to say I always felt the same way in his presence—more than any of the others in this room.

"Thank you, President Washington." She looked out across the Saloon. "My administration, like so many recently, has suffered a few setbacks—monumental setbacks, perhaps. But in a way, that just fuels my resolve to swing for the fences. What, after all, have I got to lose?"

The room applauded amidst more than a few shouts of encouragement.

With that response, she quickly added, "Before you get too excited, just wait 'til you hear what issue we are tackling."

The room came to a collective hush, and Maggie stood back and let the suspense build for a few seconds. When the moment was right, she smiled and blurted out, "Immigration reform."

The groans from the crowd wouldn't have been any louder if she had just muffed a three-foot putt on 18 to lose the Masters.

She laughed. "I've really got no choice, fellas. The mess that is our Southern border has been an open wound in this country for decades now. It is used as a political wedge issue by both sides, and what is my worth anyway if I can't attempt to forge solutions to our nation's most vexing problems."

"More power to you, Maggie," stated Obama. "I applaud you for it. But all I can say is good luck."

He smiled and shook his head. "I made it a central priority of my second term, but in the end I just couldn't reach a deal with House Republicans."

"There was a possibility of consensus," he added, "and the polling suggested the public was with us, but what we lacked on the other side was some political courage and political will—and that's always the thing in shortest supply in Washington."

"I've been down this road before too," added George W. Bush. "I know it all too well. A lot of us worked hard to see if we couldn't find common ground. We invited Mexican President Vicente Fox for a state visit and he and I met and then we addressed the nation from White House Lawn. We had bipartisan support."

Bush looked around. "Where's Jack?" The room collectively turned and looked toward a booth in the back where Kennedy was sitting with Jefferson. JFK seemed to like hanging out with Jefferson. So did I.

"Skipper," Bush said, looking at Kennedy, "I had your brother Teddy all in with me on it." He then looked at me. "And McFadden, I had your buddy McCain on it as well. Two illustrious and legendary senators there, if ever there were. We expended a good deal of political capital. In the end it just didn't work. That's a pickle you may want to avoid, Maggie."

I leaned over next to Obama. "He calls JFK Skipper?"

Obama burst into a big smile and nodded.

"How have I missed that?" I thought for a second. "Is that another Gilligan's Island thing? If so, he's really got to update is repertoire. Some of these are really tired and dated."

"No,' said Clinton, laughing. "I think it's a PT109 thing."

"You mean the boat that ran into a Japanese destroyer in the Pacific during World War II?" I asked. "Is he OK with joking about that?"

Clinton laughed. "He's smart enough just to go with it."

I couldn't stop laughing about that. And the more I thought about it the better it seemed. It worked just as perfectly in an upper crust, blue-blood, preppy, Ivy League sort of way. That Otter is a genius. At least in some ways.

While we were having this little side discussion Bush was still addressing President Bates. "The difficulty is that no matter how onerous a path to citizenship you lay out, those on the right who stand to profit most from dividing us will deem it to be amnesty, and that alone will torpedo your bill. And on the left they will challenge even your characterization of those illegally crossing the border as illegal aliens. They reject the notion that this is in any way a punishable offense."

Reagan stood up to address the group, as I kind of figured he would with an immigration discussion. I was getting much more familiar with these guys and what makes them tick.

Looking at Washington, Reagan asked, “May I say a few words on this, George?”

Before Washington could utter a response George W. Bush jumped right in. “Yes, you may, Gipper. By all means, go right ahead.” The room exploded in laughter, led by Bush himself.

I looked at Washington to gauge his reaction. His expression was priceless. I’m not sure he knew quite what to make of Otter. Even so, I think he correctly calculated that whatever it was, it was harmless and he shouldn’t be offended by it. No one else tried this kind of stuff with Washington, by the way. I got such a kick out of watching it.

Reagan laughed and waited for the room to settle down.

“When I was president a man once wrote to me to say, ‘You can go to live in France, but you cannot become a Frenchman. You can go to live in Germany or Turkey or Japan, but you cannot become a German, a Turk, or Japanese. But anyone, from any corner of the Earth, can come to live in America and become an American.

“Yes,” he continued, “the torch of Lady Liberty symbolizes our freedom and represents our heritage, the compact with our parents, our grandparents, and our ancestors. It is that lady who gives us our great and special place in the world. For it’s the great life force of each generation of new Americans that guarantees that America’s triumph shall continue unsurpassed into the next century and beyond. Other countries may seek to compete with us; but in one vital area, as a beacon of freedom and opportunity that draws the people of the world, no country on Earth comes close.

“This, I believe, is one of the most important sources of America’s greatness. We lead the world because, unique among nations, we draw our people—our strength—from every country and every corner of the world. And by doing so we continuously renew and enrich our nation. While other countries cling to the stale past, here in America we breathe life into dreams. We create the future, and the world follows us into tomorrow. Thanks to each wave of new arrivals to this land of opportunity, we’re a nation forever young, forever bursting with energy and new ideas, and always on the cutting edge, always leading the world to the next frontier. This quality is vital to our future as a nation. If we ever closed the door to new Americans, our leadership in the world would soon be lost.”

"We did manage to pass a comprehensive, bipartisan immigration bill in 1986. In exchange for legalizing most undocumented immigrants who had arrived in the country prior to January 1, 1982, providing they paid fines and back taxes, demonstrated good moral character and learned to speak English. And we toughened border security in an effort to take away any further the "back door" illegal immigration that had been becoming so prevalent. And we established penalties for hiring illegal aliens."

"A bill like that would not fly today, Mr. President," said President Bates. "On the left they'd object to the requirement that immigrants learn to speak English. And those on the far right and their media outlets would brand the bill as amnesty for law breakers, and Republican legislators would be too fearful of being primaried by them to vote for it."

"Amnesty is the very word we used to describe it ourselves," replied Reagan. "Let's face it, there's just no way you are ever going to deport 5 million undocumented aliens. It's not practical at any level."

"What was 5 million in your day has swollen to over 12 million today," added Obama.

"We have to restrict the illegal immigration," declared Calvin Coolidge, shaking his head in disgust. "New arrivals must be limited to our capacity to absorb them into the ranks of good citizenship. America must be kept American. For this purpose, it is imperative that we continue a strict policy of restricted immigration."

"I'm with you, Calvin," announced Hoover. "I cut immigration back from over 150,000 per year to just under 9,000. We had entered a great depression, of course, and I banned all immigrants who were likely to become a 'public charge.' Those we allowed in had to demonstrate that they could support themselves financially."

I noticed that Teddy Roosevelt was itching to participate.

"You limited immigration to under 9,000, did you, President Hoover?" Teddy Roosevelt asked. "It's fair to say I had a different approach. Would you like to know how many came during my years?"

He paused for a second. I had a feeling this was going to be good, "How about 1.3 million coming through Ellis Island in 1907 alone. 15 million came through between 1900 and 1915. Where exactly do you think we would be today without them, Herbert? Their effort, their resolve, their determination helped build the America that we know today.

"Yes, we let them in. But I insisted that they become in every facet an American, and nothing but American. We have room for but one language here, and that is the English language."

I had to get a word in. "Can I take a moment to describe for people some of the dynamic we now face with what has really become a crisis at the Southern border?"

Washington nodded, "Proceed."

"We simply have to summon the political courage to act," I began. "It is a crisis. Drive through the streets of Los Angeles on in the middle of any day during business hours and you can't help but see hundreds of adults of working age walking the streets, in addition to dozens and dozens of obvious makeshift homeless encampments tucked away in the city's nooks and crannies—or out in the open. I believe that number has swollen to in excess of 15,000 just in LA alone, and it is expected to double in the next four years. The State of California had to put up 50,000 of its roughly 150,000 total homeless population in hotel rooms last year."

"With all due respect, Danny," responded Carter, "let's be careful not confuse undocumented immigrants with homeless."

"OK," I responded, "that's fair, and that can be a subject for another day. But either way, I don't hear you objecting to the characterization of this as a border crisis—which desperately requires our immediate attention."

I paused, and Carter chose not to respond, apparently willing to grant my premise.

I continued. "I believe it's fair to say the climate and the realities as well as the politics are all dramatically different today than they were at the turn of the 20th Century for you Teddy. or during the Depression, or even as recently as the 80's for you President Reagan."

"Absolutely," added President Bates.

"And just like every good political wedge issue we have these days," I added. "there are vultures circling all around exploiting it for their own political or financial gain."

I saw Obama, Clinton and the two Bushes nodding with approval.

I pressed on. "The undocumented immigration most of you in this room faced, including those as recently as you President Reagan and President Bush, involved primarily adult males. Today it's young children. Think about that for a second. Unaccompanied foreign national children are being dropped at our doorstep every day. We are not equipped to efficiently and compassionately deal with that. Some have a family member in the United States, some have credible claims for asylum that need to be properly addressed, and many have neither of those. Do you simply turn them away and leave them to die in Mexico? It is an enormous crisis."

I let that sink in for a second.

"What would you say is causing this latest iteration of this problem?" asked John Adams.

"It all starts with the Northern Triangle," I responded. "That region of Central America that includes Guatamala, Honduras and El Salvador—areas replete with gang-related violence and sexual abuse, where government corruption is rampant, where there is widespread poverty, and now, devastating hurricanes that seem to appear fairly regularly. That confluence of factors triggers in families an instinctive urge to flee that is as old and true as the human race itself. They have an idealized notion of America as a sort of promised land.

"And it's amidst this backdrop that the Mexican drug cartels and other smugglers appear, selling the promise of America at a steep price that now even rivals their drug profits. And of course they spread false information about what's happening at the border. Our obligation to permit asylum seekers to apply for citizenship, and our sympathy for undocumented minors who appear at our border unaccompanied by adults is exploited by the smugglers. What results is a steady stream, not just of illegal crossings at various vulnerable spots along our porous Southern border but direct appeals to our sympathetic, compassionate nature at formal ports of entry.

"We simply don't have the facilities or the resources to properly care for them, house them and sort through their cases in any meaningful way. And the alternative is to callously refuse to permit them entry and turn them back, knowing they'll likely never be returned to their family and home, and may not even survive whatever comes next.

"Any attempt at a political solution is crushed in our divisive political climate. Politicians more interested in earning political points than forging a compromise, and media organizations laser-focused on enhancing ratings and igniting the passions of their viewers combine to create a dynamic where any meaningful compromise is dead on arrival.

"On the right, people see our rise in homeless populations—over a million now by some estimates—our rising unemployment rates, our record income disparity, and our complete lack of affordable housing options, and rightly conclude that we just have to stop the influx of migration at the Southern border—it does both us and them a disservice. On the left people tend to prioritize an idealized notion of America's role in the world, as a haven for those seeking a better life, and our compassion for those experiencing oppression, and our traditional notions of America as a nation of immigrants.

"We can't unilaterally fix that northern triangle. We can't police the coyotes without help from Mexico. We shouldn't be permitting 12 million residents to exist in a permanent state of limbo. And we have an absolute humanitarian crisis at the border. We desperately need Congress to come together and take comprehensive action to address all of this."

"How'd I do guys?" I asked, looking at the table of our modern presidents.

I got a few thumbs up and nods of approval. Many of the faces in the room looked quite perplexed.

"Where do we possibly go from here?" asked Jefferson. I could see his brain working overtime.

"Allow me to attempt an answer," said Obama, standing up at his table.

"This always comes down to people. On the one hand, most Americans, I think, want to make sure people follow the rules, and they get frustrated when they hear of people who just cut the line or try to take advantage of living in the United States without accepting those responsibilities. On the other hand, when you talk to a lot of families who have an undocumented member in them, what you discover is they work hard, may work two or three jobs—sometimes in the lowest paying jobs. And they aspire to the same things that all of us aspire to in terms of building a better life for their kids. And when you talk to the families they are fearful that a mother might be deported and not see her children. And you hear about young people who were brought here when they were two or three years old and are as American as any of us in attitude and love of country but don't have the right papers and as a consequence they can't apply for scholarships and they can't travel because they are fearful that it might mean they get deported. What you realize is that that's not what America's about.

"So what we want is a system where people are held accountable.

Where those who have broken the law are going to have to make some amends and get right with the law but also we want a system that takes into account that there are good people out there who made a mistake but are very much our neighbors, our friends, and whose kids play with our kids. And they love this country and want to contribute to its success. If we are going to be a nation of laws and a nation of immigrants we are going to have to make sure that we are giving them that opportunity. I think that's the kind of common sense solution that most Americans would believe in.

"I firmly believe we can construct a compromise that the vast majority of Americans can live with comprised of enhanced enforcement at the border, gradual path to citizenship for the undocumented already here after payment of taxes and fees."

"Yes," added President Bates. "There is plenty of middle ground with which to forge such a consensus. I believe that a comprehensive, grand bargain type of bill, that emphasizes additional border security, a gradual path to citizenship for some of these undocumented immigrants, with fees, taxes and good behavior requirements over many years, combined with workplace enforcement, could solve so much of this once and for all. We would couple that with a joint US and Mexico program to return those turned away at the border, and for prosecution of human smugglers. We need to properly fund the system we have in place to process these asylum cases so we can do so much more quickly and effectively. Additionally, I believe we need to appeal to the UNHCR—the UN Refugee Agency—to process Central American children for refugee status at safe locations near their home countries well before they would even get here. And we need to require Mexico to offer its own meaningful asylum process too, rather than simply serve as a superhighway delivering all these people to our border.

"And, finally, I'd add a refined system of obtaining VISAs for low-paying service and farm-related work that Americans traditionally are unwilling to do." She stopped there and looked around.

"Did I miss anything, fellas," she asked, looking at me, Obama, Clinton and George W. Bush.

"You know the politics of this well, Maggie," responded Clinton. "Those on the far left will say you lack compassion and those on the far right will say you are granting amnesty to lawbreakers."

"Well," added Reagan, "if both extremes are upset perhaps that's the surest sign she's on the right track."

"I do believe, gentlemen," continued Maggie, "that this will be palatable to the moderates of both parties, in addition to the 42% of independents Danny is always talking about."

"I agree with that assessment," responded Clinton.

"Me too," added Obama. "Remember, we deported over 2.5 million people during my time, and my friends on the far left called me 'The Deporter in Chief.' You are going to take plenty of incoming fire and expend political capital, but you will have to in order to forge a solution. But we all know this country desperately needs a solution. And one thing's for certain—you'll need all those independents and moderates vocally supporting you."

There was a hush on the room for several moments, allowing Obama's reference to independents to hang in the air.

"It sounds as though it needs to in fact be driven by these independents you refer to," concluded Jefferson, "perhaps rather than the two parties, each of which are comprised of many who will inevitably oppose any attempts to compromise."

George W. Bush cracked a slight smile. "Maggie, if there were just someone out there you could lean on to help you appeal to that legion of independents and moderates." He paused, and smiled a little more.

"Someone respected and revered by that group, with a track record of genuine credibility with them that they would all listen to," added Obama.

Then Clinton, with a broad smile and all eyes in the room slowly turning to me, finished the thought. "Someone not shy about seeking the spotlight and claiming the mantle of putting country first above all other political or personal agendas."

I smiled, raised my hands up in a bit of self-defense and shook my head. "If it were up to me, of course you all know I'd be all in. I'd do anything for the cause. However, I fear our Los Gatos friend might be a tad more complicated than me. But it's certainly worth a try. Good luck with that. I sure wish I could help."

"Well, I'm certainly willing to give it a shot," said Maggie. "California here I come."

I'm not sure exactly why I suddenly felt anxious but I did. I motioned to Mary Ann behind the bar. "M.A., I may need a strong cocktail over here."

“Sure thing. What can I make you?” she shouted back.

“Use your imagination.”

Chapter Forty

On a Clear Day in Boston You Can See Galway
March 17, 2023
The Saloon

I walked into the Saloon and smiled immediately at the sound of dueling fiddles racing through a particularly rousing version of "Drowsy Maggie."

Oh my God, I thought. *Could this actually be St Patrick's Day*? Who ever knew what day or month it was these days from this present station in life I found myself in this Saloon existence—if you could even call it a station in life. I'm not sure what exactly it is.

Or was this just another tribute to our new President Maggie? That would be hard to believe, since while everyone recognizes this song when they hear it on St. Paddy's Day, no one else ever seems to know the name of it, and no one in here would connect it with her, I suspect. Except me of course.

But that song being performed live and the thought of St. Patrick's Day in the Saloon fired me up like nothing else. My pace quickened as I rounded the back of the bar and caught a glimpse of the band stand. A massive Celtic harp sat unattended at the edge of the bar, waiting for just the right song and accompanist. On a bench nearby I saw bagpipes. A couple of twenty-something female fiddle players were killing it, while a similarly aged young man played piano as a couple more manned guitars. I recognized an extra-large bottle of Bushmills looking right at home and well-loved on the top of the piano. I come from a staunch Jameson family but I will happily cross the aisle, or the northern border, to the Bushmills side in a pinch. Any port in a storm, as they say.

One look at MaryAnn confirmed that my dreams had indeed come true. At least for today. She approached me in a dark green tight velvet skirt with an emerald green fascinator in her hair. With her dark complexion and deep brown eyes she didn't look the least bit Irish, but that didn't matter a lick. It melted my heart.

"Happy St. Patrick's Day, DannyMac. We've all been waiting for you."

I've asked this before, but is this not the absolute perfect bar for me?

"I wish I had known," I responded. "I'd have been here at the crack of dawn."

"Yes—I believe that's what they all feared. Otter thought it might just be better for both you and us if you didn't have any advance notice. They didn't think you'd last beyond noon. They kept the place locked until 4."

"I need to make up for lost time. I'd better get rolling here."

As I started to walk away she interrupted. "Oh, and one more thing—Otter told the band you'd sing with them."

I laughed out loud. "In that case I'm really gonna need to make up for lost time."

"Don't overdo it, sir. President Bates wants to have a serious conversation with you."

That stopped me in my tracks. "You've gotta be kidding me."

She raised her voice a few decibels. "That's what I said!" She laughed out loud. "I don't think she has any idea who you really are or what makes you tick."

"I agree with you there, M.A."

"And I'm not sure anybody does, either," she added, before turning and scampering off.

The band finished "Drowsy Maggie" and rolled right into a quite animated version of "I'm Shipping Up to Boston" that would have made even the Dropkick Murphys proud. Yes indeed, this versatile young band would have been right at home in Dublin—or New York City.

The mood in the Saloon was perfect for the occasion. The only source of light came from the dim gas lamps interspersed throughout the large room and the brilliant light emanating from the majestic backbar which extended all the way up to the tin tile ceiling and stored any type and brand of intoxicant a president could ever hope for. All that variety wouldn't be needed today, however, but it provided the perfect backdrop.

My smile broadened as I caught a glimpse of Big Time, Haskell and Slick tending bar in classic plaid lambswool kilts. Priceless. I considered for a brief moment stopping to ask if they had a spare laying around but thought better of it. I was fully aware, however, that I may be reevaluating that decision in a couple hours.

I paused at an empty table. The centerpieces consisted of gorgeous yellow St. Patrick tea roses set amongst a bed of dark green shamrocks. But what most caught my eye was the vintage weathered paper scrolls scattered amongst the center of each table appearing as if they had been plucked right from old first edition novels—each with a memorable passage of a poem or story from the likes of Yeats, Oscar Wilde, James Joyce, Samuel Beckett, Katharine Tynan, Evan Boland, Thomas Moore and more. What a perfect touch.

Now this was a proper St. Paddy's Day function if ever there had been one.

My eyes now fully adjusted to the dim light, I looked around the room to see it was mostly full, and the atmosphere electric. Ginger appeared in front of me with a shot of Jameson and a Guinness.

"I think they're saving a spot for you at this table, Mr. President," she said, pointing the large oaken table in the center of the room. One empty chair remained.

For a moment I felt remarkably like a bride at her wedding, but then this collection of wait staff always seemed to make me feel that way.

I took the empty seat and looked around. A fine collection of my predecessors if ever there was one. Reagan, Kennedy, Jackson, Polk, Buchanan, Grant, Arthur, McKinley.

"Are there seating arrangements today?" I asked as I sat down.

"This table is reserved, I believe, for those amongst us of Irish descent," answered McKinley.

That prompted me to scan the occupants of the table again.

"Both my mother and my father were born in Ireland," said Andrew Jackson.

"So was my father," added Chester Arthur.

"My father was from Donegal and my mother from County Tryrone," said Buchanan.

Kennedy looked like he was about to jump in when Reagan interrupted him. "The whole world is familiar with your genealogy, Jack."

"I'm thrilled to be at this table, gentlemen," I said. "My mom raised me to be incredibly proud of our Irish heritage. But I have to say, in my mind, the beauty of St. Patrick's Day, at least in America, is that it makes no difference whatsoever if you grew up speaking Gaelic or you if couldn't so much as pick out Ireland on a map of the British Isles, on this one day we are all Irish."

At that moment we looked at the dance floor and saw MA with Otter and Clinton with Ginger trying to do some kind of makeshift Riverdance imitation to the band's soaring version of "Finnegan's Wake."

"That's what I mean," I said, pointing out to the dance floor. Probably not a drop of Irish blood in any of them."

The group laughed at the sight of the two couples giving it their all.

"That right there is what it's all about. I really don't at all care whether you refer to it as St. Paddy's or St. Patty's. Or whether you're drinking a properly pulled pint of Guinness with the head just proud of the rim, as they say, or a cheap green beer in a tacky see-through plastic cup, it's all heaven to me."

Ten minutes later Mary Ann appeared over my shoulder.

"Otter wants you to sing with the band, sir."

"Right now?" I asked. "It's a little early for that, don't you think?"

"He thinks there's just a narrow window of time in your case, after which it will be too late."

I laughed out loud at that. Perhaps some truth lay deep within that concern. I wondered what I had done in this group that was driving this reputation I seemed to have. Or perhaps it was just written all over my face.

"Sure," I said. "Let me have a shot first."

"Certainly. Jameson? Bushmills?"

"Make it Jameson. I'm a good Catholic boy. Or at the very least a Catholic boy."

"I hate to disappoint you, Danny," said Kennedy, "but I believe Bushmills was founded by a Catholic and Jameson by a Protestant."

"Wow. How ironic. I did not know that," I responded. "But that doesn't trouble me in the least. When it comes to drinking I consider myself agnostic."

***

Moments later I was being escorted up to the bandstand and greeting the musicians. They seemed to have plenty of attitude, like most young Irish of course, but eager to get the most out of this crowd, which couldn't have been quite in their wheelhouse.

"You guys ready for karaoke hour?" I asked.

"Whatever you like," the young lead guitarist responded.

"Do you know the Waterboys?"

Several responded with a grin and a thumbs up.

"I think I could give "Fisherman's Blues" a go."

They smiled, seemingly excited by that answer. The next thing I knew the fiddles were off and running and I was giving that tune everything I had. It was kind of like an out of body experience. Jameson can do that for me. So can tequila.

The full bar staff and many of the presidents gathered on the dance floor—some to dance and some just for the sheer spectacle of it all. I took solace in the thought that there was no way possible that this would ever end up on YouTube or TikTok. At least I didn't think so.

I walked off quickly when it was finished amidst pleas for me to stay—they were begging not because I was so good but because the whole scene was quite entertaining. But once they saw Ginger take the microphone, believe me, no one wanted to hear from me again.

As Ginger started in on Sinead O'Connor's "Nothing Compares 2U," remarkably well, by the way, Mary Ann effusively congratulated me on my effort.

"You must have a little Irish in you somewhere, Mary Ann, don't you?"

"Does Mexican count?"

"Yes—as a matter of fact. It does."

"Remember, my dad was Mexican."

"I do recall that," I said. "The Irish and the Mexicans are indeed kindred spirits. Both bastions of Catholicism. Both a bit snake bitten with tragic, tormented histories. Dominated for all time by a powerful neighbor. Both hemorrhaging waves and waves of immigrants to America out of which sprang vibrant new life throughout this country. And both maintained an indomitable spirit through it all that persists to this day."

"I've always thought that too! And don't forget how St. Patrick's Day and Cinco de Mayo are really two versions of the very same day."

"Ha! And you could argue that both are more celebrated in America than in their home countries. But we each should really have a whole month to celebrate, like the Germans do, rather than just a day."

"I think we should both be thankful we don't have an entire month. Think about it."

"You're absolutely right. Of course."

I returned to the area directly in front of the bar where it looked like Otter had been trying desperately to get Skipper to take a turn at the mic with the band. Kennedy, of course, was having none of it. JFK had a certain style and class about him that would have been potentially compromised. I, on the other hand, had no such complicating issues.

Skipper and I joined about twenty presidents who had gathered by the bar enjoying the moment. Perfect timing. Washington had just raised his glass of whiskey to the group.

"To Ireland," Washington began, "that dear friend of my country in my country's most friendless days."

The group happily drank to that.

Washington continued. "Ben Franklin visited Ireland in 1772 and was received by the Irish Parliament, which was neither independent nor free, and found them very much disposed to be friends of America. Moreover, so many Irish immigrants or descendants of Irish immigrants fought valiantly for our Continental Army. In fact, half of all members of the Pennsylvania state militia fighting for us were Irish by birth or descent. So strong was their influence, that at the time, Lord Mountjoy lamented to the British Parliament that "we have lost America through the Irish."

General Grant added, "We all know of the impact of the Irish Brigade fighting against Lee's army. Their bravery at Fredericksburg was unsurpassed. We had over 140,000 Irish fighting for us. We even permitted many units to fight under an Irish battle flag. In fact, General Sumner would inquire before each battle, 'Where are my green flags? Where are my Irish?'"

"I once kissed one of those green flags in front of the troops," stated Lincoln proudly, "when I visited General McClellan's army at Harrison's Landing. As I did so I declared, 'God bless the Irish flag.'"

Grant then added, "Many of those Irish who fought so valiantly for us in the War later invaded Canada, together with many Irishmen who fought for the South, in the hopes of holding it hostage in order to coerce Britain to grant Ireland its freedom."

"What? You have got to be kidding," exclaimed Reagan.

"No, sir. It had to be one the whackiest military campaigns ever envisaged," responded Grant.

"How did they make out?" asked Reagan.

"About how you'd expect," responded Kennedy, drawing many laughs.

Wow. This was some pretty priceless stuff to witness for a guy like me. I had no idea about any of this. I'm sure a lot of Americans don't.

I wasn't sure anyone would even attempt to follow Washington, Lincoln, and Grant, but Kennedy rose to the occasion. Of course he did.

"My visit to Ireland as president was one of the most memorable weeks of my life. They were so proud that an Irish American had ascended to the American presidency. And of course I played that card for everything I could. I drew thundering applause when I told them that on a clear day in Boston, you can see Galway."

"I enjoyed a memorable visit to Ireland as president as well, Jack," said Ronald Reagan. "The highlight was the day we helicoptered from Ashford Castle to Ballyporeen in County Tipperary— the home of my great grandfather. I'm proud to say they named a pub there after me."

"There can't be any higher honor in Ireland than that," I declared.

"Unless, perhaps, it's a church," added Kennedy.

"Oh I'd much rather a pub than a church, Jack," replied Reagan. "Correct me if I'm mistaken, but I'm fairly certain you have to be dead to get your name on a church over there."

About an hour later I was still at the bar when Matty got my attention. "I'm sorry to trouble you, DannyMac, but I think President Bates is hoping to get some time with you.

"Yes, of course," I said, looking out across the room for her. I saw her sitting with George H. W. Bush and Gerald Ford in a booth at the back of the room. I made my way back to join them.

As I got closer Maggie saw me. "I hope you are sufficiently enjoying yourself, Danny. This is like Christmas morning for you, is it not? Can you spare a couple of minutes to talk a little shop?"

"Of course, I responded. I'm all yours for the duration of my next drink."

"I think I'm gonna need a lot more time than that."

"I'm surprised you aren't leading the charge today yourself—with all I've heard about St. Patrick's Day in your hometown."

"It's bigger than Mardi Gras there, Danny."

"Holy cow. Really?"

"OK, that might be a little white lie. But it is just the most precious and grand throwdown you ever did see. Been going on in Savannah since 1824 too. You really must go."

"I am ashamed that I never had the pleasure. Might be too late for me now. But something you definitely should mention to your buddy in Los Gatos."

"Well . . . I'm not sure how much of a buddy he is, but that's kind of what I wanted to talk to you about today."

"Hey, I'm no expert on that dude. I want to make that clear."

We both laughed. What a strange and absurd thing to even consider.

"How can I help you, Maggie? I'm happy to do so in any way I can."

"As you know from the other night in here, I've decided to take the plunge and try to pass something on immigration. It's just too important to the country to fix this once and for all, and political malpractice to continue to ignore it. I may well fail, but I couldn't live with myself if I didn't at least try."

"Good for you."

"But I actually really believe it has a fighting chance. The bill itself has 59% of the public in favor of it."

"Of course, but in a divided Congress it may still be an uphill battle."

"I'm going out to California to meet with your alter ego—is that the best word for it? Just as all of you have advised me to do. I think if I had his help with independents I might be able to pull this off. He has always been cordial, but we aren't particularly close, as some of my staff have been openly critical of his administration. Some of it mean-spirited too."

"But you have a meeting with him?"

"Yes."

"On the calendar?"

"Yes."

"And he knows what it's about?"

"Yes, yes, yes."

"Well I'd say that's a good start."

"I need him to be on board. I'd love him to give me some advice. Maybe even get on board."

"Well, I'd focus less on you needing him to do this and more on the country needing it. Make the case that the country needs him, in fact, desperately. And that his support is paramount in getting this to the finish line."

"It is."

"Don't be shy about telling him that. He's always up there on his high horse blathering on and on about country over party. Play that card for all it's worth. Given the ground he has staked out over time, that will be hard for someone like him to pass up."

"You mean someone like you," she corrected, smiling.

"Yes, yes, of course. Whatever." I didn't want to think too hard about it but I guess she was right. I did kind of enjoy taking shots at him though.

At that moment Otter appeared. "Peaches, you promised me you'd sing with the band."

Maggie turned and looked directly at me, as if I was somehow to blame. I laughed.

"OK, I will," she responded.

"What are you going to sing," I asked. I loved that she thought nothing of taking the mic again when asked. What a gamer. She had spunk.

"My favorite Irish song is Fields of Athenry," she responded. "I love the melody. It is terribly sad, though."

"They're all sad, Maggie. And tragic. And terribly heartbreaking. So are their novels, and their poems. And their entire history, for that matter. But I applaud that choice of song. All their national athletic teams have adopted it, and their fans even sing it in the middle of their games. It is hysterical to hear that song coming from the crowd during a match."

She stood up to go deliver her performance.

"One last thing on your meeting," I asked. "When is it?"

"This week. I am going out there. I'll tack on a little fundraising in Silicon Valley while I'm in the neighborhood."

"And where, might I ask, will this historic powwow be taking place?"

"A restaurant near his office."

"A restaurant? That seems odd," I responded.

She started to walk away.

"What restaurant?"

"Hennigans? Or something like that."

She walked away leaving me with a puzzled look.

Hennigans? I repeated it a few more times.

Then it hit me. Hannegan's. He's meeting Maggie Bates at frickin Hannegan's! Wow. I absolutely love it. I guess you could call it a restaurant rather than a pub—perhaps if you wanted to downplay the fact that it is indeed an Irish pub. I'm guessing any pub in Ireland that so much as serves soda crackers qualifies as a restaurant over there. But Hannegan's is, at its core, an epic watering hole if there ever was one.

A moment later came another revelation. *His post presidency White House office is right near Hannegan's? How utterly perfect.*

I sat there drinking my Irish Buck wondering if I'd ever had a more proud moment. I'm sure I had but it was hard to think of any at the time. This guy might be a lot more like my hero than my alter ego.

An hour later, as Jefferson was trying his hand with the band on that massive harp, I joined a group of my predecessors as they were discussing typical St. Patrick's Days in their lives, both while president and before. I was gearing up to tell my story of St. Paddy's for me back in the day, except their stories were all such tame stuff—mostly staged events designed to win political points with Irish Americans or Catholics.

After all the others had weighed in, I thought twice about whether to add my own experience to the mix, knowing it would perhaps "stand out" a bit, shall we say. Against my better judgement I just let it rip.

"Back in the day I'd get started at 8:00 a.m. slamming Jameson on the train into the city with a bunch of new best friends I just met, hit the parade hard all day, and then finish up late night at McSorley's drinking beer until we could no longer speak."

There was silence for a moment before they all burst into laughter.

"You realize of course there actually are people who do that, don't you?" Gerald Ford replied.

"Craziest thing I've ever seen," added Carter. "That is so terribly funny but also so very sad."

Then it dawned on me. They all thought I was joking.

Chapter Forty-One

My Mount Rushmore of Bartenders
March 22, 2023

I hadn't really ever seen Hannegan's like this before. It was nearly empty, except for about a dozen obvious Secret Service agents scattered throughout. The entire block was closed off as well.

When President Bates sat down across the table from me I couldn't help but smile.

"It tells me everything I need to know about you that you wanted to meet me here," I said.

"Let's just say I got some really good advice," she responded.

I laughed. "I don't think it's a particularly well-kept secret that I might be fond of this place."

I looked around. "This is quite a security presence," I said.

I didn't really recall anything quite this extensive for this type of an event when I was president.

"Ever since we took action in North Korea, the threat level has been at an all-time high. Unfortunately, I've gotten used to it."

She looked sharp as she always does, dressed much more formally than this pub generally warrants —a very charming presence in a mid-length sleeveless tan dress and her trademark pearl necklace and earrings.

My guy Gil came over to say hello.

"Welcome to Hannegan's," he said, looking at the two of us. "It is such an honor to host you."

"What was your name again, sir?" I asked.

He broke into a smile, giving me away instantly.

"Oh please don't try to act like you aren't here six times a week," Maggie said. I guess she is as smart as everyone says she is.

"This, Madame President, is Gil. He has been tending bar here for twenty years, and really runs the place for the owners. He has also earned himself a spot up there on my own personal Mount Rushmore of all-time bartenders."

"Well that is certainly high praise indeed," she responded, "given the legions of bartenders you surely have known over the years."

I nodded. I couldn't really disagree with that.

"And I think I happen to know one or two of the others who might share the face of that mountain with him," she added, giving me a bit of a look and smile.

Alright, I thought, she's clearly been to the saloon, and maybe she's similarly taken by some of the staff there. Speaks well of her. I chose not to formally acknowledge the obvious reference, however, following the precedent set by my predecessors. But it was sure tempting. God I missed that place. It's so hard to believe that even happened to me. It seems now almost as if it was all a dream. I was dying to know how Mary Ann, Otter, Matty, Teddy and all the others were doing. I can't think of them all without smiling.

"It sure is a pleasure to meet you," Gil," Maggie said. "And thank you for the hospitality."

"Don't mention it. We are happy to do it."

It appeared as if Gil was about to walk away, but he turned back toward at us. He seemed to be uncertain as to whether to say something else. Finally he just blurted it out. "I hope you don't mind me saying this, ma'am, but you are even more striking in person that you are on the television."

Maggie beamed. "Well, let's just make it crystal clear for the record that I definitely do not mind you saying so."

Gil beamed, then turned again to walk away. I felt the need to keep him with us a bit longer.

"You might be interested to know, Madam President," I said, "that while Gil might spend his nights in here, he spends most of his days ocean fishing."

"That sounds like an idyllic life to me," she said. "I've spent a lot of time on the ocean myself. I dearly miss it. Where do you fish?"

"South of here—Monterey Bay, and off of Big Sur, and as far north as the Farallon Islands. It depends on what we're looking for, and how much time we have."

"What are you typically looking for?"

“A lot of Rockfish, lingcod. Some good-sized King Salmon in the summer, and of course, the very best Dungeness Crab in the winter. Do you like deep sea fishing?”

“Yes, of course, though I’m more partial to sailing. But I’ve got some serious anglers in my family back in Georgia.”

He smiled. “What are they catching down there?”

“Oh, lots of spotted sea trout, redfish, mackerel, sheepshead.”

He looked at me. “This lady knows the ocean.” I could tell he was thrilled with the discussion. And pleasantly surprised. But not nearly as much as she was.

“I think she knows a lot of things,” I responded.

“What kind of boat do you have?” she asked.

“A 52 foot Delta Sport Fisher yacht.”

“I’m impressed.”

“Well, before you get too impressed it’s twenty years old. But it’s in great shape. Reaches about 45 knots. Nice big cockpit. Three nice staterooms. It more than gets the job done.”

“I’d love to see some of your stunning coastline from the water sometime,” she said. She was clearly focused only on Gil now.

“Well, you’re quite welcome to accompany me anytime you like, ma’am.”

“I may just take you up on that, Gil.” She looked at me with a big smile. His jaw dropped a bit as he contemplated that rather remarkable response. I could see how she had ascended through the ranks so rapidly. I thought I had a way with people, but it was clear I had absolutely nothing on her.

“I guarantee you this, you won’t be disappointed,” he responded. Good for him.

“Well then, that settles it. I’m coming back.”

“Promise me you’ll let me tag along,” I said. “I may need a healthy amount of Dramamine, but I wouldn’t miss that moment for the world.”

Again, Gil turned to leave, but this time Maggie brought him back. “Let me ask you this,” she said. I’m always fascinated by what people name their boats. What do you call that Delta cruiser of yours?”

He smiled. “*Pastures of Heaven*. I don’t expect you to know . . .”

“John Steinbeck,” she said, cutting him off.

“Oh my God,” he said.

"I go pretty deep on classic American Lit."

"Wow. Yes you do."

"And I know enough to know he's from right around here. Isn't that right?" she asked.

"Yes, indeed. Grew up right here in Salinas. And he wrote so much about this area."

"I'm not sure I align perfectly with him politically but I have to respect his literary chops. I admire what he did so much. An essential voice."

Gil smiled broadly, thrilled with this exchange. "I can appreciate that," he responded.

Then, rather sheepishly, he added. "I write a little too, and he's a bit of a hero for me in that regard."

"Fiction?"

"Yes, ma'am.

"Short stories?"

"Some yes, but a handful of full-length as well."

"Well I'll be. I would love to read what you've written."

Gil looked over and at and flashed me the most I-cannot-frickin-believe-this look I have ever seen.

"Oh, I don't think you'd be much interested in . . ."

"Describe what you write," she asked.

"Not like Steinbeck, that's for sure. I write stories about a fisherman in a fictional town on the Central Coast of California. As much as he wants to lead just a simple life, strange and sometimes extraordinary things keep happening to him."

"I love it already. I'm in. Is it autobiographical?"

"No, no, no. I'm a bit like Walter Mitty, I'm afraid to say."

"Well, I'd love to read some of it."

I'd be honored if you would, Mrs. President."

"Call me Maggie, Gil. And tell me, when on earth do you possibly find time to write?"

"I fish in the morning, write in the afternoon, and see everybody I would ever want to see in this place at night."

"What a marvelous life. Promise me you'll send me some of your writing."

"I shall do that, ma'am."

With that, he walked away—a bit dumfounded, but thrilled nonetheless. And how enlightening for me to witness that. I had no idea he was a writer and I've known him for years. And she elicited that from him in just a few brief moments at their very first meeting.

As he walked away she kept her eyes on him.

"I'm so glad you got to meet Gil," I said.

"Are you kidding me?" she responded. "A bartender, a fisherman and a novelist? Be still, my heart."

I laughed. Now I was really starting to like her.

"And I love your little bar here. I happen to know you are a bit of a saloon connoisseur."

I laughed. "And how did you come by that?"

"Oh, let's just say I've picked up a few vibes from the ghosts in the attic."

"I can't deny it. I've frequented some pretty spectacular bars in my life. I have to say I've never missed an old girlfriend like I missed an old bar."

To that, she responded with a smile, "Gee, that tells me so much about you, Danny."

Sensing her sarcasm, I added "Of course, I love Denyse way more than any bar."

"And I'm sure just knowing that warms her heart to no end."

OK, I'm fairly certain she was mocking me now and loving every moment of it but she had a very convincing way of pulling it off.

After we ordered some light lunch she got down to the business at hand.

"I came here, as you know, to solicit your help."

"Yes, I had a feeling."

"You're the one person in this whole country, sir, who can get this immigration grand compromise across the finish line."

"I am flattered by that. I don't know that that is true, however. You underestimate your own political skills. And please call me Danny."

"I will. If you call me Margaret, or better yet, Maggie. Most people I care about call me that."

"Of course. Happy to. I didn't want to appear any less formal with you than I would be with a male president."

"Have you known many of our male presidents?" She smiled, and I couldn't help but do so myself as well. But I wasn't taking the bait.

She continued. "And let me start by apologizing for the words of some of my staff about you and your administration."

"I appreciate that, Maggie, but there's no need to say that. I know politics is a nasty business and I did manage to develop a thick skin over time. People are only doing what they think they need to do politically."

"Fair enough, but they have taken it too far and I wanted you to hear that from me."

"Thank you."

"Let me get to the point. I desperately need your help on immigration. Your country needs your help. Are you willing to assist me in what certainly promises to be a bit of a street fight at times? Both the Republican and Democratic bases will fight us furiously."

"I am, depending on how we go about it. If this is truly a bipartisan effort I can see myself helping the cause. I think there are several elements necessary in order to get this done. I think you have to ignore the 10-15% on either extreme who will be the loudest voices in opposition. On the left that means the ones who simply want open borders, unlimited immigration, no new border enforcement and no consequences for illegally crossing. They'll label you as uncaring and possibly racist as well for even trying. And on the right that means ignoring those that can't stomach any conceivable path to citizenship by anyone who may have ever entered this country illegally or overstayed a visa, no matter how long ago, even if they have been gainfully employed and paying taxes for years. They'll brand it as amnesty and flood the airwaves in opposition.

"Secondly, I think you have to similarly ignore the loudest voices in Congress on this too—which will be the ones taking their cues directly from those two extremes.

"Most importantly, I suggest you take your grand compromise and go sell it directly to the people in a comprehensive campaign. If all the elements are there for both sides, you'll begin with 60-65% approval on it, and with a campaign you may be able to push that to close to 70% or higher, at which time Congress may have no choice but to come along. The key is it can't be viewed as a Democratic bill or Republican bill, but a genuinely bipartisan effort.

"I'm happy to help if you proceed in that manner and if the entire effort maintains a truly bipartisan spirit. I'll appeal to Alliance candidates to get behind it and be vocal about it. This is precisely the type of political effort the Alliance was designed to spearhead. And I'll do the Sunday News shows, the talk shows and pen op-eds about it too. And I'll encourage Hannah to push it on her new network, because it certainly will take a lot of incoming fire from the partisan cable and radio talking heads."

Maggie smiled and nodded her head.

How's that?" I asked.

"Well, you certainly seem to know that of which you speak."

"I've been down that road before."

"As for your offer to help and your conditions, I'll take it," she said, grinning ear to ear. "It's more than I ever would have imagined. Where do I sign?"

I gave her a bit of an incredulous look. "Did you think I was gonna say, 'No, Maggie, you're on your own?' If that's the case, you're really gonna need better intelligence on me."

"Oh, I can't imagine I could have gotten anyone better advising me about you."

As I started to contemplate what she was really getting at, she added, "pretty sure that wouldn't even be possible."

I think I knew what she was referring to, and it kind of blew my mind.

Chapter Forty-Two

Tina's Date
April 12, 2023

Tina stuck her head in my office. She looked a bit more gussied up than usual. She always looks good, but there was a little something extra today about her makeup and hair.

"You burning the midnight oil, Boss?" she asked.

It wasn't even 6:00 pm.

"Are you mocking me?"

"Not at all. Hey you've worked your tail off all your life and you have the results to show for it. I love that you are now prioritizing your family and yourself a bit."

"Well, I'm not doing that today. It's been wall to wall phone calls and videoconferences with congressmen about this immigration bill."

Her gaze moved off of me across the room to the big screen on my wall that was tuned into the Dodger/Mets game coming from Citi Field. Walker Buehler was in mid-windup, working on a two-hitter in the bottom of the sixth.

"Yeah, I can see that." She said, smiling. " Sure looks like you've had a rough day."

God she was hard on me.

"I just got off the phone with Senator Murkowski. I swear!"

She laughed. "I'm just busting on you. I spent a lot of time myself on a videoconference today with people from DHS and Justice. They are all in on this—and they really value our assistance. They love you now."

"They should! I'm spending a fair amount of political capital on this thing. But I'm good with that. It's all for a good cause, and it's not like there's anything else I needed that for anyway."

"How's that all going?"

"I'm finding these Congressmen are all very accepting of it. Those on both sides welcome the compromise and think it's needed. The problem is that they're all deathly afraid of being primaried over it. That seems to be the trouble with any of these folks compromising or seeking common ground these days—it sets in motion a process by the extremes to get rid of them. They all want assurances I'll have their back, and that I'll come campaign for them, and they all seek a promise that the Alliance won't run a candidate against them. It is all political calculation."

"Did you expect anything different?"

"Not really. I made some inroads though. I think we'll have the sixty votes in the Senate necessary to invoke cloture, as long as the partisan media on either side don't go all in."

"Wow. Nice work. And how about the House?"

"I think we should have 55 to 60 percent—again assuming the extremes don't start using this as a wedge issue to score political points with their base."

"Well I'm not certain that's a safe assumption at all."

"You're right. But I'm an optimist. I want to believe the very best in people."

She seemed a little fidgety.

"Are you cutting out," I asked.

"I suspect I'm going to regret telling you this, but I actually have a date. So yes, I'm getting out of here a bit early for me."

"Oh my. Good for you. And, of course, for . . ." I kind of let that trail off as I froze at whether to use "him" or "her." I didn't want to assume anything or offend her if I got that wrong.

She picked up on my hesitancy about that immediately. And chose to exploit it. As only she can.

"What were you going to say there?"

"Nothing."

"No, you kind of stopped midsentence. Finish that thought."

Then I got an idea.

"What's the name of your date?" I asked with a bit of a smile. She could see what I was attempting of course.

"Blair," she said, smiling right back. "I see what you tried to do there. I'm not sure that answer helps you at all."

I thought for a few seconds. "Who will be driving?"

"Are you so old fashioned that you think that's a telltale sign these days?"

"Let me ask you this, will this Blair person be drinking wine or beer?"

"You do realize, of course, that I'm your employee now, and what once may have been harmless, playful banter in a saloon is now actionable sexual harassment."

"Sexual harassment? Really? So you think somehow crosses a line? You could practically be my daughter."

"First of all, can you point to even one man in human history that would have passed on a woman because of her age? And secondly, no, I don't believe you are hitting on me. For God sakes, you've got Denyse of all people to come home to every night. You hit the lottery with her—smart, great mom, engaging, smokin' hot even at almost fifty, and she loves you. What would you possibly need with me?"

"Hold on a second," I said. "So somehow it's ok within workplace culture rules for you to casually reference that my wife is smokin' hot, but I'm not permitted to so much as inquire as to the name of your date—a date, mind you, that you that you happened to mention to me in the first place? It's not like I brought it up or went looking for it."

"OK, actually you may have a point there. I'm proud of you."

"Let's both be clear about this," I said, "if there's any awkwardness to these conversations it's simply because that is precisely what you're aiming for."

She didn't respond. For once I think she knew I had maneuvered her into checkmate.

"Well, I hope you and Blair have a blast regardless of who drives, what each of you drinks and which bathrooms you choose to use."

Smiling broadly now, she said, "And say hello to Denyse for me." Then she winked. I think she got that from Otter. He used to do that all the time. I miss that dude.

She started to walk out but then turned back one more time. "By the way, I think I need to know this. Were you trying to find out what sex Blair was born as or what sex Blair identifies as now?"

I looked aghast.

"I'm just messing with you, now." She laughed hard. "Love working with you, Boss."

I just shook my head. She is something else. I do get a kick out of her, though. And I much prefer that to someone who could never even try to challenge me or go toe to toe.

With that she turned and hustled off to meet up with Blair. And by the way, I'm not convinced that isn't some purposely androgynous made up name in the first place.

Moments later my phone rang. I saw it was Murph.

"Hey stranger," I said.

"Thanks so much for picking up," she responded. "Hey, I know you're doing a lot of behind the scenes stuff on this immigration effort, but I'd caution you against going all in publicly. I thought it was really important to give you that advice."

"Go right ahead. I appreciate it. As always, I really want to hear what you think."

"I think it's alright to lobby behind the scenes, and to encourage the Alliance members to get behind it publicly or privately, but I feel strongly that you should keep your own role private. Can I be candid?

"Yes, yes. Please."

"I think politically you have nothing to gain and everything to lose. If the bill passes President Bates gets the victory lap, not you. She alone will reap the political benefits. On the other hand, if it fails you fail with it, and in a way you would have attached yourself to her, and she's been struggling to get her approval ratings back up ever since her North Korea debacle. That's not really good place to be."

I didn't respond, choosing instead just to take it all in."

"And, just as importantly, I think it's a little unseemly for an ex-president as well. I think there's a reason we really haven't seen aggressive, public efforts by former presidents on bills like this."

"I know. I've thought about all that, but I'm not overly concerned about the fact that it hasn't been done much before. That to me is not a reason to stay silent if I'm convinced it's the right thing to do.

"And as for winning political points, I'm not interested in running again. I think the lack of any coherent, comprehensive policy on immigration is inexcusable for a county like ours. That alone is worth lending my efforts to get it done. One of the nicest things about being out of office is not caring about the political impact of any actions I take."

"Some might argue, Boss, that you never much cared about that to begin with."

I laughed. "And that is perhaps the reason I am living in California today rather than D.C."

"Don't get me wrong. I have always respected that moral compass of yours. But I decided long ago that it was my personal obligation to at least inform you of when it might conflict with the political ramifications, as it so often does."

"And believe me," I replied, "I rely on you to keep pointing out those political consequences. That enables me to determine those instances when perhaps I should be more guided by the politics of a given course of action and discard that moral compass."

"With all due respect, I'm still waiting for one of those instances to happen, sir. The next one surely will be the first."

Chapter Forty-Three

You Have So Much to Lose
April 19, 2023

I knew I had to go all in on this bill if it was going to stand even the slightest chance of success. That meant, of course, that I would be completely ignoring the advice of Murph and my political people. And she's absolutely right—I seem to have made a habit of doing just that. I'm surprised she had stuck with me, to be honest. And this time I didn't hold back.

ABC
THIS WEEK WITH GEORGE STEPHANOPOULOS

ANNOUNCER: From ABC News in Washington, it's This Week. Here now, is George Stephanopoulos.

George Stephanopoulos: Good morning and welcome to This Week. President Bates, doubling down on her plan to push through a comprehensive immigration plan, has turned to former president Danny McFadden, in the hopes that he can bring along his ever-expanding base of moderates and independents and help push a hesitant Congress forward to get this done. I don't know that it's without precedent, but it is certainly unusual at best for a former president to get actively involved in successor's legislative agenda, particularly one of a different party.

Former President McFadden has been a key element of President Bates' national campaign and media blitz for her bill. In addition to working specific congressmen for support, he's been doing the talk show circuit and now the

Sunday news programs as well. We are very fortunate to have him with us this morning, and he joins us now from California.

Greetings, Mr. President. It's great to have you with us.

Danny McFadden: It's a pleasure to be with you this morning, George.

Stephanopoulos: So many former presidents tend to lay low, avoid the spotlight, write their memoirs, and work on their library, and are only heard from when they have a book to sell. You are kind of rewriting the script here.

McFadden: (Laughing) Well, George, I never paid a whole lot of attention to those "scripts" in the first place. That's what our whole movement is really about. We need to throw out so many of the norms of how we have been operating recently, particularly with respect to our two parties. In this case, everyone—both the two extremes on either side as well as the middle—acknowledge we need to fix our immigration and border situation. If I can play a meaningful role in bringing about a workable solution to such a vexing problem, I am all in.

By the way, ask me how much time I've spent working on my memoirs or raising money for a library built to glorify my name and legacy.

Stephanopoulos: (Smiling) I'm pretty certain I know the answer to that question, Mr. President, so I may pass on that.

But let me ask you this—fixing this immigration mess is a massive undertaking. This promises to be a street fight. The political risks are significant. You could expend a great deal of political capital and still come up empty at the end of the day. You have so much to lose.

McFadden: Let me remind you I'm just a private citizen now. What possible good is it for me to have any reservoir of political capital if I'm not using it for the benefit of the country? And I disagree, I believe I have absolutely nothing to lose. If we are unsuccessful then we as a country are no worse off than before. If on the other hand, we never even attempt it, we'll really never know if we could have fixed it. And there is tragedy in that.

Stephanopoulos: Sure, but how about you personally? If you lend your name to this and it fails, then it could impact any future role for you in politics—for instance if you wanted to run for California Governor or President.

McFadden: (Laughing) You think I might want to be president again? I would say the clearest indicator that I definitely don't is the fact that I signed on to do this!

Stephanopoulos: Ok, I believe you. But let me circle back to the challenge in front of you. You yourself didn't even attempt this as president. There's a reason you didn't. What makes you think you can do it now?

McFadden: Well, as crazy as it may seem, George, I firmly believe I have more influence now than at any time during my presidency. We really didn't begin to formally organize our movement until that last year. And when I was president, no one from Congress bothered to come to me on their legislative agenda. They operated around me. Fast forward to today, when the Alliance is now a growing force in this country and independents are coming into their own politically for the first time. The Alliance has a political agenda and it's being taken seriously. President

Bates herself thought to reach out to me, even though some around her may not be a big fan of mine or my cause. That's telling. We weren't getting that level of respect—at least from elected leaders—when I was president.

Stephanopoulos: Those are all excellent points you raise. But even so, so many of your predecessors have either tried and failed or simply punted on this issue. Can you really get something done on immigration?

McFadden: You might ask how can we but to that I'd answer by asking how can we not? We have a form of open borders and are doing very little to effectively or even adequately stem the tide of undocumented immigrants making that trek to the border. There is a genuine crisis at the border. We lack the ability to properly house, assess, process and assimilate the hordes that make it across each year. And as for the millions who have entered over the years, they remain in citizenship limbo for the remainder of their lives. None of that is acceptable for a country like ours.

I think a centrist approach to this—appealing to the roughly 44% of the country that is neither Democrat or Republican, and picking up a good percentage of moderates who remain in the two parties, is the only realistic way of getting this passed. I think I can play a key role in getting this across the finish line.

Stephanopoulos: That may be true. But if so, that just prompts me to return to my prior question. If it's true that you have more power—or "influence" as you put it—today than you did even as president, how can you not entertain the idea of one day returning to the White House?

McFadden: Hey, I'm flattered of course that you would ask that—even as much as I know you ask that of every politician in the national spotlight. But at the moment I am laser focused on what has emerged as the two most compelling passions of my life—most importantly my family, and then playing a role in fixing our dysfunctional political dynamic. If we can pass this bill—and I expect we will—that will show me I can immerse myself in both those pursuits and balance each quite nicely right here from this beautiful spot in California.

Stephanopoulos: And on that note we'll let you go. Thank you for spending time with us this morning.

McFadden: Thanks so much for having me, George. We're gonna get this thing passed and fix this once and for all.

Stephanopoulos: We'll have you back when that happens. When we come back, our powerhouse roundtable is ready to debate the immigration bill, weigh in on its chances of success, and discuss what it means that President Bates turned to Danny McFadden to get this bill passed. Is it smart politics or a something that will only hurt her going forward even if she achieves success?

Chapter Forty-Four

The Senate Is More Complicated
April 28, 2023

My phone buzzed just as my bike and I reached the summit at Santa Teresa. I pulled it out of my pocket and saw UNKNOWN NUMBER displayed on the screen. I let it go to voicemail as I removed my helmet, sat beneath the lonely tree there at the top and chugged my warm red Gatorade. Moments later the phone buzzed again to let me know I got a voicemail. It was the White House calling to set up a call with President Bates. I made the easy decision to risk extending my mid-ride break well beyond my standard five minutes, and called the number they left me. Two minutes later I was talking again with my newest political ally.

"Did I catch you at Hannegan's?" she asked.

I had to laugh. "Not quite. Perhaps the polar opposite of that. I'm an hour into my bike ride in the Santa Teresa Hills. Let's make this a long call so I get plenty of rest before I head back."

"I'd be happy to call you back later."

"No need for that. How can I help you?"

"Our efforts are paying off. I think we've got well more than enough votes in the House, with a nice bipartisan split and all of your Alliance caucus in tow. The Senate is more complicated, as it always seems to be. We currently project anywhere between 56 and 63 votes. So while it's possible we could break a filibuster, there's no guarantee."

"It's great to hear we're making progress."

"So I wanted to fill you in on our strategy going forward. If for any reason we don't believe we can get to sixty to invoke cloture, we really believe we have a shot at accomplishing this through reconciliation. There are so many fiscal components to this, so it's certainly not a misuse of that provision, in my mind, and the Senate Parliamentarian may just approve that. But if not we still have a shot at eliminating the filibuster—either doing away with it altogether or just for immigration issues. However, since I'm well aware of what you have said in the past in support of the filibuster generally, I felt I owed it to you to let you know that is our fallback strategy to get this done. We sincerely hope you'll still be supportive of it."

"I appreciate that very much, Maggie. You are correct of course. I've spoken often about the value of the filibuster in forcing a spirit of bipartisanship. I've long felt it is good for the Senate and the country. John McCain felt very strongly about that as well, and you know how much I admire him and all he stood for. I like it because it forces us to work together, rather than allow a party to force its will with a slim majority, only to have that reversed with a slim majority when power shifts back as it inevitably will."

"You realize that the filibuster isn't a concept embedded in the Constitution by the Founders, right? It really emerged originally kind of by accident."

"I know, but regardless of its origins it has become embedded in the history and tradition of the Senate, and has been reconfirmed many times. And it forces bipartisanship."

"But remember, Danny, part of that history of the Senate includes using the filibuster to block bills that would have advanced civil rights in the country and other honorable and necessary causes."

"Yes—like any political tool, it can be used for both noble and nefarious purposes. But it has also been used at times to block bills that would have restricted rights for women, or dramatically reduced taxes for the wealthiest Americans, or sharply increased the budget deficit. It also has been used effectively to prevent Congress from doing things like packing the Supreme Court, or creating new states merely to further their majorities in the Senate."

"Fair enough," she responded. "So what does this mean? Will you withdraw your support if we were to proceed with this by way of reconciliation to avoid a filibuster?"

"Yes, I'm afraid I would have to. Not because I oppose the merits of the bill, but because preserving the filibuster and the spirit of bipartisanship it forces is one of the core tenets of what I believe and what our supporters advocate. That overriding principle is too important to cherry pick one bill in particular and carve out an exception just for it, no matter how tempting it may be."

"I see. I must admit I'm disappointed but I understand."

"If you do go that route, let me know. Even though I'm opposed I promise I won't make a spectacle of withdrawing my support."

"No – I'm prepared to say right now we'll stay the course and push for sixty votes. Full steam ahead."

"That's great to hear."

"And speaking of full steam ahead, when are we hitting the high seas out there with your friend Gil?"

Chapter Forty-Five

May 23, 2023
Lawrence Olivier and Vivian Leigh

Denyse and I sat in Adirondack chairs on the veranda outside our stately cottage and marveled at the breathtaking views of the Channel Islands. Not a cloud in the sky. The powerful late afternoon sun glistening off the rich blue ocean water gave my sunglasses all they could handle.

"What island is that?" Denyse asked.

"It kind of looks like one but it's really a few of them. I think that's Santa Cruz in front of us and Santa Rosa to the right of that."

"I'm sure I'll feel differently when Hannah and Martin tool us around the Greek Iles on the *Que Será, Será*, but this is just about as close to paradise as you can get in this life."

I laughed. "You know Hannah. I think all we have to do is say the word and we can set sail with them tomorrow."

"Danny! What are we waiting for?"

"Really? That's not us, right? And the last thing I want to do is overdo it with her."

"Perhaps you are right, but maybe it can be us. You're always redefining yourself. Maybe you can become a yacht person. I know I can. Perhaps that's something you can shoot for."

"Is this place not swanky enough for you?"

I had whisked her away to the San Ysidro Ranch Resort in Montecito, a little slice of heaven tucked away in the hills just below Santa Barbara. It had been a favorite getaway years ago for some of the old Hollywood crowd, with vine-covered cottages scattered in the hills amidst verdant gardens, sycamores and majestic oaks, all offering spectacular views of the Pacific.

"No. This is absolutely perfect."

I pointed up to a deck on a bluff about a hundred yards from us. "You see that clearing up there?"

Denyse looked up.

"That's where Lawrence Olivier and Vivian Leigh got married one night here at midnight."

"Lawrence Olivier? Wasn't he gay?" she asked.

"I have no idea. How does anyone know? Maybe it was just a Hollywood publicity marriage."

"Did the marriage last?"

"I don't think so."

"Maybe he was gay if he left Scarlett O'Hara."

"I'm not sure she was a picnic." I said. "I think Scarlett and Vivian may have had a lot in common."

"I'll bet these gardens around here could spin a yarn or two."

"No doubt. This old place is oozing with history. I read up on it. Churchill, Chaplin, Groucho Marx, Bogie and Bacall, Audrey Hepburn, Bing Crosby, Sinclair Lewis—they all stayed here. So did JFK and Jackie—they came here on their honeymoon. In fact, I think they actually slept in our suite."

"Did he sleep with anyone else while he was here?"

I laughed. I guess I forgot about Denyse's disdain for JFK given some of his more notorious habits. She's not a big fan of infidelity, to put it mildly. She chose the right guy, though.

"Did any happy marriages frequent this place?" she asked.

"Yes," I said emphatically. "Danny and Denyse McFadden stayed here in May of 2023. You can't find a more solid marriage than those two! How about that?"

"Good answer, McFadden!"

Having worked the conversation to a positive note, I went inside to shower before dinner.

Denyse was still on the veranda when I emerged a half an hour later to find she had replaced me with a glass of Chardonnay.

She was reading on her cell phone. It looked like something was up.

"Is something wrong?" I asked.

"More troubles for your girl Maggie."

"What now?" I asked. "The immigration bill? Her husband again?"

"Neither. Wait 'til you hear this."

"Not sure I want to hear it."

"Evidently her son Cade got in a bit of trouble at Dartmouth."

"What happened."

"I guess he was at an off-campus party that got a little bit out of control. And I think he got a little out of control too. There's video of him leaping onto a beer pong table in front of at least a couple dozen kids. Actually, there's several different videos from various cell phones. The table instantly collapsed. He suffered a concussion and some internal injuries. He and eight others were arrested for underage drinking. They confiscated some cocaine as well which they are still sorting out."

"Is he gonna be OK?"

"He is still in the hospital for evaluation. Looks like they are keeping him for a day or two of monitoring."

"Where was the Secret Service detail?"

"The Post has a long story about it and they delve into that. I guess his agents view their job as keeping him safe from others, but not necessarily from himself. I think they were providing him some latitude.

"The story also suggests Dwight is spending an awful lot of time back at their home in Atlanta, and might be maintaining a presence in the White House every so often just for show. They allude rather cryptically to some other rumors about him and the marriage but they chose not to detail those."

I shook my head. "I am so sorry to hear that. That poor kid. This stuff happens all over but in his case half the world will probably hear about it. And poor Maggie. This isn't how she mapped it all out when she decided to run. I can't imagine how she's coping with it all."

"Nothing like having your dirty laundry splashed all over the papers."

"I have to say though if she and Dwight have split it might be the best thing that's happened to her. I'm not a fan. Still, how brutal to have it all happening while she's in that fishbowl. And no wonder the kid is acting up a bit."

"Geez," Denyse replied, "with that husband and that Vice President she seems to have a bit of a knack for attaching herself to the worst possible men."

"I'm not sure why it is but for some reason many of the finest women seem to go for the bad boy type."

Moments later, I added, "Except you, of course."

"Are you implying you're not a bad boy?"

"Yes. Yes I am. I've seen some of them in my day, and I'm definitely not."

"I think there was a point in time you really could have gone either direction on that. I like to think I played a role in steering you onto the right course."

As I often do with her, I thought it best just to stop talking.

"I'm just glad you lumped me in with 'the finest women.' And I'll do you a favor and I won't ask you to define that term."

She handed me her phone and I read the article, which was being reported everywhere.

I read the whole thing, as painful as it was to get through. "I feel so sorry for them all."

"It is so heartbreaking. How do you even begin to pick up the pieces and move on after something like that?" Denyse added.

"I can only hope she's availing herself of all the expert advice and sympathetic ears available to her in that position." I said.

"I have no faith in any of those White House staffers she has surrounded herself with."

"I agree completely. But I wasn't referring to them . . ."

Chapter Forty-Six

May 27, 2023
The Inevitable Media Blitz

So we did manage to piece together sixty senators to vote for cloture to avoid a filibuster. As part of the deal reached by the majority and minority leaders, four more amendments were permitted and there would be no more than thirty hours of remaining debate.

While getting sixty to invoke cloture nearly always means the underlying bill will pass, with all that time still left on the clock and the prospect of more amendments to come I was nervous, to say the least. And then, of course, there was the inevitable media blitz from the two ends of our political spectrum.

FOX NEWS

THE SEAN HANNITY SHOW

Sean Hannity: Alright. Well folks, buckle up. We have an incredible show for you tonight.

I need to start with what happened in your United States Senate today. The "Upper House" of our Congress today took one step closer to passing a bill that would amount to complete capitulation to the liberal Democrat agenda. Led by many of the RINOs who always tend to be leading the way these days, the usual suspects we're all too familiar with, we appear headed toward enacting a bill that would be a travesty, and would provide amnesty to at least 15 million illegal aliens who have thwarted our laws and stepped in front of the line of all those around the globe who would have loved to immigrate to America in the proper and lawful manner.

Moreover, this is being done before the border has been sealed—which is the one thing we have demanded for years that must come in advance of any immigration bill. Close the border to illegals before we even consider what they refer to as a "path to citizenship' —which is just a fancy way of describing amnesty. If we don't secure the border first, we will one day simply be right back where we are today—facing the very same type of pressure to grant amnesty to all those thousands of criminals who still come illegally every day and aren't going to stop until we've established proper border enforcement. The truth of the matter is that liberals don't want any border enforcement because all of these illegal immigrants and their legal children born here will be adding to the ranks of the Democratic party.

Border agents have told me they've captured illegals crossing who have ties to Yemen, Iran and Sri Lanka. Even one suspected terrorist who can obtain access through the weak spots in our border is far too great a risk for America to assume. Today's actions in the Senate should be enough to frighten every American citizen. And let's face it, many others who enter are in fact criminals hoping to evade justice in their country by starting over in our country. Do we expect them to somehow magically morph now into model citizens?

Beyond that, just look at the impact on our economy of these actions. Illegal immigrants drive down wages as it is, creating more competition for lawful citizens seeking employment in this country. Just wait until they are all granted citizenship.

America is the only country that leaves its borders wide open and the results are obvious. The other side makes an emotional argument about deporting children but the truth is that's what all countries do—they have to maintain their sovereignty.

I think it's clear that so many pushing this bill simply want to be in favor of anything that could be referred to as immigration reform. I doubt they've even taken the time to read so many of the most troublesome aspects of this massive bill.

Finally, it is hard to stomach that this bill was driven by a Republican president. And I think this episode puts to rest the notion that McFadden was ever a moderate. Bates and McFadden have shown themselves to be every bit as liberal as Obama and Hillary, and it's time we start thinking about them in those terms. Let's call McFadden's vaunted "Alliance" what it really is—an extension of the Democrat party.

While right now it may appear that President Bates may have the votes, I am not going to stop shouting from the highest mountaintop about this until we turn this around. I'm not conceding defeat on this bill and neither should you. There's still time to change some of these Republican minds about it. And perhaps encouraging new candidates in their districts to take them out in the next primary is in order. I am happy to use my platform and megaphone to bring that about.

One thing is for certain—we'll be doing our part every night on this platform. I hope you'll stick with us. There's still time to win this thing.

MSNBC

THE WOKEN SAMANTHA STOKEN SHOW

Samantha Stoken: It's Tuesday, May 27, 2023, and you're watching The Woken Samantha Stoken Show—the progressive soul of America.

The Senate today moved one step closer to passing President Bates' controversial immigration bill. A version has already passed the House. Unless ten or more senators have a sudden change of heart, we may soon be codifying some of the very worst elements of the Republican agenda on immigration.

Don't get me wrong, we desperately need to fix our immigration system, but this bill is downright dangerous. Where do I even begin?

This bill places the annual refugee cap at just 40,000. In Obama's last year that cap was well over 100,000 – right where it needs to be. So much for America being a nation of immigrants. We need to remain a safe haven for the world's refugees. That's part of the promise of America—what made us great.

The workplace enforcement aspects of this bill will certainly lead to additional discrimination against anyone who speaks Spanish or appears in any way to be Hispanic. Punishing businesses for hiring undocumented workers is just bad policy all around. We can't allow this to be enacted. It encourages and rewards racism against Hispanics.

All of the stepped-up border enforcement mandated by this bill will simply contribute to the ever-increasing militarization of the border. Our Southern border shouldn't

> resemble a war zone. That's a not only a bad look, it's un-American, and utterly lacking in compassion for our fellow man.
>
> Additionally, I am shocked that there is so little contained in the bill to pay for medical care and attention for border crossers. Border Patrol officials need more training in health care and the additional resources necessary to effectively care for all those who require it.
>
> Perhaps worst of all, this bill doesn't do nearly enough to address the root causes of the crisis in the countries that make up the Northern Triangle. We need to be working with them and providing the support and resources necessary to improve the conditions in those nations and reduce the need for their citizens to flee their country. The money they earmark for sealing the border should be used to improve conditions in those countries.
>
> In short, I'm appalled by this. This is not compromise at all, but Democrats caving in to some of the most heartless and misguided demands of Republicans. Don't be fooled by this. Merely because Danny McFadden and his Alliance have signed on to this doesn't make it a moderate or reasonable compromise. I think this is evidence that his movement is not so much in the middle after all but squarely within the most extreme conservative wing of the country.

***

The nightly drumbeat from these media mouthpieces made me nervous. I remained hopeful, however, that a majority of Senators were solidly behind us and would not buckle to the pressure.

But then of course, this happened.

NEW YORK TIMES

OFFICER SHOT AND KILLED BY UNDOCUMENTED AFRICAN IMMIGRANT FOLLOWING DOMESTIC ALTERCATION

(New York, May 28, 2023) By Shelly Carr

A New York City police officer was shot and killed by an undocumented African immigrant he was pursuing on foot following a domestic disturbance yesterday evening in Queens. The suspect, Lukeny Goncalves, who also incurred gunshot wounds during the chase, is in critical condition in the ICU at NewYork-Presbyterian Queens Hospital.

Police were called to the home of the suspect's girlfriend in The Rockaway section of Queens following reports of a domestic disturbance. The suspect fled the scene as officers arrived at the apartment of his girlfriend, who had telephoned police earlier to report that Goncalves was threatening to harm her and was armed.

The suspect is an undocumented immigrant who came to America from Angola on a VISA that expired in back in 2017.

NYPD has indicated that there is bodycam video from each of the three officers involved that they anticipate will be released in the coming days. Witnesses say the officer fired at the suspect while pursuing him on foot through a city park, and a brief gun battle ensued, but there are conflicting accounts on the issue of who fired first.

The incident comes just as the Senate appears poised to pass a comprehensive immigration reform bill, and while

> the nation continues to grapple with a number of high profile incidents of police shooting of young black men. It also comes as the nation continues to struggle with how to curb gun violence.
>
> The deceased officer, Rodrigo Garcia, a 43-year old and an 18-year veteran of the force, leaves behind a wife and three children.

***

I walked in the door from the garage after picking up Jack from baseball practice. Denyse looked crushed.

"Have you heard any of the news today?" she asked.

"You mean about the shooting in Queens? My phone's been blowing up. I glanced at it, but I haven't yet really read anything on it."

"It's all over the news. The only thing anyone is talking about. I'd say it really touched a nerve with so many different segments of the country for very different reasons."

"Tragedies like this really tend to do that."

"You know already it's being used by some people to attack your bill."

"Of course, I saw that coming. It really shouldn't though. If anything, our bill provides stricter limits on VISAs, and does provide very real border enforcement and particularly enforcement pertaining to overstaying VISAs, which never gets talked about but is a big piece of this. While we do provide path to citizenship for certain undocumented immigrants who clear all the hurdles, my guess is that this suspect wouldn't have been eligible for that path in the first place if he had an expired VISA and hadn't done anything to seek an adjustment in status."

"I'm not certain everyone will pick up on that nuance."

"Yes, not in this simple, soundbite news cycle. But if this does really hurt the bill, as I suspect it will, it's really ironic because in some ways our bill will prevent some of this from happening in the future."

"Would it help you to get out there and make that point?"

Ha! I love how invested you are! I married the right girl."

"You can say that again."

She picked up the remote and turned on the tv. "Would you like to see any of this?"

"I'm not sure I do. Maybe we could see how Hannah's channel is covering it."

"Sure," Denyse responded. "I've been taping Elizabeth Peters' show every night at six. That's the former Virginia Congresswoman. She's pretty fair. And she always has a fresh take on all this stuff. She doesn't just spew the talking points."

Denyse pulled up her show as I settled in on the couch. Montana leapt up by my side. What followed was an honest, comprehensive presentation of the facts known about the incident, and the implications, including for the pending bill and the national discussion on immigration, on guns and on race. And, most importantly, her political analysis included not just the liberal and conservative views—both of which were using the incident to attack the bill—but she also offered a more nuanced middle view, explaining how the pending bill so opposed by both extremes might have actually prevented an incident like this had it been passed years ago.

I don't know how many eyeballs were tuning in—I would think the more sensational stuff perhaps attracts a stronger viewership. However, at least with respect to this show, I applaud Hannah for what she was doing—threading that very difficult needle—providing the unvarnished truth and a comprehensive look at all the possible implications, devoid of all hate or judgement or political agenda. I decided there can't possibly be any money in that format, of course, but God it was refreshing to see. Good for Hannah.

I wondered if it would make a difference.

Chapter Forty-Seven

Dios Te Bendiga
June 1, 2023

An elderly Hispanic woman approached the counter. She looked back into the kitchen where I stood with Jack and nine of his classmates, flipping pancakes, frying bacon, scrambling eggs, arranging bagels, donuts, cereal, strawberries, bananas and blueberries for a tiny cafeteria room filled to the gills with homeless women and children.

"Dios te bendiga." she said, placing her right hand on her heart. It was only 7:05 a.m., and we hadn't even set the food out yet.

I looked at the kids, many of whom were looking at me, expecting me to answer her. I looked back at the students and pointed to them. This was all about them engaging, not me.

Jack's friend Ally looked at me and mouthed, "Should I answer in English or Spanish."

"Either," I mouthed back.

"We are happy to provide it for you," she answered. Then, her brain working overtime, she added, "Nosotros . . . somos felices . . .traer deyunas."

The woman beamed.

"De que iglesia vienen?," she asked.

"What church are we with?" Ally said, repeating the question. "We are not with a church. Um, no iglesia. Una escuela. Jesuit College Prep en San Jose." She then pointed at all her classmates.

"Muchas gracias," said the woman, now addressing all the students. As she walked away I flashed Ally a thumbs up.

We were at the InnVision women and children's homeless shelter—Georgia Travis House—in downtown San Jose, at our twice monthly visit to prepare a nice meal. I had my green ND hat pulled way down and kept my sunglasses on, channeling my guy Bono a bit. It seemed to work for the most part in here, where people are already so preoccupied with some of life's most existential crises—and not just homelessness and unemployment. Through our intermittent visits over the years we had seen it all in here—mental health issues, substance abuse, domestic violence victims, unwanted pregnancies, suicidal tendencies, life threatening illnesses—you name it. You would think that with the place Silicon Valley has etched out for itself in the business and cultural landscape of this country that this is one spot that wouldn't have to grapple with pervasive homelessness. Unfortunately, and heartbreakingly, that just isn't the case.

Our day had begun at 5:15 with a trip to Safeway to stock up on all the food we'd be preparing. These kids loved going up and down the aisles freely tossing items in the baskets. Those who do this with us regularly knew how appreciative the residents of this particular shelter were—which was always so apparent in the looks on their faces when they entered the cafeteria room and saw our group behind the counter and a huge spread of food before them. Beats the heck out of oatmeal and Cheerios, their regular daily fare. Luckily many groups like ours filled in to supplement so many meals each week.

The doors officially opened to the residents at 7:00 but many filed in early. The smell of bacon and maple syrup tends to trigger that response. Later, when the room was full, the students displayed the food along the counter, led us all in a prayer, and then positioned themselves to assist in serving the residents as the line formed. A few of the kids took food to the tables to serve those who were less than fully mobile.

It was a little like pulling teeth, but I encouraged all the students to mingle with the crowd as they came around with more coffee and orange juice and served seconds. The homeless children especially seemed thrilled at the change of pace from the daily routine.

About 45 minutes later, as people began finishing up, the room broke into a spontaneous round of applause for their student chefs. Now it was the students' turn to beam. I had asked them all to introduce themselves, which they did with varying degrees of assertiveness. I think everyone there was better off for the experience. As the room began to clear out, Ally surreptitiously got my attention to make sure I saw the many women filling the plastic storage bags we had left out with the leftover breakfast food to take with them. They were even packing the pancakes and scrambled eggs—perhaps the most telling sign of the need.

As the students began scrubbing the kitchen, two of the women appeared and grabbed dish towels.

"This is our day to clean up after breakfast," said a young woman who couldn't have been older than 25. She appeared to have bruises on her face. I'm sure so many of the backstories of the residents here are heartbreaking.

"My friends and I will take care of it," said Jack, attempting to wave them off. Good for him.

"There are no exceptions," she responded. "It is our day and our assignment. Otherwise we'll get in trouble."

Jack turned to me. "Tell them you'll gladly help them out then," I said.

A few of the other students went out to the small play yard behind the facility to play with the children while the rest of us cleaned up with the two women. The facility had to be completely cleared out by 8:30 am. At that time most of them would simply cross the street to another facility where they could spend the day, get medical attention, counseling, assistance seeking employment and home schooling for their kids.

I felt my phone buzzing in my pocket. I pulled it out and saw it was Denyse.

"Your timing is perfect. We are just finishing up."

"Successful breakfast?" she asked.

"Yes—very much so, I would say. A few of the pancakes stuck to that ancient griddle but all in all it was win-win for everyone involved. I think it was really valuable of course for the students to see the extent of the need and the genuine appreciation the women and children had for them being here."

"And how about you?" she asked.

"It's the absolute best. There's nothing like it. Such a pick-me-up. Makes me want to do a lot more than breakfast, though. I will. In time."

"I have no doubt you will," she responded. "Meanwhile, are you following this final vote in the Senate on your bill at all?"

"No, not at all. It's actually kind of nice to completely immerse myself in other things for a few hours. I love that about this experience too. I actually hadn't even thought about it at all."

"Do you want to hear how it's going?"

"Only if it's good news. Don't bring me down from this high."

"It's fascinating, really. There's bipartisan support of course but there is also bipartisan opposition —the extremes on both sides are opposing it. It's a nail-biter. But you've got a chance."

I laughed. "So you're saying I've got a chance."

"Maybe. It looks like it's coming right down to the wire. Many of the networks are covering it."

"What are you watching it on?"

"C-SPAN."

"That's my girl. No bias or slant there. Can you put your phone on speaker so I can hear it live?"

"You sure you want to?"

"Yes. At this point I do."

"Alright. Wow, 48 Ayes. All it needs is two more."

"Or three, really."

Mr. Van Hollen.

Mr. Van Hollen, Aye.

Mr. Whitehouse.

Mr. Whitehouse, No.

Mr. Wicker.

Mr. Wicker, No.

Mr. Wyden.

Mr. Wyden, Aye."

"Alright – so it's 50-50," Denyse proclaimed. "Wow."

"What's happening now?"

"I'm watching. People are just standing around talking with one another. A split vote should be good enough, right? With the VP breaking the tie??

I didn't respond.

"Right?"

Then, moments later, she resumed her play by play. "OK, Margel just made a grand entrance. He is approaching the chair. Alright. A woman just came up to Margel with a big proclamation-like sheet and she's directing him to take the gavel. Now she's holding the sheet up for him to read off of."

I could hear Margel read the proclamation through the phone. "On this vote the yeas are fifty, the nays are fifty. The Senate being equally divided, the Vice President hereby votes in the negative and the motion is denied."

For a brief moment I was certain I had heard that wrong.

"That snake!" Denyse screamed. That's when the gravity of it all hit me.

"You have got to be kidding me," I exclaimed. "He voted it down? Now I've truly seen everything."

"He just pounded the gavel, and you should see the look of defiance on his face. And he's mugging for the cameras."

"I know it well—I'd rather not see it, thank you. I get it. The folks he is appealing to—they just love him stirring it up. They're so sick of Washington and how it has operated for decades. They feel they're being left behind in all the wokeness. They have such intense distrust for government that they just love sticking it to the man whenever they get the opportunity. I think this is driven more by that than anything else. The irony in my mind is that this was an example of how Washington can really work for them, and actually solve some of the vexing problems that they've complained about for years. The enhanced border security, limitations on undocumented immigrants, limitations on pathways to citizenship and employer compliance requirements are exactly what they've been asking for. At some point you have to settle for very good even if it means you can't obtain the perfect."

"Interesting how you phrased that."

I knew her well enough to know exactly where her mind was going. And she wasn't thinking about politics. "Of course, I've personally never settled for anything less than perfect—certainly not in any of my major life decisions. Thank god I held out for 'the perfect' with you."

I couldn't see her face to see how she took that. Maybe that was a good thing. There was a brief silence, then she just moved on. At least I had thought to work that in.

"What is Margel's endgame on this?"

"I think Margel has made the calculation that Bates can't be re-elected and he wants to stay viable by distancing himself from her. No better way to do that than this. What a colossal F-you."

"There's some world-class loyalty for you there."

"And it may actually be much more than that. I actually think it's possible he's considering running against her and unseating her. He chose the most visible and dramatic way possible of breaking with her. And I can bet there are those in the media/news/entertainment industry willing to make a name for themselves by going all in alongside him and drawing attention to themselves. They'll feed off of each other. And raise a ton of cash."

"How pathetic. But beyond that, how truly sad."

"Haven't you heard me say a thousand times politics is a nasty business?"

"You're not kidding. I know some of President Bates' staff have hit you pretty hard and I do really fault her for that but I have to say I kind of feel sorry for her."

"Don't underestimate her. She's savvy—a political force to be reckoned with. But he's always been uncomfortable with her willingness to make deals with Dems and seek compromises. I think with this he wants to divide the party, forcing Republicans to choose between him and her. And which side do you think Tucker and Hannity and all the rest at that end take? He's banking on the hard core going to him."

"But she'll have all the more moderate Republicans."

"So many of those have left the party to become independents, and they can't vote in the primaries. That's why the more extreme candidates these days tend to fare well in primaries.

"This is terrible news for someone like me—even aside from the huge loss on immigration. I really worry about the next presidential election. The last thing this country needs in Margel versus Clayton —the very far right versus a self-described 'Democratic Socialist.' If it's those two we are absolutely screwed."

"Gee Danny, if only there were a viable third party the others could gravitate to . . . Someone should really do something about that one of these days."

I chose to let her sarcasm hang in the air without a response.

"So what do you do now?" she asked.

"Me? I'm going with our car caravan to drop these kids at school, then I'm off to ride the Santa Teresa trail, and then I'm coming home to enjoy a nice lunch with my wife out on the deck."

"No—I mean on immigration. What do you do now?"

"You're forgetting it's not my problem, babe. I'm off the clock, as they say."

"Oh I know you a lot better than that, McFadden."

"Ha! That was before I was retired. It's all my friend Maggie's problem now. I'll happily leave it in her capable hands. Look, we've gotta get out of here. I'll see you at home for lunch."

"Nice dodge there. You're in mid-campaign form."

I let that hang in the air too.

***

On the way out I ran into the older woman who had interacted with us at the beginning of breakfast.

"Gracias." She said, grasping my arm with her hand.

"Como se llama?" I asked.

"Eugenia."

I repeated it, "Eugenia." That always helps me to remember a new name, but I also wanted to make sure I was pronouncing it correctly. It was one of those names that sounds dramatically different in English.

She smiled, and said, "Si," nodding her head.

Before walking away she pointed to the students and whispered to me, "Son angeles."

I looked and saw that so many of the students were now engaging with the women and children who remained in the room, led of course by Ally, who seemed to have gotten to know them all.

I let Eugenia's words sink in as I walked out to the SUVs.

Later in the back seat with Jack on the way back to Jesuit Prep I attempted to strike up a conversation.

"What'd you learn today, dude?"

He thought for a second. "I think I learned they're in need of a lot more than just breakfast."

"No question," I answered. "We provide them a brief moment of joy and perhaps a little hope. Maybe we restored a little of their faith in mankind."

"Dad, do you think that younger woman with the bruises on her face had been beaten?"

"I think so. Since this is women and children only, it gets the domestic violence victims as well."

"God that sucks."

I watched his mind processing it all.

"When can we come back?" he asked.

Jackpot. That question made it all so worthwhile. Precisely the response I was hoping for.

In this moment of father-son bonding, I did what I always seem to do. I took it one step too far.

"I like your friend Ally very much."

"Yeah, she's nice."

Then, after a few seconds, I asked, "Does she have a boyfriend?"

He shot me a look. "Ally? Really? Dad, she's not my type."

I considered letting it go at that, but sometimes that life advice gene I inherited from my father kicks in, and I had to seize the moment.

"Well, I don't know exactly what qualifies as 'your type,' but all I'm saying is that you could do a whole lot worse than a girl who has a big heart for the homeless. That's a priceless quality in any person right there, and might be worth adding to your list of qualities that make up 'your type.'"

"You're sounding a lot like Mom right now."

"Good. If you're hearing things like this both from her and from me then perhaps it will start sinking in. If you won't listen to me, listen to her. After all, she brought you into this world."

I looked over and saw that he had pulled out his ever-present ear buds and inserted them, shockingly choosing his music over my sage life advice.

Apparently my ideas for any type of future for Jack and Ally were as improbable as the ones I had for the passage of a true immigration fix for this country.

The difference, of course is, that Jack, I suspect, unlike our country, had many other viable options.

Chapter Forty-Eight

Cleopatra and Catherine the Great
August 10, 2023

And then came another first in American history for a US president. Maggie's challenges seemed to be piling up, although this could be a step in the right direction for her.

ATLANTA JOURNAL CONSTITUTION

PRESIDENT BATES FILES FOR DIVORCE

(Atlanta, August 10, 2023) By Jeffrey Selzer

In a move without precedent in US history, President Margaret Bates has filed for divorce from her husband of twenty-one years, Dwight H. Bates. In a petition for dissolution of marriage filed in Fulton County Superior Court in Atlanta, her lawyers stated very simply: "The marriage is irretrievably broken."

The divorce filing, which states that the couple have no minor children, comes just days after their only child, Cade, recently turned 18.

This move follows a series of revelations and rumors that have gradually come to light over the course of the last few years, including a sexual harassment action filed against Mr. Bates by an employee of his corporation. After that matter was exposed, several other women have come forward with additional allegations of workplace sexual harassment and infidelity. Additionally, Mr. Bates' name appeared many times during legal proceedings involving British socialite Ghislaine Maxwell, charged with enticement of minors and sex trafficking for Jeffrey Epstein. One of Epstein's victims listed Mr. Bates among many others with whom she was directed to have sexual relations. Mr. Bates' name appeared often in various depositions and other discovery taken relating to the various legal actions involving Mr. Epstein and Ms. Maxwell.

While Mr. Bates appeared in public many times with the President in her first year in office, over the past eighteen months such appearances are far less frequent, and he seems to be spending most of his time at their home in the Randall Mill neighborhood of Atlanta, and at his corporate headquarters in New Orleans.

While many US presidents have had less than perfect marriages, and allegations of infidelity have been asserted with many of them, no US president has ever been a party to divorce proceedings while in the White House. Ronald Reagan divorced and remarried many years before becoming president. Reports of infidelity dogged President Bill Clinton throughout his political life, and accounts of affairs involving other presidents, most notably John Kennedy, have emerged in the years following their presidencies, but no marriage involving a sitting president has ever been dissolved while in office.

***

Tina heard me arrive at the office and was waiting for me when I entered the suite.

"Good for her," she pronounced. "I like this lady more and more each day."

Of course I knew exactly what she was referring to.

"I feel for her," I responded. "To have all this family dirty laundry aired publicly—in every corner of the world—has got to be heartbreaking for her."

"But god is she tough," I added. "I give her credit. How many times is the woman asked the swallow their pride and any sense of dignity and stand by their man for political or public relations reasons."

"Yes, indeed—but what you are referring to is really completely different, though, isn't it? Those women I believe you are referring to all had some power, but their power was still subservient to their husband's. Hillary Clinton, Jackie Kennedy, Eleanor Roosevelt. Here's a case of the woman having the real power in the marriage. It's still the man cheating, of course—it always is—but in this case the aggrieved spouse has the power."

I hesitated to act in any way as devil's advocate. Against my better judgement, however, perhaps just to stick up for my gender, I blurted out, "Of course, it's not always the man who is at fault in every case."

Her response was fast and furious. "Hold on there, cowboy. I know you are Mister Middle-of-the-Road and all, but there's just no middle ground here. And don't try to tell me there is. Name a woman—even one woman—in a position of great power who cheated on her less powerful spouse or otherwise used her power for sex."

I thought for a second.

"Go ahead," she added, now seemingly delighted by my hesitation. "Name one."

"Alright," I said. I thought a bit more.

Then, moments later, "Cleopatra." I intended to say it a lot more confidently than it came out.

"Ha!" she screamed. "Really? That's the best you can do? You have to go all the way back to ancient Egypt? Are you kidding me right now?"

She laughed longer and harder than I think I've ever seen her laugh. Maybe than I've ever seen anyone laugh.

She wasn't finished. "This might just be my favorite conversation I've ever had with you." She laughed again.

"Cleo-fucking-patra? That was before Christ, you know. Nothing could possibly prove my point better than that pathetic response."

I had clearly touched a nerve. Squarely. And yes, the more I thought about it, the more I realized that I deserved this.

"Not to mention," she added, "I'm not so sure it's even considered cheating when your husband is actually your 12-year-old brother and you had to marry him. I'm not even willing to concede your point, however feeble it was."

I was racking my brain for another example or a better example and the best I could come up with on the fly was Catherine the Great. I made a snap judgement that it would not be in my best interests to utter that name at this time. Sometimes my instincts do protect me, although in this case those instincts were a little late to the party. In defense of my thought, however, Catherine the Great was several hundred years more recent than Cleopatra, but I surmised that it wouldn't exactly help my cause.

Tina wasn't done yet. In fact, she was just getting started. "This is precisely why we need more women in charge. When you remove all potential for decisions being made based solely upon the possibility of sex, there's no telling what can be accomplished. And with promotions based exclusively on merit, only the most talented people will occupy the key positions. Just imagine a world—"

Cathy walked in, causing Tina to pause for a second.

"What's going on in here?" Cathy asked.

I laughed. "Our girl's on a bit of a roll."

Tina just took a breath and jumped right back in. "Name an organization or industry that wouldn't be much better off if women were in charge. Let's start with the Catholic Church, shall we? How's it working out for them? Maybe then venture to Hollywood, Wall Street, Washington, the Boy Scouts, professional sports, Silicon Valley, higher education . . . And then consider this—as bad as it is—and it's bad—it's so much better here in this country than so many other places in this world."

Cathy smiled. "I'll just come back later."

She started to walk away.

"Wait, wait." I said. "Don't I have that call I need to get on?"

"Which one was that?" she responded.

"You know . . . the one we scheduled yesterday."

She looked a bit lost, but then responded, "Oh, yeah. I forgot about that. Yes. You need to get on that call. The one we scheduled yesterday."

Tina looked at the two of us, then pulled out her phone to look at the time.

"You mean that call that starts at 9:43 in the morning? Is that a weekly 9:43 a.m. Tuesday call you have?"

"Sorry, I've gotta run." I said. "I apologize. I would have loved to stay and finish this conversation. Thank you for the reminder, Cathy."

I walked away quickly, knowing full well everyone knew there was no phone call to take. God love Cathy for that by the way. But a part of me—not a part I'm proud of—kind of enjoyed the fact that by leaving this way I would only tend to rile Tina up even more. Again, I'm not proud of that.

The most painful part, of course, was that she had a point. She always does. Love her.

Chapter Forty-Nine

Y'all Are Growing on Me
August 12, 2023
The Saloon

So I found myself sandwiched at table between Nixon and Garfield, a most unlikely pair. The two of them were in the midst of a fiery discussion about the merits and pitfalls of the gold standard.

Nixon was making his case. "Departure from the gold standard enables the use of monetary policy to address unemployment. While there may then be inflationary pressures, I've never seen a president beaten on inflation in the United States. I've seen many beaten on unemployment."

"It played a role in my defeat, Dick," added Jimmy Carter, sitting across the table from us.

"To be fair, Jimmy, you had both high unemployment and high inflation."

Garfield spoke up. "Any party which commits itself to paper money will go down amid the general disaster, covered with the curses of a ruined people."

"While I don't concede your point," General Garfield, responded Nixon, "Jimmy here might be the finest Exhibit A to prove your argument. I just maintain there was a whole lot more contributing to that unprecedented stagflation during his term than just monetary policy."

Garfield looked confused. I'm not sure he had heard the term stagflation before. Carter looked a bit exasperated, but chose not to respond.

"Are you suggesting, Dick, that you attempted to influence monetary policy purely for political reasons?" Lyndon Johnson asked.

"That has to be the most naïve and inane question ever uttered in this saloon," responded Nixon. "You would have had a fine career as a White House correspondent, Lyndon."

I saw that Ike sitting nearby was clearly enjoying this back and forth. This conversation, which had been rather dry and boring, was getting more interesting,

At that moment I saw the door from the White House open. We hadn't seen Maggie here in weeks. I hoped everything was alright and that perhaps she was just too busy.

Maggie entered, but without that smile we had grown accustomed to seeing. In fact, from our table not too far from her I noticed that she looked a bit like she had seen a ghost—and by that I'm not referring to any of the ones that frequent this saloon, including me.

Mary Ann evidently saw something alarming too. She set her drink tray down and made a bee line to Maggie. I swear, Mary Ann possesses the most powerful basic human instincts I've ever seen in a person—that and a legendary reservoir of compassion. Mary Ann took Maggie's hand and they sat down immediately on the small bench next to that entrance.

We had a full house in the saloon that night, in addition to a very versatile six-piece cover band. They had been on a break, and Otter and Clinton and a few others were at their side spoon-feeding them songs for their playlist. Word spread throughout that Maggie had arrived, and the energy in the crowded room picked up.

Bush whispered to the lead singer, and the band started in on the prelude to "Midnight Train to Georgia." I then read his lips as he appeared to say to Clinton "I'm gonna go get Peaches."

I felt as if I might be able to head off a disaster if I could just get to Bush before he could got to her.

I peeled myself away from that riveting discourse about the gold standard, and tried to navigate a path through the congested tables and the crowd to intersect with Bush well out of earshot of Maggie. I excused myself often as I tapped on shoulders or elbowed my way through a veritable obstacle course presented by the men standing and conversing in groups amidst the tables. I suddenly developed a much greater appreciation for the wait staff which has to navigate this nightly.

Just when it appeared as if I would successfully intersect with Otter's path, I hustled past a table with Washington, Monroe, Lincoln, John Adams, Jefferson and the two Roosevelts.

My buddy Teddy motioned to me. "McFadden, sit with us for a second." I turned to look at the table and saw all these on these consequential figures focused squarely on me, eager for my response. I had to make an instantaneous decision.

I hesitated for just a second and George W. Bush slipped past. While I could have easily said no to most of the men at that table, knowing Washington was there, and seeing the look on his face, proved to be too much for me. It was certainly the esteem I had for him, but also the reverence people in this saloon seemed to have for the Father of our Country.

I took the empty seat between Washington and John Adams. Lincoln addressed me. "We are curious, McFadden, in your estimation what constitutes the single greatest threat facing our republic at this time?"

While I could seamlessly deliver that answer—even in my deepest sleep—I knew it would be anything but brief. As the words started rolling off my tongue, I saw Otter leading Maggie to the stage. Her patented smile had returned to her face. She willingly grabbed the microphone as Bush coaxed Obama up on the stage as well next to Clinton. Maggie then belted out "Midnight Train to Georgia" with these three presidential stooges filling in behind as "The Pips." Priceless.

As compelling as my little monologue on the country's threat assessment may have been, I felt I had to put a halt to it. One of my better decisions. "We've gotta listen to this, right?" I asked.

None of them seem convinced, but they went along with me. We looked at the stage to see Otter synchronizing a little dance with Obama and Clinton. Maggie looked behind her just as the three of them raised their right arms high and mimicked an engineer pulling a train whistle as they all in unison belted out "Woo, woo." I laughed so hard I had tears in eyes, but that was nothing compared to Maggie. Upon seeing those three presidential pips she absolutely lost it, doubled over in laughter, and was physically incapable of singing for at least a half a minute as the band behind her ad libbed without missing a beat. She was clearly loving every second of it though. I thought for a moment that I had completely misinterpreted her mood upon entering the bar. It's a good thing. I have to say, as a stand-in for Gladys, she wasn't bad. And what does it say about her to be able to stand up there and do that in front of a room full of old men who all started out as skeptics.

I've never wished so much for a song to be longer. And my gosh, if the country could see that bipartisan effort that went into producing that moment...

At the end the band and 'the Pips' swarmed around her as the rest of us stood and applauded. I'm not sure half the room really understood it fully but they've all come to find humor in some of Otter's shenanigans—some of them—and that speaks well of them.

"Thank you so much, Maggie said to the crowd, still holding the microphone. "That was good for my soul. You have no idea. And y'all are growing on me."

"And *this* one here," she added, pointing at Bush and shaking her head. "I'll proudly answer to 'Peaches' any time, my friend. But only from you."

I'm pretty sure Bush is the only one who would ever even attempt to call her that.

Maggie waded back into the crowd which eagerly congratulated her as if she was making a grand entrance into a joint session of Congress for a State of the Union. The wait staff went into overdrive to meet the sudden demand for drinks following that infusion of energy in the room. I had seen this dynamic play out many times. I knew what was coming next. I would have bet my entire presidential pension that we were all now on the midst of an epic, raucous bash destined go deep into the night.

I couldn't have been more wrong.

Chapter Fifty

Georgia on My Mind
August 12, 2023
The Saloon

I was trying to make sense of what just happened—seeing Maggie seemingly in a moment of extreme vulnerability and perhaps despair, but following that with a very energetic and memorable rendition of that Georgia anthem that brought down the house. I didn't know quite what to make of it all.

I watched Mary Ann as she was scrambling to fill drink orders, but she herself was keeping an eye on Maggie the whole time. And I watched Maggie, who was bathing in the adulation of the room in the aftermath of that song, enhanced also by the fact that we hadn't seen her in a little while. It was great to have her back amongst us.

It had been a few minutes and the band hadn't yet attempted to follow that up with anything. Otter had been in discussion with the lead singer. After talking with the rest of the band, they began playing a slow, stirring version of Georgia on my Mind. That stopped Maggie in her tracks. She was surrounded by the Harrisons, Chester Arthur and Franklin Pierce, but I could see her mind was suddenly a million miles away.

My table had moved on to another subject. During Maggie's song, Teddy looked at Washington and asked, "Tell me, General, what was your closest brush with death during battle?" That struck me as such a classic Teddy question. A man's man if ever there was one.

Washington, with a slight smile, began his response by saying, "Where would you like me to begin, President Roosevelt?"

That response seemed to excite TR.

Washington then carefully described the events leading up to the Battle of the Monongahela in 1754, where he led British forces against the French in the Ohio Valley at the tender age of 22. He then recounted a costly, ugly battle where he had not one but two horses shot out from under him, leaving him with four bullet holes in his coat and another in his hat but not a blemish on his body. "Death was leveling my companions on every side of me," described Washington. "But for some reason, it couldn't touch me."

Roosevelt beamed.

Although I suspected the great general was far from finished, and I desperately wanted to hear all that followed, I felt compelled to leave this engrossing conversation and check in with Mary Ann about Maggie, or perhaps Maggie herself.

Turns out, there couldn't be a better time to slip away unnoticed than when Washington is telling war stories. Such was his ability to captivate the attention of all these men who followed him. I managed to slither away absent any commotion.

I caught up with Mary Ann on her way back to the bar. She approached me and leaned in close so no one could overhear.

"I may need your help. I think our girl needs us."

"What's going on with her? Is she alright?"

"She's going through an awful lot."

"In what sense? Personally? Professionally?"

"I think in every sense."

Our whispering was causing some others around us to take notice. Mary Ann picked up on that. She looked at me, tilted her head toward the bar and then quickly walked away. I followed her lead.

Once out of earshot of the crowd she turned back to me. "You may be able to help her, Danny Mac."

"Me? Happy to do anything I can. I mean, that's what we're here for after all."

"Great. She may not want to open up to you—or any of you guys. I think she feels a women demonstrating emotion would be judged much more harshly than a man. But I think it may be just what she needs."

"Great. That's good to know. I'm on it. Thanks for all you do for us in here."

"I do more for some of you than I do for others." She laughed. "Good luck."

***

I made my way over to Maggie. "Can I have you for a few minutes?"

"What? I'm not singing another song. I was taught to go out on top. I caught lightning in a bottle there, and I could never replicate that. You and George W are gonna have to find someone else."

"No, not that," I responded. "I promise. But I do need you for a few minutes."

She scanned the room, I'm sure looking for Mary Ann—who did happen to be watching us but immediately looked away. Maggie was as sharp as I thought she was.

We walked to an open booth in the back and sat across from each other.

"We're all here to help you, Maggie. Whatever you may have going, you've got a support system right here."

"I don't know. I think they'll view it as a sign of weakness. And on the personal stuff, I'm not sure they experienced some of the same type of stuff I'm going through."

"You'd be surprised. I'm not saying they can be of any help with what it's like being a woman in that office, but some of these guys experienced devastating personal tragedy while serving as president, in addition to disastrous political defeats. And you know what? Many of them fought those battles on both fronts and not only persevered but conquered them in the end."

She looked at me and started to tear up. "I don't know—I think it might just be different for a woman. A lifetime of experience and observation has taught me that."

I took her hand across the table. "Here's what I can do for you," I said. "I can assemble these guys and kickstart a conversation that gets you all you need to hear without any necessity of you sharing what's going on or exposing yourself in any way. You share only what you are comfortable with, or nothing at all. We're here for you. It's the very least we can do for you and it certainly can't hurt. I promise you'll feel a renewed kinship with them and be inspired."

"And besides," I added, "this is the ultimate safe space. Nothing leaves this place. Unless you want it to."

Her face brightened ever so slightly.

"Were you ever in sales?" She asked. Now she was smiling.

"Is that a yes?"

"It might be."

"You'll be amazed by what you hear."

I wished I could shoulder some of that pain for her. For the first time since I began this saloon existence, I was nervous. But it felt right. I think this is what we spirits are supposed to be doing.

Chapter Fifty-One

I've Had a Rather Rough Go of It Lately
August 12, 2023
The Saloon

I returned to the tables near the bar where so many of the presidents were. Washington's table was now surrounded with perhaps a dozen and a half presidents, including many of those who had served as generals. It looked like Matty had delivered them a large tray of hard drinks and had stuck around to listen to the conversation. Lincoln was in the midst of describing an incident from the Civil War.

"Mary and I came under fire when we travelled to Fort Stevens to visit the troops defending the capital and inspect the site of the bloody battle that had happened that day. A rebel sniper in a nearby tree began shooting when he recognized me. An Army surgeon beside us was hit by the sniper. He survived, but the shock of it and the blood caused Mary to faint. They all hollered at me to get down."

"Did the rebels know it was you?" asked Teddy.

"Yes. I believe the shooter recognized me by my stove-pipe hat."

"You wore your big stove-pipe hat on your head on a simmering battlefield?" The whole gathering burst into laughter, led of course by Teddy—laughing the loudest amongst them.

"I have to admire that!" declared Teddy. Then he looked up and shouted to an imaginary tree above, "Here I am. Come and get me you sons of bitches!"

The surrounding presidents howled with laughter. The look on Lincoln's face made me think he wasn't certain whether he was being mocked or celebrated.

I whispered to Matty, "Are these guys still trading brush-with-death-stories?"

"Yes," he replied. "This is classic. All these 19th Century guys have them. They could go all night. This is really entertaining."

"Which one of these characters has had the best story?" I whispered.

"Wow, great question. Maybe General Hayes. Or Monroe."

"Better than Teddy getting shot in the chest and insisting on delivering a speech before going to the hospital?" I asked.

"He didn't tell that one. He told a few others though."

"That dude must have dozens."

I wondered how many times bullets had altered the course of human history. The ones that hit their target as well as the ones that didn't.

Someone tapped on my shoulder from behind. I turned and saw it was Otter.

"I saw you and Peaches having a moment."

I think she's goes by 'Gladys' now," I said.

"I rarely go back on a nickname, Rook." He smiled. "Although I applaud your effort. That's a good one . . . I'll have to think about that one. Proud of you."

Then, looking more seriously, he added, "Is everything alright with her though?"

"Do me a favor," I responded. "I think she feels everyone here kind of had nothing but smooth sailing in their family and personal life to make the rougher political moments more palatable. Would you possibly be able to work your magic and arrange a bit of a discussion of the boys dispelling that myth without putting her in any way on the spot?"

"I'd be honored, my friend." He seemed thrilled to be asked. "I'll talk to Big Daddy and a few of the others, and we'll tee that up for her. Give me a few minutes and I'll let you know when to join us."

"You are the best," I said. "What would this place be without you?"

"I know my role, Rook. It's all about knowing, accepting and executing your role. Don't you worry. I got this."

Wow. What expert life advice.

Twenty minutes later I was sitting at the bar with Wilson, Harding and Cleveland, chatting with Ginger when Haskell appeared at my side.

"President Bush says to tell you he has assembled the troops." I looked over and saw about a dozen of our colleagues seated around two tables in the back that had been joined together. The music, which had been rather lively, now consisted of slower, instrumental songs at low volume. Background music.

I looked around the room for Maggie. At first I feared she had left, but after a few moments I spotted her behind the stage talking with the lead singer. I walked over nearby and motioned to her. She excused herself and joined me. I told her the conversation we discussed had been arranged and asked if she was still up for it. She nodded, and a few moments later we settled in to the two empty seats left open in the center where the tables met.

To my surprise, Maggie herself kicked it off. "I've had a rather rough go of it lately, fellas. Personally, I've had some terribly troubling family challenges. And that's putting it mildly. Politically . . . how should I phrase this? My Vice President just betrayed me by casting a tie-breaking vote in the Senate against me. I can't imagine that's ever even happened before."

"I can imagine it," replied Andrew Jackson. "It happened to me too—by my Vice President John Calhoun—who voted down my appointment of Martin Van Buren as Minister to the United Kingdom." I heard some audible gasps of incredulity amongst the others at this revelation.

"To add insult to injury," Jackson added, "the Senate had the votes to deny the appointment outright, but enough members abstained purposely just to enable Calhoun to cast a dramatic vote against me."

"You can't be serious," cried Maggie. "You poor thing."

"Politics is not an industry for the feint of heart," Truman added.

"He displayed a want of every sense of honor, justice or magnanimity," added Jackson.

"Thank you for sharing that, President Jackson," said Maggie. "It does help to know I am not the only one who has had to suffer that particular slight."

I was thrilled that this conversation had gotten off to a start like this. I'm so glad Jackson shared that, especially since I wasn't sure what he thought of Maggie in the first place. I don't think he was thrilled at first about a woman in this role but I think this shows he was coming around to her. And he had to be proud that she was a fellow southerner.

Maggie wasn't done opening up.

"I feel like I should add that my political problems may seem tame compared to the manner in which my family life is being upended more and more by the day. I'm afraid to say I have reached a low point—and not just in my presidency."

I looked at Mary Ann over by the bar. The look of profound empathy in her expression said it all. That admission from Maggie left us all rather stunned—even those like myself who may have had a vague inkling of what she was going through.

Franklin Pierce, now observing the conversation with a group of others who had migrated to our table and were standing around us, stepped forward to be closer.

"Just as you are not alone in having a Vice President vote against you, President Bates," began Pierce, "neither are you alone if you are also experiencing in the White House the sadness and depression that accompanies family tragedy."

I was thrilled that Pierce was speaking up, even though I had no idea where he was going with this.

"Just a month before my inauguration I was traveling by rail with my family near Andover, Massachusetts when an axle broke and our train derailed. Our carriage descended down an embankment."

He paused.

With his voice now cracking, he continued. "Our 11-year old son, Benny," pausing again, "was killed instantly before our eyes." He stopped talking, his eyes closed now.

My heart sank. Oh my god.

Moments later, he continued. "Our other two children already having passed in their childhood, Benny had been our only surviving child. The light of my life."

He paused again. I teared up. How could you not? I looked around—I was not alone.

"It was a devastating blow. How could I possibly summon my manhood and gather up my energies for all the duties that lay before me, with our country teetering on the brink of being torn apart. It left me unprepared to properly execute the leadership required, and my own party replaced me on the next ticket."

"What a terribly heartbreaking tragedy, President Pierce," said Maggie. I am so sorry to learn of it. Thank you from the bottom of my heart for sharing that."

"Unfortunately, Franklin, I know that feeling as well," said Coolidge. "When I was president, my son, Calvin Junior, developed a blister on his foot playing tennis on the White House tennis courts. We thought it nothing.

Soon it became infected, and to our eternal shock, developed into blood poisoning that took his life."

He let that sink in, looking around the room.

"When he went, the power and glory of the presidency went with him. For the remainder of my time in the White House, whenever I glanced out the window, I would always see my boy playing tennis on that court there."

He paused a few more moments before continuing. "I couldn't understand why such a price was exacted for occupying the White House."

I looked around and saw that all of the presidents and as well as the bar staff had now gathered around us. I'm certain so many could sympathize—certainly with the mental anguish of holding the job, even if they hadn't experienced personal tragedy while in the White House.

I could see that Lincoln was keenly interested in the discussion. I knew he lost his mother when he was quite young, and I recalled that he had sons that died young too. His mannerisms and demeanor struck me as those of a man who had battled depression. He had to have. His default expression seemed to be one of sadness. I had hoped he would join the discussion.

He leaned forward in his chair and looked at Maggie. "Mary and I experienced profound family tragedy in the White House. My poor Willie died in February of 1862. It was so hard to see him die."

His voice now cracking, he paused to compose himself.

"Such a sweet-tempered, smart, thoughtful boy. He was Mary's favorite. He was too good for this earth."

He stopped again. Then, moments later, gathered himself again, and looked straight at Maggie.

"In this sad world of ours, sorrow comes to all. I am anxious to afford some alleviation of your present distress. Perfect relief may not be possible, except with time. You cannot now realize that you will ever feel better. Is not this so? And yet it is a mistake. You are sure to be happy again. To know this, which is certainly true, will make you some less miserable now. I have had experience enough to know what I say; and you need only to believe it, to feel better at once."

Maggie seemed quite moved. "Thank you so much, President Lincoln," she replied, "for sharing that and for your words of encouragement."

"So well-stated, President Lincoln," said John Quincy Adams. "I too experienced extreme sorrow which I managed to prevail over. When my eldest son, George Washington Adams, took his own life, I was overcome with despair. In time, to assuage my grief, I made a vow to employ the remaining days which God has allotted me on earth to purposes approved by God and tributary to the well-being of others. Rest assured, there is light to be found after the darkness."

"Unfortunately, that is something else John and I have in common," said the elder Adams. "His brother, Charles, died while I was in office."

"I lost my darling wife, Letitia, during my presidency," added Tyler. "She had been disabled some years before, and confined to a wheelchair, such that when I ran as Vice President our plan was simply to stay in our house in Williamsburg and only come to Washington for official duties as needed. This would allow her to continue to stay at home where she was comfortable and our family could properly care for her."

"That right there tells you all you need to know how about how 'indispensable' the job of Vice President is," cracked LBJ. I questioned the timing of that quip, but a few managed a laugh.

"Yes, indeed, Lyndon," replied Tyler. "It was wholly undemanding. But all that soon changed when I suddenly had to assume the presidency. We reluctantly moved into the White House. Letitia remained in her bed and wheelchair on the second floor at all times. Sadly, we lost her to a stroke a year and half later. But her condition never altered her cheerful disposition. Nor her beauty."

"Thank you for sharing your memories of her, President Tyler," said Maggie. It sounds as if she was a remarkable woman."

Tyler's solemn expression brightened at that complement. However, with his emotions gearing up he chose not to respond.

William Henry Harrison filled in. "She was indeed," he declared. "I will testify to that."

Harrison's son Benjamin spoke up. "I lost my wife Caroline during my presidency. To tuberculosis. I must mention that this mansion was quite rodent-infested upon our arrival. We all have Caroline to thank for taking it upon herself to have them eradicated."

"While that may be true," remarked Jackson, "I have to say I've still seen more than a few rats around this place."

That drew some laughter.

I sat there rather dumbfounded at all these revelations. I could not believe how many of these men had experienced such profound tragedy while holding this office.

"Let me add something here, if I may," said Obama., who was standing behind me. "Whether or not you experience a tragedy while in office, and whether or not you suffer from clinical depression or some other form of mental illness, all of us know there is a certain loneliness to the job. That, you know, you'll get advice and you'll get counsel from a whole host of people. But ultimately, you're the person who's gonna be making those decisions, and you're the person who will be owning the consequences, good or bad—especially the bad. That is a considerable burden."

Nodding of heads throughout the room indicated near unanimous agreement with his words.

"But in spite of that loneliness, and that burden, and the undeniable anxiety it produces, so many presidents have achieved great things from that office—often while experiencing depression, battling mental illness or coping with great personal tragedy."

Wow, I thought. This was the most beautiful part of this great saloon—as an invaluable learning tool and mechanism for coping in this all-encompassing job that has become all but impossible as the world and the country evolve into ever-more complex entities.

Teddy Roosevelt, sitting across the table, raised his hand. A burst of energy and anticipation coursed through the room.

May I add a few thoughts?"

Maggie's expression brightened. All of ours did. "Oh, please do, President Roosevelt."

"Thank you for that, President Obama," he began. "Take heart, my dear Maggie. Well before I was president, I found myself in a dark place, and pretty well convinced that all was lost in my life. On Valentine's Day, 1884, I lost both my mother and my young bride. My darling wife, Alice, was beautiful in face and form, and lovelier still in spirit. As a flower she grew, and as a fair young flower she died. None who ever knew her did not love and revere her for her bright sunny temper and her saintly unselfishness. Fair, pure and joyous as a maiden; loving, tender and happy. As a young wife, she had just become a mother, when her life seemed to have just begun, and when the years seemed so bright before her. Then, by a strange and terrible fate, death came to her. And when my heart's dearest died, I feared the light went from my life forever—that my life had been lived out."

"Then, later, after finishing a distant third place in the New York City mayor's race, I considered myself finished in politics too. Devasted both personally and professionally, I was a beaten man."

He paused and looked around. The room hung on his every word.

Then, ever so slowly, he arose.

"But courage, my fellow leaders, is not, as some would assume, having the strength to go on. No sir. It's going on when you don't have the strength."

The room applauded long and hard. Maggie beamed.

"Yes, I licked my wounds and for a brief time. I even felt sorry for myself, I am ashamed to say. How utterly soft. Shameful of me."

Then, steadily raising his voice, "But I came back. Oh, indeed did I come back."

The room began to applaud and he paused to allow it to swell, playing the room as skillfully as Arthur Fiedler in front of the Boston Pops. This was vintage Teddy.

"I dealt with potentially debilitating sorrow by pouring myself into work, with activity filling my days. As arduous as the task confronting me may have been, I was driven relentlessly by this truth—nothing in this world is worth having or worth doing unless it means effort, pain, difficulty."

The room kept applauding, and shouting encouragement. I was awash in goose bumps—and I never get goose bumps.

"We must dare to be great. And we must realize that greatness is the fruit of toil and sacrifice and high courage. We must show the qualities of practical intelligence, of courage, of hardihood, and endurance, and above all the power of devotion to a lofty ideal—which made great the men who founded this Republic in the days of Washington," he looked around the room to acknowledge some of the early presidents among us, and nodded his head when he came to Washington. "And made great the men who preserved this Republic in the days of Abraham Lincoln." He then looked at Grant, then Hayes, then Garfield, Benjamin Harrison, McKinley, and finally Lincoln.

The room was applauding loudly now.

"Yes, my dear Maggie, today I say summon the courage to carryon even when you don't have the strength. And dare to be great. For it is only due to that zeal and drive on the part of so many of your predecessors in their time of personal turmoil and tragedy that our country has achieved greatness."

The room was now standing and applauding. I looked at Maggie and she smiled back at me. How could she not? Teddy was working the crowd and it was working him.

No one wanted to even attempt to follow that display. The room was abuzz with energy and enthusiasm. The band, with a world-class sense of the mood and the moment, started playing a muted version the "Battle Hymn of the Republic." Wow. So many emotions stirred deep inside of me.

I was practically on the verge of tears when Big Time took the empty seat next to me. I had never seen him sit at a table before. He looked at me and then pointed at Teddy. "How priceless is that dude?" he asked.

"Nobody like him. No one even comes close," I responded.

"We've all heard this stuff from him many, many times," he added, "but that doesn't diminish it one bit. I could listen to that same speech every night and be just as inspired." He then arose and headed back to the bar—perhaps evidencing that work ethic Teddy inspires in us.

I turned again to look for Maggie but she was gone.

Mary Ann noticed me looking around. "I managed to catch her briefly as she left."

"Do you think this helped her?" I asked.

"Are you kidding? Yes. Absolutely. That was perfect. I've never seen them all open up quite like that."

"Great. I don't know exactly what she had intended in visiting the saloon tonight, but what she stumbled upon I would venture to say could not have possibly been replicated in any other manner. No amount of therapy or medication could have reset her mind and mood quite as effectively as that outpouring of empathy, compassion and inspiration."

It felt so right to be a small part of something that was clearly so invaluable. I think I was beginning to not only accept this new role and purpose for myself here, but embrace it and even relish it as well. Maybe that's how all these guys have come to terms with this existence. This night, like every night here, was all about Maggie, but I too was walking away feeling like I was on top of the world.

"It'll be awfully hard to top tonight," I said to Mary Ann..

"Oh, I'm not so sure about that," she responded.

"Really? How on earth are you gonna engineer that?"
"Easy," she replied. "She promised me she'd come back soon,"
"Yeah? So?"
"And that she'd bring her dogs with her."
Wow. Jackpot. That fired me up like nothing else.

Chapter Fifty-Two

A Big Proposition at Big Sur
September 3, 2023

"What bridge is that?" asked Maggie pointing up at the structure high in the hills along the coastal highway that connected one cliff to another. "That's rather famous, isn't it?"

"Bixby Bridge," answered Gil. "That's probably the most photographed spot in Big Sur. It's almost 100 years old now. Imagine what it must have taken to build that thing way back then. And that was completed before the road was done, too."

"What a gorgeous site. This is precisely the view I had hoped for, Gil," said Maggie. "Thank you so much for making this happen for me."

"Hopefully you'll see us get some fish pretty soon as well."

"That would be nice, but after seeing Monterey Bay from off the coast and now Big Sur, I really couldn't care less if we catch anything."

This little excursion, first discussed at Hannegan's months ago—where so many consequential plots are hatched, and some not so consequential—was months in the making. It took quite a bit of planning to bring it about, and world events had intervened twice to postpone it. But it was well worth the wait. We launched out of Moss Landing, just north of Monterey, and so far the entire three hours had been like a rolling panoramic postcard.

Denyse and I were enjoying the view from inside in the boat's cabin across from Gil and Maggie, who were chatting it up like they'd known each other for years. Gil's brother Wally and his cousin Ty were above us navigating from the open flybridge. Our view out the tinted windows on all sides of us was spectacular, and we benefitted from the cabin shielding us from the wind. We were moving pretty good.

"How fast are we going?" Denyse asked.

"I'd say at least 40 knots," answered Gil.

Denyse leaned in to me and whispered, "I have no idea what speed that really is."

Reading her mind, Maggie added, "It's a little faster than 40 miles an hour. Closer to 45."

Gil was thrilled to see her pounce on a nautical question like that.

"We're just trying to get a little south of here and then we'll see what we can catch. I expect we'll find some rockfish and lingcod. Some people have reported whitefish the past few days, but those are usually down south by the Channel Islands and Catalina."

We weren't exactly alone on the high seas. We certainly felt secure, with a few helicopters flying above us, and several boats surrounding us. We had three Secret Service and two Coast Guard officials on board. It all struck me as an awful lot, compared to what I had gotten used to in office. Wally up top had a bloody mary going—he may have been the one they were most watchful of at the moment. For good reason, as far as I could tell.

A little while longer we stopped, still within eyesight of the majestic Big Sur coastline in the distance.

"Alright, said Gil. "Let's go give it a shot."

"Aye, aye, Captain," Maggie shot back jumping up to accompany him.

They headed out to the mezzanine. As we followed I saw Denyse flash me a bit of a look.

"What?" I asked. "You've got something on your mind."

She shook her head and tried to brush it off.

"No, seriously, what?" I asked again.

"You don't see what's going on here?"

I didn't respond, not knowing quite what exactly to say.

"I would surmise that's your friend Maggie might be aiming to hook a little more than just a few rockfish and lingcod on this little excursion."

"What?" I laughed. "You're crazy."

"Am I? All I know is that I've got some pretty powerful instincts, which you should know by now, and they are all pointing to one conclusion."

"I don't see how you can—"

"My goodness I thought you were smarter than that, McFadden."

"OK, they are both uncommonly personable, charming, attractive people that others just naturally gravitate to, so of course they'll get along famously. But she's the frickin Leader of the Free World and he's a bartender at Hannegan's. Of course, I would love to live in a world where that could happen but I just don't think it's this world."

"Wow. Did I hear that right? You are literally the last person on earth who I would think would speak disparagingly of a bartender. Especially one at Hannegan's. Unless, of course, you were implying the opposite—that a president is beneath a bartender, which kind of sounds a lot more like something you might actually think."

"No—I'm not saying they aren't enjoying each other's company. But c'mon. Even if they wanted to have anything beyond that it might just be far too impractical logistically. And besides, I think she's technically still married to that squid."

"Squid?" She howled.

"That's how Brett and Jack usually refer to Kelly's boyfriends," I replied. "I thought it would only be appropriate with our Mr. Bates too."

"Those boys are too much. They are so protective of Kelly. But in this case I would think their description is spot on. But as to these two," she pointed out at Maggie and Gil and paused. "Look, let me just say I love you dearly but you have a blind spot when it comes to these things. You have a few blind spots."

"You seem to be the expert on my blind spots."

"While that may be true, I'm also the expert on your multitude of endearing and charming qualities too, which more than make up for the few, insignificant blind spots."

We stepped outside the cabin, and saw Wally and Gil preparing to cast their lines.

Before we were near them she leaned in to me. "Care to make a little wager on the truth of my intuition?"

"Sure. Whatever you like."

"Anything?"

"Yes."

"OK. If I win, you have to serve dinner and tend bar all night for my old bunko group girlfriends and wait on us hand and foot. I'll reassemble them just for that. It's been about ten years. And if you win, I'll do the same for your old poker group."

"Ha! I love it. Of course. But I'm not sure we'll ever really know when one of us has won."

"Oh, I have a feeling we'll know . . . "

Gil turned toward us. “We’re in about 170 feet of water right now. There’s some action 100 feet down and below. We’re gonna drop our lines and give it a shot.”

Just moments later Gil cried out, “Wow. Fish on.”

“Holy shit,” yelled Wally. “Me too.”

“These lings and rockfish love bait,” added Gil, maneuvering his rod. “They are aggressive at live bait.”

“What did you use for bait?” asked Maggie.

“Octopus. And squid.”

Denyse busted out a laugh. I ignored her but I, too, thought it was hilarious.

“Feels like a rockfish.” added Gil. “He’s a fighter. These rockfish are.”

He glanced back at Maggie with a big smile. “Care to take over, Madame President?”

“Oh no, thank you. I prefer the view from right here.”

Denyse shot me a look. I just shook my head.

“Fishing for these guys at these depths is not always fun but that’s where they are today,” said Gil.

I know Gil sensed Denyse and I were a bit out of our element. He addressed his running narrative right at us, assuming, I’m sure, that Maggie didn’t need it.

“I’ve got a great reel, here, see? It’s got a big handle. I’m pulling in 30 to 36 inches with each crank. It makes a difference in these deep waters.”

When his fish became visible in the water we could see it was bright orange. He pulled it up and grabbed a hold of it, with one hand in the mouth. It had huge, exaggerated bug eyes.

“Vermillion rock fish,” he pronounced. “Beautiful fish. I’m guessing 8 pounds.”

“Was it squid or octopus you used there?” asked Denyse.

“Squid.”

“Good,” she responded. “I was hoping you’d say that.”

Gil looked confused for a brief moment.

I looked at Denyse and shook my head. “Stop.”

Then all of the sudden Ty yelled, “Fish off. Get the gaff. Get the gaff.”

As Gil was setting down his fish, Maggie spotted the gaff nearby, grabbed it, plunged it into the water, speared the bright orange rockfish on her first try and brought it up herself.

Wally quickly grabbed it from her and brought it to the cooler. But then he turned around, kneeled down, and, raising his hands above his head, pointed in her direction and bent over signaling "we're not worthy."

Gil shook his head, looked at Maggie, and exclaimed, "that was a sight to behold, Madam President," while Denyse and I applauded together with Ty.

"Oh, please," Maggie protested. "Don't tell me you've never seen a woman who knows her way around a proper fishing boat before."

"You have an open invitation to join us on any future voyage of the Fields of Paradise, ma'am," said Gil.

"Look, fellas," said Maggie, "the poor thing was barely moving in the water. It was floating away, not swimming away. If you're impressed by that—"

"Why is that?" asked Denyse. "I thought they said it was fighting pretty hard."

"When you reel these guys in from deep water their bladders fill all the way up and their eyes bug out," responded Gil. "They become docile. That happens with rockfish."

Maggie sat down, exhaled, and looked at Gil. "On second thought, I think I will take that bloody mary, thank you."

"Coming right up," responded Gil immediately. "You certainly earned it, ma'am."

Moments later he handed her a pint glass full of bloody mary, garnished with nothing less than a small lobster tail.

"My goodness," she said, taking a big sip. "Classy. And a heavy pour, too. Why am I not surprised?"

Denyse caught my eye, smiled, and then quickly looked away. I knew exactly what that meant. I could sense her already planning the guest list in her mind.

About an hour and a half and roughly a dozen rockfish and lingcod later, not to mention a few more bloody marys all around, Maggie looked over at me. "Can I get a few minutes, Danny?"

"Of course."

"Why don't we go back inside." She got up and walked back into the cabin.

As I followed, I looked back and Denyse. She was very discreet about it, but her brief look told me she was just dying to know what this was about.

I took a seat inside the cabin next to her. We could see the mini armada of boats around us."

"Look at all the men on those boats required just to allow you a little cruise of the ocean," I said. "There must more than a dozen following you."

"Oh, honey that's nothing. Most of us Georgia ADPi girls are quite accustomed to that kind of attention."

She delivered it with a straight face, but before I could even process it she let out a southern howl that I'm sure they could hear out on the deck.

I laughed. Moments later her face quickly turned serious in a way that kind of startled me.

"Uh oh," I said. "Do I need a cocktail for this?" I asked. "I know enough not to have too many on a boat. Learned that the hard way deep sea fishing off Fort Lauderdale on Spring Break back in college."

Her smile returned. "Not necessary. Maybe a hot ale flip if they serve those here."

I laughed. That told me everything I needed to know about her and the saloon. Suddenly I became a tad jealous.

"No thanks," I said. "But I can recommend a place where they serve up some pretty good ones,"

"I have a feeling I know the place you refer to. I think they need to attract more ladies among their clientele. Those hot ale flips aren't exactly packing them in."

As much as I enjoyed poking around this particular issue, I chose not to bite any further, considering how it was just a pleasant memory, never to be revisited in person again. At least I didn't think so.

She moved on. "But I need your full attention for a few moments."

"You have all of that and then some," I responded. Now I was really intrigued.

"I have an ulterior motive for being here."

OK—maybe Denyse was right, I thought. Is she really gonna ask me about Gil?

"As you know," she said, "Margel is killing me in the party, and he's going hard after any other Republican who tries to compromise with Democrats."

"I can see that."

"There's much more to gain for him politically by ranting and raving and seeking division than by playing nicely in the sandbox with others."

"Yes. And it gets him attention and money. There are so many out there who are bitter and resentful that they have been ignored for decades and he's riling them up by framing everything as an existential battle between them and the wokest of the left, ignoring that there's a massive constituency in the middle that doesn't even seem to have a voice in the discussion."

"Well, I managed to have a long meeting with him last week at Blair House. He's going to resign as Vice President."

"Good. Why hasn't he resigned to this point?" You long ago cut him completely out of anything official."

"He has been demanding a full pardon before he'll resign. I finally convinced him that my Justice Department is just not interested in going after him. I'm pretty sure he's only agreeing to step aside now in order to free himself up to run against me full-time."

"Yes, ever since he broke that tie in the Senate I had a sense he was aiming to unseat you."

"No question about that."

"That son of a bitch."

"No—I wouldn't say that. A wise man once told me politics is a nasty business. I'm a big girl. No one owes me anything in life."

"Did you hear that in the saloon?"

"I did, as a matter of fact."

"I think I know the man to which you refer. Wisdom wouldn't exactly be the first word I'd use to characterize that dude's words."

"Oh, I beg to differ."

I felt a little bad making light here. She appeared more vulnerable in that moment than I had ever imagined I'd see her. Silhouetted against the cliffs of Big Sur in the distance behind her, her eyes cast a shade of blue somewhere in between that of the sky above and the dark Pacific below.

"Your movement, Danny, really helped get me elected in the first place, as people viewed me as a much more moderate and feared what they viewed as Clayton's more, shall we say, socialist tendencies. People like Margel have now caused a lot of true conservatives to get frustrated with the more extreme and divisive elements in the Republican party and become independents. That only makes my challenge in getting re-elected more unlikely, particularly since those Republicans who left the party won't be voting in the primary. I don't know how I'd survive the primary."

"Here's what I'm getting at, Danny. I'd like to name you my Vice President when Margel steps down, and have you run with me on the ticket next year. I've thought about this long and hard, and consulted with my political team. I firmly believe that if you can't help me, the country may be looking right down the barrel of an election where both choices are equally unpalatable—Margel on the right versus Clayton again on the left. And that will only fuel more of the polarization and divisiveness you're always talking about."

Maybe I should have been expecting that but I clearly wasn't. It floored me. I'm not sure what my expression conveyed but from the looks of hers I'd say she was disappointed.

"Before you say no, think about it for a little bit. I acknowledge it might not be the best thing for your family, but I'm suggesting it's the best thing for your country. As a matter of fact, it may be the only hope left for your country."

I sat back, more than a little bit stunned.

"I know you revere some of our nation's greats who rose to the occasion when the country most needed them, even at great personal hardship to themselves. Many of whom I happen to know you count among your heroes—people like George Washington, Thomas Jefferson and Teddy Roosevelt."

Now I knew she was parroting conversations with my doppelganger in the saloon.

"Of course," she added, "there are countless others who have answered that call as well, like Clara Barton, Eleanor Roosevelt, Harriet Tubman, and Ruth Bader Ginsburg. The list is endless. And impressive. These are all heroes. Household names."

"As strong as our democracy and our foundational documents are, we just don't survive as a republic without countless actions by people of integrity and character who went above and beyond the call of duty for this country. Their actions have kept our democracy intact through the years."

I smiled. "You're certainly speaking my language here, Maggie." It was easy to see how she got to where she is. She's a tough one to say no to.

"And you are sure you want to take a chance on me? I mean really, you hardly know me."

"Oh, I'm pretty sure I know you. I think I know you a whole lot better than you think I know you."

That set my mind on fire again. I wondered how my saloon spirit was interacting with her. If he respected her, tried to help her, harbored any jealousies toward her. What I wouldn't give to know how some of those conversations went. But if this is any indication, apparently they've been going well.

I promised her I would consider it and decide soon. She was encouraged by that.

"By the way," she added, "do you have any additional advice for me?"

"Additional?" I asked.

"Yes," she responded, smiling.

"OK. Here's one. Charm the press like you've charmed everyone else your whole life. Even the ones who've been kicking your tail since your Korea decision—especially those."

"Charming them is the last thing I want to do with them. I refuse to be nice to those that have been so truly despicable."

"That may be. I completely understand that. I'm just saying there's monumental value in it. And it's your greatest asset. It may feel as though you are letting them win, but if it results in even a little better coverage you win even bigger."

"I think you know I've experienced some depression in the last few years for the first time in my life. More than some, I should say. My husband has a lot to do with that, and you can see how it has impacted our son. But surely the press has a lot to do with it as well."

She had a look less of anger now than profound sadness.

"Well, no, I was unaware of that," I responded. "That is certainly understandable, but I must say you've hidden it well from public view."

"That's a bit of my mama's influence. God rest her soul. She was always just as sweet and delightful as can be no matter what manner of havoc was being wreaked around her behind the scenes. Are you familiar with the term highly functioning depression?"

"Yes, of course."

"I suspect a good portion of the country is experiencing one or more forms of depression regularly. A good deal of that I believe is hidden from view."

"Have you thought of bringing the country in on it—to shine a light on it?"

"I don't think I'm quite ready for that, Danny. Nor is the country. And some in the media would be relentless about making it a gender issue. As the first woman president I can't have that be a part of my legacy. That would do a terrible disservice to women. And girls."

"I don't doubt that. "

"Enough talk about this. Today has been helpful. What a lovely day. I'm so glad we did it. Thank you for your role in this."

"I had nothing to do with it. This is a Gil production."

"Either way, thank you. This is therapeutic. Now let's go join our shipmates."

We reemerged on the back mezzanine, and saw the fish haul seemed to be growing exponentially.

Denyse stood right alongside Wally helping him reel in a lincod. She saw us right away.

"Did he give you his 'we're better than this' speech, President Bates?" Denyse asked Maggie. "I could deliver that in my sleep. I'm pretty sure I have."

Maggie laughed. "Actually, I sort of gave that speech to him, but I'll leave it to him to fill you in."

"Talk about preaching to the choir," answered Denyse. "That's preaching to the choir director, there. I can't imagine you got any pushback."

"Well, we'll have to see about that," said Maggie. I certainly hope not."

I could see Denyse's mind spinning. But even so I'm sure she had absolutely no idea what just transpired. I'm not altogether sure I even did.

***

The sun was getting low on the horizon as we approached Moss Landing at the conclusion of a very long day. As we got closer to the harbor we could see as many as a dozen otters bouncing around in the water seemingly loving life as only otters can.

Ty was bringing us in up top and Wally was in the cabin with the rest of us. He looked over at Denyse and me.

"So McFadden, are you up for Hannegan's tonight?"

"I don't think I can answer the bell tonight," I said.

"How do you know I wasn't talking to the other McFadden?" he said, laughing.

Denyse completely missed that little exchange. I could see she was singularly focused on trying hard to hear the conversation across from us between Maggie and Gil. It really wasn't hard, they were plenty loud enough for anyone who cared to hear them.

"Which of your novels should I begin with?" Maggie asked.

Gil responded quickly. "Definitely not the first one. Not the second, either. The third is when I started to hit my stride. They say we all have one great one in us. That was mine. Try that one."

"Sure. What's the name of that one?"

"Red Sky at Morning."

"I'm in. Sounds ominous."

"That's intentional."

"Let me ask you this," Maggie said. "Does that simple, Joe Lunchbucket, fisherman protagonist of yours have a love interest?" She smiled, thrilled to have asked that question.

"Maybe," replied Gil grinning back. "I'd say it's something he's presently working on. And getting increasingly optimistic about by the minute."

"Oh, is he now?" she responded, with more than a hint of delight.

Denyse whirled and looked me right in the eyes with a big smile. "So, Danny, I think my bunko ladies would like to begin with a nice array of healthy yet tasty appetizers, preferably with an assortment of martinis—just to get the evening started, perhaps accompanied by a Billy Joel playlist."

"Hold on now," I said. "I really think you're jumping the gun here."

"Oh, I couldn't disagree more. I like my chances. Actually, McFadden, I'd even go so far as to say I've got you on this—hook, line and sinker."

Chapter Fifty-Three

College Danny
September 8, 2023

My phone vibrated in my pocket just as Denyse, Kelly and I were entering the gates at the Jesuit Prep High School's football field for the first game of the season. Some of Jack's friends on the football team had convinced him to give it a shot for his senior year and it didn't take too much to convince him. I love that about him. The baseball coaches weren't too happy about that but somehow that may have only increased his desire to play. I wasn't sure how much playing time he was going to get, but I was thrilled that he gave it a shot and was enjoying it.

My phone buzzed as we approached the bleachers. I considered ignoring it, but pulled it out of my pocket just to check and see who it was.

Satch. I had to take that. I motioned to Denyse and Kelly to go ahead and I walked around the track beyond the end zone to get a little privacy. Brent followed, while Ricky accompanied the girls into the stands. Aaron and a few others I didn't recognize dispersed amongst the crowd.

I skipped the hello and greeted him instead with a challenge. "Are you not streaming this game? What kind of unofficial uncle are you, anyway?"

"I am so sorry—does Jack have a game? I'll find it right now."

"No big deal. It's football not his baseball team. I don't even know if he'll start. I only have a few moments. They're gonna kick off in about ten minutes."

"I won't take up much of your time, then. Christie saw a report on the internet that you took our president for a fishing trip and I had to call and see how you two got along."

I laughed. "I wouldn't say I took her. I'm no man of the sea. A friend of mine arranged it all. Denyse and I were just kind of along for the ride. But it was great day. A unique and interesting day, but a fun one."

"How did it go with her and you?"

"Very well. I like her more every time I meet her. I feel very badly for her with some of her personal and political challenges. I really do enjoy her company—I don't think I was prepared to be won over like that."

"She is a delightful person. Are you planning on spending a lot more time with her?"

"Why do you ask? What have you heard?"

"Let's just say I'm aware of some advice she's received to possibly attempt to hitch her wagon to your star politically."

"And how on earth would you find that out?"

"She may have solicited my advice, knowing of our friendship."

"And that's not something you felt you should give me a heads up about?" I was somewhat surprised, though not annoyed.

"To be honest, sir, I want you to join forces with her. Like you, I am so deeply worried about the polarization in this country, and I don't see many paths out of it without direct involvement by you, given all you stand for and the unique following you've carved out in this country. I love you to death, sir, but as a Marine, my obligation to this country comes first."

"Well, let me tell you, I called her yesterday and respectfully turned her down. Jack's a senior now, and not only do I not want to move him again but I want to be here right alongside him for every bit of it. He's in a really good place. If I mess this up for him he'll never get this year back, and neither will I. Just look at the way Maggie's son has been impacted by all their craziness. Additionally, politically speaking, I just wouldn't feel right attaching myself with either party in light of all that I've done to lead and help organize this independent movement."

"I respect that decision, sir. And I wouldn't dream of trying to talk you out of that."

"But I told her that just because I'm not joining the ticket doesn't mean the Alliance won't be helping the cause. I am guessing that if it's Clayton who starts to emerge from the far left, and Margel gains traction from the far right, the Alliance will work overtime on her behalf to help defeat Margel to secure the nomination and then beat Clayton to earn a second term. She does, however, face the same type of challenges I did in getting re-elected. That's the trouble with the middle."

"I understand and appreciate that. I would add only that I do encourage you to get involved in this upcoming presidential election in the greatest capacity you can given your other family priorities. We're still as a country trying to right this ship, and we need as much of you as you are willing to offer. Please don't completely sit that one out."

I made my way back to the home bleachers. As I got nearer to Denyse, sitting at the far end of the crowd, I could hear her voice in what seemed to be a lively conversation. Ordinarily that wouldn't be anything to be alarmed about. Denyse is about as friendly and chatty as they come. As I got closer, however, I noticed that I recognized the woman sitting next to her—who seemed to be talking every bit as much as Denyse. I hadn't seen her in about twenty years, but there was no mistaking who this was, and the thought of her next to Denyse without me there shepherding the conversation sent a shiver down my spine. It was Lori Summer—who used to run with my crowd in college and was a fixture in my dorm. I knew she was a Jesuit High parent and I had a vague recollection that her son played football.

Ricky was in the row directly in front of them and motioned for me to sit there. Brent stood momentarily in the aisle perusing the crowd. I noticed a few other familiar Secret Service faces nearby. The ladies looked at me and smiled broadly. I could tell that introductions were no longer necessary. The looks on their faces led me to believe considerable damage had already been done. I plopped myself directly in front of Denyse and Lori, hoping to manage any of the fallout.

"Lori – oh my God," I said. "It's so great to see you. You have not aged a bit. How are you?"

"I'm great, Danny. It's certainly been a while. I've often wonder what ever happened to you."

I laughed and so did she. "A lot," I responded. "A lot has happened. Too much has happened."

"Lori was just filling us all in a bit about 'College Danny,'" said Denyse. "I must say I'm not altogether sure I would have fallen in love with that Danny."

"How on earth did you possibly get that much information in just five minutes? What did you tell them, Lori?"

"I told them the truth. I told them you were really, really fun to hang with, Danny. You really were. I can't emphasize that enough. But you may have still had a little maturing yet to do back when I knew you."

Denyse howled. Kelly had been mid-sip on her Diet Coke, and almost spit it back up through her nose.

"You and your girlfriends kept coming back to hang with us, Lori! That must not have bothered you too much, then," I protested.

"We actually kind of felt sorry for you guys." She laughed, but not nearly as loudly as Denyse and Kelly. "But, yes, Danny, it was highly entertaining."

"I admire how diplomatically you phrased that, Lori," said Denyse.

"Can I suggest that maybe it wouldn't have been nearly as entertaining if I—or really all of us— were more mature. How boring would that have been?"

"Ha," she laughed. "I will grant you that."

I looked at Kelly. "Lori and her friends came to all our parties, tailgated with us and sat with us at football games, shuffled around among us as dates for all our dances, and they were always there for masses on Sunday Night in our hall chapel."

Kelly smiled. "Well at least you were going to Mass back then, Dad. Who would have thought 'College Danny' would have something on 'Ex-President Danny.'"

That triggered another round of laughter.

"Back then I didn't need a security detail to attend church."

"OK, Dad," Kelly responded. "You just keep telling yourself that's the reason you're neglecting your weekly obligation."

Lori laughed out loud. "I love both your wife and daughter, Danny."

I shook my head. "I think both of them are enjoying this way too much."

Kelly had another question. She was suddenly full of them.

"So it sounds like Mom's convinced she wouldn't have liked College Danny. Why aren't we asking if College Danny would have fallen in love with College Denyse back then?"

"Great question, Kelly," I quickly interjected. "The answer is of course I would have. I would have absolutely fallen head over heels for your mother at any age, in any era of history, in any country, on any planet, and under any other conceivable circumstances."

"Wow," said Lori. "What an answer, Danny. Nice of your daughter to tee that up for you."

I saw Denyse with a look of exasperation whispering to Kelly, but in a voice plenty loud enough for me to hear.

"Then please ask him why it took him all of five years to ask me to marry him?"

Kelly just laughed and looked over at Lori. "Could he talk like that back in the day?"

"At a certain point in the night, when the party got to full tilt, he kind of came into his own and there was no holding him back. He could get rolling pretty good and we would just sit back and take in the show."

Kelly, just a year removed from college, had another question. "Please tell me he was respectful of women?"

"Oh, yes. He just wanted to make sure everyone was having the most fun possible—beginning with him."

I thought hard to determine if that was a compliment or a shot. I chose to take it as a compliment and move along.

Lori mercifully changed the subject. "I heard you were fishing with the President a few days ago."

"Yes. Right off of Big Sur. We had a great day."

"Did President Bates catch anything?"

"I think she was trying to land a lot more than just a fish," Denyse answered.

"Oh really," responded Lori. "Perhaps a little political alliance, so to speak?"

"Maybe," I said, "although I'm not sure that's what my lovely wife was referring to."

I looked at Denyse, shook my head, and turned back to the game.

Chapter Fifty-Four

Have You Ever Heard of James Madison?
November 23, 2023

Unfortunately, Maggie couldn't seem to catch a break. Each week seemed to bring new frustration.

POLITICO

SENATE REJECTS PRESIDENT'S NOMINATION OF KASICH TO FILL VP ROLE

(11/23/2023 2:05 PM EST) By Fredrika Kramer, POLITICO Reporter

In an embarrassing rebuke that promises to have reverberations well into the upcoming election year, the Senate today voted down President Bates' nomination of former Ohio Governor and Congressman John Kasich to be Vice President. The President had hoped to have Kasich, a Republican viewed by many as a moderate, fill the role left vacant by the resignation of Vice President Charles Margel. Only 48 Senators voted in favor of the nomination. Opposition came from many progressive Democrats, following the lead of Senator Clayton of Massachusetts, who argued that Kasich's strong anti-union views should disqualify him. Perhaps even more surprising, however, nearly two dozen Republican senators voted in opposition to the nomination of their fellow Republican, after being lobbied to do so in the last few weeks by former Vice President Margel himself, evidence of a deep division emerging within that party. Both senators who belong to the Alliance Party supported the President's nomination.

It is unclear where President Bates intends to go from here in her search for a replacement to fill the vacancy. Thus far the White House has not released a public comment on the defeated nomination and calls to the Press Secretary today were not returned. White House aids speaking off the record expressed disappointment bordering on anger at the result of the vote.

***

MSNBC

DEADLINE: WHITE HOUSE

Nicole Wallace: President Maggie Bates paused to take a few questions this evening on her way to Marine One on the back lawn of the White House prior to embarking on a trip to Dallas. I think you'll find her responses to a few of the questions posed to her by members of the White House press corps to be interesting, and perhaps even mildly entertaining. Let's roll the tape.

> *(Video)*
>
> **Newsmax Reporter Roger Barrington**: *Madam President, if you can't get a nomination for vice president appointed through Congress, and end up serving the remainder of your term without anyone in that role, is that not by itself an indicator of a failed presidency?*
>
> **President Bates**: *Who asked that?*

(Barrington raises his hand.)

President Bates: *Let me ask you something. Have you ever heard of James Madison? He served without a Vice President—for nearly four years. How about Teddy Roosevelt? Have you heard of him? He spent more than three years without a vice president. He's on Mount Rushmore, by the way. John Tyler served his entire presidency without a vice president. McKinley, Truman, Coolidge, LBJ—all of them spent months and years without vice presidents. I appreciate your concern, but we'll be just fine, thank you. I think I'm in good company on that score.*

Washington Post Reporter Rachel Niven: *If you don't fill the Vice President role, Madam President, the Speaker of the House would be first in the line of succession to you. Are you comfortable with Speaker Crawford, a member of the Alliance Party, being first in line to you?*

President Bates: *Are you actually asking me to speculate about my own death? Bless your heart. Perhaps you know something I don't. That reminds me I need to schedule my annual physical. Let me get back to you on that.*

But to answer you more directly, yes, I would be happy and I think the country would be well served if Speaker Crawford were to find himself as President. The Congress would miss him in his Speaker role, but he would make a fine President, and would be a unifying force in Washington. That said, let me just say at the same time here for the record that's not an outcome I am presently rooting for.

Nicole Wallace: How about that? She certainly has a sense of humor now, doesn't she.

Chapter Fifty-Five

There Is Nuance in the World
three months later
February 23, 2024

Denyse, Jack and I and tuned in to the first Republican Presidential Primary Debate together with seemingly all of America. I was a rarity in US politics—someone who had ascended to the presidency without ever having to take part in one of these time-honored spectacles. I always kind of felt they were as helpful at picking great presidents as the Westminster Dog Show is at picking great dogs. And they seem to employ remarkably similar criteria.

I had a big rooting interest here. Not only had I come to know and like Maggie very much, I felt she really had begun to embody the country-over-party mantra—and that had become all the more important as Margel's campaign message seemed to consist mainly of spouting a laundry list of complaints and wedge issues intended to divide not only the country but the Republican Party as well. I may have been a little skeptical of Maggie at first, but I was a full convert now.

PRESIDENTIAL DEBATE

REPUBLICAN PRIMARY

Al McGuire Center, Marquette University

President Margaret Bates

Former Vice President Charles Margel

Moderator for Segment 1: Brett Baier

Brett Baier: *Welcome to the first presidential primary debate of 2024. I'm Brett Baier, and we are coming to you live from the Al McGuire Center on the campus of Marquette University in Milwaukee, Wisconsin. Our two Republican primary candidates tonight are President Margaret Bates, the former Governor of the State of Georgia, and former Vice President Charles Margel, who also served as a Senator from the State of Ohio. Welcome to each of you.*

We want to get right to it. I know how candidates detest raising your hands in a debate when asked to answer just yes or no, so we will only be asking you to do that with two questions tonight. But we begin our debate tonight with those two questions, as they are both questions that seem to be coming up often these days.

The first is as follows: do each of you pledge that you will support the other in the event you are not successful in seeking the nomination of the Republican Party? Please raise your hand if your answer is no.

(President Bates raises her hand, the crowd groans.)

Baier: *To be clear, President Bates, by raising your hand* *you are stating that you do not pledge that you will support the Republican nominee for President if it is not you.*

President Margaret Bates: *I do understand that, Brett.*

Baier: *So you are standing on the debate stage of the Republican Presidential Primary, as part of the process by which the Republican Party will determine who the nominee of the party will be, and you can't say that you will support the nominee of the party if it's not you.*

(audience boos)

Bates: *Let me be clear, Brett, I expect that I will support our nominee, but Mr. Margel has been very unpredictable, and has a knee-jerk tendency to act as provocateur on so many issues, further dividing us as a country. I fully expect that I will be the candidate, but I want to see how he conducts his campaign first before I pledge my blind support for him no matter what he may choose to do or say.*

We're on a precarious path here as a country. Some of our internal issues threaten us in my view even more than the international ones. I cannot see myself voting for Senator Clayton, and I will happily pledge that tonight. But I'm unwilling to pledge blind support to Mr. Margel, and neither should our party.

(A mixture of applause and boos)

Baier: *Mr. Margel, do you pledge to support the candidate who successfully wins the nomination of the Republican Party following the primaries?*

Charles Margel: *I do. Of course I do. That should be a a bare minimum requirement of all candidates seeking our* *party's nomination.*

(Applause)

Baier: *Secondly, perhaps more importantly, do each of you pledge not to run an independent campaign if you are not the successful Republican candidate? Yes or no? First you, President Bates.*

Bates: *Let me put it this way, Brett, If I am not the nominee—*
Baier: *Please, Madam President, just yes or no.*

Bates: *I can't do that. I'm sorry, some things just can't be packaged nicely into one of two boxes and wrapped up in a bow. That's how we got where we are today in this country. It's that kind of thinking. There is nuance in the world—and there needs to be a lot more of it in our political discourse.*

Baier: *But you have to realize that by choosing to run as an independent, you would be virtually assuring that the Democratic candidate—which appears to be Senator Clayton, who calls himself a Democratic Socialist—would most certainly wind up in the White House. How can you give that message to Republican voters tonight and yet ask for their support?*

Bates: *I take issue with your premise. If the 2016 election taught us anything, it's that when the two parties select extreme candidates whose popularity outside their own party is virtually non-existent, as was the case with Hillary Clinton and Donald Trump, a lane is created in the middle for a competent moderate. In that election you'll recall that independents wouldn't stand for those two choices, and mobilized to put Danny McFadden in the*

White House. Since then his movement has only gained steam, and they now have a foothold in both the House and Senate. It's no longer a given that an independent will merely swing an election for one side of the other. 48% of voters do not identify as being either Republican or Democrat—the highest numbers in over 100 years. I'm not saying I would run as an independent if it's Mr. Margel versus Clayton, but I will tell you someone certainly will using Danny McFadden's playbook, and no, I'm not willing to pledge that it won't be me.

(louder boos mixed with louder applause)

***

Watching all this unfold was fascinating but nerve wracking.

"What do you think, Danny?" Asked Denyse. "Did she just blow any chance she had?"

"To get the nomination or win the election?"

"Both."

"Well, she hurt herself with the more ardent conservative base that won't appreciate her unwillingness to support the party if she loses. But that same positioning may help establish a predicate for a run as an independent."

"Do you think she'll do that? Would you support her? And would your movement get behind her?"

"I would. I like her, and I can't stomach either Margel or Clayton. I have a visceral reaction to Margel, and Clayton is just way too far left for the majority of the country. This 'Defund the Police' stuff is just batshit crazy. I think our people would support her if she took both of them on. However, a lot of people are still disillusioned by the mess that happened in Korea and its repercussions. That's been a bit of an albatross around her neck."

"Is there any part of you that's wants to get back in if it's Margel versus Clayton?"

"A part of me? Yes, but just a small part. I would however, publicly support her if she chose that route. Perhaps I could end up as Ambassador to

Ireland."

"Really? Wow. I never even thought of that. How about Italy or Greece instead?"

"I don't think those Embassies are located in Tuscany, the Amalfi Coast or Santorini."

"Not now they aren't."

I laughed. "I'm pretty sure they might want someone who can actually speak Italian or Greek. Besides, wouldn't it be a lot more fun just to have Hannah and Martin take us there on their boat? We could stay as long as we want and then come back home and live here."

"OK, party pooper."

The debate didn't get a whole lot easier for Maggie. Margel hammered her on everything, but she held her own. She definitely came off as more likable, and more pragmatic. But Margel excoriated her for Korea, and hit her with a steady stream of our most divisive cultural wedge issues, most of which could never realistically come before Congress or the president in a viable bill in the first place.

"Do you think she has a shot?" Denyse asked, as the candidates shook hands following the debate.

"I do. Her main problem is that so many of the moderate republicans have left the party now and won't even be voting in these primaries. Our movement has a little bit to do with that. We've given those people a place to go and candidates to vote for. She would clearly win among all voters, but that's not how these things work. The primary will be very close, but she does have a chance."

"I wonder what they are saying on Fox," Denyse said.

"Great question. That will be telling."

I grabbed the remote. Just as I was about to change the channel the camera zoomed in on Maggie's friends and family in the second row. I recognized her son, Cade, and her sister, Dr. Loretta Griffin, President of Emory University.

Then Denyse screamed. "Oh my god, Danny, look at that!"

I looked closer at the screen. There, three people to the right of Dr. Griffin, not engaging with anyone around him, sat Gil. Our Gil. Hannegan's Gil. It was the first time I'd ever seen him in a coat and tie. Perhaps he felt like that, for him, was an effective disguise.

The camera stayed on Maggie as she approached the front row. They all stood and applauded. Maggie embraced Cade and then her sister, then shook hands with several of the others. When she came to Gil she extended her hand they greeted each other ever so briefly, but the exchange was unremarkable.

Denyse was positively gleeful. She immediately pulled up her calendar on her cell phone. “Here, let me give you some dates that will likely work for me and the ladies.”

I had a decision to make. I could concede right there, which clearly would be the right and fair-minded thing to do, given the clear evidence in front of us. Or I could stoop to putting up some lame and feeble defense that we still don’t have any real proof of anything.

She looked at me awaiting any sort of response.

After a few more moments of thought, I blurted out, “I really don’t think that proves anything.”

Her jaw dropped immediately, evidencing sheer and utter incredulity. I guess I’m not a good loser. I think I knew that. I wondered how long I could legitimately maintain this charade. But she’s so cute when she’s mildly agitated. Was that so wrong of me?

Chapter Fifty-Six

Politics Is a Nasty Business
March 2, 2024

Like many campaigns in our history, this one turned decidedly ugly the longer it went on, with both candidates running commercials and phone calls excoriating the other. It was troubling, and terribly depressing to watch. And there was an element of misogyny of course as well, because now there could be.

LOS ANGELES TIMES

REPUBLICAN RACE TURNS NASTY AS SUPER TUESDAY DRAWS NEAR

(March 2, 2024) By Jason Darby
The Republican primary race has taken a decidedly nasty turn in the final days before Super Tuesday, when 16 states will go to the polls, and nearly 20% of the delegates will be up for grabs. Residents of those states have been inundated with a barrage of negative campaign commercials, questionable robocalls, and social media disinformation. Some robocalls this week are making insinuations pertaining to President Margaret Bates' sex life decades ago.

Last night, Congressman Max Wiley, a supporter of Margel, was asked about recent robo calls circulating through many states that hint that Margaret Bates may have used sex as a tool to get ahead early in her career. Rather than disavow the calls, he seemed to only double down on that message. Responding in the hallway outside of his office to a question posed by CNN's Manu Raju about his comments, the congressman responded, "Maybe she should have tried sleeping with Kim Jong-un, rather than bombing him—that would have been more up her alley, so to speak. Make love not war, isn't that how it goes?"

Some women's groups have uniformly expressed outrage at the congressman's words, in addition to the robocalls. The former Vice President has yet to disavow the calls, claiming no responsibility or knowledge of their origin.

Negative ads produced by the Bates campaign target Mr. Margel for the many congressional inquiries initiated that are examining various allegations of ethical and financial impropriety. When reached for comment, Alice Hostry, a spokesman for the Margel campaign, noted that despite many months of investigation, no indictments have been brought. It should be noted that Mr. Margel has refused to cooperate with any of the congressional investigations, ignoring all subpoenas for testimony, documents and records.

Chapter Fifty-Seven

Settling for Matt Damon
March 6, 2024

Super Tuesday did not exactly go Maggie's way, causing her to concede the primary and suspend her campaign. However, that didn't mean it was over for her. Necessarily . . .

***

HOUSTON CHRONICLE

BATES CONCEDES IN REPUBLICAN PRIMARY RACE AMID SPECULATION ABOUT NEXT MOVE

(March 6, 2024) By Stuart Coombs

President Maggie Bates suspended her presidential re-election campaign today, a move not too terribly surprising in light of the results of Super Tuesday, with challenger Charles Margel edging her out to claim victory in eight states, virtually assuring himself of the Republican nomination. The president does continue to enjoy general popularity in the country, with an approval rate holding steady at 54%, but Republican primary voters are indicating a clear preference for her former vice president. Mr. Margel does not, however, have the type of support in national polls that the president has. Political observers will be watching now for any signs that President Bates might seek re-election as an independent. She has not as of yet provided a direct answer to that question. She is thought to have a remaining war chest of as much as much as $185 million, which could be used in a general election, though that is merely a fraction of what might be necessary to mount an effective campaign for the November election. A recent poll conducted by Quinnipiac shows her leading nationally among likely voters in a three-way race with Mr. Margel and Massachusetts Senator Robert Clayton.

***

Maggie's appearance on Jimmy Kimmel that night went viral, and the video clip of their discussion was viewed more than 27 million times over the course of the next ten days.

***

ABC

JIMMY KIMMEL LIVE

Interview Between Former Talk Show Host Jimmy Kimmel and President Margaret Bates. March 6, 2024

JIMMY KIMMEL: Our guest tonight shattered a nearly 250-year-old glass ceiling by becoming our first-ever female president. She recently suspended her campaign for re-election, but I suspect she is far from done here. Please say hello to the 46th President of the United States, Margaret Bates.

(rousing ovation, Maggie walks out with a broad smile.)

KIMMEL: Good evening, Madam President.

(More applause, eventually morphing into a standing ovation.)

KIMMEL: That has to make you feel good, right?

MARGARET BATES: Yes, of course, but long ago I realized it's just not about my feelings anymore. That's kind of a survival strategy I adopted in my line of work.

KIMMEL: Well thank you so much for coming on. I know we booked this a long time ago and I believe at that time there may have been an expectation of a different result on Super Tuesday.

BATES: Well, to be honest some of my team advised me to cancel, but I felt it was particularly important for me to come on precisely because of that result. It's important for me to convey to the country that no one is closing up shop just yet. So much work still lies ahead of us, with many achievable goals in sight.

KIMMEL: Well thank you for honoring the commitment. Had you not shown we would have really had to scramble to find someone to fill the spot. We probably would have had to settle for someone like . . . well, like Matt Damon.

(laughter)

KIMMEL: As you know, we've been trying to book you for years now.

BATES: I did not know that.

KIMMEL: Why don't you just give me your cell phone so we can make sure that doesn't happen again.

BATES: Sure. And why don't we just put it up on the

screen too, for the people at home as well.

(laughter, hen applause.)

KIMMEL: Well I like that a little political setback hasn't diminished your sense of humor.

BATES: We have to be able to laugh, Jimmy. It sustains us. I suspect you know that better than anyone.

KIMMEL: Yes. Good for you. That's one of many things people love about you.
So much has been written about you breaking that gender barrier. Do you think about the impact of your election on women, particularly on girls?

BATES: I do, but I don't dwell on it. I am relentlessly focused on achieving our goals. If I'm not viewed as successful in this role, my presidency will be considered a setback for the cause, rather than a triumph. That may only make it harder on the next woman.

KIMMEL: How much would you say women are still held back in the workplace in this country today, and is it getting better?

BATES: Well it certainly remains an issue, although I suppose I'm the last person who should be complaining about it. I've tried hard not to wrap myself in that. I just tend to consider it unbecoming of me to fixate on such issues. I do think my election is evidence of some considerable progress. However, just as the election of President Obama didn't mark the end of racism, neither does my election mark the end of sexism. But clearly the "Me Too" awakening has ushered in a new era of accountability across several industries. And to that I can only say it's about time.

(applause)

KIMMEL: Before we leave this topic I feel compelled to ask you about how you view comedian Billy Ratner calling you a PILF? Are you aware of that?

BATES: I don't know who that is.

KIMMEL: That doesn't surprise me. It speaks well of you, actually. He's a bit of a shock comedian. You've no doubt heard of the term MILF, have you not?

BATES: Yes. And gosh, I'm so eager to see where this is going . . .

KIMMEL: Well, as he and others explain it, a PILF is a President I would love to—.

BATES: (now shaking her head) How darling. Can I retract my earlier statements about how far I think we have come as a country now?

(laughter)

BATES: I wasn't necessarily saying that to be funny.

KIMMEL: Yes, it is boorish, but at some level a compliment?

BATES: Oh, I suppose, in a twisted, misogynistic way, but the trick is to get men to think of us first as something other than just an object to try to sleep with.

(applause)

Someone to hire perhaps, or partner with, or run your business . . .

(more applause)

. . . or possibly even lead your country.

(tremendous applause now)

KIMMEL: I think they like what they are hearing.

BATES: These are hardly original ideas.

KIMMEL: There is obviously still considerable support for you.

(pointing up to the crowd)

(applause)

KIMMEL: Many are speculating that you could still make a run.

BATES: At the moment I am going to focus on some of our more pressing issues. We've come so close on a comprehensive border security bill. I do believe we still have a chance at it, even in an election year.

KIMMEL: Much was made of the fact that you refused to commit not to run as an independent when you were questioned about that in the debate. Do you regret saying that, and have you ruled out a run as an independent?

BATES: No, I don't regret it. Not because I think I'm going to run, but I want to keep these two candidates honest. I fear we have the two extremes lining up for this race—leaving that majority in the middle out in the cold. If people view them both as unpalatable due to their extremist tendencies, I'll evaluate our chances sometime this summer. I don't anticipate that, but I'm not ruling it out either.

KIMMEL: Promise me you'll come back then.

BATES: Sure. Just call me directly on my cell phone. (Smiling)

(tremendous applause)

Chapter Fifty-Eight

Dog Day Afternoon
March 12, 2024
The Saloon

At about 3:00 p.m. the door from the White House to the Saloon flew open and two good sized dogs on leashes dragged our suddenly helpless president into the saloon. She let go immediately as a pack of more than a dozen dogs converged on the newest members of the presidential dog club in an historical greeting ritual every bit as traditional and our inaugurations. And almost as peaceful.

As Maggie just stood there in the doorway dumbfounded, Mary Ann looked up from her place on the floor in the middle of the room where she sat immersed in canine love and let out a joyful scream. She knows every dog's name—she and Washington. Remarkable, since I'm not even sure Washington knows all these presidents' names. Mary Ann was clearly as delighted as the dogs were to have these two new additions.

There is nothing quite like Dog Day in the saloon. The place is overrun with dogs—all the dogs who served alongside the presidents while in the White House. They scamper about in packs controlled only by their stream of consciousness in a search for instant gratification—much like our modern political parties, now that I think about it. It is the only time in the saloon that the presidents are not in complete control of the agenda or the conversation, and are forced to take back seat, yielding all the attention to man's, and now woman's, best friends.

Many moments later Maggie still looked like she had seen a ghost—but a happy, welcome ghost at that. Her first instincts spoke volumes. She paused to kneel down and greet a few of the dogs running by her at their level. Of course. How telling.

I enjoyed seeing my big, chill, fluffy collie, Montana, again. But all I could really do is observe him from a distance as he darted about the room trying in vain to keep up with the others. He's not nearly as fast as so many of these—the retrievers and labs, Tyler's greyhound and Washington's hunting dogs. Montana was older and a little more fragile than many of the others, just like his namesake in his final few years in the NFL with Kansas City.

Maggie approached Mary Ann and Washington. I figured I had to hear this conversation, so I decided to join them.

Mary Ann leapt up and hugged Maggie. "I love your two precious babies! Thank you for bringing them."

"Make no mistake about, they brought me here."

"Please keep one thing in mind for next time," asked Mary Ann.

"What's that?"

"No leashes. There's no leashes in dog heaven."

Maggie howled. "Is that what this is? Dog heaven?"

Mary Ann scanned the room. "Look around. You tell me. Have you ever seen such joy and sheer happiness in one place?"

"Forget about dog heaven," Maggie replied, "maybe this is heaven."

"Yes!" cried Mary Ann. "I knew I liked you."

"I can tell one of those guys is a bulldog," I said to Maggie. "What's the other?"

"Oh, honey we have no idea. She's a rescue. A mix, of course. Some Golden Retriever, I suppose . . . lab, perhaps. Maybe some pointer."

"Sounds a lot like me," Mary Ann declared proudly.

"Whatever it is that went into that mix, Mary Ann," I said, "what came out was just pure love. Not an ounce of anything else. I've never met someone quite like you."

"You'd be surprised," she answered. "I suppose there's one or two people I love a little less than others."

"I'll believe that when I see it," I responded.

"Hey I've got a question I've been dying to ask you," I continued. "Do the dogs in the saloon appear because the president is bringing her dog or does the president's dog come with her because all the dogs are in the saloon?"

"I learned long ago not to ask questions like that."

I laughed. "That's smart of you."

"I had an old boyfriend who disagreed. He spent a lot of time contemplating life's unsolvable mysteries, and had a fair amount of anxiety about it all. When I told him I didn't waste time thinking about such things, he told me that was because I'm not smart. The truth is, it's precisely because I am smart that I decide not to spend a minute thinking about that."

"Whatever happened to that boyfriend?"

"I don't know. That was last time I ever saw him. Never spent another minute thinking about him either."

"Is he one of those people you love a little less?'

"Yes. It's a short list but his name is right at the top."

Maggie and I laughed.

"What are your dogs' names, Maggie?" I asked.

"I named them for my two favorite characters in literary fiction. The bulldog is Atticus, of course. He's a fine Georgia bulldog. Just like Uga, our University mascot."

"How perfect."

"And the mix is Jo."

I thought for a second. "Well I know about Atticus, of course. But who is Joe named for?"

"Jo is a female. I don't suppose you've read Little Women?"

"No—I don't go real deep in literature."

"Ask your buddy Gil about her."

She smiled and started to walk away.

"Gil?" I said, shocked. "Gil from Hannegan's?"

She ignored me. Purposefully, and perhaps gleefully. I had to hear this story. There had to be a story.

At that moment there was a bit of a three way dustup between FDR's bullmastiff, Blaze, Rutherford Hayes's German Shepherd, Hector, and Harding's bulldog, Old Boy. Matty, sensing trouble, darted out from behind the bar to intervene. I think he's probably the only one in the room big enough to garner the respect of all these guys. And Taft, perhaps.

As many other presidents and staff gathered around to help them, I saw Buchanan's massive Newfoundland, Lara, slip behind the bar, plop her front paws up on the counter, and, standing on her hind legs, engage several of the taps with her teeth. Soon she was joined by a dozen or so of her comrades, many of whom leapt up on the counter and began lapping up the flowing beer as it spilled all around them. What a priceless spectacle. I stood just a few feet away, but I had no desire whatsoever to try to put a stop to this hilarious moment. Not that I would have been successful even if I tried.

Some of the other presidents joined me in spectating, each equally amused by the scene unfolding before us.

"Look at all those hounds devouring that beer." remarked Chester Arthur.

"In all my years around saloons, I've never seen anything quite the equal of this," declared Van Buren.

"Shouldn't we really cut them off?" asked Coolidge. Spoken like the prohibition-era president he was.

"If they react anything like Cleveland does when he gets cut off, I'd prefer not to be here for that." responded Benjamin Harrison.

"What's the harm here? None of them are driving," I added.

"Do you suppose they're all working together?" asked McKinley.

Kennedy laughed out loud. "Are you actually suggesting those three over there acted in concert with these fellas to create a diversion to enable them to take over the bar?"

"Many of these breeds are highly intelligent," responded Jefferson, clearly contemplating that very notion.

"I suppose it demonstrates all that can be accomplished by working together, rather than opposing one another in organized factions," commented Washington.

"If you think this is something, you should see Lyndon's beagles drink whiskey," added Kennedy.

"How on earth can they possibly get a whiskey bottle open?" asked Polk.

"They don't need to," responded JFK. "He just pours it right into their bowls."

Everyone got a kick out of that.

Franklin Pierce ventured into the canine mob behind the bar in an attempt to bring some order to the mayhem. That only brought on more laughter.

"He seems to be having about as much success leading them as he did the country," deadpanned Grant.

I noticed Lincoln trying hard not to laugh at that but he just couldn't help himself, which broke up all the others even more.

I decided it was a good thing that everything in this saloon was so secretive, I don't think anyone would ever believe it anyway. Another classic Dog Day in the saloon.

Chapter Fifty-Nine

Me and Bobby McGee
April 18, 2024
The Saloon

I couldn't help but laugh as I entered the saloon and heard the music. That Nashville band was back. After hearing them a few times now they were really growing on me, and so was country music.

Big Time called to me as I approached the bar. "Danny Mac!" Mary Ann and Slick instinctively whirled around toward me and broke into big smiles. God I loved just walking into this place.

"You know, they're playing your song, sir." said Mary Ann.

I listened for a second with a bit of a puzzled look on my face.

"I don't believe I know this one," I replied.

"Listen closely," she directed.

I paid close attention to the lead singer's words.

"I like my truck. I like my girlfriend . . . but I love this bar."

I laughed out loud. "That is hilarious. I'm not sure about the girlfriend part, but I can identify with a guy who just really loves a bar."

"Is that a real song?" I asked.

"Oh, yes. Toby Keith."

"What's it called?"

"I Love This Bar."

"Of course. Stupid question. Might be my new anthem, however."

She laughed. "Some of these guys don't understand country music, but they all seem to love that one."

"Is Maggie here?" I asked. I'm not sure she would like it as much. At least not that line."

"No, she's not here yet." Mary Ann responded. "Something tells me she'd get a kick out of it, though. Now Tina of course would be offended by that."

"No doubt. I miss Tina around her."

"So do I!" she responded.

"Hey, you should get out there," Mary Ann added, pointing to the large oak tables in front of the bar. They're all assembling to discuss Maggie's future. You'd better go join them."

"Oh really? I don't want to miss that."

I hustled over to join the group. I remember how helpful their perspective had been when I sought their advice on seeking a second term.

The discussion, of course, was being led by the some of the real heavyweights—FDR, Jefferson, Teddy, Washington and Reagan, but everyone seemed to have an opinion. What I loved most was how they all, to a person, seemed to want only the best for her. It may have taken four years, but she clearly had won them all over. No small feat with this crowd. Unfortunately, the collective forecast for her prospects, in light of everything we knew—which was limited of course—was not positive.

After a good ninety minutes or so of that, the door to the White House flew open and Maggie emerged, stylish as ever, sporting a conservative, emerald green coat dress with satin lapels.

"Peaches!" yelled Bush, causing Maggie to break out a huge smile. Mary Ann hustled up to greet her while Matty instinctively whipped up a martini. Haskell and Slick hustled to rearrange chairs at the head table to prepare a preferred spot for her. She had the room in the palm of her hand as she approached the table. She seemed happy and at peace.

Bush jumped up to greet her. "We are prepared to provide you our best political advice."

"Why, thank you. That is mighty kind of y'all."

Washington took over from there.

"We have convened to discuss your political predicament. Would you care to hear our advice and counsel?"

"Oh yes, please, although I'm not sure the specifics of my challenges have much precedent in our history."

"The prevailing view of this group seems to be that your challenges mimic the ones which confronted your predecessor, President McFadden, four years ago."

"We don't believe your situation is unprecedented," added Teddy Roosevelt. "In fact, it is nearly as old as the country itself."

Maggie looked skeptical.

"I was a very popular figure in 1912 but found myself outside of the two major parties. I, like you, lost the Republican nomination, but undaunted, I chose to establish and run in a third party. The Bull Moose party. I can attest that it is terribly difficult to run against the two major parties in this country. I merely handed the election to Woodrow here. No offense, President Wilson, but had I not run you would have lost to Taft."

"Oh, but you did run, Teddy. Everyone in this room can point to moments of good fortune or bad fortune beyond their control that helped seal their fate. We all play with the hand we are dealt, my friend. But did you ever consider that it may have been my genius that lured you into the race in the first place, thereby throwing the election to me?"

"You certainly possess an active imagination, Woodrow," replied TR.

Washington looked annoyed. "Please excuse our family squabbles, President Bates."

"Oh, we have those where I come from too, Mr. President. Fighting back against my brothers made my sister and I the tough women we are today. And I like to think it shaped their view of girls too. But our bond of love was far more fierce than our quarrels."

"The salient point here, Maggie," added George H. W. Bush, "is that while you may have had some success fighting your brothers, and I don't doubt that for a second," he flashed a smile, "it's virtually impossible to fight the two parties in this country as an independent. So many have tried and failed. Ross Perot and John Anderson, to name just a few, and many become spoilers in the process."

Van Buren then raised his hand. Washington nodded his head and motioned for him to proceed. "In 1848, well after leaving the White House, I was drafted by the Free Soil party to challenge the two established parties. I did about as well as any third party candidate had ever done, but fell way short."

"Your presence in the race, my dear Martin," said Zachry Taylor, "helped me win New York by taking votes away from Cass, without which I would not have been elected. I am forever grateful."

"How pleasant for me to know that all my effort and anxiety accrued to someone's benefit," responded Van Buren, now smiling.

Millard Fillmore, seated at a table in the back, stood up. "In 1856, while I was away in Europe the American Party nominated me as a third party candidate for president. People who opposed Fremont, the Republican candidate from California, felt that a vote for me took away a vote from Buchanan and would only serve to elect Fremont. We won more than 20% of the vote and the State of Maryland, but that was not nearly enough."

Grant leaned in to me and whispered, "There were no good choices in that disaster of an election. I voted for Buch—even though I had never voted for a Democrat before. Such was my disdain for Fremont."

Being from California, I was aware of Fremont's participation in the mass killing of Native Americans in the West but didn't recall learning that he had also run for President. Considering how poorly Buchanan's presidency is viewed by historians, that choice between Buchanan and Fremont certainly presented the country with a classic Cornelian dilemma, as so many elections these days seem to.

Fillmore then added, "It is so inherently difficult to go up against the two major parties in this country. I would caution against it."

"Let me add my thoughts, for what they are worth," said Eisenhower. "I was recruited by both Democrats and Republicans to run for president after World War II. I had not been political before in any Washington sense of that word. In fact, I had never even voted in any election."

That statement generated some looks of astonishment and a few chuckles.

Ike looked at Washington. "I benefitted mightily from the notion that I was a reluctant candidate—just as you did, General Washington. And you as well, McFadden."

Then, with a bit of a smile, he added, "The truth may have been more complicated. I harbored some political ambitions, largely because I believed deeply in a solid alliance between America and Western Europe, and I feared the isolationist views of Taft and many others in the extreme right wing of the Republican party would diminish that critical partnership. Perhaps I didn't fit into either party. I viewed myself as moderate leaning conservative, believing in balanced budgets, and that government should not be called upon to do for individuals that which they should do for themselves. But to block Taft and the isolationist views I needed to run. And to win I knew I needed to run with a party, rather than as an independent."

"Is it true, Harry, that you offered Ike the Vice Presidency?" asked Clinton.

Truman and Eisenhower immediately looked at each other. "I did him one better than that," responded Truman. "In 1948 I feared I would not win re-election. In an attempt to keep the streak of Democrats in the White House which had begun in 1932, I offered to take a step back and give Ike the top spot on the Democratic ticket."

"My goodness," responded Clinton. "That is astonishing."

"It is a rare and admirable man who would make such an offer," added Madison, "Most presidents, I would posit, possess an ego which would preclude even consideration of such a possibility."

"I wasn't aware that there were any small egos amongst us in this room," said Lyndon Johnson— who seemed to have one of the biggest of them all.

"I did it for the good of the country," responded Truman. "My ambitions for the nation exceeded any personal ambition I had at the time."

"How truly admirable of you, President Truman," said Maggie. "even heroic."

"But he declined, and then you went out and won anyway," cheered Clinton.

"Proving the whole world wrong, and much to the embarrassment of the Chicago Trib," added Obama.

"Back to my point," said Eisenhower, "Even as popular as I was, I needed to align with one of the two parties to have a chance to win the presidency."

Washington turned to Maggie. "And I'm afraid that, my dear, best sums up our considered opinion about your present circumstance."

Maggie nodded but didn't appear completely convinced. With all eyes on her now, the room could sense her hesitancy. In light of that, a few more of them jumped in.

"I think this group is just trying to protect you, Maggie," said Carter.

"Yes," added Obama. "Certainly without the political infrastructure behind you—an established national footprint, the data bases, fundraising lists, social media presence and television and print media support, it would just be too uphill a climb. If you had all of that, or even some of that, perhaps our advice would be different."

"I believe we had almost this precise discussion in advising McFadden not to run again four years ago," added Clinton. "Nothing has changed."

The room went silent as Maggie took it all in. She paused and looked around. The moment was becoming more awkward and uncomfortable by the second.

Then Maggie spoke. "I thank you all for your thoughts. And for being candid. I do appreciate it so, and I'm not offended."

She then turned to Mary Ann. "Do you have an opinion," she asked.

"I don't pretend to know what's going on out there, but I firmly believe if anyone can pull this off, it's you. I would not bet against you, ma'am."

Maggie smiled. "Let me tell you all why I think it might just be different this time around." She paused for effect. She had such great timing.

"All those things you mentioned, President Obama, that I would need to pull this off—the infrastructure, the fundraising lists, social media presence and media support, which haven't ever been there before for an independent have now been developed. I'll tell you what's changed. So many things."

She then looked over at me. "Danny, it's all there now. That infrastructure is there. Your Alliance has taken off. It is organized and operating in all fifty states. Better yet, it has now even established roots in Congress—with two seats in the Senate and twenty-two in the House, and with that number ready to multiply in this coming election. It also has four governors and over a hundred legislators in statehouses across the nation. It has a social media footprint, and even has an influential media empire cheering it on. And, perhaps best yet, more and more people are fleeing the two parties every month. Now more than 50% of the country refuses to identify as either Democrat or Republican. Whatever circumstances y'all may have faced in your time, I think it's fair to say things are different today. Vastly different."

I looked around and saw many people nodding in approval.

"And I'd like to thank both President Truman and President Eisenhower for their words, which really resonated with me. Like you, President Truman, my ambitions for the country exceed my own personal ambitions. If I run, it will be to save us from these two deplorable choices we have in front of us. Like you, President Eisenhower, I fear what the country might end up with if I don't run and win.

"On the left we have a candidate who calls himself a Democratic Socialist—as if that's a badge of honor. I'm sorry, capitalism is not a dirty word. It built this country and set us apart. Some in the far left really have no regard for the budget, the deficit or the debt—which, by the way, sits at

29 trillion right now, and growing each year. It's all Monopoly money. Every issue is couched in moral terms as a question of just how much more government can do and spend for the people. I admire their compassion, but if we follow them we go the route of Greece, with no EU to come bail us out.

"On the right, my party, the leadership is absolutely and unapologetically gaslighting America—just repeating one lie after another over and over and relying on Americans' healthy distrust of government and institutions and their general cynicism about everything these days. More interested in culture wars and wedge issues than any real progress as a country competing on the world stage. Moreover, this latest version of my party seems to be similarly ignoring our massive national debt. There's nothing conservative about that. Pick your poison, fellas.

"You mentioned, President Bush, that your advice for me not to run was for my own protection. While I do appreciate the concern, with all due respect, protection from what? What do I possibly have left to lose? I've lost my husband, any semblance of a family, my happiness, my personal and professional reputation, and in many ways my dignity. I'm the subject of the most vile and hateful attacks on Twitter and the internet every day. I stand here today much like Bobby McGee—with nothing left to lose. That's some freedom, baby. Me and Bobby McGee.

"So to some degree I don't care if I try and lose. I'm doing the right thing. I go back to my fights with my brothers. If I knew I was in the right, as I most often was, I'd punch back. Ferociously. I knew at times I stood little chance of winning, but knowing I was in the right assured me, fueled me and made the cause and the inevitable injuries I'd suffer worthwhile. From a risk/reward standpoint, this isn't even close. I risk nothing by running, but our country stands to gain everything.

"Y'all might disagree on whether there's a path there for me, but I'm fixin' to find out. And like those fights with my brothers, I'm coming out swinging!"

The room applauded, many of them stood up. I had goosebumps. I'm guessing everybody did.

When the noise finally settled down, Teddy Roosevelt arose and approached Maggie. "Madam, I have never been more inspired by the words of a woman."

"Well, sir," she responded, "I'm not sure that actually qualifies as a compliment—in fact I'm fairly certain it doesn't—but let's just say I appreciate the sentiment just the same. But you really should pay more attention to the words of women around you."

The room settled down, but it was clear we still had work to do.

"It all sounds well and great," said Reagan, "and inspiring, of course. But how can you as a Republican who ran unsuccessfully in the Republican primary, suddenly a few months later become embraced by independents, and somehow piggyback on the Alliance?"

Many in the room nodded their heads.

"I have the same question, President Reagan," said Jefferson, who was seated at the main table with Maggie but had been silent to this point. "I don't pretend to know the dynamics of politics today, but, as much as I'd like to keep a fellow Southerner occupying the White House, that strikes me as an unlikely occurrence."

"With all due respect, Mr. Jefferson," Maggie replied, "in Georgia we all consider Virginia to be part of the north."

The room erupted in laughter. I love this lady. Hilarious that she would feel no compunction about taking on Jefferson like that. And Virginia. I looked at Madison and Monroe—they both enjoyed that as much as the others.

"But that's a fair question, Mr. President," she added, now looking at Reagan. "Perhaps this esteemed body would care to offer some advice on that."

She scanned the room. "Let me begin by saying I'm probably more philosophically aligned with independents at the moment. The movement of both parties to the polar extremes has caused unprecedented hemorrhaging as more and more reasonable, pragmatic people abandon the parties to become independents. As a result, even the two parties' modern standard bearers—Kennedy for the Democrats and Reagan for the Republicans, would be tossed out by today's parties as much too moderate."

"I don't dispute that," said Ford, "but I would suspect there may be reticence by the leadership of the Alliance about drafting someone who ran and lost in the Republican primary."

Maggie nodded. "Of course. I didn't say I thought it would be easy. Few things in life truly worthwhile come easily."

Bush, cracking a smile, chimed in. "Gee, if we only knew someone who had intimate knowledge of the Alliance and how it operates . . ."

All eyes in the room now turned instinctively my way.

"Don't look at me!" I protested. "I've been out of touch and truly out of the loop now for four years. I didn't even know about the great success the Alliance has had nationally since I left office. I simply set the boat afloat. Someone else raised the sails and is at the wheel."

"I think it's clear we are all looking to the wrong Danny McFadden," said Kennedy. "Should you not be focusing on the one in California?"

"Oh, I don't think I'd trust that dude," I said, laughing.

"I do think you are on to something, Jack," added FDR. "Who better to deliver the support of the Alliance? Engage him. Determine what goals and vision he has which align with yours. Offer him a spot on the ticket—for either him or someone of his choosing."

"What is the extent of your relationship with him?" asked Obama.

"I think he was skeptical of me at the outset, but I believe I have won him over. And I've gotten quite close with a good friend of his."

"Who is that?" I asked.

"I think I better save that for later," she responded. That set my mind racing.

"I do believe we are friendly enough and there's enough respect there that I could go to him for advice," added Maggie. "And of course if he's willing to come along for the ride all the better."

"I'd say it's a tall order to ask a former president to join the ticket in the second spot," noted Nixon.

"No question," replied Clinton. "But it sounds like Harry was more than willing to do it."

"McFadden might be one of the more likely amongst us to entertain such a notion, given his passion for the cause," added Bush. "He may view it as a watershed moment for bipartisanship to have a Republican and former Democrat united on a national ticket in the name of his Alliance."

"You and he got pretty close, Otter," said Clinton. "How would you suggest she approach him? The setting might be critical."

I could only laugh as they sat there talking about me as if I wasn't right there. Which I guess I kind of wasn't.

"Doesn't he have a place at a lake in Northern California up by Mount Shasta?" asked Reagan. "Go meet him there."

"Do it on the back lawn at Mount Vernon, with the Potomac as a backdrop. I defy him to say no to you in that particular setting," said Obama. I saw Washington crack a smile at that comment.

"How about Shangri-La?" said FDR. "I had it built precisely for this sort of thing. A secret presidential hideaway."

There was silence in the room and blank looks.

"I had it renamed 'Camp David,' added Ike.

"Oh is that so," asked FDR. "Why the name David?"

"After my father and my grandson, both of whom were named David."

"I see," replied FDR, with a rather puzzled look. "David. Sounds utterly appropriate."

Laughter gradually ensued as the room decided Roosevelt was mocking the great general.

"I hosted Winston there," added FDR, "as well as Princess Martha of Norway. And Princess Julianna of the The Netherlands. No one named David however."

More laughter. Ike managed a grin when he realized the joke was on him. At least a little.

"How about on Cemetery Ridge at Gettysburg next to the statue of Father Corby—the chaplain of The Irish Brigade and future president of Notre Dame?" asked Kennedy. "That statue and that spot, looking out over the scene of Pickett's Charge, seemed to have deep meaning for McFadden."

"Use the Oval Office," said Nixon. "Still the power center in the world after all these years. No true American could say no in that setting."

I couldn't sit idly by without chiming in. "Do it in the bleacher seats at Wrigley some weekday afternoon," I added. "Maybe wait until the 7th inning stretch so he's had a few Old Styles."

Maggie turned to me with a classic wtf look on her face. "What, not Hannegan's?"

I laughed hard. "Just the fact that you even suggested that tells me you're gonna land your man—wherever you do it."

"OK, gentlemen. That settles it. I'll find the right time and place, and I'll go make my best case. The consequences of not doing so would be dire. For me, for all of us, and for the country."

The room applauded. What a night.

As Maggie approached her exit escorted by Truman, I saw George W.

Bush talking with the band. The next thing I knew the musicians scrambled to get into position, and then went right into the chords of a very familiar tune. On cue, the female lead singer took the microphone, and started singing.

Busted flat in Baton Rouge, waitin' for a train

When I was feeling near as faded as my jeans . . .

How absolutely perfect. Janis Joplin herself couldn't have sounded much better. I looked up at Maggie, who recognized it instantly, of course. Smiling broadly, she blew Otter and the band a kiss.

"Me and Bobby McGee." I love this bar.

Chapter Sixty

The Voices of Reason
May 2, 2024

"Is your phone blowing up, Danny?" Denyse asked as I walked in the door with Jack. I had just watched him perform a Moot Court competition at his high school, reenacting the Scopes Trial.

"I've had it off for a couple hours—actually both of them. What's up?"

"I guess the roundtable tonight on 'The Voices of Reason' had quite a discussion of the possibility of your friend Maggie embracing your Alliance and making an independent run for re-election."

"First of all, as you know, it's not my Alliance, It belongs to the entire country, with an effective organization that really doesn't actively involve me. And secondly, the fact that Maggie might run as an independent has been openly speculated about even before she ended her primary race. The papers are all over it."

"That's not the part I'm referring to. There's a new wrinkle."

OK. She had my attention. I played along. She grabbed the remote and pulled up the show.

Denyse had become quite a fan of Hannah's new network, labelled "The BFN," short for Bias-Free News. She tuned in nearly every night to catch a new show called The Voices of Reason—a nightly panel discussing the news of the day, promising balanced and independent commentary untethered to any political agenda.

I didn't recognize any of the panelists. Hannah's team had brought on a lot of new faces and was specifically avoiding the likes of those who frequently made the rounds of the political shows on MSNBC, Fox and CNN and Sunday mornings on the networks.

BFN

THE VOICES OF REASON

Political show on cable television with a panel discussion format moderated by Drew Mapes. May 2, 2024

DREW MAPES: Welcome back to The Voices of Reason.

Many pundits are speculating that President Margaret Bates may be planning a late re-entry into the race with a run for re-election as an independent.

While she remains popular nationally, with approval ratings hovering between 52 and 58 percent, our country's political structure creates a challenge for her, just as it did for her predecessor, President McFadden. As you know, she suspended her campaign for the presidency when it became clear she would not secure the Republican nomination, but has not ruled out an independent run. She continues to collect donations, and many of her public statements can be interpreted as hinting to independents and specifically to the Alliance movement about a run.

National polls have her leading in a three-way race, but no candidate achieves a majority. State by state polling about the possibility of her candidacy is not really available yet. National polls are not as valuable in a presidential election as state polling, given the electoral college system we have for electing presidents. National popularity isn't the issue. A candidate needs to carry a sufficient amount of states to earn a majority of the electors. It's not clear right now what if any states Bates would win.

National approval ratings don't always mean a lot when it comes to securing the nomination of a particular party, do they, Francis.

FRANCIS CANTOR: No, they don't, Drew. And while her political pivot toward the middle may have resonated with the country generally, that only made her more vulnerable in a Republican party that has moved further right as more and more people are abandoning the party to become independent.

MAPES: But that might not stop her, though. What are you hearing, Lucy?

LUCY REGINALD: Political people and some elite donors are encouraging her to make a run as an independent. It's fair to say a good deal of the country is frightened by the prospect of a race where Margel and Clayton are the only two choices—neither of which can boast national approval ratings exceeding 50 percent. And both hail from the far ends of the political spectrum.

MAPES: But do you really think she'll actually jump back in?

REGINALD: History suggests that once someone rises to the presidency, it's pretty intoxicating, and terribly hard to pass up an opportunity for another shot at it.

MAPES: The President is still hampered a bit by some of her early foreign policy missteps. She may never live down her decisions in Korea, though that region seems to be stabilizing. But is it possible for someone who lost in the Republican primary to navigate a path to success as an independent?

REGINALD: Here's what I'm hearing from sources close to her. You heard it here first. Look for her to run as an

> independent, and to make an overture to Danny McFadden to join her on the ticket and appeal to the growing Alliance political movement that has certainly been gaining steam nationally each year.

Denyse let out a shriek. "Get a load of that!"

All I could do was laugh.

Denyse stared at me, waiting any sort of more meaningful reaction.

"Well . . ." she said.

"It's a bit crazy, but the fact that she wants to piggyback on the Alliance—if that's even true—just serves to demonstrate how the movement is becoming a legitimate political force. I don't mind hearing that."

Denyse turned the sound back up.

> **MAPES**: Do your sources suggest that McFadden has in fact been approached?
>
> **REGINALD**: No. I don't believe so. Nor do they have any idea whether McFadden would take it. But he's an unconventional politician. And who knows, perhaps it would be viewed as another giant leap forward for his political movement.

Jack walked in the room.

"What's mom screaming about now?"

I laughed.

Denyse turned to him. "Oh, nothing really—just that your father and I might be returning to Washington."

"Running for president?"

"Well, not exactly," she responded.

"It's not true," I said, "It's all speculation. She hasn't asked me to be her VP and even if she did we're not interested. We're pretty happy with our life right here. We're not moving again."

"Vice President?" responded Jack. "Sounds cool. A lot less work too.

Hey, don't stay here on my behalf. I'll be off at college. Far off I'm sure. I'm outta here. You guys do whatever you have to do. I'll be just fine."

"By the way," he added, "has any president ever come back as a vice president?"

"No," I answered. "A Senator and Congressman, yes. And a Supreme Court justice as well. But none have ever returned as a VP, nor will that ever happen."

"C'mon now. I would think that would be such a better job than the President, Dad. You get to play golf with Tiger Woods, fly around on a private jet, go see the Olympics in person if you want, and generally just share in the credit for the good things but avoid all the blame for the bad things."

"I don't think that's quite how it works, Jack, but thanks for your thoughts."

"Just my two cents, that's all."

I laughed as he walked away into the kitchen. I'm sure to make a bowl of cereal.

Once he was out of earshot, Denyse added. "You know, he may have a point."

I shot her a look. Then I borrowed a phrase from Tina. "Are you kidding me right now?"

She didn't respond.

Chapter Sixty-One

Shangri-La
May 19, 2024

"You know what FDR's original name for this place was, don't you?" asked Maggie.

Challenged by this bit of history trivia, it killed me that I couldn't come up with an answer. I stalled for time.

The Camp David servers had just come around as we finished up dinner to offer us our choice of port or Irish coffee. I chose both. Why not? All I had on the agenda for the following day was a late morning meeting with Maggie, where presumably she would ask me to be her running mate on an independent ticket.

Denyse and I had helicoptered right in to the compound just a few hours earlier and, we believe, had managed to do so under a shroud of secrecy. Most observers, however, were anticipating that a meeting like this would take place between us at any moment.

We were dining with Maggie and Gil on the large flagstone patio just off of the President's Cabin. It was a hot and muggy evening, with dozens of crickets and a collection of mockingbirds serenading us. The view of the Maryland countryside from atop this hill was spectacular.

"I give up," I said.

"Shangri-La," answered Maggie, impressed to have stumped me. A power move—perhaps to set the tone for what was to come this weekend.

Gil, quite shockingly, then attempted to one-up her.

"Anyone know what that's from?" he asked.

"What Shangri-La comes from?" asked Denyse.

Gil nodded, and looked right at Maggie, as if to challenge her specifically. They seemed to know each other even better than I knew them to.

"Something from Buddhism?" suggested Denyse.

"You are close," responded Gil.

Maggie smiled. “Did you really think I wouldn’t know this?”

Gil laughed and shook his head.

“I am a world class bibliophile, and you of all people should know that. It’s from Lost Horizon. James Hilton—the British author.”

“I will never doubt you again,” replied Gil.

Maggie sat back, satisfied that she had just bested both of the men at the table.

What do you guys feel like doing tonight?” asked Maggie.

“Nothing involving trivia,” I responded immediately. They laughed.

“Is there still a pool table in the Holly Cabin?” I asked. I’ve spent many a night through the years shooting pool with or against Gil—each one a story unto themselves.

Denyse shot me a look. “Really, Danny? You have to be joking?”

Maggie howled. “C’mon, Denyse, let’s let these boys show us how it’s done.”

Denyse couldn’t really say no to that. I had a feeling I was being set up.

Maggie alerted the staff and then we jumped into two golf carts—really nice golf carts—and headed down the hill toward Holly Cabin, Gil and I following Maggie and Denyse.

“Do you suppose we are underestimating their billiards prowess?” Gil asked me.

“I know I’m not underestimating my wife’s!” I laughed. “Is it possible that the first female president in history is also a pool shark?”

“Nothing about that woman would surprise me,” responded Gil. “But I’ve never heard her utter a word about pool. She has mentioned darts though, now that I think about it. That might be telling, actually.”

“She was shockingly quick to say yes to this.”

As we entered the cabin we saw the staff frantically setting up to anticipate whatever needs we might have.

“I don’t think we ever used this cabin, did we Danny?”asked Denyse.

“You mean you guys didn’t routinely shoot pool in here during your term?” replied Maggie. She was enjoying this. She really struck me as much happier and more relaxed than the few times I had ever seen her before in person. It was great to see.

“I came here with Bibi and President Al Sisi to commemorate the 40th anniversary of the peace treaty between Egypt and Israel negotiated by

Carter," I said. "That negotiation took place largely in this cabin."

I pointed to the photo of Sadat on the wall with the quote "When the bells of peace ring, there will be no hands to beat the drums of war."

"You and Gil won't find the atmosphere in here tonight nearly as peaceful," remarked Maggie.

I laughed. I guess it was Game On.

We proceeded right to the pool table as the staff laid out appetizers and took drink orders.

"We're not really doing girls versus guys, are we?" I asked.

"Scared?" replied Maggie. "How unlike you, Danny."

"Alright," I said. "Bring it on."

"Care to lag for break?" asked Gil.

"You guys can break," responded Maggie. "Us girls might not hit it hard enough."

"Care to do the honors?" I asked Gil as he racked the balls.

"Go for it." he responded.

It was a tight rack and I broke hard, scattering the balls all over the table as some continued to collide with one another two and three times, but nothing landed.

Maggie handed Denyse a pool cue.

"I'm not going first!" she complained.

"I insist," replied Maggie.

Denyse approached the table. She evidently listened to this president more closely than she did the last.

"Now which end of this stick do we hit the ball with?" asked Maggie. Now I knew we were being played. But I also knew Gil was pretty damn good. He excels at everything that can be done in bars. And I'm not bad. And I know Denyse has many talents but this is definitely not one of them.

There was no shortage of low hanging fruit out there on the table but Denyse kind of mishit the cue ball and it very slowly glanced off another one before coming to rest, leaving every ball remaining on the table.

She walked past us and whispered to me, "You owe me, McFadden."

Gil acted like he hadn't heard that.

As she walked away she turned to me again. "You so owe me."

As soon as she looked the other way Gil looked at me and smiled.

Gil took my stick and then seized the moment. So many opportunities before him. He worked quickly, sinking shot after shot, with the cue ball always seeming to magically line up to leave him a perfect shot at the next one. He finally missed trying a bank shot to sink the last solid left on the table.

Maggie took the cue stick from Denyse and paced around the table, deep in thought. "Looks like we're in big trouble, Denyse."

I leaned in to Gil. "If she's any good," I whispered, "she's got an awful lot to choose from."

"I'm afraid we may have outkicked our coverage," he responded. "But only if she knows what she's doing."

One shot answered that. She drilled a stripe hard into a corner pocket, then executed a brilliant cut shot to put another in the side pocket.

"We're in big trouble," she muttered again shaking her head as she walked to the far end of the table. Then she sunk a third, the cue ball hitting the bank and tapping a second stripe, which came to rest right in front of another pocket. She finished it off for her fourth in a row.

Denyse looked positively gleeful.

Maggie studied the table. There were no obvious shots left. One of our solid balls was blocking what would have been a decent line on a stripe.

"Can I use your ball?" asked Maggie.

As I was about to tell her to go ahead, Gil emphatically answered, "No, You've gotta hit yours with the cue ball first." I know Gil is competitive, but I wasn't sure what the strategy was there. It may have been the best approach to get us a win, but it pretty much assured himself he wasn't gonna get much of anything else in the foreseeable future.

Maggie then struck the bottom part of the cue ball. It elevated immediately, popping straight up and then completely clearing the solid ball in its way before hitting a stripe and knocking it cleanly into the corner pocket. A perfectly executed jump shot.

Denyse shrieked.

"Wow," I said. "That is impressive."

"Is there a reason you were hiding this from me?" asked Gil.

Maggie didn't stop to acknowledge our comments or even look up. Chilling.

Another stripe slammed into the back of a pocket. And then another one, leaving only the 8 ball and our last remaining solid on the otherwise empty table. Forget about me and Gil, this lady belonged with Fast Eddie and Minnesota Fats.

The 8-ball sat up against an edge on the far side of the table. There were no obvious plays. Maggie called a bank all the way back to the near corner. Her only realistic chance, but a long shot, for sure.

She took aim and let it ride. The cue ball struck the 8 right where it needed to, and it came off the bank hot and headed right for that corner. It looked clean nearly the whole way, but just as it neared the pocket it glanced off the cushion and redirected, missing the pocket and then banking all the way back to the other end.

Denyse nonetheless applauded and ran over to give her a hug, which Maggie reluctantly accepted. But I could tell she was fuming inside. I knew she was competitive, but I had no idea. Wow.

I knocked in the last solid easily, but left myself way too much green between the cue and the 8. My shot at the 8 never really had a prayer, but I didn't leave Denyse anything easy either.

After plenty of counsel from our president, her shot was errant.

Gil took the cue from me. I could tell he sensed he had played this way wrong. And that's an understatement. "What's my obligation here?" he whispered to me.

"I think we're already in way over our heads. I think the worst possible thing to do is let them win, and have them know that you did. That's a make-able shot, and I think you've gotta make it. But let me be clear, either way we've already lost."

Gil lined up the shot and sunk the 8 ball easily. I chose not to look at the girls, pretending to look at my phone instead.

As Gil walked over to me I whispered, "Who's bright idea was this, anyway?"

"I don't know, but I may be sleeping with you and Denyse tonight in your cabin."

"Be my guest," I replied. "After all this I'm fairly certain you won't be interrupting anything anyway."

Chapter Sixty-Two

A Big Ask at Laurel Lodge
May 20, 2024

The following morning Maggie and I met in a meeting room at Laurel Lodge—the new Laurel Lodge. The old Laurel Lodge is now Holly Cabin where we were last night. And speaking of last night, I thought it best not to even reference that with her, but she brought it up right away.

"Did you enjoy yourselves last night?" she asked.

"Oh yes, we love it here. It's great to be back."

"Gil seemed to enjoy himself," she added.

"He always does."

"He knows his way around a pool table."

"He's a bartender," I said. "And you've certainly played a little pool before in your life, I gather. I think it's fair to say you both underestimated each other."

"I apologize for being so intense last night. I get a little carried away. And I'm afraid I'm not a good loser."

"Well you know what Vince Lombardi said about good losers, right?"

"What's that?"

"Show me a good loser and I'll show you a loser."

"Well, I don't know the first thing about Coach Lombardi but I think he and I would get along just fine."

"Ha. I actually disagree with that quote. I think there is some honor in being a gracious loser—at least on the outside. But maybe that's just because I've lost so many times."

She smiled.

"Did that primary campaign hit you hard?" I asked. "You seem to have handled it as well as can be."

"I'm in a much better place than I was. Cade is my rock. He is so much better now too. He and I have gone through all this together and it's brought us closer—closer than I ever imagined we'd be. We speak at least twice a day.

"My marriage falling apart was like a death in the family. A bad dream that just began all over again every morning when I'd wake up. I took some meds for a few months," she added, "mostly to settle me down and take the edge off but I swear it just made me worse. More than anything making a clean break with Dwight, as devastating as it was, there was a sense of relief when I finally ended it. I gave up trying to think it would get better and then I gave up thinking I'd have to just put up with it. Since then I've became much more calm. Now it's just me and Cade. And of course my babies."

I gave her a quizzical look.

"My dogs."

"Of course."

"And Gil has been a godsend, He's been great at getting me to fend off my impulse to fixate on the demons and the problems. He's helped me to just let the bitterness wash right off me. And I have you to thank for him."

I laughed. "I had nothing to do with it! Setting you up with a Hannegan's bartender was the last thing on earth I thought I was doing."

"He's a lot more than a bartender—not that that's not enough."

"Have you read his stuff?"

"Yes! Most of it now. And I love it. He's deep, and I treasure that. I can't read it at the end of each night—I require something light and breezy on my bed table then. But when I want something smart, something to challenge me and cause me to really think about life's most pressing issues, he's about as good as anyone—and I've read them all."

"Let me ask you this," she added, "do the patrons at that Irish pub of yours have any idea what he does on the side."

"By that do you mean secretly dating the leader of the free world?"

She laughed, and it appeared like she may have even blushed a bit.

"No, I mean his fascinating little side gigs."

"They all know he's an accomplished fisherman. And I think many know he's a writer too, but I don't think they know the half of it. But they don't need to. They just relish having a wise, witty, chill old bartender to interact with a few times a week. It doesn't seem to matter whether you are reading him or ordering drinks from him, either way he has an uncanny ability to connect with you."

"Fascinating. Of course. But the writer in him deserves a much, much bigger audience."

"I think you might just be able to help with that, ma'am."

She smiled. "In time, maybe. I don't get the impression he particularly minds. That's another thing I adore about him. I'm too used to men with massive egos. Or maybe just one or two men . . .

"But no, exiting the primary was not devastating to me. Stop me if I'm sounding too much like you, but I just wasn't willing to alter my positions and philosophy just to hold on to power. What good is it to have power in the first place if you aren't able to use it for good?"

"Good for you. And yes that does sound like me. I wish all our politicians sounded like that. Heck, I'd even settle for ten percent of them."

"That doesn't mean I've given up the fight, however," she replied. "That energizes me—even if I'm not successful. Fighting for the right cause is exhilarating. And besides, I think we're on the verge of something—all kickstarted by you, not me. The consequences this time of either of the two parties' choices getting into office would be dire. I can't sit back and let that happen when I can be a factor in bringing us out of this polarization."

"It sounds like you've decided to run."

"Well, yes and no."

She paused for a second. I was intrigued. She appeared to be choosing her thoughts and words very carefully.

"We've gamed this out pretty good. I've got an effective team conducting sophisticated focus groups and polling."

"What are they finding?"

"The good news is that there may in fact be a scenario to avoid the inevitability of one of these two national party candidates getting in the White House."

"How can I help? I'm happy to do so, you know. I do have some sway with Alliance folks, and with other independents and other disaffected Republicans and Democrats generally."

"Yes—and that is borne out in our data. And yes, I would like your help."

"You've got it. I'm honored to be asked. What can I do for you?"

"Well," she said, pausing just a second, "it's a big ask, but I'd rather you view it as a request coming from the country, rather than from me."

I laughed. "You should have been in sales, my friend."

"Danny, if you don't already know by now that all politics is sales then you are not as smart as I thought you were."

I smiled, knowing all the while she was methodically maneuvering me into a position where I couldn't easily say no, but I was well aware of that. And fine with it.

Eventually she just came out with it.

"I'd love for you to be on the ticket with me." She let that sink in for a second.

Then she stood up and looked up at a photo of FDR on the wall. It showed him sitting on the deck here at Camp David admiring the view off the Presidential Cabin.

Then she added, "I think it's the only hope we have of avoiding a really disastrous result—either of these two extremes gaining control—and all the chaos, divisiveness and paralysis that would ensue. And our findings confirm that I need you in order to pull it off."

"I'd love to see some of that polling data, if you don't mind."

"Of course. My numbers took a dive after our intervention in North Korea, but they have gradually been recovering ever since—but broadly across the entire electorate, not necessarily within the party.

"And since I bowed out of the primary I've been speaking more freely, and that seems to be resonating with voters as well."

"How telling is that? That's my whole point about the shackles the parties tend to impose on their candidates."

"I have to say a weight seems to have lifted from my shoulders when I did start speaking my mind."

"What do you anticipate the most compelling talking points of your campaign will be?"

"Fiscal responsibility. China and the global threat it presents. The border. Global warming. Crime. So many issues are screaming out for bipartisan compromise. Neither of these candidates can pull that off. How would you frame the issues?"

"Your description is a good start. Fiscal responsibility to begin with. Neither party seems to care about that anymore. That's frightening. And so is the amount of debt we are taking on. We seem to be inching closer and closer to a European-style social safety net with government funding all sorts of new things. All that spending is becoming normalized. I think it's a recipe for disaster, but beyond that, that's not America to me.

"I agree with China being a focus. They'll have both the most powerful economy and the most powerful military very soon.

"Global warming of course. And all its manifestations—the fires, the hurricanes, farming conditions, sea levels.

"I'd add one more to that core list, however—the most important one. And I think you have to put this first: uniting the country. Make polarization generally a core issue—the key issue. The cultural and political divide. It can and should provide the salient case for your candidacy. We've completely lost any sense of common identity as Americans. What a tragedy that is. And people have no faith or trust in their government unless their party is in power. For good reason, by the way. That must change too."

"Yes, of course," she responded. "Our divide is now one of our biggest threats."

"I firmly believe it's the biggest. And nothing tees this issue up for you better than these other two candidates you are running against.

"It's batshit crazy out there. Politics has become the WWE. We desperately need a return to truth telling, and empathy and understanding of each other. And it would help if people would shed their air of superiority that serves to separate us even more and stifles any inclination to reach across the aisle. 'With malice towards none,' right? Lincoln knew what he was talking about."

She nodded. She was obviously listening intently. That was encouraging to me.

I am happy to be on the ticket, but I'd really want that to form the core issue and message driving the campaign."

She nodded in apparent agreement.

"So who was it that gave you the advice to ask me to join the ticket?"

"I have a pretty good political team. They all pointed to the fact that your Alliance support and vote helped me win four years ago."

"Did you seek advice from anyone else?"

She smiled. "Whoever could you be referring to?"

"Anyone else—either of this world or any other?" I laughed.

"Ha! Yes, as a matter of fact. I got some expert opinions from some characters you might be familiar with."

"And that group suggested you reach out to me?"

"They did indeed."

"It couldn't have been unanimous."

"Close. You have some friends in that room."

"I doubt any of them, as former presidents, would have ever considered coming back and running in the VP slot."

"Funny you should mention that. I learned that Harry Truman in 1948 asked Eisenhower to run with him and offered to let him head the ticket. So Harry Truman was willing to take a back seat."

"Wow. Really? I had no idea. I would think with all those egos it would be a rare president who would even consider it."

"Yes, I agree. I think it both rare and admirable."

"That sounds like Truman, though. Speaks well of him. Well, I think you've asked the right ex-president. I'd have no trouble assuming that co-pilot role for this particular cause. I'd relish the challenge. I won't say no to you—or the country." I smiled. "Give me a day to talk to Denyse about it. But now that Jack just finished up high school, that's no longer a huge issue. And I'll want to see what a few of my political people have to say. I regret that I can't run it by those 45 advisors you've got at your beckon call.

"But back to the original point—no, my ego doesn't preclude me from considering making a run of it in the VP slot if that's for the good of the country."

"Well, that's nice to know, but that's not what I was asking."

"I'm confused now. You do or don't want me to join the ticket?"

"I do."

"OK."

"But one caveat."

"What's that?"

"Not in the VP slot."

I paused, more than slightly dumbfounded.

"You've gotta be shittin' me."

I saw instantly that she wasn't.

"What do you think?" she asked, as seriously as I'd ever seen her. "My polling people believe this is the only scenario with an actual shot at winning. And I'd love to join forces with you and go make this happen. God this country needs you and me right now. No one else can pull this off."

I couldn't muster any semblance of a response. My head was spinning.

I sat there in thought for more than a few seconds. "And how about your drinking buddies? What do those guys think of this part? Is this what they advised you to do?"

"They don't know about this part."

Several moments of silence transpired as I contemplated the enormity of this stunning proposition.

"And I thought it only appropriate to approach you about it at this particular place. Heck, if Egypt and Israel could come together here to map out a path for peace between their two nations, what better place than here for you and I to come together to craft a path to unite our hopelessly divided country."

We both sat for a few seconds in silence. I admired how she put that—invoking that bit of world history combined with this iconic setting—all making it really hard for a guy like me to say no. She was really good.

"So what do you think?" she repeated.

"I think one day of running this by Denyse won't be nearly enough. Better give me two days."

"You got it," she laughed. "Take three."

I took a deep breath.

Holy shit.

Chapter Sixty-Three

I Hope You Really Heard Her, Sir
May 23, 2024

Two days later I was back on my Rockhopper mountain bike, dripping wet, attempting the Fortini Loop mid-afternoon amidst a Bay Area heat-wave. For some reason I always seemed to relish this grueling ride even more on these scorching hot days. As I approached the Loop coming in along the Calero Creek Trail off of Harry Road, my adrenaline was pumping as fast as my mind was racing. I was hoping this ride would do something about all that. The guys followed along in the SUV on the roads as close as they could get to me, but they weren't riding with me on this 97-degree day, and I don't blame them.

The hills were golden now—barely a hint of green. Yellow and brown sagebrush desperate for water attempted in vain to fill the vast empty spaces between sporadic oaks. No wonder the fires ravage this state every summer like a Biblical plague. The whole scene cut a stark contrast to the verdant grounds at Camp David, with its unbridled vegetation teeming from every conceivable crevasse of open space creating a sea of green everywhere you look.

In many ways this particular ride had become like an old trusted friend. I recalled coming here at so many consequential moments in my life. Upon learning my mom had passed—this place was the perfect salve for my emotional wounds. After I learned I had a large tumor that required immediate surgery—it ended up being benign but those are some scary moments for a young father of three. The first time I had an offer to sell my firm—I'm so glad I held on but it killed me to turn that first offer down. And right before I proposed to Denyse, the first time—more on that story at some later date. That last one was hardly a difficult decision for me to make but I almost felt I owed it to this place, which has meant so much to me through the years, to allow it and all the wildlife here to have an opportunity to chime in. The

Loop and I always seem to agree on these decisions. I needed its counsel today as much as I ever did. I figured it would clear my mind enough to come to a thoughtful decision, and, in the best case, may even be gracious enough to offer me a sign.

I was dying to find out how my family felt. They have absolute veto power over this, but I had a feeling they'd be supportive. Denyse was assembling them all for a family meeting tonight. And I wanted to determine what my political people thought. If they felt it to be too much of a long shot I stood the risk of doing the cause much more harm than good. But first I needed to determine unequivocally if I really wanted to undertake all this again.

As I approached the summit my quads were singing, and not a happy tune. A trail like this has no switchbacks. I fought through it, knowing that if I stopped or slowed down the momentum lost would just make it all the harder when I tried to get going again. As I got to the top I looked up, and, sure enough, there was my bald eagle, on cue, circling in all its glory. If that wasn't a sign I don't know what would be. It came to rest atop a huge oak and then proceeded to circle again when I paused at the summit and took my helmet off for a nice long drink. The view did not disappoint. I said a prayer of thanks that I had this spectacular spot in my life that seemed to be all my own on days like today —those pivotal life moments. And I thanked God for once again placing me in a position to make a real difference in this world.

The Loop delivered, as it always does. My mind did indeed clear. From this vantage point all the inevitable chaos, stress and anxiety that lay ahead seemed well worth the effort if it moved the dial even a bit to make us better. I thought of all the others who had made just such a calculation—most notably Washington, Jefferson, Lincoln and FDR. Service to the country for each of them was no picnic, but made us infinitely better.

On that note I bade farewell to my eagle buddy and began my descent with a renewed energy. I peddled harder than usual on the back side, being eager to get back home and get a sense of where the family was on this. The angle of decline is significant on this side—which I am well aware of— and can be dangerous even if when one is just tapping the brakes the whole way down. I felt myself losing control on a sharp turn. I quickly applied the brakes. The wheels skidded to a stop but the momentum carried me and the back of the bike forward and in the direction away from the turn. Thrown from the bike, I proceeded to slide another 20 feet down the side of the hill.

I sat there for several minutes just taking stock of it all. Erik wouldn't be coming up on me anytime soon. He positioned himself back at the beginning of the loop. It was way too hot for him to be taking this ride with me.

I hadn't hit my head on anything, but my legs were torn up pretty good. My right elbow and shoulder were beat up as well—bruised and sore, and I'm sure would be swelling soon. My back felt tweaked. And the whole thing scared the hell out of me. But I did not believe I was in shock, and really felt like I hadn't broken anything. But several times in my life on various playing fields I have tried to convince myself that I didn't break something when I really had.

Even though I calculated I was alright, I continued to sit there a few more minutes. I may have been partly afraid that getting up and walking would expose an injury I hadn't contemplated.

Then I heard a voice from the trail.

"Are you alive?" It was a teenager's voice. A question only a young teen could phrase quite like that.

"Yes, I am, thank you."

"Do you need any help?"

"I just might," I said, picking myself up and standing upright for the first time. "Maybe you can wait here while I see if my bike is OK."

"This is a pretty gnarly hill. I've seen lots of new kids lose it at this turn."

I could only laugh at that. Me and the new kids.

He stood my bike up and rolled it back to the trail as I did some deep knee bends and raised my arms above my head. It felt like I really was going to be OK.

"I think you are correct about this being a trouble spot," I said reaching down and picking up an old dirty plastic Gatorade bottle close to where I lost control. I spotted something shiny reflecting the sun beneath it. I decided to pick it up too – a quarter.

"Here's a little something for your trouble," I said, tossing the quarter to the kid.

He caught it on the fly. "Gee thanks."

I had kept my helmet on, half hoping he wouldn't recognize me. This was embarrassing enough as it is. As I approached the bike he looked at me more closely.

"President McFadden?"

"Yes, that's me, as much as I'd like to deny it."

"Awesome. My Dad says all the time that he wishes you were still president."

"Well tell him I appreciate the support."

"And you are . . . ?" I asked.

"I'm Shane. Hey, do you mind if I take a selfie with you?"

"Sure. One condition though. Please promise you won't mention anything about my little spill here."

"Deal. My Dad is gonna love this."

I took my helmet off and posed with him for a couple of photos.

"What is a kid like you doing all the way up here all by yourself on your bike? I rarely see kids your age here. And never in this heat."

"My Dad and I are training for a 40-mile bike ride to benefit pancreatic cancer research. He rides after work but that's when I'm usually at baseball practice."

"Have you lost someone to that terrible affliction?"

"Yes. We lost my mom a year and a half ago."

My heart sank. "I am so sorry to hear that. How are you holding up?"

"I'm doing alright. I'm listening to my dad. We are staying busy, and doing our best to be positive. We are figuring this out together."

"Good for you. How is your dad?"

"I don't know. He tries to be good around me, but I can tell he's sad—about mom, about money, about our country these days. This has made us best friends though."

"When is your ride?"

"It's a week from Saturday."

Where is it taking place?"

"It goes from Monterey to Santa Cruz."

"Wow. I love both of those places, and all of the in-between. Care if I join you?"

"Are you kidding—we'd love to have you. That would be awesome."

"That way you can tend to me again if I fall."

"Wait 'til I tell Dad!"

"What's the name of the organization? I'll go online and try to register as soon as I get home."

"They call it PanCAN, but I don't know what the real name is."

"I'll find it," I said. "Let me have your father's cell phone number too. I want to check with him first, as there will be some implications of me tagging along. I'll want to clear it ahead of time with him and the organization. And I'll give you my number. Don't give that to anyone, of course, but call me if you are ever struggling with the loss of your mom or get really worried about your dad."

He seemed genuinely touched. "That is so nice of you. Thank you."

He airdropped me his father's contact info and the photo we took. We then traded cell phone numbers. As we said our goodbyes, I added. "You'd make a good Samaritan."

He looked at me with a bit of a blank stare. I guess that was a bit of a reach for a kid these days.

The bike, thankfully, seemed to have made it through the incident much better than me. I took a seat, gathered myself, and rode about ten yards, pumping the brakes the whole time. Shane stayed behind me, lacking any confidence in me—for good reason evidently—but that only added insult to injury. Even so I'm glad I met him, and hoped I could add a little ray of light to his life.

***

Forty-five minutes later after throwing on some sweats to cover my bruises I stepped up to the counter at Nine Lives. Santa Cruz Avenue was crowded and people had seen me come in. A group of onlookers gathered in front of the store. Erik and Brent sprung into work mode.

A large photo of me with baristas Martina and Kaitlyn from three years ago now hung on the wall. I always began my visit there by glancing up at that photo—not to admire it, but because it listed their names, and I wanted to make sure I got those right.

"Hey Kaitlyn," I said to the server, generating a big smile.

"What's up, Mr. President?" she responded.

We chatted for a few minutes—mostly about Brett—as another barista whipped up several "Presidential Power Smoothies"—my regular custom order I've been doing here now for the past three and a half years.

"How does that drink sell?" I asked Kaitlyn.

"A lot of people who come in order it," she responded, before adding, "once." She laughed. So did I.

"I don't blame them one bit," I said. "I'm not sure anyone else would put all that in one drink. It works for me, though."

"Your support is has made this place pretty gas."

I knew enough to act like I knew exactly what that meant. Given the context, it had to be good, as awkward a choice of adjective that may have been for an establishment that serves food and drinks.

I walked out with a tray of four Presidential Power Smoothies—for me, my two SUV buddies, and Denyse back home. A small crowd of maybe a dozen and a half people had gathered on the sidewalk, many of the faces obscured by cell phones as they took pictures and videos. Many yelled words of encouragement.

"Thank you for all the support," I said as I stepped off the curb toward the SUV. Brent held the door open and made sure the path was clear.

As I stepped into the car I heard a woman cry out from across the street, "Danny McFadden, we need you now!"

Her voice was crystal clear amongst the chatter of the people behind me on the sidewalk and the cars going by in between us. It had a plaintive, almost desperate tone.

I set the drinks inside the vehicle, reversed course and stood up for a moment beside the car scanning the opposite sidewalk for the source. I instantly spotted her—a young woman pushing a baby in a stroller. I flashed her a thumbs up sign. The crowd on both sides of Santa Cruz Avenue applauded.

As we sped away, Erik turned to me and said, "I hope you heard her, sir."

"I did," I responded.

"I know you heard her words, but I hope you really heard her, sir."

I thought about those comments on the drive home—both hers and his. I think I was underestimating the intense desire of so many in this country for someone to usher us out of this political death spiral.

Chapter Sixty-Four

A McFadden Family Meeting
May 23, 2024

I walked into the house following my ride and saw that Denyse, all three kids and even Montana had gathered out on the deck awaiting my return. Although I fully expected that they had started without me, and if so that was just fine. The kids may have feelings about this they wouldn't want to share with me. Heck, Denyse may have feelings on this she wouldn't want to share with me—but in her case merely out of support for me, and not wanting to stand in my way.

I walked outside and handed Denyse her drink as Montana greeted me as he always does—as if he hadn't seen me in years.

"What did you glean from your trail?" she asked. "Did your precious Fortini Loop speak to you?"

I laughed off the sarcasm. "It may have."

"Did it offer you a sign?"

"I think so."

"Care to share it?"

"Well, you know I don't really believe this stuff."

"What did it say?" She seemed eager now to hear.

"Well, I saw a bald eagle."

"That was it?" she responded.

"That's a pretty big deal, I would say. And it is the symbol of our country, for god sakes."

"But don't you see that guy every time you take that ride?"

I hesitated. "I don't know about every time. I don't know that I would say that."

"Dad," added Kelly, "that's like going to tip of lower Manhattan and saying that seeing the Statue of Liberty was a sign."

Denyse howled. "Are you looking for a sign, or just affirmation of a decision you've obviously already made?"

"No one's made any decisions here. That's what this meeting is all about."

I slipped off my sweats to take a look at my right leg.

"Good god, Danny, what happened to you?"

"Oh nothing," I answered. "Just a little fall on the bike."

She looked at Kelly. "Quick—go bring us a wet washcloth, some soap and Neopsorin. And grab of few of those big bandages from the cabinet."

"You fell on the bike? Here, let me see that."

I took a seat and put my leg up on another chair as she came over to examine my leg.

"Honey, that doesn't look good. What happened?"

"I kind of lost control on the way down and took a bit of a tumble."

"I'll say. Are you hurting?"

"Other than my pride? Not really. But I do feel it a bit in my shoulder. Don't worry. I'll be OK."

"Have you ever fallen on that trail before, Dad?" asked Brett, checking out the damage to the side of my thigh.

"Never."

Kelly started laughing. "You mean to tell me, Dad, that this once in your lifetime fall wasn't a sign, but a bald eagle that hangs out right there every day of the year is?"

"Yes, Kelly!" Denyse replied, laughing our loud again. "Are you kidding me? You nearly kill yourself and that's not a sign? Danger ahead. Proceed with extreme caution." Then, pointing at my leg, "This isn't a sign but that old bird is? You are absolutely priceless." She laughed some more.

"OK, I get it. You two may have a point."

Denyse slipped back into caring mode as she tended to my wounds. I liked this version of her a lot better.

Jack looked up from his phone. "Hey Dad, I just saw a picture of you on Instagram from today."

"Wow," I responded. "That was quick. I assume it was the kid on the trail? He was so nice stop and come to my aid."

"No—it's from Nine Lives. Someone took a couple pictures of you leaving with your drinks."

"Wait," said Denyse, "did you say a kid came to your aid on the trail?"

"Yes. I didn't really need it, but he saw me down and was nice enough to stop and see if I wanted help."

I found the photo on my phone and handed it to Denyse. "Here's the selfie we took. The poor kid lost his mom to pancreatic cancer last year."

"Good lord," exclaimed Denyse.

"I offered to participate in a bike ride/fundraiser with them next week."

"Of course you did," responded Denyse. "What's that he's got in his hand?" She zoomed in on his right hand.

"I don't know," I said. What is it?

"It's a coin, A quarter. That's George Washington. Why is he holding that in his photo with you?"

"I found that on the ground in the spot I fell . . ." I stopped to contemplate that for a second.

"That's interesting," Denyse said. She was thinking hard too.

"Was the Washington bust side face up or down when you found it?"

"Definitely face up."

"Now we might be getting somewhere," she said.

"And the kid said his dad wishes I was still president."

"OK, I think I'm prepared to say *that* might be the sign you were looking for. A Washington coin. I know how important that is to your little make-believe world."

"What make believe world?" asked Jack.

"Never mind," I barked back. Then, looking at Denyse, I added, "And, if it makes any difference, when I got into the car on Santa Cruz Avenue in front of Nine Lives, a woman from across the street yelled out, "Danny McFadden, we need you now."

"Alright. There you go. If you're looking for a symbol from above that may outweigh the terrible fall you took. There's mixed messages here. Maybe the fates are telling you, it's terribly complicated, and it certainly won't be easy, but go for it if you feel compelled. Which, by the way, is precisely how I would sum up my own feelings on it."

"Well, to be clear, I don't actually believe in signs and the fates of course . . ."

"Nobody's buying that, Dad," said Kelly. "C'mon. You live for that stuff."

I laughed.

"I have not made up my mind yet. But thank you for your support, Denyse."

"Would you move from here?" asked Brett.

"There'd be no immediate need for that. The nice thing about jumping in now as an independent is there's no two-year grind to win a primary. I've managed to miss all of that. This will be four months, at the very most. That's the way we should pick presidents. These endless election cycles are killing us. Why would we even want to elect anyone who would be willing to abandon their lives for two full years and campaign round the clock?"

"If we win, and I'm not saying we would, but if we did of course me and your mom would move, but we'd keep this place."

"Do you guys have a chance to win?" asked Jack.

"I would think so, but these things are so hard to predict. We both have higher national favorables than either Margel or Clayton. To win a primary, as they both had to, you really need to do and say things that make you unattractive to the other party and to independents. That's an advantage for us. It also helps that I already won as an independent, so there shouldn't be much fear among voters that an independent can't win in the first place and would be a wasted vote."

"It would be really weird to be in college with you and mom living in the White House."

"You'll have secret service living in your dorm with you posing as students," said Kelly. "You'll get used to it. Hopefully you'll get some that you like who know when to leave you alone."

"Jack, in your case I'm gonna need a whole team of those guys to be at your side round the clock." I laughed. I don't think he saw the humor.

"In all seriousness, this move would put you all in a fish bowl—even more so than the one you're in right now. And of course there are dangers. It just seems that all the various fringes in this country keep getting crazier and crazier every year. But we'll get some fairly sophisticated protection."

"I love your guys, said Jack. "Those guys are total units."

"But this is my point. We don't have to do this. The last thing I want is to put you in an untenable situation in the midst of some pretty important years in your life. You saw how tough it was for Cade Bates."

"I think we understand all that really well, Dad," added Kelly, "but there's another aspect of this that needs to be pointed out. Kids today can't even talk about politics. It's just an ugly, distressing topic that bums everyone out. No one wants to see it on television, or discuss it with friends or family members. Most of my friends don't even want to think about it. That all changes with you. They all relate to you, and respect you as someone with integrity and character who isn't caught up in all the political games, and someone with a keen sense of America's place in the world. I know I've been spoon-fed this stuff by you and mom since I was in the crib, but I believe it. You make people love America and have hope for its future. And I believe you are literally the only person in America in a position right now to do something about it. And a lot of people feel that way. You've already a made massive difference. If the three of us have to undertake some sacrifices that's a small price to pay for the chance to let not only my generation but the rest of the country experience an America they can be truly proud of. That's your life's work, your legacy. We've discussed it and decided we're in."

Denyse applauded. "Bravo, Kelly. So well-stated. I couldn't agree more."

Then Denyse turned to me. "As for me, let me tell you something, I signed up for it all—the fun, and boy has it been fun. The dysfunction and anxiety—and there's been plenty of that. The love—my god the love in this family is electrifying. The magic moments—every Christmas, every Fourth of July, every trip to Lake Almanor, every opening day, every Notre Dame/USC game, every Thanksgiving, every St. Patrick's Day, the birthdays—our birthday traditions rock. All of it. And, as importantly as all the rest, the sense and belief that we are here for more—that in the end, it's not purely about our happiness, though that's a big piece of it. Together we discovered that life at its core is really about impacting others and how we can make a difference in this world."

She was on a roll like I've rarely seen her.

"I know how you idolize and revere your make believe friends—Washington and Jefferson and Lincoln and Teddy Roosevelt—and how desperately we need another one like those right now. And I hear your concern about the optics of the first woman president in our history deciding to take a back seat to a man, but let me tell you something— that is one truly extraordinary specimen of a woman there. Do not patronize her with that narrative. She's knows exactly what she's doing. She has done just fine for herself, thank you, and doesn't need you or any other man to tell her what's best for her. She can fend for herself. And if she's saying she wants it this way, then take her at her word.

"So the question in my mind isn't what would make you happy or what would make us happy, but rather what are we called to do at this place and time. I think you started something special four years ago. You caught lighting in a bottle. And now against all odds that lighting is striking again.

"We could remain in our cushy life here in Los Gatos and accept our yacht invitations, and spend all our time artfully navigating our decidedly first world problems, and we'd be really happy doing so. How truly idyllic. But think for a second. What would your guy Teddy say? A soft life is hardly one worth living, right? I don't know what the exact quote is but it's something like that. Right? I think I've even heard you rattle that off in your sleep many nights.

"Do I look forward to all the venom and hate that will be coming our way, and the impossible standard you'll have to live up to? No.

"But if you decide you are up to it—a decision you need to make for yourself, let me tell you I am in. Not because I have a burning desire to return to that fishbowl and be judged day in and day out and have the world literally riding shotgun with my family through every twist and turn of our lives, but because all that pain and heartache and anxiety might—just might—be a means to a better end—a more perfect union—or at least one remotely like the one your guy Jefferson laid out on paper so many years ago. And without you we just keep slipping ever father away from it. To the point soon where we run the risk of never being able to get it back. For whatever reason fate has made you the instrumental linchpin in this whole thing. That's a mighty big responsibility. But I think you might just be up to the task."

Kelly, Brett and Jack stood up and applauded.

Wow. Holy cow. God love her. I began to think maybe she should be the one to be running for president. I wondered if FDR ever felt that way. Maybe John Adams did.

"What do you think, Dad?" asked Jack.

"I think if I'm smart I'll convince Mom to do a heck of a lot more campaigning than she wants to do."

"I think if you're really smart you won't," replied Denyse. She was smiling though, which I took as a good sign.

"Is it decided then?" asked Denyse.

"I've got one more call to make," I answered.

"To who?" asked Brett.

Moments later Denyse responded. "I'm pretty sure I know who."

Chapter Sixty-Five

You Son of a Bitch!
May 24, 2024

"I've been expecting this call," said Satch, answering on the first ring.

"Have you really, now? And why would that be?"

"I got a fairly reliable tip. From a very powerful source."

"Denyse?"

He laughed. "Another brilliant, strong woman you've become close with."

"Tina?"

"Someone almost as smart but even more powerful than Tina."

"That's not a large group." I thought for a minute. "Maggie?"

He laughed. "Winner."

"You heard this from Maggie and you didn't tell me?" I wasn't so much annoyed as I was curious.

"There are a few reasons for that, sir. First of all, I am a Marine—always—and she is my Commander-in-Chief. She sought my counsel, and I chose to respect the confidentiality of that discussion."

"Alright. I can appreciate that. Every time I entered a foreign embassy around the globe as President, without exception, the first person I interacted with was one of our Marines standing guard. I can't say I have a problem with that."

"Secondly, you might also forget that I have an intense rooting interest here. I have a keen sense of what's best for the country. I believed our best chance to have you run again was to have our President directly ask you to do so. How could you, or anyone else for that matter, possibly say no to her? I felt this was our country's best chance of having you answer the call."

"You son of a bitch!" I exclaimed. I was only half joking.

He laughed. "And it tells me everything I need to know about her that she would even consult me before approaching you."

"Oh, she is formidable, that's for sure. It doesn't surprise me in the least. What did you tell her?"

"I told her that while I know you put country over party, the question would be can you put country over family—the two things you value the very most."

"That is precisely how I break this down."

"And where are you on that now?"

"The family has given me their blessing, but that doesn't mean it's the best thing for them. Kelly said the benefit to the country would be worth the personal challenges to them. Jack is off to college in a few weeks so Denyse and I will be empty nesters. The boys I believe are both OK with it, but it will make their college experience vastly different than most."

"Their college experience was going to be different anyway. And Denyse?"

"Hard to really tell for certain. She says she all in—and says so enthusiastically. Her reasons are similar to Kelly's. But I just have to think behind it all, knowing her, she wouldn't tell me if she didn't want me to do it anyway, so she'd rather say she's all in and get 100% behind it."

"You know her better than me, but I suspect she'd tell you straight if she didn't want you to do it. But even so, is that so wrong that she might just want to be really supportive of you and that may be driving her decision?"

"No, I suppose not. She always has been."

"So you've told me where the family is on it. How about you?" he asked.

"Well, I know how hard it will be. There will be stress and anxiety, and plenty of struggle, heartache and many failures for every success. It won't be a picnic. But it's no picnic standing on the sidelines watching all the misinformation, gaslighting and sheer hate that our politics has devolved into."

"But you have to realize that you kickstarted a movement that is beginning to make a difference," he said. "You lit a fire, and it's spreading. So many people have left the two parties. Your movement now has a national organization, and seats in Congress, and even a media empire sympathetic to your cause. Conditions for you today this time around are so much better than they were when you were first elected.

"And, more importantly, there's still unfinished business. And that may come easier this time around too. Sure, it's still a tall order, as you like to say. But how wonderful that you have a chance to fill it.

"And one more thing. Our country has persevered for all these years not only due to its foundational documents and the system the founders created, but because of the admirable people of character who were manning the ship in the times of storm. The Constitution wouldn't survive on its own without people of moral fiber choosing time and again to make decisions in the best interest of the country as opposed to their self-interest.

"I think our country is now on the verge of one of those storms. Margel is definitely not the right person for this moment, and neither, I would offer, is Clayton. You and Maggie offer us precisely what we need at this critical crossroads.

"And last but not least, Christie and I would be thrilled to welcome you two back to the East Coast."

"I'll do you one better than that," I responded. "If I do this I'll demand that you come rejoin the cause."

"Perhaps we can come in the months Dom is away at college."

"We'll make you permanent occupants of the Lincoln bedroom. We won't ask you to do any work, I just need to have you around."

"OK sir. We'll play catch in the Rose Garden every afternoon."

"I'll settle for that. Or better yet," I replied, "how about we coach a DC Little League team together?"

"Perfect. I'm on board. Just give me the pitchers, and we'll do just fine."

Chapter Sixty-Six

A Republic, If You Can Keep It
June 4, 2024

I notified Maggie that I was in. All in. But I had one request. I really wanted to honor my commitment to Shane and his father to ride with them at their fund-raiser for pancreatic cancer research, and requested that we hold off any announcement until after the event. That was a big ask, and certainly wasn't ideal, but she honored that request. And, to my eternal shock and delight, we managed to pull it off. News of our plan miraculously did not leak. I decided that had to bode well for our future partnership together. If there was to be a future . . .

***

CBS EVENING NEWS

NORAH O'DONNELL: Good evening. Tonight, we are standing by to bring you the President live from historic Independence Hall in Philadelphia, where we expect her to declare whether she will be running for re-election as an independent candidate for president. Having lost her bid to win the Republican nomination, speculation is running rampant that she will now run outside of the party.

This is a live shot of Independence Hall, the site of the signing of the Declaration of Independence in 1776, and the drafting of the U.S. Constitution in 1787. As we pan back you can see the massive crowd that has gathered on Independence Mall—the large grass fields in front of Independence Hall. A spillover crowd fills nearby

Washington Park, and large video boards are interspersed throughout both sites.

I want to bring in our election expert, John Dickerson for his thoughts. John, there wouldn't be this degree of fanfare would there, and this historic venue selected, if she were merely announcing that she wasn't running, right?

JOHN DICKERSON: Ordinarily I would agree with you, Norah, but let's remember it was just four years ago that we covered an eerily similar scenario at another historic venue—Mount Vernon—where President McFadden did precisely that. Even so, I have to say it sure seems unlikely that she would be doing all this just to announce she is not running.

O'DONNELL: Speaking of President McFadden, political pundits are speculating wildly about the possibility of him joining the President on the ticket as her running mate.

DICKERSON: Yes, indeed they are, Norah. It may be the least well-kept secret in Washington that she is reaching out to him. McFadden on the ticket could be a difference-maker for her. He would bring with him a solid and growing base of support among independents as well as disgruntled members of both parties. And who better to join her on the ticket than someone who himself successfully navigated that independent path to the White House.

O'DONNELL: A former president coming back as a Vice President would be unprecedented, would it not?

DICKERSON: Yes, but remember, John Quincy Adams came back as a Congressman, and Andrew Johnson later served as a Senator. And of course Taft became Chief

Justice of the Supreme Court. It would not be the craziest thing for McFadden to serve in another capacity.

O'DONNELL: We're getting the one minute warning signal here. We are going to take you now live to Philadelphia's Independence Hall, an iconic venue well steeped in our nation's history, for an address by the President which promises to add a new chapter to that lore.

(*President Margaret Bates steps up to a microphone on a stage in front of Independence Hall.*)

MARGARET BATES:

Good evening. Two hundred and thirty-seven years ago, the Constitutional Convention wrapped up its four months of work drafting our seminal founding document in the venerable building behind me, As Ben Franklin, who some like to refer to as "The First American," emerged from that gathering, a woman promptly demanded to know what type of government he and the other delegates had crafted in that four months of secrecy. His answer? "A republic, madam, if you can keep it."

As I stand here tonight, our nation is tearing itself further and further apart. That gap that separates us grows ever wider by the day. Indeed, the notion of a truly *united states* of America is a fiction— a thing of the past. That division now comprises the lens through which we view every issue.

In fact, in the last 150 years we have never been closer to *not being able to keep it*—that Republic constructed by Franklin and his colleagues—than we are today.

Historians believe the woman whom Franklin was addressing was Elizabeth Willing Powel, a prominent society figure and the wife of Philadelphia Mayor Samuel Powel. So while I wasn't the woman he was directly addressing, I am nonetheless a woman who hears him loud and clear, even today— a few centuries later—and who heeds his caution. And I am a woman who is doing something about it. In fact, that's precisely what tonight is all about.

Our two-party system appears poised to present our country with a choice between two nominees who are each polarizing figures at the far ends of the political spectrum. And both have negative national favorability ratings that exceed their positives.

But that's our system. In this country the two parties are the gatekeepers along the path to the White House. This in spite of the fact that more and more people abandon the parties every year and independents now far outnumber either of the two parties. The only person to have broken through outside of the two parties in the last 175 years is Danny McFadden.

My political people are convinced I could mount a successful independent run for re-election. But I am here tonight to declare that, after a great deal of thought, I have decided not to do that.

(*Audible gasps of disappointment in the crowd.*)

No, no, no—hear me out. I have something far better up my sleeve. Something that gives us the very best shot at once again becoming a collection of truly united states. And who knows, the way these things go, we may only have one shot at that. And to quote another one of our Founders, I'm not throwing away my shot.

I truly believe both Alexander Hamilton and Benjamin Franklin would be proud of what I'm about to do here—in addition to Madison and Washington and many of the others who were highly suspicious of political parties when they drafted the Constitution.

Ladies and Gentlemen, I am about to bring out the one person who, more than any person on earth, has the authenticity, credibility and gravitas to unite this country again. Someone with whom you are already quite familiar.

So while I am declaring tonight that I won't be a candidate for president, I have agreed to be this person's running mate, and will be seeking the vice presidency on a new independent ticket with our next president—who happens to also be our last president—Danny McFadden.

(*Long applause as Danny McFadden emerges from inside Independence Hall to the sound of Frank Sinatra singing The Best is Yet to Come. He embraces President Bates, then they face the crowd smiling amidst thunderous applause. As the song fades out, McFadden takes the microphone, then pauses through another round of applause.*)

DANNY MCFADDEN:

Thank you, Madam President. I'm so thrilled to be standing here alongside you. A former Democrat linking arms with a former Republican—creating a powerful imagery apropos of the work that will be required ahead to fix this county.

A republic if you can keep it. Those words of Ben Franklin sum up so concisely our case for the presidency.

I'd say for most of our nation's history, thankfully there has been little or no question as to whether we can keep it. For nearly 250 years we have kept it, but it's threatened now as much as it ever has been since the Civil War. And the threats, unfortunately, are coming from inside the house. Not some foreign adversary, they are of our own doing.

And Dr. Franklin didn't ask the most relevant follow-up question, but it needs to be asked today as well. Even if we do manage to keep this republic, how strong can we possibly be as a nation if along the way we manage to become our own worst enemy, with every election contested, every issue politicized, political advantage routinely and reflexively sought over political compromise, hate trumping love, and disdain for one another replacing genuine understanding of each other. We may still have that Republic that Franklin and his fellow visionaries constructed, but each passing year seems to bring more impotence upon this once great nation. As Lincoln, quoting the Bible, once famously said, "a house divided against itself cannot stand." No, it cannot.

Our enemies, who so desperately seek to sow division and doubt in our democracy, don't even need to bother anymore. But they happily use our own social media platforms to exacerbate our internal contempt for one another. And division is now big business in America. Indeed, it is one of our most lucrative career paths. And division is also fueling our social media mega companies. Nothing generates likes and clicks like divisive content triggering outrage. Those seeking to unite us have to fight Silicon Valley's algorithms too.

It's worth a few more follow up questions tonight. In this divisive environment, can we possibly still achieve our most audacious ambitions? Would we have had the wherewithal to save the world, as we did in 1944? Could we have led the world in putting a man on the moon?

And perhaps our greatest contribution to civilized society—our values and ideals—which for more than two centuries have formed a shining example and a standard for others to seek to emulate, appear to be rapidly eroding with every passing year.

To top it off, in what is perhaps the biggest body blow of all, one of our nation's most cherished and distinguishing features is now squarely at risk – our expectation every four years of a peaceful transition of power.

The 9/11 Commission Report, in analyzing the reasons terrorists were able to breach our shores and wreak unspeakable havoc upon our nation, cited a "failure of imagination" as a major contributing factor to the United States allowing itself to be blindsided. The same could properly be said of Pearl Harbor. As devastating as each of those events were, what we are faced with now, I would posit, could be even more destructive to our democracy. We simply cannot afford to be caught flatfooted.

Our two-party system in this country has run its course. Worst of all, the parties are complicit in this problem. Circumstances now compel us to imagine a better system. If the best of America—the values, the leadership, ingenuity, work ethic, and model for the world—is to return, we must rid ourselves of the worst of America.

Addressing this dysfunctional dynamic must be our top priority going forward. Unfortunately, I think that you'll find that your other two choices this election—the ones that our two-party system manufactured and produced in a terribly flawed and dated primary process—simply offer more of the same division, with little or no hope of addressing this massive elephant in the room.

Martin Luther King, speaking about racism in 1964, famously said "We must learn to live together as brothers or perish as fools." Those words are just as instructive to our condition in America today.

When you sent me to the White House in 2016 in the most unlikely of elections, the seeds of this movement were sown. Eight years later the problem still persists but our prospects of defeating it are infinitely better. That movement we started has become a juggernaut, and is our only hope of reversing course as a country.

I stand here tonight in partnership with President Bates. We are two U.S presidents hailing from opposite ends of this great country, one a former Democrat and the other a former Republican, one from what is traditionally viewed as a blue state and one from what is thought to be red, to offer you an alternative path forward to a new united future for us and for this nation.

The challenge before us is formidable but nothing that America can't achieve. Together. But I promise you we will never do so if we don't try.

We are better than this America. So much better. Let's prove that to ourselves and to the world on November 5th.

CNN ANDERSON COOPER

ANDERSON COOPER: Well that was a truly extraordinary scene we just witnessed. The President of the United States, whose re-election effort stalled when she bowed out of the Republican primary, had been expected to announce tonight that she would be running as an independent. Instead, she shocked the crowd here in front of Independence Hall and the world by announcing that she would be running instead as a Vice Presidential candidate on a ticket with former President Danny McFadden.

Let's go to Kaitlan Collins who's in Philadelphia with the President. Kaitlan, what was the reaction of the crowd to this turn of events.

KAITLAN COLLINS: Wow. Anderson this crowd is energized by this announcement. I think there was a feeling among Bates supporters before tonight that they would be behind her, but that she would really struggle to get re-elected as an independent. I would say based on the enthusiasm I see right now that they are thrilled with this development.

COOPER: David Gergen, what did you think watching this tonight?

DAVID GERGEN: It was wonderful political theater. And I felt their messaging was spot-on. In their brief, elegant remarks they have completely upended this race. You notice they didn't mention any of the issues the other two candidates are fixating on. It's as if they'll be running a completely different campaign. They have elevated the discourse while the other two appear in contrast stuck in the mud.

DAVID AXELROD: I couldn't agree more, David. While the other two candidates are reading right from their same old playbooks, citing one wedge issue and cultural issue after another, that actually plays right into the hands of McFadden and Bates, as their core message is to get us beyond that exact back and forth. The more those other two bicker about those issues, the better McFadden and Bates' message appears in contrast.

And I would add this too, Anderson. McFadden is situated so much better to pull this off today than he was eight years ago. There is a sophisticated organization he can tap into, well financed, with supporter networks set up, and now there are politicians in place all over the country with allegiance to President McFadden, many of whom he helped get elected. But most of all, his candidacy is no longer a pipedream. He said it himself tonight —that last election he won may have been unlikely. No one tonight is questioning whether he can win.

GERGEN: McFadden used the word audacious tonight. This is indeed an audacious proposition. I think everyone in this country, no matter what your political views, recognize that our present divisions in this country are killing us. That message can have appeal for every voter in this country.

COOPER: What a truly stunning turn of events we have witnessed tonight. A presidential race that really began in

earnest 14 months ago has been completely upended with
only five months remaining until election day.

***

Hours later, when I finally made it to my hotel room at the Lotte New York Palace Hotel in Manhattan, I took a deep breath and let it all sink in. Tomorrow we would begin with The Today Show—and the next four months leading up to the election promised to be a whirlwind. I was remarkably at peace with it all, however, even in the face of all the chaos I knew lay ahead. For a moment I thought of the Saloon, and what my old buddies there would think about all this. I wished I could have access to them in this moment, and in many of the others that would soon be headed my way in this campaign. I took comfort in the thought that they'd all be solidly behind us, and thrilled that Maggie and I were taking it upon ourselves to confront this systematic dysfunction in our system head on.

I did, however, have a tinge of nervousness. Denyse and I had certainly been happy with our admittedly cushy life in California these past four years. This wasn't necessarily in the gameplan. But sometimes it's less about your gameplan and more about taking what the defense gives you. In my case, I seemed, for whatever reason, to have stumbled into an offense that actually stood a realistic chance of getting us beyond all this polarization, and that was a rare thing indeed. I couldn't afford not to give that my all.

Chapter Sixty-Seven

Neville Chamberlain
October 5, 2024

While I had never been shy about appearing on the national political shows with these nightly talking heads, and was proud that I could be found on any one of them on any given night regardless of where they were positioned across the political spectrum, I had never done Rachel Maddow or Tucker Carlson. Murph implored me to stay far away from both. Tina, on the other hand, saw merit in attempting to have an honest conversation with Tucker Carlson. After much thought, I took her advice. I'm glad I did.

FOX NEWS

TUCKER CARLSON TONIGHT

TUCKER CARLSON: I am actually excited about our next guest, independent presidential candidate Danny McFadden. I give him credit for coming on Fox News, which he does from time to time, unlike Senator Clayton, Nancy Pelosi, and most Democrats. He's been on with Brett Baier and with Martha MacCallum recently. I'm pleased that he is making time for us.

Welcome, President McFadden.

DANNY MCFADDEN: Happy to be with you, Tucker. Thanks for including me in your show.

CARLSON: Let me begin by asking you why are you venturing over to this channel. I'll be honest with you, you are not my own preferred candidate, and I would venture to guess you might not be the preferred candidate of many of our viewers. Although I'm certain my audience would prefer you to Senator Clayton.

MCFADDEN: That's easy, Tucker. I'm not afraid to have a spotlight on my record or my positions. I'm running to be a president for all of the people. The days of everyone watching Walter Cronkite at night are long gone. Today people get their news and opinions from a wide variety of sources. If I'm not showing up where they are tuning in, they'll never get exposed to me and have a chance to learn what I'm all about. I'm not afraid of speaking my mind about all the issues to the liberal media or the conservative media. I know I won't win them all over, but I surely won't win any of them if I'm not showing up where they are tuning in.

CARLSON: OK. Fair enough. That's admirable. And smart.

While I can appreciate some things about you, like the fact that you are opposed to Senator Clayton and the Democrats' massive multi trillion dollar cradle-to-grave safety net proposal, there are many things nonetheless that I dislike about your positions, and I think my audience may as well. At the top of my list is immigration. Before we retroactively grant citizenship to any illegals that crossed our borders in abject violation of our laws through any sort of amnesty program, we need to properly secure our borders. I'm not in favor of moving one inch on the former until we have accomplished the latter.

MCFADDEN: I understand your position, Tucker, and I can't say I wholeheartedly disagree in principle, but the practical realities are such that much of America and

Congress feels differently, and no immigration bill that solely funds border security without addressing the other part has any chance of success. Not even close. So in the end, were does that leave us?

This issue is emblematic of so many others today. If we had passed the immigration bill I campaigned for with President Bates this past year we would already be well on our way to securing the border in a meaningful way. Your all-or-nothing approach merely ensures further legislative gridlock, and that we'll continue to have a chaotic immigration policy and a perpetual crisis at the border for decades to come.

CARLSON: But people who have come here illegally should not be rewarded with citizenship, no matter what hurdles these bills make them jump through. That's not right or just.

MCFADDEN: Again, I understand your position. As much as you believe fighting for that principle is the right approach, I'm saying your unwillingness to compromise, coupled with the far left's unwillingness to compromise, just serves to ensure we'll have a mess on the border for years and possibly generations to come, and we'll have to continue to address all the multitude of collateral economic and social issues that inevitably leads to throughout our country.

I am offering practical solutions to problems like these which can help us move forward as a nation. But we'll never get anywhere if people in Congress decide they need a perfect bill in every instance and that any bill that's not perfect, even if it is very good and fixes a problem, is unacceptable and dead on arrival.

CARLSON: Well that sounds to me like the kind approach that led to Neville Chamberlain's demise in Britain.

MCFADDEN: Ha! (*laughing out loud*) Wow! That's precisely what I'm talking about. God no. All compromise is not surrender! The fact that you use that analogy makes my case for me. Our whole Alliance movement, which if you haven't noticed, is gaining momentum with every passing day, exists now because the two parties have become increasingly intransigent and increasingly extreme. Our independent approach now represents our country's only realistic chance for actual progress as a nation. Without us leading the way, we'd be doomed, and destined to surrender our place on the world stage to China and others.

Perhaps the most telling example of that dysfunctional dynamic and its destructive effects is in our ever-expanding national debt. Republicans' never-ending quest for further tax relief on the right, and Democrats' efforts to institutionalize a cradle to grave safety net, to use your words, on the left, have left us in position where literally no one is acting to stop the financial bleeding. I saw that first hand as president when Congress went around me to pass a budget bill over my veto that only served to make the deficit substantially worse.

CARLSON: Well, if your so-called independent approach is so special, why didn't it work for you as president? You didn't get your economic program passed, because, as you say, Congress just went around you. And, as we all know, the gridlock you faced was so insurmountable you didn't even bother to seek a second term.

MCFADDEN: OK. All that's true, and fair, perhaps. But

that ignores the fact that we planted a seed in that last year. We were forced to, but we did. And it spawned a national independent movement. And that movement now has established a beachhead in Congress with 22 House members including the Speaker, and 2 senators. And those numbers will only increase with every passing election. And those legislators will find they are increasingly powerful precisely because they occupy the center, and both parties will desperately need them to get any bill to the finish line. But they will, and progress will be made again.

We did not have any of that when I was president. We were just getting started. We have it now. Boy do we have it now. And thank god, for the country's sake, we have it now. Not a minute too soon.

Chapter Sixty-Eight

It's Kinda Like Our Wedding
Election Day, Tuesday November 5, 2024
7:58 p.m. PST Fairmont Hotel San Jose

"Where are you?" I asked Denyse. I was calling her from a private room off of a large suite on the 20th floor at the Fairmont Hotel in San Jose, as the polls in California and much of the West Coast were about to close. The suite was packed with all the top people associated with the campaign. We controlled the entire floor. Maggie and Gil were here, but no sign of Denyse. And, by the way, how absolutely priceless it was for me to have my buddy Gil here with us amongst all these official people and political folks. I still can't get over that. Classic.

I hadn't seen Denyse in ten days, as Maggie and I had been crisscrossing the country, largely via Air Force One, in the waning days of this heated campaign. We did Good Morning America in Manhattan this morning then Afternoon Chicago. We voted by mail. Denyse hadn't wanted to campaign, and I honored that. I didn't blame her, by the way.

"I'm so sorry I'm not there yet," she responded.

I could hear a lot of commotion in the background.

"Where are you?" I asked again. She seemed to be avoiding answering that.

"I can be there in about a half an hour."

"Sure," I said. 'That's fine. I was just getting worried."

Just then I heard through the phone what sounded like a huge crowd around her erupt in cheers. Moments later I heard hooting and hollering in my hotel coming from the suite next door.

I looked at the television in my room just in time to hear George Stephanopoulos declare "The polls have closed in California, and ABC News can now project that the State of California and its 55 electoral college delegates will go to Danny McFadden. Exit polling indicates a wide margin of victory for the former president." They displayed a little photo of me in a white box next to an outline of the state with the number 55 inside.

Denyse screamed into the phone. "We won California Danny! Oh my god I can't believe they called it that quick. I'm so proud of you!" I could barely hear her above the background noise.

The noises coming from the room next to me suddenly grew louder too. I heard someone banging at my door.

"Come in," I yelled. It was Murph—Christina Murphy—who served in my administration as one of my top advisors and was now heading our election effort.

"The networks are calling both California and Arizona for us."

"I saw California. Wow. Great news about Arizona."

Just then I saw the Arizona news being announced on ABC.

"I'm talking to Denyse. I'll be out there in a minute."

"Were the heck is she?" Murph asked. "We need her tonight."

"She knows," I responded. "She'll be here soon."

I could hear more cheering through the phone.

Where the hell are you?

"Somewhere you're at least a little bit familiar with."

"Not Hannegan's?"

"Yes! It's packed. I swear everyone we've ever known is here. You'd be in your element."

"Really?"

"All my Bunko babes convinced me to meet them here for a drink. They thought this would be the perfect place to be tonight. But Kelly and her friends are all here too. All the old Little League parents. The Holy Spirit parish people. Your old mountain bike crew. So many of your former co-workers from Aengus. The crowd has spilled over outside too. They've got the entire street blocked off like they do for St. Patrick's Day.

"Oh, and your brother Brendan and his buddies are here too. It's kind of like our wedding . . . that is, if it had just been your wedding. Which is kind of what it was actually now that I think about it. But that's not important now."

"How much have you had to drink?"

"By the way," she added, ignoring my question completely, "I'm pretty sure they all think you're gonna show up here tonight."

I was momentarily speechless.

"Danny? Did I lose you?"

The truth is, I had never been more conflicted in my entire life. I needed to be two places at one time. Kind of ironic, considering that I am kind of two places at one time already, though I try not to think about that. But now I needed to be in three.

"No I'm still here."

"Are you disappointed in me?"

"No—in fact, I don't know if I've ever been more proud."

She screamed again. "I knew you wouldn't mind! I am coming over. I may have just one more with the girls. A small one . . ."

"Oh God, you sound just like me. And I know that means I won't be seeing you here tonight."

"When do you need me there?"

"This thing is far from over. It's already 11:00 o'clock on the east coast right now. We'll come out to address the crowd here either way eventually. It's going well, though. I think we're the only ticket with a shot left to actually get to 270, but if we come up short who knows what will happen if this ends up in the House. We need to win it outright or we'll lose the House vote."

"Have fun," I added. "You deserve it. If you make it over here great, but I'm good either way."

"I'm sorry I'm not there yet. You sure you're not disappointed in me?"

"No. The truth is I've never been more turned on."

I laughed as I said it—but just to make her think I was joking.

Chapter Sixty-Nine

Steve Kornacki
November 6, 2024
Election Night 12:45 a.m. EST

MSNBC NEWS

ELECTION NIGHT COVERAGE

(*Split screen Rachel Maddow and Brian Williams on the left, Steve Kornacki on the right in front of a map screen of the United States.*)

RACHEL MADDOW: Let's check in now with our resident political junkie slash human calculator slash energizer bunny, Steve Kornaki. He's been in his charging station but we have him back.

BRIAN WILLIAMS: Steve, you are a national treasure. Please tell us the latest.

STEVE KORNACKI: Well, we are beginning to get some clarity at this hour. As we look at our Big Board, this much we know. Neither Margel nor Clayton have a realistic mathematical path to 270. It's a been a big night for McFadden and Bates, but the question remains will it be big enough. So I want to explain what I mean by that, break that down right now and then focus on the House race nationwide too, because that may become relevant to this presidential election as well.

Let's go to our map. You'll notice a sea of white emerging. Those are all states we have called for McFadden—totaling 212 Electoral College voters. He's leading by stitching together the same type of coalition that carried him to the White House eight years ago. Back then he garnered 86% of independents. This year exit polls suggest he's getting 93% of independents. And that's a bigger group than it was eight years ago. He's also getting 67% of voters who are either registered Democrats or registered Republicans and indicate that they are disillusioned with the direction of their party. He's also carrying the youth vote again. He's doing well with women again, and he is getting the Catholic vote.

But he does not have this thing locked up, and there is some reason for concern despite his success. We have Clayton now with 112 electoral college delegates—which you see in the states colored in blue, and Margel with 98 from the states colored in red. That leaves 116 votes yet to be assigned. So, as you can see, even if either Margel or Clayton were to run the table and take all the undecided states, it still wouldn't be enough to get them to 270.

MADDOW: But they are not conceding the race.

KORNACKI: Exactly, Rachel. You don't see either of them conceding. And here's why. If we were to assume that all of the remaining undecided states will break the way they are currently leaning—a huge assumption but let's play this what-if game for the moment to illustrate a point—this is how the map would look. You see McFadden still clearly leading, but he only has 267 electoral college delegates—three short of what is needed to win.

If none of these candidates makes it to 270, then our system dictates that the US House of Representatives selects the next president from among these three.

MADDOW: So whatever party controls the House of Representatives will win the White House.

KORNACKI: Well, it's even more complicated than that. Let's turn to our House map. All 435 House races are up for grabs today, but the reality is 165 or thereabouts are safe Democratic seats, and 145 are safely Republican. Another 60 or so seem extremely likely to break for the Alliance or Independent incumbents. That leaves about 65 truly contested seats. If the present leader in the polls wins all those races—again, an unlikely scenario but let's game this out—we'd have 179 Democrats, 153 Republicans and 103 who are either Alliance or Independent. No party would have a majority.

WILLIAMS: What a mess that would be.

MADDOW: Those Alliance and Independents would seem to have some power, as neither party would have a majority and would need those votes.

KORNACKI: Maybe not as much as you might think, though. The voting tally set up for the tie breaker in the House is actually one vote per state. The delegations in each state vote to determine who their state's one vote goes to. Most states have either a Republican or Democratic majority in their delegation, so that independent influence might be minimal. Using the assumptions we have been making for this exercise, Republicans would control anywhere from 23 to 26 states, Democrats 21, and Alliance or independents controlling between 3 and 6.

MADDOW: Wow. Fascinating. So while all those new independent seats in Congress as a result of this Alliance wave we are seeing will wield a great deal of power in the

House going forward, the way the rules are written they would not likely be in a position to get McFadden across the finish line.

KORNACKI: Correct, Rachel. They would not on their own be able to get McFadden elected. They would need to work some magic by aligning with one of the two parties. But if Republicans end up controlling 26 states, they would have a majority and would presumably elect Margel.

But you make a good point about the power they'll wield in the new Congress. It appears that their support will be necessary to get any bill passed from now on, and they'll likely retain the Speaker of the House. But the way our presidential elections are set up, they might not have much sway with this election if this thing gets thrown into the House.

MADDOW: Wow. Just wow.

KORNACKI: Let me caution you that the early voting returns can be very deceiving. I offer these what-if scenarios only to illustrate that, despite McFadden leading by a large margin in both the popular vote and the electoral college, there are realistic scenarios where any of these three candidates could still wind up as president if this goes to the House.

MADDOW: We are in for a wild ride indeed.

KORNACKI: I'll be right here to break it all down.

MADDOW: You are the best in the business, my friend. We will be checking back with you again soon. America is hanging on your every word.

Chapter Seventy

Tom Joad
November 6, 2024
3:05 a.m. EST

"Give me some good news, Murph."

"You've got real a shot at this, Boss. You crushed them in the popular vote—getting more votes than the two of them combined. No one anticipated that."

Her tone and demeanor, however, seemed to scream moral victory.

"What's the bad news?"

"The bad news is that the House races seem to be breaking in a way that Republicans will control 26 state delegations, so if we fall short of 270, they can combine to elect Margel."

"It's not entirely clear they would all do that, however," added Maggie. "Some are just as frustrated with Margel and the direction his wing of the party as anyone."

"But either way," I replied, "that's not something we'd be confident rolling the dice on."

"Right," responded Murph. "We want to win this thing with 270. At this point that's maybe only a 50-50 proposition at best."

"So you're saying we've got a chance."

Murph didn't laugh. Denyse did though. I married the right woman—for that and many other reasons.

"What's the latest on Georgia?" asked Maggie.

"Still too close to call," said Murph. "But we are improving with each new traunch of votes that comes in. Not sure we can close the gap with Margel though. But that won't be called at least until the morning, if not later."

"I think you should say something now, Danny Mac," said Tina. "You can't claim victory but holy cow what a night we've had. The Alliance now has 100 seats in the house? No one can call your movement a fluke anymore.

The two parties are scared shitless."

"Alright," I said. "Maggie, are you up for this?"

"I'm with you, chief." She smiled.

"Do you want to say anything?"

"No thank you. I've got Georgie on my mind on my mind right now. My heart's twisting and turning on with every new development there. Besides, Tina's right. This moment is yours. Even without 270 you can take a victory lap for your cause."

"Alright, let's do it."

"We'll alert the networks," said Murph.

All the staff left my room, leaving just me, Denyse, Maggie and Gil.

Do you know what you're gonna say?" asked Denyse.

"As much as I want to wing it, I can't help but think this could be perhaps my final political speech. Unless one of these last undecided states breaks our way. I need to do justice to our cause with this, whatever I say. Something inspiring to lead people to pick up the torch from here and move us beyond all this dysfunction. In light of all that, this needs to be something memorable."

"I've got an idea," said Gil.

***

Twenty minutes later the service elevator opened on the second floor. We stepped out and I could already hear Sinatra's "The Best is Yet to Come" blaring from the Regency Ballroom. It energized me as it always does. Such a great anthem for our campaign. I was hoping it would also prove prescient for our election night.

My cell phone buzzed as we were being escorted through kitchen to get to the ballroom. I looked down at the phone and then laughed.

"Who was that?" inquired Denyse.

"Just Kelly." I said. "She wants to know what time we'll be getting to Hannegan's."

"She's your daughter alright."

"Let me remind you that you're the one who just came from there tonight, not me."

Moments later I stepped up to the microphone to address the jam-packed room full of supporters, staff, volunteers and media. Denyse, Maggie and Gil were at my side. Just before I started to speak, I recognized Satch and Christie in the back of the room. They are so unassuming. I would have been honored to have them with us up in the suite tonight. Seeing him there in person however, provided me a burst of adrenaline—that little extra I needed to try to try to hit a really high mark with this address.

> We've always told you the truth in this campaign and I will tonight. We're not sure if this is going to break our way tonight.
>
> *Crowd groans.*
>
> Although it just might.
>
> *Cheers.*
>
> But either way we won't know for many, many hours. And I had to come out here and thank you.
>
> If it doesn't go our way, I'm here to say tonight that that's not the end of the world. Look what we started. We've taken on an entire political and media industrial complex that profits from and indeed exists because of our polarization. That is a massive undertaking. But look what we've done tonight. We're crushing the two parties in the popular vote.
>
> *Cheers.*
>
> And when the dust settles in the coming days we'll have over 100 House seats and possibly 10 senators. And 8 governors. And today more than 55% of the country now identify as independents.
>
> We're not only moving the dial we are ramrodding it for-

ward at warp speed. Whether we get the White House tonight or not, we are now a force to be reckoned with. A force built solely around the simple notion that we are better than this. Indeed we are. My god we are. And we are starting to show it.

Cheers.

That work doesn't stop if I'm not the one out front giving the speeches. This is it for me. If you see me again behind a microphone it'll be because I'm president and this thing broke our way.

But either way this is my last campaign speech.

Groans.

Oh, c'mon. I've gotta let others take the wheel.

Some boos.

But even if this is the end of the road for me tonight, in a very real way you'll still be seeing me. You'll see me in so many different pressure points along the fault lines of our great political divide. I'll be there. And so will all of you.

Mild applause.

We'll be there whenever a first time Congressman is getting squeezed by a party boss but stands firm to vote his or her conscience.

Applause.

Whenever anyone with a media platform chooses truth and enlightenment to fight forces pushing misinformation and division for profit, I'll be there too. And so will all of you.

Applause.

Whenever politicians, facing challenging political issues, choose to cross the aisle in zealous pursuit of genuine problem solving, rather than resort merely to political advantage and division, we'll be right there at their side.

Applause.

Whenever an elected official picks up a phone to talk directly to a political opponent about a difference rather than fire off a nasty, hateful twitter bomb, we'll be there too.

Applause.

Whenever legislators summon the courage to ignore the PACs, the lobbyists and special interests of the world, look real close and you'll see all of us.

Applause.

Whenever public servants insist on doing what is right in the face of powerful partisan forces bullying them to do otherwise.

Applause.

And whenever officeholders face a primary fight from within their own party funded out of spite, for having the audacity to vote according to their conscious instead of choosing unyielding fealty to the almighty party line, look deep in their eyes and you'll see all of us.

> *Applause.*
>
> No sir. If this thing does indeed end for us tonight, it's by no means the end of the line for all of us, for this cause and for the impact we will have, which isn't going to stop until every American realizes that we are indeed so much better than this, and starts embracing that notion. Just imagine what America will be on that day. What potential. All the very best of us, working together. Limitless potential. The living embodiment of Jefferson's idealistic vision of an Empire for Liberty in the world. We owe that to the world.
>
> *Raucous applause.*
>
> Thank you so much for being at our side in this campaign, and in this cause. We'll see what happens tonight. But be proud either way. What a monumental impact you have had. Good night and God bless America.

I felt that was as good a stopping point as any. The four of us stood there soaking up the applause for several minutes.

I noticed Shane, his father and many of those I rode with in the PanCAN Monterey to Santa Cruz bike ride fundraiser there all dressed in their purple. Wow. How very touching.

I glanced off stage. Murph was smiling and Tina gave me a big thumbs up.

Then Gil leaned over to me and said, "Tom Joad himself couldn't have delivered that any better. Or Steinbeck."

"Thank for the suggestion," I replied.

I smiled. Whatever was to happen next, I was remarkably at peace with it all.

Chapter Seventy-One

An Irish Goodbye
Ten Weeks Later, Inauguration Night
January 20, 2025
The Saloon

The saloon exuded even more energy than usual as I entered. Energy fueled by sheer anticipation. No night in this place ever exceeded January 20 every fourth year, when a new presidency begins and often a fresh face joins our exclusive, secret club. We hadn't seen much of Maggie in these past several months. The tradition in this place is that the current president never spoils the surprise, allowing the new one to just stroll in to great fanfare and celebration. No group appreciates and celebrates the peaceful transition of power more than these folks. In this case we weren't even sure if President Bates was in fact running. She had listened to all of our advice but in return shared so little.

"What do you know?" I asked Mary Ann as I took a seat at the grand bar. It appeared that about half the presidents were in the saloon.

"I'm so nervous I can't stand it," she replied.

"Me too," I said. "I've really come to respect Maggie. I want nothing but the best for her. And I think she's just great in that role."

"I always worry about the next one coming through that door. Although we've now had four in a row that I really, really like."

Moments later she added, "And I want someone who likes dogs."

Matty came over to join us. "How are you betting here tonight, Danny Mac?"

"I don't think I would touch this bet," I answered. "And like M.A. suggested a moment ago, I'm fearful of some of the options."

Ford was seated next to me and overheard our discussion. "I hope it's not a bitter rival of President Bates. That can create further complications in this room."

"This group in this saloon seems to have a remarkable ability to move beyond that stuff," I said. "That's not the case in Washington DC."

"No need to make up your mind on them right away," added Carter. "Sometimes it helps to let them grow on you."

"Whoever it is," added Obama, "I hope it's someone who's ready to be president—not just someone who wants to be president."

"What makes somebody ready, in your mind?" I asked Obama.

"My instinct is that the people who are ready are folks who go into it understanding the gravity of their work, and are able to combine vision and judgment. Some people respond and some don't."

I saw that Washington had been in a serious conversation with George W. Bush. When they were finished Otter approached me.

"Hey Rook, Big Daddy wants to make sure there's no awkwardness like last time when we are doing toasts tonight to the new guy, or lady. If we need you to step up and offer a few witticisms, can I count on you."

"You got it," I responded.

"But really," I added, "now that we've had another president follow me and will likely have yet another one tonight, when do I shed the "Rookie" nickname."

"These things have a life of their own, my friend. You have the nickname until you don't."

"OK," I answered. Who could possibly argue with that logic?

As more presidents made their way in, a very versatile band started warming up. I think they needed to be prepared to play almost anything, depending on who walked in that door.

I pulled Mary Ann aside. "If we see Maggie come in using the former presidents' entrance, then we know she didn't get re-elected. Do I have that right?"

"Correct," she answered.

I thought some more. "Let me ask you this. Since Grover Cleveland's two presidential terms were not consecutive, does that mean there were two Clevelands in the saloon when he came up the second time as president?"

"Great question. No. Washington and Cleveland decided it was best for the former president to stay away those four years, so only the current one was actually here in the saloon at night during that time."

"Fascinating," I said. "This place kills me."

"I know, right?"

***

A half an hour later I saw Maggie enter the Saloon through the doors used by myself and the other presidential spirits. *OK*, I thought to myself, *this is Maggie the spirit now*. We hadn't seen her in several months, but obviously this meant that the real Maggie was no longer president. Her entrance from that door caused a bit of a hush to come over the room. She was immediately embraced by Washington, Jefferson, Kennedy, Reagan, and a few of the others.

As Mary Ann joined them I saw her wiping a tear from her eye. President after president lined up to express their sympathies. Maggie's cheerfulness, however, disabused us of any notion that comfort was necessary. She was clearly upbeat.

As the room continued to fill up, I made my way over to that receiving line and took my place at the end. Maggie appeared to be displaying all the charm and good nature we had come to expect of her. My mind was awash in hypotheticals pertaining to who might be walking in that venerable old entrance from third floor of the White House.

The band played indistinct jazz as people continued to mingle. But there seemed to be a great deal more anticipation of the arrival of our newest club member than I recall from four years ago.

As I finally made it to the front of the line, Haskell arrived to take drink orders.

"Can I get you two anything?"

"Sure, said Maggie, "a French martini please."

I was caught flatfooted on the drink order because I had been trying to think of the perfect sentiments to express to Maggie in this moment.

As I stalled for a second, Haskell tried to fill the void.

"I think the two of you have to go down as two of the greatest one-term presidents this country has ever seen," said Haskell.

I laughed. That may have been the first outright miss of any Haskell complement I had ever witnessed in this saloon. But after so may hundreds that hit the mark, I figured he was entitled to that.

"I think you are mistaken, sir," replied Maggie. "I surely am, but I don't think the same could be said of Danny here."

I thought that a very odd statement from her, but I chose not to dwell on it.

At that moment Bush, standing next to the White House third floor entrance, motioned to Haskell behind the bar, who let out a piercing whistle. The band stopped, and a hush came upon the entire room as all eyes turned toward that entrance.

I kept looking over at Bates who remained poker faced.

The door cracked and began to open slowly.

I stole another glance over at Maggie.

Finally, breaking character, she shot me a smile and a big thumbs up. I had no earthly idea what that meant.

Otter let out a shriek that could have doubled as a proper hog call back home in Crawford as a big fluffy collie barreled through the door.

I could not believe my eyes as our newest president followed sporting a huge Cheshire cat smile.

I was as overcome as I was the first time I set foot in this bar.

I think then I completely blacked out. Moments later, when I had regained my wits about me, I saw that our guy Haskell was still in front of me, patiently awaiting my drink order. Man, he's good at what he does.

"Jameson, I said, before adding, "Better make it a double."

Then, looking up at our new very familiar-faced president, I added, "Why don't you make that two of those."

I looked around and found Mary Ann. She was literally screaming with delight. She just kept looking up at the figure in the door, then back at me, and then up again at him. I know her so well. She was frozen there—so conflicted, not knowing which of us to run and hug. God love her. But I saw tears running down her face. It warmed my heart like nothing else. I pointed to the door, and mouthed to her, "Go see him." She patted her heart in response.

I looked back at Maggie. She clearly relished seeing the expression on my face. "Wait 'til you hear the rest, Danny," Maggie said. "It gets even crazier from here."

"Crazier than this? That can't possibly be true."

Seconds later, as I was still in a daze, utterly dumbfounded, I asked, "How the hell did this happen? I had no idea this was even a possibility."

"This is really only half the story," she responded. "If nothing else, this is gonna be a really fun four years."

The room had exploded in a long applause that wasn't dying down anytime soon. That warmed my heart too. Teddy Roosevelt sprinted up to embrace our new president. I wish I had a video of that moment. But what made me even more proud, perhaps, was seeing all the patrons instinctively head for the bar to get themselves drink—and so, by the way, did the staff.

On cue a group of new bartenders and waitresses suddenly emerged. Reinforcements. It was all hands on deck tonight. The band played "Hello Danny" to the tune of "Hello Dolly."

Well Hello, Danny. It's so nice to have you back where you belong . . .

Then, demonstrating that versatility, they went right into "Let's Get It Started" by the Back Eyed Peas—somehow a surprisingly smooth transition.

This was gonna be a party.

***

In spite of all that I knew what I had to do. I'm all about our traditions, and I had my marching orders. Cleveland had created the precedent, and no one was going to accuse me of bucking a sacred American tradition. I needed to do the right thing.

I finished my Jameson first, of course, and decided to just slip away unnoticed. I didn't want to steal a moment's attention from the new president. Washington saw me starting to exit, and extended his hand.

"Good man," he said. "Thank you for honoring the tradition. It's not goodbye forever."

I walked past the bar on my way out and Kennedy spotted me.

"An Irish Goodbye, McFadden?"

"That's such a misnomer," I replied. "No Irishman I've ever known ever left a party before last call. In my mind, a real Irish goodbye is being kicked out an hour after closing time."

"I can't argue that point," he replied with a smile.

"Farewell," he added. "Four years goes by in the blink of an eye in this country. But another four years of you at the helm seems just what the doctor ordered for this nation."

"And this saloon," he added.

"I appreciate that very much," I answered. "God willing."

Just as I neared the exit I heard a familiar voice.

"Hey Rook."

I turned to see Otter hustling to catch me in time.

"I thought of a new nickname for this president," he said.

"Oh ya?" I answered.

"Yes, no more Rook. That's officially retired."

"Good. Lay it on me," I said.

He smiled broadly, clearly relishing the moment. And evidently quite proud of himself.

I'm ready," I repeated.

"Lazarus."

I thought for a second and then laughed out loud. "Perfect. I love it."

"Thanks for all you do, here, Otter," I added. "I mean that. You really hold it all together in this place for everybody."

"Don't mention it, Laz," he replied, with a huge smile on his face.

That dude is priceless.

Before I walked out that door, I took one last look back. What a wonderful scene this was in front of me. And maybe, just maybe, this nation was actually beginning to right itself. And not a moment too soon. That very real possibility made walking away and checking out for the next four years so much more palatable.

God I was proud of this country.

And petrified for our new president.

Chapter Seventy-Two

Happy Parts

Four Months Later – May 12, 2025

Evidently White House weddings take place less frequently than U.S. wars. But what a spectacular place to get hitched. Following an elegant ceremony in the Rose Garden, where Tricia Nixon and David Eisenhower had once wed, we began making our way inside the White House for the cocktail reception in the East Room, to be followed by a sit down dinner in the State Dining Room.

Denyse and I walked into the East Room with Satch and Christie. By order of the bride there was no receiving line. The newlyweds preferred to make their rounds during the dinner.

I was summarizing for Christie a bit of the history of White House weddings when I overheard Satch talking to Denyse. I strained my ears to try to pick up every word.

"How is our guy doing with accepting Michael into the family? Has he come around?" asked Satch.

"After a rough start I think he's gettin there," she replied.

"I'm proud of him. Both of them. I know this was a challenge for each of them."

"But really, Satch, do you think God has ever created the young man who would be good enough for Kelly in the eyes of Danny and the two boys?"

"Your boys are priceless, ma'am. All three of them."

"Michael *is darling*," added Denyse, "and Kelly is happy. He is perfect for her. I think they are all happy for her even if they might not show it as much as I'd like."

As we entered the East Room I sensed the energy immediately. At least twenty of Kelly's friends from Santa Clara had made it in for this, many with dates, and many of Jack and Brett's close friends were here too. It was so nice to see all that joyful youth bouncing about in a room usually filled with such stodgy old characters.

I heard the band and immediately felt the lead singer sounded familiar.

"Who booked the band?" I asked Denyse.

"Tina offered to take care of it all. I figured since she was on the staff that did a State Dinner for the Queen, that would be good enough for Kelly and Michael's wedding."

I looked over at the band. I thought I recognized that base player too.

"Satch lent a hand too. That whole hospitality staff reported up through him for a few decades."

"Interesting."

"Hey are you planning to say anything at the reception?" asked Denyse.

"I've gone back and forth on it," I replied. "I am mortified at the thought of being viewed as trying to steal her thunder."

"Danny, you're the father of the bride."

"I know, but I'm deathly afraid of coming off as attempting to grab the spotlight."

"You have a bigger spotlight on you every time you walk out that door. If the focus of your remarks is on her, it only adds to her spotlight."

"Your right. I'm just fearful people say of me what they did about Teddy Roosevelt."

"What was that?"

"How he needed to be the bride at every wedding and the corpse at every funeral."

"Ha! That's hilarious. There's an element of that with all guys like you."

"That settles it. I can't do it."

"No, no – I'm kidding. People will want to hear it. More importantly, Kelly will want to hear it. So will I. You will only add to a cherished moment in the most loving and appropriate way."

Forty-five minutes later as we were taking our seats in the State Dining Room, Denyse grabbed my arm.

"Danny, look at Tina," she said.

I looked over and saw Tina taking her assigned seat at the table with some of my former White House staff.

"Is her date the gentlemen seated to the left of her, or the lady to her right?" Denyse asked.

"I have no idea," I said. "I only know she is here with a date."

"Because if it's that guy to the left of her, all I can say is good for her. You go girl."

Now that statement put me in a bit of a pickle. I saw that I could say the very same thing back to her about the sharp looking young lady to Tina's right, but not only am I conditioned not to say such things about employees and their dates—as someone who values my job—but, perhaps more importantly, I knew that if I so much as uttered the very same sentiment about the young lady next to Tina—or any other lady for that matter other than Denyse—I would be living a life of celibacy for at least the next few weeks. So I kept quiet. I'm not stupid. I know how this works. I learned as president there are certain things you just can't change. And you shouldn't even try.

As we were finishing up our dinner, Kelly came over and looked at Denyse.

"Is he going to say anything?" she mouthed.

"Yes," Denyse responded.

Denyse then turned to me. "Danny, it's time."

I stood up at the table as many people began tapping their spoons against their glasses.

"And make sure you say something nice about Michael," Denyse added.

"You have such little faith in me," I responded.

The room got quiet fairly quickly.

"Thank you all for coming," I said. "We're delighted you could all be here with us for this wonderful moment. We are beyond thrilled to be adding Michael to the family. He's a homerun."

Satch, seated to my right, looked up at me and whispered. "And I'm pretty sure he knows what that means now."

I laughed, but resisted the urge to repeat that line. Another wise move.

I continued. "Believe it or not, Thomas Jefferson utilized a part of this very room in the White House as his office. He had his desk in that corner over there." I pointed to the space used by Jefferson. "Jefferson, of course will forever be known for penning those immortal words that all men are created equal."

I paused, then added, "He didn't mention women, however."

Some laughter.

"I have some advice for young Michael here. Take it from this president," I pointed to myself, "rather than that one," I pointed to Jefferson's corner. "This strong young woman you have married today is absolutely an equal, and I would suggest it's in your best interests to treat her as such."

Laughter and clapping.

"I have to add one more thing for these two today if I might," I added.

"When Kelly was a toddler, back even before she could utter a complete sentence, she just adored the movie *Beauty and the Beast,* and wanted to watch it over and over. She was the cutest toddler ever, by the way. She'd ask for it by just saying to me 'Belle, Belle'—the name of the beautiful heroine. And she'd get so excited as I'd set it up for her. Many times I'd watch the whole thing right alongside her holding her hand in mine. But sometimes I'd walk away for a few minutes to do something in another part of the house or take a phone call. Now that movie has many wonderful moments featuring pretty dresses, dancing, and pure joy. But like so many Disney flicks, it also has many really frightening segments too—like when the Beast is in the woods terrorizing people.

"If I happened to be in another part of the house when one of those scary moments came on the screen, complete with frightening music intended to scare the bejesus out of kids, Kelly would simply start calling out, as loudly as her cute little panicky voice could muster, 'Happy parts, happy parts, happy parts.' Eventually I'd hear her and come sprinting in to the room to the rescue. I'd look at her and see her hands pressed hard against her cute little face to hide two eyes closed as tightly as a human's can possibly be. As quickly as I could, I'd grab the remote and fast forward to the happy parts. Then I would yell 'happy parts,' and Kelly would cautiously remove her hands and slowly let her eyes open back up. Her look of terror would immediately dissolve into a big smile when she saw Belle in her beautiful yellow dress. We would both applaud and cheer loudly as all was right again with the world—for Belle and for Kelly. And for me."

I paused and looked over at Kelly and Michael. I laid my hand on Denyse's shoulder and she instinctively grasped it in hers.

"I know both of you realize how incredibly fortunate and blessed each of you have been in your lives. And there is so much joy awaiting you in the future. More than you can even imagine.

"But inevitably there will be bumps in the road, and tough challenges, and moments that will really test you. In those most difficult times, remember you are not alone in this life. You have people who love and care for you. Lean not only on each other, but on all those in this room who adore you so very much. Your mom and I will forever be there for you too, sweetheart, when you most need it.

"What I'm getting at, of course, is that all of us here—everyone in this room, and so many more—will be there for you always in times of need to help you fast forward to the happy parts. And just like those precious moments between us back when you were a toddler on that couch, do not be shy about seeking our help when you most need it. With all the support of this veritable army of people behind you, you'll find that the happy parts are always well within your reach."

People spontaneously started applauding.

"Let's here it for the happy parts. And by the way, you have provided so many of those to your mom and I and everyone in this room your whole life. You and Michael enrich all of our lives immeasurably.

"I know I speak for everyone in this room today when I say, here's to a lifetime full of happy parts, Kelly and Michael. Cheers!

"And one last thing. Belle has nothing on you, Kelly."

As glasses clinked together at every table, I looked over at Denyse. She was sobbing.

Chapter Seventy-Three

A Heavy Pour
May 12, 2025

Well after the other toasts, and the first dances, as people were moving about and mingling, Maggie came over to our table with her glass of Pinot and sat next to me in Denyse's empty chair. We watched as Denyse danced with Brett and then Jack. I was so proud of those boys for even thinking to dance with their mom with all of Kelly's beautiful friends so eager to dance.

"Nice toast, Danny. Happy parts. I like that. Very touching."

"Thank you. I'm rather surprised I made it through that."

"So when you think about it, that Saloon of yours really functions as a provider of "happy parts" for presidents, doesn't it?"

"My saloon?" I laughed. "I think many others could lay claim to ownership well ahead of me. Beginning with Otter. But yes—you could certainly say it performs that function well. Although you can get a lot of sage advice there too."

"By the way," I added, "I've been meaning to ask you, Maggie. Did the presidents in the Saloon advise you to approach me with the offer you did at Camp David?"

"No—I came up with that myself."

"Why on earth would you do that?"

"Don't get me wrong—they give great advice, but sometimes you've got to trust your own intuition no matter whose advice it goes against. I knew I couldn't have won without you at the top of the ticket. Not this time around, at least. And I really think Margel and Clayton would have been a disaster for the country. I had a feeling I could talk you into it. And besides, this VP thing is not such a bad gig. And I go down as not only the first female President but the first female VP as well. Not bad."

"Well then maybe I'll have to make you the first female Chief Justice too."

"I don't know," she responded. "Our Beltway politics might be child's play compared to what's going on with the Court."

We looked over and saw Gil dancing with Kelly.

"I think Gil knows Kelly and her friends a heck of a lot more than you realize, Danny."

"Yes, I get the feeling she and her pals are a little more familiar with Hannegan's than even I knew."

"You think?" She smiled. "The apple doesn't fall far."

"Ha! So true. Hopefully she got a few good qualities from me as well."

"And just so you know," she added, "Gil sees Michael a lot too, and he really likes him."

"That's good to know. I do too."

"By the way," I added, "since we're being so honest with each other about all these sensitive subjects, I think I should caution you that your favorite bartender-fisherman-novelist also happens to be quite woke. I'm guessing you've figured that out by now."

"I knew that from the start. Steinbeck is not exactly Rush Limbaugh, you know."

"I certainly don't mind," I added, "but I wasn't sure how you felt."

"Honey, that doesn't bother me a bit. I'm not asking him to be my running mate. Or my senior policy advisor. I'm looking for other things out of him." She smiled.

I laughed. "You deserve it all, Maggie. I'm so happy for you."

"Both of you gentlemen have provided me precisely what I need."

"We are happy to be of service to you. There can be no possible higher calling."

It was great to see her so happy. She did deserve it.

"And let me add this as well," she said." I know now why the two of you are such friends. In the words of Thoreau, you both 'live deep and suck all the marrow out of life.'"

"In my case I'm afraid all too often it sucks right back."

She laughed. "That's what you have Satch for. And that adorable family of yours. Gil is my Satch."

Just then Brett lifted Denyse's hand up high and she gracefully spun around underneath.

"Your girl knows her way around a dance floor," said Maggie. "But that boy's got some game, too."

"Some lessons he is learning from sources other than his father," I replied. "And that's a good thing."

The song began to wind down, and Maggie, anticipating that Denyse would be coming back, stood up.

"Hey one more thing before you go," I said. "Thanks for trusting your intuition."

"Don't mention it. We women are known for that."

***

As the hour drew late, and the party began to wane just a little, Kelly approached Denyse and me at our table.

"Dad, you really need to thank Tina. The service staff has been unbelievable."

"That's great to hear. I will make sure I do that."

"And they're so caring," added Denyse. "One of the young men went on and on to me about how I am a model mother for all of America to emulate and I've been such a wonderful first lady."

"And one of the waitresses burst into tears upon meeting me and mom," said Kelly.

OK, those comments made me really, really, suspicious. And scared me a little bit, too.

"Tina and Satch arranged the service staff?" I asked.

"Yes. They insisted," said Denyse.

"I have a feeling I know where they got them."

"Who was the one that cried upon seeing you?" I asked.

"Let me see," said Kelly. She scanned the room and then pointed to one talking with Maggie and Gil by the windows.

I looked closer. It was Mary Ann.

"I can't imagine why someone would be that emotional upon meeting us," said Denyse.

"My guess is that it's just because we're all in the news so much and the whole country kind feels as if they know us," I answered.

I quickly looked around the room. "Let me guess," I said, pointing to one of the male servers. "That's the one that complimented you, Denyse, on being such a great mom and First Lady."

"Yes, that's him."

It was Haskell.

"I think I know what's going on here." I said. "I'm gonna go find Tina and Satch."

"What for?" asked Denyse.

"Oh, just to give them a proper thank you," I said.

"I'll come with you."

A full bar had been set up in the Blue Room, which is off the hallway between the East Room and the State Dining Room. In this room the party was definitely still going strong. These were the "closers." I saw Satch holding court as he does, with Christie by his side, and Tina with a group nearby. A closer look revealed Matty, Slick and Ginger working away behind the bar, along with another older gentleman with his back to us. I approached Tina, shaking my head, as Denyse stopped to chat with Christie.

Tina greeted me with a big smile on her face. "Such beautiful ceremony, Danny Mac."

"It was," I answered. "And such stellar service, too. Where on earth did you find some of these characters?"

She laughed. "You noticed that, did you? And how about that band?"

"Of course. I knew I had seen them before."

"By the way, Danny Mac, I've dying to ask you how are you enjoying your time back in the saloon?"

"Let me tell you, it is so great to be back amidst all those characters. I wish the whole country could feed off that camaraderie as I do. But this time around I really don't plan to be up there all that much."

She shrieked.

"No, I'm serious."

I could see I wasn't going to get her to stop laughing.

"No really," I said. "Last time I desperately needed it as an escape," I said. "I was a bit like a deer in headlights in this job. This time around we've got some momentum, and some genuine support. I see a real opportunity to finally make some progress as a country. I really don't think I'll get up there very much."

"Yeah . . . right," she responded, still laughing. "I'll believe that when I see it."

I'm not quite sure how or when it was she got to know me so well . . .

As Denyse joined us, we could hear Matty yell over to the older bartender. "Hey Old Kinderhook, we need a couple more dry martinis here."

"Coming right up, Big Time," the older man responded. I looked at him more closely and did a doubletake. It was Martin Van Buren. Old Kinderhook himself. Born and raised in a saloon. I wanted to laugh out loud but I didn't dare.

Tina saw my reaction. She leaned over to me and whispered, "He works so hard behind the bar in the saloon so many nights we thought we'd give him a bit of a treat and bring him down here."

Denyse looked at both of us. "Old Kinderhook? Is that what he called the older bartender? Isn't Kinderhook that little town in New York where one of the presidents lived? You dragged us all there that summer when we brought the kids to Cooperstown."

"I'm not sure," I answered, as Tina looked away to shield her laughter. I tried hard to keep a straight face.

"Yes, it is as a matter of fact," she said. "We went to one of the president's homes there. Which one was that? Filmore? Buchannan?" It was the one you said you idolized because he was raised in a saloon."

"It's sounding vaguely familiar but I can't be sure."

Denyse mildly exploded. "You're lying to me, McFadden!"

Just then Matty yelled out to me, "Hey, Laz, can I get you anything to drink?"

I happily diverted all my attention to him.

"See if the old guy can get me a hot ale flip," I yelled back.

"Wait, what did he call you?" asked Denyse.

"I'll explain all this later tonight."

"I'm not sure I really want to know, to be honest."

I looked over at Tina, who was now laughing hysterically, but still trying to do so surreptitiously. I'm glad somebody was getting a kick out of this.

Denyse shook her head. "I will just choose to focus on the things I love most about you, Danny, and ignore some of this other stuff." There it is again—don't ask, don't tell.

"That's actually a bit like how I feel about Jefferson," I responded. "And Kennedy really. Not to mention Washington, Madison, Jackson,

Monroe . . ."

My old college history teacher Arnold Harris and his wife Carol approached. The professor leaned in close and said to me, barely above a whisper, "I've been watching the old gentleman back there behind the bar. The one with the crazy looking hair. His appearance, the way he's dressed, the manner in which he speaks— if I didn't know better I would swear he is trying to imitate Martin Van Buren. But in this case, sir, I do in fact know better. And I'm willing to believe that this gentleman is in fact President Van Buren himself. So having said that, Carol and I are retiring for the evening. Thank you for the invitation and a wonderful time, but I am determined never again to be stuck here in this old mansion with the ghost of one of our former presidents. Fool me once, shame on you. Fool me twice . . . Enjoy the rest of the evening, sir."

I laughed out loud.

"I will invoke my fifth amendment right here," I responded, "which I'm only able to do thanks to my good friend James Madison."

"Oh dear. Is he around here too?" responded the professor. "We really have to be on our way, sir."

With that, he and Carol turned and walked briskly away. Now that was amusing. To me at least.

"Do you mind if we go sit down over there?" Denyse asked, pointing to the couches near the windows. "My feet are killing me."

Moments later Satch and Christie joined us, followed closely by Maggie and Gil.

"Well, there's half your bucket list checked off today, sir." said Satch.

"You have a bucket list, Danny?" Denyse asked. She seemed half perturbed, half amused that Satch knew and she didn't.

"Just a couple of life goals."

"Oh really? I'd love to hear them."

"I think I told Satch a while back my two remaining goals were staying healthy and alive long enough to be able to walk Kelly down the aisle, and seeing Normandy."

"You could have had them just get married at Normandy," said Gil. "They could have simplified it for you."

"Oh believe me Gil, I'm not convinced he didn't suggest that to her," added Maggie.

"If seeing Normandy means that much Danny, well let's go," said Denyse, perking up. I loved that about her. Always up for anything.

"In this role now I think I really need to wait for an anniversary. But let me tell you, Satch, I had one more item on that list I was really too afraid to even mention out loud on our hike that day—both because it was so audacious as to be borderline arrogant to even suggest, and because the mere mention of it could jinx it."

I had their attention.

"You have to tell us now, sir." said Satch.

"I told John McCain the last time I saw him that I would do something bold to bridge the debilitating political divide in this country. Actually, I more than told him—he made me promise, so I did. I couldn't say no to that guy. Not at that time in his life and not at that place. We were at his favorite haunt—The Up The Creek Bistro in Cornville, Arizona.

"For whatever reason, Satch, I didn't have what it took to say that out loud to you that day on our hike."

"Well sir," said Satch, "in that case I would say very respectfully that I was mistaken a moment ago. You don't have half of your bucket list checked off, you have two-thirds of it.

I smiled.

He continued. "The first McFadden presidency could always be considered by some to be a fluke—the chance result of two candidates whose campaigns were imploding. And you were simply there in the right place at the right time.

"This one however," he paused searching for the right words, "this one had to be real. For this to happen, your Alliance must have taken root, and started making meaningful inroads in permeating our political divide. People at each end of the political spectrum had to lay down their arms and extend their hands to the other side. You offered our country a much better path forward and they took it. They not only elected you but they also elected more than 100 others who were inspired by you. I'm not saying your work here is done—far from it. But your idea and philosophy has taken root and inspired people and changed our culture, our politics, and our potential as a country. We have turned a page. There's hope again in America. And mutual respect. And justifiable pride.

"I knew John McCain," he continued. "Loved him as much as you did, maybe more. John McCain would be over the moon about these developments. I'm sure he is."

Denyse jumped up on her sore feet and leapt over to give Satch a hug. Yes, she had consumed a few glasses today but the wine was not driving this spontaneous act.

The whole wedding party came bouncing in. Most went to the bar, but Kelly came over to say hi.

She looked at Denyse. "Did Dad tell you what he said to me as he was walking me down the aisle?"

"No," replied Denyse. "But now I need to know."

"He said 'Your Mom and I really love Michael."

"Oh, that's so sweet of him."

"But then immediately after that he said, 'Now remind me, which one of those guys up there is Michael?'"

Denyse punched my shoulder. Hard. "Danny!"

I laughed. So did Kelly.

"It looked like she was going to cry, and I just wanted to put a smile on her face. And mine, by the way."

Mary Ann came over to take our drink order. "Another round, Mr. President?"

I laughed. She never called me that.

Looking right at me, she asked, "Is it true you tried to order a hot ale flip?"

"Yes, I did."

"I think there's only one place in America you can still get those, and it's not here. At least not on this floor."

Satch laughed out loud at that.

"I was just kidding with that order," I said.

"Can I get Old Kinderhook to make you something else? He's dying to serve you."

"Heck, I've barely had anything to drink all day. Just have him pour me a Jameson."

"A double?"

"I don't know about a double." I smiled as Denyse looked over at me.

"Let's just say a heavy pour. How about that?"

"A heavy pour?" Denyse laughed out loud. "Is that what you're calling it now?"

A few minutes later I had my drink.

As the night wound down I surveyed the scene in front of me. The wedding party soaking up every last moment of this lovely celebration, seemingly without a care in the world—a feeling that can only really come with youth. Kelly and Michael gleefully embarking on the journey of life together. My two boys apparently making some inroads with a few of Kelly's friends. That saloon staff—and Old Kinderhook—where do I even begin with them? Can't imagine any of them without smiling. They are each so perfect at what they do. And then there was my girl Tina—love her—enjoying herself nearby. Whether she was with that strapping dude at her side to her left, or the stunning young lady in the skin tight dress on her right, she seemed really happy. More so than I ever saw her in the Saloon. Heck, perhaps they're both with her—I would never even for a moment underestimate that woman. And Maggie and Gil, certainly the most unlikely couple in America, but the living embodiment of how vastly disparate people can come together with magical results. And as for Satch and Christie—sometimes life has a way of placing the answers we've been searching for so desperately right in our path before us. And that's kind of what happened with me, I think, and the country.

I reflected on the great day we'd just had, on the past eight years, and on what did appear to be a new direction for America—one far away from that dysfunctional, self-destructive, path we've been stuck on lately. Independents in America—a plurality now that outnumbers both parties—finally have a real political voice, and are using it to unify us and rein in our extremes. We are indeed finally proving to ourselves that we are better than this. I knew it all along.

Denyse, studying my face, seemed to sense that I was taking stock of it all.

"What are you thinking, Danny?"

"How unbelievably blessed we are. But at the same time how very easily it all could have gone in such different direction if we hadn't acted boldly."

"Who? You and me? The country?"

"Yes and yes. All of it." I answered.

Mary Ann brought me another 'heavy pour.'

"You have never been more correct," Denyse said, grasping my hand in hers. She looked deep into my eyes. "Life has certainly served up a heavy pour, McFadden. Both to you and to this country of yours."

I laughed. But she was absolutely right. She always is.

At that moment a warm and wonderfully serene sensation came over me about the whole thing. For the very first time I was remarkably at peace with it all, and deep in my heart I had the distinct and unmistakable feeling that we were in fact finally moving beyond all the hate and divisiveness, and that all would once again be right with this grand experiment we call our Republic. What a wonderful feeling.

Or perhaps that was just the Jameson . . .

SOURCES AND NOTES

While this is a work of fiction, much of the dialogue is taken from actual words of the presidents that appeared in their speeches, letters, memoirs, interviews or other papers, and has been adapted to fit the context of the novel. References are provided in such instances to allow for examination of the original quote and context. In addition, dozens of other citations are provided to many other historical references that were relied upon to write this novel that may be of interest to some reading this. I thank all those who did the work referenced in these Sources and thus made a novel of this style possible.

Chapter One

Bruce Springsteen's quote about a fan yelling to him following 9/11 is taken from: "My City of Ruins: Cover Songs Uncovered," *The Pop Culture Experiment*, Patrick Garvin, September 11, 2017. https://popcultureexperiment.com/2017/09/11/my-city-of-ruins-cover-songs-uncovered/

Bruce Springsteen's quote about living in a new world following 9/11, adapted from Bruce Springsteen television interview with Ted Koppel, "Bruce Springsteen & "The Rising," *ABC News Nightline*, July 30, 2002.

For more on the unique genetics of the Solomon Islanders: "Naturally blond hair in Solomon Islanders rooted in native gene, study finds," *Stanford Medicine News Center*, Roseanne Spector, May 3, 2012.

Chapter Two

Abraham Lincoln uttered the phrase "This too shall pass away," in a speech delivered at the Wisconsin State Fair on September 30, 1859. He was not claiming the phrase to be his own, but the words of an "Eastern monarch." Address before the Wisconsin State Agricultural Society, *Abraham Lincoln Online*. http://www.abrahamlincolnonline.org/lincoln/speeches/fair.htm.

On Martin Van Buren not mentioning his wife once in his 800-page autobiography: Rubel, David, Mr. President, *The Human Side of America's Chief Executives*, (Agincourt Press, 1998) 54, And his memoirs, *The Autobiography of Martin Van Buren*, published sixty years after his death, do not cover his White House years.

On Martin Van Buren knowing both Alexander Hamilton and Aaron Burr as a youth growing up, being the child of parents who ran an inn and saloon in Kinderhook, New York that was frequented by politicians on the way to Albany: Joel Silbey, "Martin Van Buren: Life Before the Presidency," Miller Center, University of Virginia. https://millercenter.org/president/van-buren/life-before-the-presidency

Chapter Five

On Susan B. Anthony casting her ballot for Grant and subsequently being arrested: Godfrey D. Lehman, "Susan B. Anthony Cast Her Ballot For Ulysses S. Grant," *American Heritage*, December 1985, Volume 37, Issue 1.

On Anna Strong's involvement in Washington's spy network on Long Island: "Anna Smith Strong: Member of the Culper Spy Ring," History of American Women: Colonial Women.
https://www.womenhistoryblog.com/2011/07/anna-smith-strong.html.

John Quincy Adams' wife Louisa wrote in her autobiography, which she never completed, that her husband was cold and insensitive to women, like all Adams men were. David Rubel, Mr. President: *The Human Side of America's Chief Executives*, (Agincourt Press, 1998), 42.

On journalist Anne Royall obtaining an interview with John Quincy Adams by staking him out during his morning swim: K. Thor Jensen, The First Woman to Interview a President Got Him in the Nude," Observer, April 24, 2017. https://observer.com/2017/04/the-first-woman-to-interview-a-president-got-him-in-the-nude-john-quincy-adams-anne-newport-royall/

John Quincy Adams quote about Anne Royall, "Her pen was as venomous . . ." is adapted from a headline that appeared in the Washington Post about the journalist years after her death. Jeff Biggers, "Meet Anne Royall: The Muckraker Who Made Washington Bow Down in Fear." *HuffPost*, The Blog, September 4, 2013. https://www.huffpost.com/entry/meet-anne-royall-the-muck_b_4381394.

Grant's quote, "God gave us liberty and he gave us Lincoln . . ." adapted from a toast Ulysses S. Grant offered on February 23, 1864 before the Vicksburg campaign. Edward Deering Mansfield, *A Popular and Authentic Life of Ulysses S. Grant*, (Cincinnati: R.W. Carroll and Publishers, 1868).

Lincoln's quote about Grant drinking whiskey is adapted from the following quote that appeared in the New York Times October 30, 1863: "When someone charged Gen. Grant, in the President's hearing, with drinking too much liquor, Mr. Lincoln, recalling Gen. Grant's successes, said that if he could find out what brand of whiskey Grant drank, he would send a barrel of it to all the other commanders." Ronald G. Shafer, "Trump called Ulysses S. Grant an alcoholic. Here's what historians say about that." *Washington Post*, October 16, 2018.

George W. Bush's quote "One reason ..." is adapted from: "Statement by President George W. Bush on the Passing of Harper Lee," February 19, 2016, George W. Bush Presidential Center.
https://www.bushcenter.org/about-the-center/newsroom/press-releases/2016/president-bush-statement-on-harper-lee.html.

Kennedy quote about Margaret Chase Smith is adapted from his quote appearing here: Eileen Fitzpatrick, "The Unfavored Daughter: When Margaret Chase Smith Ran in the New Hampshire Primary," *The New York*

Times, February 6, 2016.

Chapter Nine

John Quincy Adams quote, "There's nothing more pathetic . . ." adapted from his quote which appeared here: Gregory Korte, "What Will Obama do after the Presidency?" *USA Today*, July 26, 2016.

Nixon quote about actions of the president not being illegal was uttered in his May, 1977 David Frost interview: "Transcript of David Frost's Interview with Richard Nixon," Teaching American History. https://teachingamericanhistory.org/document/transcript-of-david-frosts-interview-with-richard-nixon/

Chapter Ten

This Week With George Stephanopoulos is a national weekly television show broadcast on Sunday mornings by ABC hosted by George Stephanopoulos. The transcript which appears in this chapter is a completely fictional interview for this story.

Chapter Eleven

C B Hannegan's was an epic Irish pub and restaurant in Los Gatos, California on Bachman Street just off of Santa Cruz Avenue, which opened in 1979 and stayed in business for 38 years before closing on December 28, 2017. It was a Los Gatos treasure.

Chapter Thirteen

Washington's quote "I do not think myself equal to the command . . ." adapted from quote appearing in: "George Washington's Address to the Continental Congress, June 16, 1775," Founders Online, National Archives. http://founders.archives.gov/documents/Washington/03-01-02-0001. And Washington quote "rely on the goodness of the cause," adapted from: General Orders, July 2, 1776, Founders Online, National Archives.

http://founders.archives.gov/documents/Washington/03-05-02-0117.

John F. Kennedy quotes about the Bay of Pigs adapted from quotes appearing here: Steve Adubato, "JFK: A great leader learned from a terrible failure," NJ.com, March 30, 2019.
https://www.nj.com/business/2013/11/jfk_a_great_leader_learned_fro.html.

Chapter Sixteen

Newday is a national cable show broadcast by CNN that in March of 2021 was co-hosted by Alisyn Camerata. The transcript which appears in this chapter is a completely fictional interview for this story.

Chapter Twenty-Two

On Washington's friend and pub owner Samuel Fraunces: "Samuel Fraunces," George Washington's Mount Vernon.
https://www.mountvernon.org/library/digitalhistory/digital-encyclopedia/article/samuel-fraunces/

John Garner quote about FDR being the "most destructive man in all American history": Nathan Miller Nathan, FDR: *An Intimate History*, (New York: Doubleday & Company, 1983) 395.

John Garner's quote about the "worth" of the Vice Presidency: "U.S. Presidents, Franklin D. Roosevelt, John N. Garner (1933-1941)," Miller Center, University of Virginia. https://millercenter.org/president/fdroosevelt/essays/garner-1933-vicepresident

LBJ's "goddamn raven hovering" quote adapted from LBJ quote appearing in: David M. Oshinsky, "Fear and Loathing in the White House: Why couldn't L.B.J. and Bobby Kennedy just get along?" *New York Times*, October 26, 1997.

Chapter Twenty-Five

On John Quincy Adams beginning each day with a swim in the Potomac: David Rubel, *Mr. President: The Human Side of America's Chief Executives*, (Agincourt Press, 1998), 41.

On Truman's morning shot of Bourbon and brisk walk: "The Daily Schedule," Harry S. Truman, Little White House. https://www.trumanlittlewhitehouse.com/guide/the-daily-schedule.

Eisenhower on taking up painting, and being a "deliberate dauber": Piers Brendon, *Ike, His Life and Times*, (New York: Harper & Row, 1986) 203.

On Teddy Roosevelt regularly boxing in the White House and losing sight in one eye while in the ring, Sudiksha Kochi, "Fact check: Theodore Roosevelt's eyesight was permanently damaged by military aide during boxing match," *USA Today*, November 5, 2021.

Teddy Roosevelt quote on exploring nature: "Ten Presidential Quotes About Exploring Nature," Cloudline.
https://www.cloudlineapparel.com/blogs/cloudline/10-presidential-quotes-about-nature-in-america

Teddy Roosevelt Yellowstone quote and background of his trip: Sean Reichard, "Old Yellowstone: President Theodore Roosevelt's 1903 Trip," *Yellowstone Insider*, April 8, 2016.

On the importance of sailing to FDR and JFK: Michael Beschloss, "Sailing Was More Than Respite for Roosevelt and Kennedy," *New York Times*, September 12, 2015.

JFK quote about going to Hyannis Port "to be revived." adapted from: Will Hide, "On the trail of JFK in New England," *The Guardian*, November 11, 2013.

On FDR considering himself an "ancient mariner," and FDR's quote comparing politics to sailing: Michael Beschloss, "Sailing Was More Than Respite for Roosevelt and Kennedy," *New York Times*, September 12, 2015.

Chapter Twenty-Six

College Gameday is a national weekly Saturday morning television show broadcast by ESPN during the college football season hosted by Reece Davis and featuring Kirk Herbstreit, Desmond Howard and Lee Corso. The transcript which appears in this chapter is completely fictional created for this story.

For background on US presidents who played and coached college football: Timothy Brown, "Three Football Coaches Who Later Became US Presidents," *Fields of Friendly Strife*, February 13, 2018. Woodrow Wilson is also listed in this article as having coached football at Wesleyan in the 1880's.

Chapter Twenty-Nine

For the true origins and playing rules of the "Split the Room Game," something the Coonan extended family has been playing at holidays and on vacations for thirty-five years, see https://dancoonanauthor.com/split-the-room-game. It was not created at Monticello.

For more on The Nina, which was Columbus' nickname for his favorite ship, formally named The Santa Clara: Jolie Lee, "Whereabouts of Nina and Pinta Remain a Mystery." *USA Today*, May 14, 2014.

On Jefferson's favorite wine being from The Hermitage: James A. Bear, Jr., "Reforming the Taste of the Country," 1984, reprinted in: The Jefferson Encyclopedia, Wine.
https://www.monticello.org/site/research-and-collections/wine

On Jefferson and Madison's relationship and feelings about Ben Franklin: "On this day, Benjamin Franklin dies in Philadelphia," Constitution Daily, National Constitution Center, April 17, 2021. https://constitutioncenter.org/blog/benjamin-franklins-last-days-funeral-and-a-u-s-senate.

Thomas Jefferson's quote, "No one can replace him . . ." is from the eulogy he gave for Ben Franklin: "On this day, Benjamin Franklin dies in Philadelphia," Constitution Daily, National Constitution Center, April 17, 2021. https://constitutioncenter.org/blog/benjamin-franklins-last-days-funeral-and-a-u-s-senate.

Jefferson's quote, "A walk about Paris , , ," adapted from Jefferson quote appearing here: Madelyn, "Thomas Jefferson in Paris," Paris Perfect, September 29, 2020. https://www.parisperfect.com/blog/2013/07/thomas-jefferson-in-paris/

Jefferson's quote, "Man has not yet created a work of art . . ." is a completely fictional quote for this novel inspired by a somewhat similar sentiment expressed by the character Gil in Woody Allen's 2011 movie *Midnight in Paris*—as a homage to that film which inspired Presidential Spirits and this sequel. Gil's exact quote in the movie is, "You know, I sometimes think, how is anyone ever gonna come up with a book, or a painting, or a symphony, or a sculpture that can compete with a great city. You can't."

On Madison and Jefferson's "literary cargo: "James Madison and Thomas Jefferson," Steve Allen Books, September 16, 2016. https://stevenallen-books.com/james-madison-and-thomas-jefferson/

Madison specifically referred to the books Jefferson sent him from Paris as "literary cargo" in a letter to Jefferson of March 18, 1786: "To Thomas Jefferson from James Madison, 18 March 1786 From James Madison," Founders Online. https://founders.archives.gov/documents/Jefferson/01-09-02-0301.

On James and Dolley Madison moving into the White House (then called the Executive Mansion) with Thomas Jefferson at first upon arriving in Washington in 1801: Noah Feldman, *The Three Lives of James Madison*, (New York: Random House, 2017) 444-45.

Chapter Thirty-Two

Ulysses Grant quote, "one of the most unjust wars . . .": Sherman Fleek, "Grant in Mexico: 'One of the Most unjust (wars) ever waged.' " U.S. Army, January 31, 2019
https://www.army.mil/article/216806/grant_in_mexico_one_of_the_most_unjust_wars_ever_waged

On Grant's admiration for Zachary Taylor and the original Grant quote, "The general here was known . . .": "A Personal Example" - Zachary Taylor's Influence on the Leadership Style of Ulysses S. Grant," The Zachary Taylor Project. https://www.thezacharytaylorproject.com/post/a-personal-example-zachary-taylor-s-influence-on-the-leadership-style-of-ulysses-s-grant

On Winfield Scott: Professor Carol, "Robert E. Lee and Winfield Scott," June 8, 2016. https://www.professorcarol.com/2016/06/08/robert-e-lee-winfield-scott/

Grant quote on Robert E. Lee "I could never see in his achievements what justifies his reputation . . .," ʹRon Chernow, *Grant*, (New York: Penguin Books, 2017) 517; *New York Herald*, May 28 1878.

Grant quotes on advantages the South had in the Civil War: : Ron Chernow, *Grant*, (New York: Penguin Books, 2017) 517; *New York Herald*, May 28 1878.

Grant quote on Southern generals: Ron Chernow, *Grant*, (New York: Penguin Books, 2017) 516; *New York Herald*, May 28 1878.

Grant quotes on Appomattox: Ron Chernow, *Grant*, (New York: Penguin Books, 2017) 505-11; Interview with John Russell Young, Ulysses S. Grant

Homepage. www.granthomepage.com/interviews.htm; Ulysses S. Grant, *Personal Memoirs of U.S. Grant, All Volumes*, (Independently published, 2020).

On Grant's groomsmen including Longstreet (best man), Cadmus Wilcox and Bernard Pratte, all of whom would surrender to Grant at Appomattox: Ron Chernow, *Grant*, (New York: Penguin Books, 2017) 62. There is a dispute amongst historians as to whether Longstreet was indeed Grant's best man, but Chernow concludes that he was.

On Robert E. Lee's interaction with Ely Parker, the Native American (Senecan) on Grant's staff at Appomattox: Ron Chernow, *Grant*, (New York: Penguin Books, 2017) 509-10.

On Eisenhower giving tours of Gettysburg to Churchill and others: Felix Belair, Jr., "Eisenhower and Churchill Tour Gettysburg Farm and Battlefield; and: "CHURCHILL TOURS PRESIDENT'S FARM," *New York Times*, May 7, 1959.

Chapter Thirty-Three

The Michael Smerconish Program is a national radio show broadcast by SiriusXM on the POTUS channel, hosted by author, lawyer, television host and journalist Michael Smerconish. The transcript which appears in this chapter is a completely fictional interview for this story.

Chapter Thirty-Four

On Teddy Roosevelt running with the Progressive Party in 1912: H. W. Brands, *T.R.: The Last Romantic*, (New York: Basic Books, 1997) 718-29.

Lincoln quote "I was an old line Whig . . ." adapted from quote appearing here: David Herbert Donald, *Lincoln*, (Simon & Schuster, New York, 1995) 222.

On Lincoln and Johnson running with the newly formed National Union

Party: Arthur Schlesinger, Jr., *History of U.S Political Parties, Volume II 1860 – 1910* (New York: Chelsea House Publishers, 1973) 1287.

On FDR's tendency to refer to a refill of alcohol as "another little sippy:" Mark Will-Weber, *Mint Juleps with Teddy Roosevelt: The Complete History of Presidential Drinking*, (Washington D.C.: Regnery Publishing 2014) 255.

At one point or another in his political life, John Quincy Adams identified with the following parties: Federalist, Democratic-Republican, National Republican, Anti-Masonic, and Whig.

Reagan quote, "I didn't leave the Democratic Party . . ." adapted from Reagan quote appearing here: "Top Ten Political Defections, the Ol' Switcheroo, Ronald Reagan" *Time Magazine*.
http://content.time.com/time/specials/packages/article/0,28804,1894529_1894528_1894525,00.html.

On Churchill switching parties: "Churchill Critiques: Changing Parties," The Churchill Project, Hillsdale College, March 21, 2016.

On FDR's response upon learning that Churchill was England's new Prime Minister, and for much of the background of Churchill and FDR described here: Jon Meacham Lecture: "Winston Churchill and Franklin D. Roosevelt in the White House," White House Historical Association, conducted in partnership with The National Churchill Library and Center at George Washington University, June 7, 2017

On Churchill favoring an invasion in central Europe rather than Normandy: John T. Correll, "Churchill's Southern Strategy," *Airforce Magazine*, January 2013.

On Churchill wanting to cross the channel with the invasion on D-Day: Dan Snow, "D-Day 70 – 24 Facts about D-Day." BBC.
https://www.bbc.co.uk/programmes/articles/Q9YNVD851WHmGm6jy9mx1X/24-facts-about-d-day

Truman quote about Churchill saying FDR was the greatest American friend England ever had: "Roosevelt and Churchill: A Friendship That Saved The World," National Park Service.
https://www.nps.gov/articles/fdrww2.htm

FDR's quote, "It was great fun to be in the same decade with him," adapted from FDR quote about Churchill appearing here: Edwin McDowell, "Roosevelt-Churchill Letters Depict Tensons," *New York Times*, July 11, 1984.

On Eleanor Roosevelt believing Franklin's polio condition made him more empathetic toward others, his condition not being a secret, his Rochester speech, and his polio being used as a political advantage: "Roosevelt's Polio Wasn't a Secret; He Used It To His Advantage," *NPR News*, November 25, 2015. https://www.wbur.org/npr/247155522/roosevelts-polio-wasn-t-a-secret-he-used-it-to-his-advantage. Historian James Tobin argues that the "splendid deception" theory put forward by Hugh Gregory Gallagher about the extent of the deception concerning FDR's polio is a false narrative.

David B. Woolner, "Franklin Roosevelt's battle with polio taught him lessons relevant today," *The Washington Post*, April 28, 2020.

On FDR's birthday balls to raise money for polio, FDR not accepting the finality of the diagnosis, the actions he took to overcome it, and forbidding cameras from taking photos of him in a wheelchair: Jeffrey Kluger, "The Legacy of F.D.R.," *Time Magazine*, June 24, 2009

On political opponents of Roosevelt using his disability against him, and the Mussolini quote about Roosevelt: Cecil Adams, "Did Americans Really Not Know About FDR's Disability? The president did his damnedest to keep people from seeing him wheel around." *Washington City Paper*, August 16, 2016.

On the Secret Service confiscating film from cameras taking photos of FDR in a wheel chair: Cecil Adams, "Did Americans Really Not Know About FDR's Disability? The president did his damnedest to keep people from seeing him wheel around." *Washington City Paper*, August 16, 2016.

On John Adams jailing reporters for being critical of his administration: Scott Bonboy, "Can the media be jailed for criticizing a president?" Constitution Daily, National Constitution Center, October 6, 2017. https://constitutioncenter.org/blog/can-the-media-be-jailed-for-criticizing-a-president.

On Wilson pushing to pass The Sedition Act of 1918, restricting the free speech rights of US citizens during wartime, resulting in hundreds of convictions: Scott Bonboy, "Can the media be jailed for criticizing a president?" Constitution Daily, National Constitution Center, October 6, 2017. https://constitutioncenter.org/blog/can-the-media-be-jailed-for-criticizing-a-president.

On Congressman Matthew Lyon being thrown in jail for criticizing John Adams, and then winning re-election from prison: "Matthew Lyon," Freedom, A History of US, Biography. https://www.thirteen.org/wnet/historyofus/web02/features/bio/B10.html

George H. W. Bush quote about the Americans with Disabilities Act, "It was powerful in it's simplicity . . ." adapted from Bush's quotes contained here: "Remarks of President George H. W. Bush at the Signing of the Americans with Disabilities Act, July 26, 1990.
https://www.ada.gov/ghw_bush_ada_remarks.htm

Chapter Thirty-Nine

Reagan's quote about uniqueness of American immigration adapted from his quote appearing here: Kathy Rittel, "Reagan celebrated Immigrants in his final speech," *The Island Now*, July 22, 2019.

Calvin Coolidge quote, "New arrivals must be limited to our capacity to absorb them . . ." adapted from his quotes appearing here: "We're All in the Same Boat Now: Coolidge on Immigration," Coolidge Foundation, February 19, 2016. https://coolidgefoundation.org/blog/were-all-in-the-same-boat-now-coolidge-on-immigration/; "President Coolidge signs Immigration Act of 1924," This Day in History—May 26, History.com. https://www.history.com/this-day-in-history/coolidge-signs-stringent-immigration-law.

On Hoover limiting immigration and banning immigrants who would become a public charge: "The United States and the Nazi Threat – 1933-37," United States Holocaust Memorial Museum. https://encyclopedia.ushmm.org/content/en/article/the-united-states-and-the-nazi-threat-1933-37.

On 1.3 million immigrants passing through New York's Ellis Island in 1907 alone: "Immigration act passed over President Wilson's veto." This Day In History – February 5, History.com. https://www.history.com/this-day-in-history/immigration-act-passed-over-wilsons-veto.

Teddy Roosevelt immigration quote, "We have room for but one language . . ." adapted from Theodore Roosevelt, *Works* (Memorial ed., 1926), vol. XXIV, (New York: Charles Scribner's 11 Sons) 554.

Obama quote expressing frustration on immigration reform adapted from: Video interview with Barack Obama, "Pushing for Change – President on Frustration Over Immigration Reform," *CBS This Morning*, April 17, 2014. https://www.cbsnews.com/video/obama-expresses-frustration-on-immigration-reform/

Chapter Forty

On Irish whiskey and religion: "Ask Your Bartender: Protestant vs. Catholic Whiskey," Jeffrey Morganthaler Website, March 17, 2019. https://jeffreymorgenthaler.com/ask-your-bartender-protestant-vs-catholic-whiskey/

For a listing of U.S. presidents with Irish heritage: "US President with Irish Heritage," The Irish Emigration Museum. https://epicchq.com/story/us-presidents-with-irish-heritage/

Washington quote about Ireland constructed from background info appearing here: Matthew P. Dziennik, "Ireland and the American Revolution," Journal of the American Revolution, May 12, 2014.

Lord Mountjoy quote about losing America through the Irish: "The Irish of 1776," *The Christian Science Monitor*, March 17, 1983.

Background supporting some of Ulysses S. Grant's words about the contributions of the Irish to the Civil War, Kate Hickey, "Abraham Lincoln's Irish Brigade letter to sell at auction on St. Patrick's Day," Irish Central, March 16, 2016. https://www.irishcentral.com/roots/history/abraham-lincolns-irish-brigade-letter-to-sell-at-auction-on-st-patricks-day

On Lincoln's appreciation for Irish involvement in the Civil War, and kissing the Irish flag: James O'Shea, "When Abraham Lincoln kissed the Irish flag and praised the Irish," *Irish Central*, December 12, 2012.

The complete story of the attempt by Irish Civil War veterans to capture Canada and hold it hostage to secure Ireland's freedom from Britain is told here: Christopher Klein, *When the Irish Invaded Canada: The True Story of the Civil War Veterans Who Fought for Ireland's Freedom*, (Doubleday, 2019).

On JFK's address to the Irish Parliament in 1963, and Ben Franklin's address to the Irish Paliament in 1772: "John F. Kennedy – "Address to the Irish Parliament," AmericanRhetoric.com.
https://www.americanrhetoric.com/speeches/jfkirishparliament.htm.

John Kennedy quote "on a clear day in Boston, you can see Galway," adapted from a JFK's speech given at Eyre Square in Galway on June 29, 1963. "John F. Kennedy: Remarks at Eyre Square in Galway," The American Presidency Project, University of California, Santa Barbara. https://www.presidency.ucsb.edu/documents/remarks-eyre-square-galway. (On that day he actually conveyed the reverse of this quote.)

On Ronald Reagan's trip to Ballyporeen: Ronald Reagan, *The Reagan*

Diaries, Edited by Douglas Brinkely, (Harper Collins 2007) 244.

Chapter Forty-Three

This Week With George Stephanopoulos is a national weekly Sunday morning television show broadcast by ABC, hosted by author, journalist and former political operative George Stephanopoulos. The transcript which appears in this chapter is a completely fictional interview for this story.

Chapter Forty-Four

For a brief overview of the origin and history of the filibuster: "About Filibusters and Cloture: Historical Overview," Powers and Procedures, United States Senate. https://www.senate.gov/about/powers-procedures/filibusters-cloture/overview.ht

Chapter Forty-Five

References to the Hollywood history of the San Ysidro Ranch, and of John and Jackie Kennedy honeymooning there: Michael Redmon, "The San Ysidro Ranch – The San Ysidro Was Originally a Working Ranch," *Santa Barbara Independent*, October 19, 2017; and: Jeff Coyen, "Where is America's Best Hotel?" *NBC News*, February 3, 2009.

On Lawrence Olivier and Vivien Leigh getting married at midnight on a bluff at the San Ysidro Ranch: Kendra Bean, "Revisiting the San Ysidro Ranch," Guest Post, VivienandLarry.com., March 15, 2010. vivandlarry.com/classic-film/guest-post-revisiting-the-san-ysidro-ranch/.

Chapter Forty-Six

The Hannity Show is a nightly national cable television show broadcast on Fox News, hosted by Sean Hannity. The transcript which appears in this chapter is a completely fictional interview for this story.

Chapter Forty-Eight

On divorced presidents: Brittany Wong, "There's Only Been One Other Divorced President In History Before Trump," *Huffington Post*, November 11, 2016.

Chapter Forty-Nine

Nixon quote: "I've never seen a president beaten on inflation , , ," adapted from, Burton A. Abrams & James L. Butkiewitz, "The Political Business Cycle, New Evidence from Nixon Tapes," *Journal of Money, Credit and Banking*, Vol. 44, No. 2/3 (March-April 2012).

Garfield quote, "Any party which commits itself to paper money . . ." adapted from, Burton T. Doyle and Homer S. Swaney, *Lives of James A. Garfield and Chester A. Arthur*, (Brutus H. Darby, Washington DC, 1881).

Chapter Fifty

Washington quote on the Battle of Monongahela, "Death was leveling my companions on every side of me . . ." adapted from quote appearing in: Joseph J. Ellis, *His Excellency* (Vintage Books, 2004) 22.

Chapter Fifty-One

For background on Lincoln and his wife, Mary, coming under fire while surveying the battlefield at Fort Stevens, David Herbert Donald, *Lincoln*, (Simon & Schuster, New York, 1995) 519; and, Christopher Klein, "Abraham Lincoln's Battlefield Brush With Death," History.com, May 7, 2020. https://www.history.com/news/lincolns-battlefield-brush-with-death

Andrew Jackson quote about Calhoun, "want of every sense of honor . . ." adapted from: John Meacham, *American Lion*, (Random House, New York, 2008) 193.

Background for Franklin Pierce account of losing his son Benny: Hayley Glatter, "TBT: President Franklin Pierce's Train Wreck," *Boston Magazine*, January 4, 2018.

Franklin Pierce quote, "How could I possibly summon my manhood . . ." adapted from the words of Franklin Pierce contained in a letter to Jefferson Davis, dated January 12, 1853, cited in: Robert E. Gilbert, "Presidential Disability and the Twenty-Fifth Amendment: The Difficulties Posed By Psychological Illness," *Fordham Law Review*, Volume 79, Issue 3, Article 5, 2010.

"Presidents Who Lost Children While in the White House," Shapell Manuscript Foundation. https://www.shapell.org/historical-perspectives/curated-manuscripts/tragedy-in-the-white-house-u-s-presidents-who-lost-children/

Calvin Coolidge's quote, "the power of the presidency went with him . . ." adapted from a passage in Coolidge's memoirs, Calvin Coolidge, *The Autobiography of Calvin Coolidge*, (Cosmopolitan Book Corporation, New York, 1929)

Additional background and quotes pertaining to Calvin Coolidge on the death of his son adapted from: Benjamin Shapell and Sara Willen, "Calvin Coolidge Jr.'s Death," Shapell Manuscript Foundation, July 6, 2017. https://www.shapell.org/historical-perspectives/between-the-lines/death-calvin-coolidge-jr/: and from: Jude Sheerin, "The mental rigours of being US president," *BBC News*, April 15, 2019.

Lincoln quotes about the death of his son, Willie, adapted from quotes appearing here: "Family: William Wallace Lincoln (1850 – 1862)," Mr. Lincoln's White House. http://www.mrlincolnswhitehouse.org/residents-visitors/family/family-william-wallace-lincoln-1850-186; and, "The Death of Willie Lincoln," Abraham Lincoln Online. http://www.abrahamlincolnonline.org/lincoln/education/williedeath.htm

Lincoln's quote, "In this sad world of ours . . ." adapted from a letter from Abraham Lincoln to Fanny McCullough, who was experiencing severe depression upon the death of her father, December 23, 1862. "Letter to Fanny McCullough," Abraham Lincoln Online, Speeches and Writings. http://www.abrahamlincolnonline.org/lincoln/speeches/mccull.htm

John Quincy Adams quote, ". . . employ the remaining days which God has allotted me on earth . . ." adapted from quotes appearing in: Joshua Kendall, "The First Children Who Led Sad Lives," *Smithsonian Magazine*, February 11, 2016.

For background on Letitia Tyler passing away during John Tyler's presidency: Allida Black, "Letitia Christian Tyler," The White House, First Families, The White House Historical Asssociation, 2009. https://www.whitehouse.gov/about-the-white-house/first-families/letitia-christian-tyler/; and, "Letitia Christian Tyler," William & Mary Libraries, Special Collections Research Center. https://scrc-kb.libraries.wm.edu/letitia-christian-tyler#:~:text=Letitia%20Christian%20Tyler%2C%20born%20Letitia%20Christian%20%28November%2012%2C,two%20years%20when%20her%20husband%20unexpectedly%20became%20President.

On Caroline Harrison eradicating rats from the White House, Carl Anthony, "Rats in the White House: Pestering Tales of Barbara Bush in the Pool & Others," Carl Anthony Online, June 1, 2014. https://carlanthonyonline.com/2014/06/01/rats-in-the-white-house-pestering-tales-of-barbara-bush-in-the-pool-other

Obama quote on the loneliness of the presidency adapted from quote appearing here: Emily Friedman, "Presidency Can Feel Isolated, Lonely," *ABC News*, November 17, 2008. https://abcnews.go.com/Politics/President44/story?id=6273508&page=1.

Teddy Roosevelt quote on losing his wife adapted from quotes appearing in his diary and in a tribute he wrote to her: "Theodore Roosevelt's diary the day his wife and mother died, 1884," Rare Historical Photos. https://rarehistoricalphotos.com/theodore-roosevelts-diary-day-wife-mother-died-1884/

Teddy Rooevelt quote, “Courage is not having the strength to go on . .” adapted from a quote in the speech TR gave at Harvard, his alma mater, on June 28, 1905.

Teddy Roosevelt “dare to be great” quote adapted from: Drake Baer and Richard Feloni, “15 Teddy Roosevelt quotes on courage, leadership, and success,” *Business Insider*, February 14, 2016.

Teddy Roosevelt quote, “the qualities of practical intelligence, of courage, of hardihood, and endurance, and above all the power of devotion to a lofty ideal . . .” adapted from Teddy Roosevelt’s Inauguration Speech delivered March 4, 1905.

Teddy Roosevelt quote, “Nothing in this world is worth having or worth doing unless it means effort, pain, difficulty . . .” adapted from quote appearing in Teddy Roosevelt’s American Ideals in Education Speech, delivered November 4, 1910.

Chapter Fifty-Four

On presidents serving without vice presidents: Arlen Parsa, “18 American Presidents Didn’y Have a Vice President For All of Part of Their Term,” Forgotten History Blog,
https://forgottenhistoryblog.com/18-american-presidents-didnt-have-a-vice-president-for-all-or-some-of-their-terms/

Chapter Fifty-Eight

On the presidents’ dogs, names and breeds: Roy Rowan and Brooke Janis, *First Dogs: American Presidents and Their Best Friends*, (Algonquin Books of Chapel Hill, 2009); “List of U.S. Presidents and their Dogs,” Dogtime.
https://dogtime.com/dog-health/general/5668-list-of-us-presidents-and-their-dogs

Chapter Fifty-Nine

On Van Buren, the Free Soil Party and the election of 1848: "The Election of 1848: Free Soil, Free Labor, Free Men," National Park Service, December 9, 2020. https://www.nps.gov/mava/learn/historyculture/the-election-of-1848-free-soil-free-labor-free-men.htm

Grant's quote, "I voted for Buch . . ." adapted from Grant's letter to his father, Jesse Root Grant in September of 1859; and from Ron Chernow, *Grant* (Penguin Books, New York, NY, 2017) 99-100.

On Eisenhower being recruited by both parties to run in 1952, and having never voted before then: Chester J. Pach, Jr.. "Dwight D. Eienhower, Campaigns and Elections," University of Virginia, The Miller Center. https://millercenter.org/president/eisenhower/campaigns-and-elections

On Truman offering to let Eisenhower lead the Democratic ticket in the election of 1948: Chester J. Pach, Jr., "Dwight D. Eienhower, Campaigns and Elections," University of Virginia, The Miller Center. https://millercenter.org/president/eisenhower/campaigns-and-elections.

On FDR naming the presidential retreat in the Blue Ridge Mountains Shangri-a: "Camp David," National Archives, Prologue Magazine. Winter 2008, Volume 40, No. 4.
https://www.archives.gov/publications/prologue/2008/winter/camp-david.html

On Eisenhower renaming the presidential retreat in the Blue Ridge Mountains "Camp David," after his father and his grandson: David Eisenhower and Julie Nixon Eisenhower, *Going Home to Glory: A Memoir of Life with Dwight David Eisenhower, 1961-1969* (New York: Simon and Schuster) 31.

Chapter Sixty-One

On FDR naming the presidential retreat in the Blue Ridge Mountains Shangri-La, after the fictional Himalayan paradise in British author James Hilton's novel, *Lost Horizon*: "Camp David," National Archives, Prologue Magazine. Winter 2008, Volume 40, No. 4.
https://www.archives.gov/publications/prologue/2008/winter/camp-david.html

On the Egypt/Israel deal being negotiated by Carter, Sadat and Begin at Camp David's Holly Cabin: "Holly Cabin – The Original Laurel Lodge," About Camp David, September 8, 2010.
https://aboutcampdavid.blogspot.com/2010/09/holly-cabin-original-laurel-lodge.html.

Chapter Sixty-Two

On the naming of the new Laurel Lodge at Camp David and the old Laurel Lodge becoming Holly Cabin: "Holly Cabin – The Original Laurel Lodge," About Camp David" September 8, 2010.
https://aboutcampdavid.blogspot.com/2010/09/holly-cabin-original-laurel-lodge.html.

Chapter Sixty-Six

On Ben Franklin's response to the question posed by Elizabeth Willing Powell, as he emerged from the Constitutional Convention: Gillian Brockwell, "Did Ben Franklin really say 'A republic, if you can keep it?' *The Washington Post*, December 18, 2019.

Chapter Sixty-Seven

Tucker Carlson Tonight is a nightly national cable television show broadcast on Fox News, hosted by Tucker Carlson. The transcript which appears in this chapter is a completely fictional interview for this story.

Chapter Sixty-Nine

On the vote in the House of Representatives for president following a failure of any candidate to achieve a majority in the Electoral College, being one vote per state: United States Constitution, Twelfth Amendment.

Chapter Seventy-One

Obama quote about presidents, "My instinct is that . . ." adapted from his quote appearing here: David Remnick, "Testing the Waters," The Political Scene, *The New Yorker*, November 6, 2006.

Chapter Seventy-Two

On weddings taking place at The White House: "How many weddings have been held at the White House?" White House Historical Association. https://www.whitehousehistory.org/questions/how-many-weddings-have-been-held-at-the-white-house#

On Jefferson having his office in a portion of what is now the White House State Dining Room: "The State Dining Room," The White House Historical Association. https://www.whitehousehistory.org/white-house-tour/state-dining-room.

Chapter Seventy-Three

Maggie Bates' quote of Thoreau comes from: Henry David Thoreau, *Walden; or Life in the Woods*. (Boston: Ticknor and Fields, 1854).

ACKNOWLEDGEMENTS

I had barely finished writing the first few chapters of my first novel, *Presidential Spirits*, when it first dawned on me that I would be doing this again. Not because I thought I'd sell a lot of books or that I had such compelling stories to share, but because I loved it. So much. It's the journey, not the destination—although I like that too.

And while I was certain I'd write another, initially at least I was not inclined towards a sequel. I didn't set out to write this as a series. I was happy with the first one, how it ended, and the message it conveyed, and didn't think I left anything on the table, as we'd say in my life as a fundraiser. And I had no shortage of other novel ideas.

But I began to reevaluate that when I started doing bookclub events and began hearing from some of the people who related most to that novel. So many asked me to do a sequel. All that was wonderfully flattering, of course, and prompted me to start thinking about it more and more. The two stories that most inspired this—*Field of Dreams* and *Midnight in Paris*—are two of my favorite movies, and I've often wished they had sequels. That can be tricky though. I didn't want to even begin without a really compelling concept for a story that I loved, and I didn't want to detract in any way from the first. And if I was going to spend a thousand hours on it, I wanted to absolutely believe in it, and convey a message that is not merely a regurgitation of everything about the first.

I started jotting down ideas and sketching out plotlines. After a full three months of brainstorming, I arrived at what I considered a compelling narrative that I loved and decided to give it a shot. Then came the truest indication that I was doing the right thing—I had that same feeling come over me as I was writing each day that this was precisely what I needed to be doing. Once again, I felt that regardless of whether I finish, or how it gets placed, or whether it sells as well as the first one, this is exactly what I needed to be doing.

And if you're wondering why this one is longer than the first it's because I just didn't want it to end.

Perhaps in the end I wasn't quite ready to be done with these characters. And I like to think a few of them at least weren't ready to be done with me. (I used to hate it when writers talked like that. Get over yourself, I thought. Now I've come to accept that it's perfectly normal.) And, most importantly, the core message of the novel is perhaps even more urgent than when I wrote the first one.

There are so many people to thank—both for the success of the first one and for contributing to this. Thanks to my beta readers on this novel—Maryalice Whalen, Kathy Kale, Tom Preston, Mike Noyes, Kevin Appleby, and my brother Terry. Kevin and Terry provided a good deal of expertise on immigration issues, and Terry helped again by reviewing some of the military history. My friend Angie Zaremba, my buddy's sweet southern bride, assisted a little in this California boy's attempt to make the character of Maggie Bates as authentic as I could. And my friend and former co-worker Christina Martinez reviewed my conversational Spanish. Sarah O'Connor provided input with some of the younger political perspectives.

Thanks to my friend and fellow author, Lelita Baldock, and to Michael Hutchinson of Directing Design for their roles in producing the cover. And, of course, a huge thank you to my publisher, Goose River Press and Deborah Benner for believing in me again.

I also want to thank both St. Bernard High School and the University of Notre Dame for embracing the novel as they did and spreading the word to their alumni base. I never could have expected such a wonderful response from those two schools which have meant so much to me in my life, but how truly heartwarming—precisely what one might wish for from an alma mater but never realistically dream of.

And last but not least, thanks to my wife and biggest supporter, Donna Coonan, the former Donna Denyse Kreter, for providing a sounding board from start to finish, and graciously allowing me to devote all the time and effort necessary to produce this story. I'm still loving every new chapter of our journey.

Of all the really remarkable rewards that came with writing *Presidential*

Spirits, the most heartwarming has to be how it reconnected me with hundreds of people from every decade and every nook and cranny of my life. Classmates as far back as first grade at St. Anthony's in El Segundo, teammates from every team I ever played on, dozens of old friends from high school and college, in addition to many other fellow alumni I never had the pleasure of knowing until now. Coworkers from every job I ever had in a career that has seen a whole lot of stops in four different fields. Parents with whom Donna and I bonded while raising our kids, in both Northern and Southern California and in Connecticut. And many fans, alumni and former athletes that I served while working at Cal and Santa Clara. As someone who really values friendships, I have relished reconnecting with all of these people whose lives intersected with mine at one point or another, especially those I had long ago lost touch with.

When I wrote the first novel I could never have imagined that it would be enjoyed by teachers who taught me at various stages of my education, including some who really had a profound impact on my life. Thank you so much Paul Giannini (St. Anthony), Sylvia Rousseve (St. Bernard), and Dr. Peri Arnold (Notre Dame). What a truly remarkable thing a great teacher is in a person's life.

And while I'm mentioning great teachers. let me add a few more. Elizabeth Christman was a novelist and screenwriter who taught me Fiction Writing at Notre Dame. I needed special permission to take her course because it was offered by another department, but I am so grateful I did. We wrote a short story every week and I told her I'd write a novel one day. It took me more than three decades to get around to it, but, as George Eliot (the pen name for Mary Ann Evans) once said, "It's never too late to become who you might have been." I would see that quote hanging outside the office of my friend and co-worker, Zoe Segnitz, at Santa Clara University, and always felt it was speaking right to me. We lost Professor Christman many years ago. While I can't thank her personally, she certainly merits mention here.

One last teacher needs to be acknowledged as well. I saved the best for last--my mom, Kathleen McFadden Coonan, the former English teacher, lover of literature, Library Board Member and literacy advocate, who was forever encouraging me to read books as a kid and placing vocabulary lists in front of me to memorize. She and dad would pack the station wagon on Saturday afternoons and take all the kids to the El Segundo Public Library.

What a wonderful academic environment they created for us. Such a gift—one that clearly keeps on giving.

Mom could recite every time any of us Coonan kids ever received any sort of recognition for something we wrote, no matter how small or insignificant. None of it was to her. Those were the most special moments of her life. We lost her just three months after my novel was released, but I'll always cherish the photo my dad took of her opening up that book for the first time and reading the dedication to her. She was every bit as excited about the novel as I was. She had a right to be. She put in just as much effort and hours to making that a reality as I did. More.

And lastly, thank you to all the readers. And not just for reading it. Thanks for mentioning it to or purchasing it for friends, putting up such great reviews, and posting about it on social media. And thanks to all the book clubs, magazines, podcasts, author shows and others who featured it. Your overwhelming response has enriched my life beyond measure. I'll keep writing these as long as you keep reading them. And, I suspect, even if you don't.

Cheers!

ABOUT THE AUTHOR

In addition to being a history lover and political junkie, Dan Coonan has been a leader within the field of intercollegiate athletics for over twenty years. He took over as Commissioner of The Eastern College Athletic Conference (ECAC) in 2017 after eleven years as Director of Athletics at Santa Clara University. He has also practiced law, managed a congressional campaign, and spent four years as Chairman of the Board of LifeMoves, the largest homeless shelter network in the San Francisco Bay Area. He published his first novel, Presidential Spirits, in 2020. He resides in Connecticut with his wife and three children.

Website: DanCoonanAuthor.com

Facebook: @DanCoonanAuthor

LinkedIn: www.linkedin.com/in/dan-coonan/

Instagram: @DannyfromtheDock

Twitter: @DanCoonanAuthor

CPSIA information can be obtained
at www.ICGtesting.com
Printed in the USA
BVHW052140230622
640205BV00001B/3